STAR
WARS™

40

THE EMPIRE STRIKES BACK

FROM A CERTAIN
POINT OF VIEW

TOM ANGLEBERGER   JOHN JACKSON MILLER

SARWAT CHADDA   MICHAEL MORECI

S. A. CHAKRABORTY   DANIEL JOSÉ OLDER

MIKE CHEN   MARK OSHIRO

ADAM CHRISTOPHER   AMY RATCLIFFE

KATIE COOK   BETH REVIS

ZORAIDA CÓRDOVA   LILLIAM RIVERA

DELILAH S. DAWSON   CAVAN SCOTT

TRACY DEONN   EMILY SKRUTSKIE

SETH DICKINSON   KAREN STRONG

ALEXANDER FREED   ANNE TOOLE

JASON FRY   CATHERYNNE M. VALENTE

CHRISTIE GOLDEN   AUSTIN WALKER

HANK GREEN   MARTHA WELLS

ROB HART   DJANGO WEXLER

LYDIA KANG   KIERSTEN WHITE

MICHAEL KOGGE   GARY WHITTA

R. F. KUANG   BRITTANY N. WILLIAMS

C. B. LEE   CHARLES YU

MACKENZI LEE   JIM ZUB

DEL REY

NEW YORK

FROM A CERTAIN POINT OF VIEW

Star Wars: From a Certain Point of View: The Empire Strikes Back
is a work of fiction. Names, places, and incidents either
are products of the authors' imaginations or are used fictitiously.
Any resemblance to actual events, locales, or persons, living or dead,
is entirely coincidental.

Copyright © 2020 by Lucasfilm Ltd. & ® or ™ where indicated.
All rights reserved.

Published in the United States by Del Rey,
an imprint of Random House, a division of
Penguin Random House LLC, New York.

DEL REY is a registered trademark and the CIRCLE colophon
is a trademark of Penguin Random House LLC.

Illustrations on the following pages by Chris Trevas: vi–vii, 13, 25, 39, 57,
93, 131, 145, 239, 251, 265, 341, 353, 373, 387, 417, 447, 511, 531, and 543

LIBRARY OF CONGRESS CATALOGING-IN-PUBLICATION DATA
Names: Angleberger, Tom, author. | Chadda, Sarwat, author. |
Chakraborty, S. A., author.
Title: Star Wars: from a certain point of view / Tom Angleberger,
Sarwat Chadda, S .A. Chakraborty [and others].
Description: New York: Del Rey, [2020]
Identifiers: LCCN 2020029555 (print) | LCCN 2020029556 (ebook) |
ISBN 9780593157749 (hardcover; alk. paper) | ISBN 9780593157756 (ebook) |
ISBN 9780593159712 (international edition)
Subjects: LCSH: Science fiction, American—21st century. | Star Wars fiction.
Classification: LCC PS648.S3 S626 2020 (print) | LCC PS648.S3 (ebook) |
DDC 813/.0876208—dc23
LC record available at https://lccn.loc.gov/2020029555
LC ebook record available at https://lccn.loc.gov/2020029556

Printed in the United States of America on acid-free paper

randomhousebooks.com

2 4 6 8 9 7 5 3 1

First Edition

Book design by Elizabeth A. D. Eno

CONTENTS

Contents

A long time ago in a galaxy far, far away. . . .

FROM A CERTAIN
POINT OF VIEW

EYES OF THE EMPIRE

Kiersten White

"**P**ick any of the last ten transmissions you've looked at. You have to live there for the rest of your life. Where are you?" Lorem said, her voice ringing through the small processing room where they all worked.

Maela admired how Lorem could multitask, sorting through data while keeping up a steady stream of chatter.

Dirjo Harch did *not* admire it. "Just do your job." He deleted whatever he was looking at on his screen and pulled up the next data packet. Maela wished they could work individually. Or better yet, in small groups. She'd pick Lorem for her group. And Azier. So really, she'd make a group that was everyone except Dirjo, with his sour expressions and his pinched personality.

"I *am* doing my job," Lorem said, chipper as always. Sometimes she wore her cap at a jaunty angle over her dark curls. Just enough to be off dress code, but not enough to give Dirjo an excuse to report her. Maela liked the uniform, liked what it meant. That she was here. That she did it.

A light flashed near Maela's face and she flipped the switch, accepting an incoming transmission and adding it to the ever-growing queue. She had spent so long with the Vipers, infinite rows of them, round domes and legs like jointed tentacles. She used to stare into their blank black eyes and wonder where they would go. What they would see.

Now she saw everything.

"But *while* I'm doing my job," Lorem continued, and Dirjo's shoulders tensed, "I don't see why we can't have some fun. We're going to be looking through a hundred thousand of these transmissions."

Azier leaned back, stretching. He rubbed his hands down his pale face, clean-shaven, wrinkled. Maela suspected working on the Swarm transmission recovery and processing unit was a demotion for him, though she didn't know why. Dirjo and Lorem were just starting their Imperial service, like her.

"Lorem, my young friend," Azier said in the clipped, polished tones of the Empire, the ones Maela was still trying to master to hide that she came from somewhere else, "the man we report to is serving on the *Executor* as part of Lord Vader's Death Squadron. Do you really think *fun* is a priority for any of them?"

Lorem giggled, and even Maela had to smile. Dirjo, however, scowled, turning his head sharply. "Are you criticizing Lord Vader?"

Azier waved a hand dismissively. "They're bringing death to those who would threaten the Empire. I lived through a war none of you remember or understand. I have no desire to do it again. And Lorem, to answer your question, I'd rather stay in this floating tin can forever than visit any of the forsaken rocks our probe droids are reporting from."

"Not a hundred thousand," Maela said softly.

"What?" Lorem asked, turning around in her chair to give her full attention to Maela.

"Project Swarm sent out a hundred thousand. But some won't make it to their destinations. Some will crash and be incapable of functioning after. Some might land in environments that make transmission impossible. If I had to guess, I'd say we'll receive anywhere from sixty-five thousand to eighty thousand transmissions." Vipers were tough little wonders, and their pods protected them, but still. Space was vast, and there were so many variables.

"In that case," Lorem said, grinning, "we'll be done by the end of the day. And then we can decide which planet we'll live on forever! Though none of my prospects are good. You're from the Deep Core, aren't you? Any footage from your planet so we can add it to our potential relocation list?"

Maela turned back to her own work. Her accent attempts hadn't been as good as she thought, after all. "No footage. We didn't send droids to Vulpter."

Azier snorted a laugh.

"Why?" Lorem asked. "Why is that funny?"

Dirjo hit a button harder than necessary. "Half the probe droids we have are made on Vulpter. Back to work." His tone was brusque, but he looked appraisingly at Maela. "You came from the manufacturing side. I would like to speak about it, sometime."

Maela went back to her screen. She knew this work wasn't sought-after. That it was either washouts like Azier or those who hadn't managed to climb up the ranks yet like Dirjo. But she had specifically requested it and had no desire to move elsewhere in the Empire's service. She slipped her hand into her pocket and rubbed the smooth, rounded surface of a probe droid's main eye. How many times had she traced these eyes, longing to see what they saw? Imagined flinging herself through the reaches of space alongside them to uncover sights untold?

And now here she was. As close as she could get. The fates and visions of tens of thousands of probe droids at her fingertips. It was an actual dream come true.

For her, at least.

"No," her mother said, not bothering to take off her mirrored goggles. "Absolutely not."

Maela felt the pout taking over her face, which made her angry. She was past pouting age, and *definitely* past being teased for the way her lips refused to allow her to hide any emotions.

"It's not fair," she said, gesturing at the prototype her mother was tinkering with. "There's so much out there, and they see everything, and all I see is this factory." Maela leaned close, looking at her distorted reflection in the probe droid's main eye. She knew it wasn't an eye, not really, but she always thought of it that way. She would walk down the lines of droids, hanging like fruit from mechanical vines, making certain she saw herself in every single eye. That way, when they went out into the galaxy, flung to places and planets she would never visit, at least part of her would be taken. A ghost in her mother's machines.

"You think you'll see so much, working for the Empire?" Her mother made a face like she had a bad taste in her mouth. "You don't want any part of them."

"How can you say that?" Maela threw her hands in the air, astounded at her mother's hypocrisy. "You work for them!"

"I do not work *for* them. I design and manufacture droids. Which is not an easy business to be in after the Clone Wars." She sighed, leaning back and running her hands through her wild curls. They were more gray than black now, and Maela knew beneath the goggles she'd see the fine lines of age slowly claiming all the skin around her mother's eyes. "This is what I'm good at. It's what keeps our family safe."

"And keeps us locked up here on this lifeless planet in this lifeless factory!" Maela kicked the table, and the prototype parts went skittering away. "At least if I were working with the Empire, I'd be doing something."

"Yes," her mother said, in a tone like a door sliding shut. "You would be doing many things." She walked away, leaving Maela alone with the metal that was not yet a droid.

Maela picked up the eye and stared at her reflection. She didn't want to be a ghost, a memory, a prisoner. The eye fit perfectly in her pocket, tucked alongside the decision Maela had made. She would send herself out into the galaxy, flung to new and unknown destinations by the same Empire that claimed these droids.

7

Maela's eyes were grainy, so dry she could hear her eyelids click when she blinked. She didn't know how long she had been watching footage, dismissing transmissions that offered no useful information. The others had wandered out at some point, to eat or sleep, she didn't know.

She didn't need her mother's droids to carry her ghost into the galaxy, because she was connected to them now. They were at her fingertips, and she stared out through them at countless new sights. She was *everywhere*.

Plants as tall as buildings, towering overhead, glowing in colors human eyes couldn't have discerned. Desertscapes so barren she could feel her throat parching just looking at them. A depthless ocean, eyes and teeth and fins exploring her as she sank into darkness. World after world after world, and she was seeing them all.

She was so blinded by the infinite white ice of the newest planet that she almost missed it.

"Someone made those," she whispered, tracing the even, symmetrical mounds rising out of the snow. They were metal, and, according to the droid, they were generating power. Which meant they were being used. But before she could make the connection active and direct the droid, the screen flashed and then the feed was dead.

Her droid had self-destructed. Which could only mean it had been attacked. Maela's heart began racing. This was it. She had found what they were looking for, she was certain.

She pushed her comm. "Dirjo, I've got them."

His answer crackled with static and sleepiness. "Got what?"

"The Rebellion."

Within minutes he was at her shoulder, leaning over. The rest of the team had joined them, the space too tight to accommodate all of them at her station. "Are you certain?" Dirjo asked. "There are a lot of settlements out there."

"Not on Hoth. The only things I've found are snow and the occasional animal." She had gone over the entire feed from the droid, searching backward, but other than the generators and the attack, all she had found was snow, ice, and lumbering beasts that ran on two legs, with small arms and powerful, thick tails. They were cute, actually. She had spent more time looking over the images of a herd, imagining what they must sound like, what their fur would feel like, how those curling horns would function, than she had worrying about the Rebellion.

"Besides," she said, trying to focus, "those generators are too big for a settlement. And someone shot at the droid." That one hurt. She wanted the connection back. She didn't want her droid, her *eyes*, lying dead in the snow.

Dirjo bit his lip, frowning. "If we're wrong . . ."

"If we're wrong, then we keep looking."

Azier snorted. "Being wrong in the Empire is never that simple."

Maela didn't care. She was certain she had found the Rebellion. And it felt right, that she was the one who had succeeded. Her droids, her eyes. All that time she had spent wishing and putting herself inside them. It had worked.

Dirjo took a deep breath, then nodded. "I'll send it to Piett." Maela moved out of the way as Dirjo took over her station.

Lorem frowned. "Maela is the one who found it. She should get the credit."

"It's not about credit," Dirjo said. "It's about the Empire."

"If it's not about credit, then why are you insisting on being the one to personally send it to Piett?" Azier muttered.

Maela had already moved to another station. If it turned out she was wrong, they would need to keep looking. So she might as well get a head start on it. But she couldn't stop thinking about those creatures she had seen. Or the flash of light and then the end of the transmission. A violent end for her mother's creation, and an abrupt end to her trip to Hoth.

While everyone was distracted waiting to hear from Piett, Maela searched through countless transmissions. A surge of triumph flooded her when she found it: Another probe droid had crashed into Hoth. Which meant that she could still explore.

She shouldn't. Either Hoth was their target or it wasn't, and she should move on.

But Hoth felt more real than anywhere else she had been. What she had seen there mattered, and she was irrationally angry at the abrupt end of the transmission. Probe droids were lost all the time. But this one had been *destroyed*.

Later—it was hard for her to know how long, because she was frantically watching transmissions, hoping for something special, trying to forget how badly she wanted to return to Hoth—word came from the *Executor*.

"Yes, sir. Thank you, sir." Dirjo leaned against the workstation, relief and smug joy warring for dominance on his face. "We were right. They're on Hoth."

Lorem clapped a hand on Maela's shoulder. "You mean Maela was right."

"This will be a huge victory for the Empire. It's already a victory for Project Swarm." Dirjo stood up straight, tugging on his uniform jacket and pushing out his chest. "We should go celebrate."

"Anything to get me out of this cell," Azier grumbled and stood, not bothering to straighten his rumpled uniform.

Lorem laughed, grabbing Maela's hand and dragging it away from her station. Maela looked longingly at the flashing lights, the square buttons beckoning her with the promise of other eyes. She shoved her hand in her pocket and rubbed the smooth surface of her eye. She would tell her mother. Send a message of this triumph. Proof that not only the droids deserved to be sent out into the galaxy.

She dreamed of ice. Couldn't stop thinking about it, wondering about it, missing her too-brief sojourn on a planet that actually mattered.

A few days later, when everyone else was on a sleeping shift, Maela slipped back into the Swarm processing center. Her chair was cold and the lights were dim, but the room disappeared around her as she assumed manual control of the remaining probe droid on Hoth.

She slipped inside its metal frame and let the screen fill her whole vision. The cold of her chair became the cold of that barren landscape. She was there.

Gliding along the glaciers and snow dunes, she hoped to find a herd of the animals. But something else caught her eye. Smoke. She drifted toward it, her metal limbs never touching the ground. The smoke billowed from tremendous carcasses of the Empire's machines, ruined and blasted, scorched and melted. They'd gotten here before she did.

But it wasn't a "they" and a "her." She was part of the Empire. She turned toward their target. Whatever had happened here was finished. She told herself she was looking for any information left behind that might help the Empire, but really, she wanted to see this place she would never visit, this place she had discovered, this place she had given to the Empire. It was her victory, too, wasn't it?

The entrance to the base wasn't hard to find, blasted and twisted just like the Empire's machines. She carefully moved inside, navigating places where the roof had collapsed and left chunks of ice and snow to block her way. It was dim, so she adjusted the specifications for the transmission. And then she saw.

There was a taste like metal on her tongue, and a ringing in her ears.

Imperial uniforms, and others. Bodies left behind, broken and ruined. She drifted above them, touching nothing.

There, another body. A different one. She extended an arm. Trapped beneath a tremendous weight of ice and snow, only the creature's head was visible. Her arm connected with one of those funny curling horns, but—

But it wasn't her arm. It was the droid's arm. And she'd never know what this felt like, what any of it felt like. The droid spun and spun and everywhere there were blast marks and bodies and broken machines, and it didn't matter whether the bodies were rebels or Empire or creatures that should be running on the ice. They were all equally ruined. Destroyed.

She had flung herself through the stars, and she had thought all she was doing was seeing. But an eye was never just an eye. It was connected to a body.

She was the eyes of the Empire. And its hands had done this because of her.

11

Dirjo leaned against his chair, updating them on the Empire's prog-ress after Hoth and reminding them—yet again—of Piett's successes. Lorem would say Dirjo was droning on, but Maela thought that was unfair to drones. They didn't choose to be that way. They were made, and they did what they were told.

They looked where *she* told them to look.

Her hands twitched, imagining the feel of a curling horn. Project Swarm had succeeded, but it wasn't over. It would never be over, not as long as the Rebellion lived to hide again. The droid eye stared dully at her from where she'd set it on her workstation. She looked at her reflection, distorted, then went back to her screen. Feed after feed after feed. Hundreds of them, blurring together.

A moon filled with ancient forests, the droid coming in hot enough that it ignited the vegetation around itself, the feed turning into one swirling inferno.

A planet devoid of light, so dark that no setting on the droid could penetrate it. Only repeated motion-sensor triggers hinting that somewhere out there, something was lurking.

An asteroid as big as a planet, the probe damaged upon landing so that it could only stare, motionless, powerless, as it was carried along.

A swamp planet, a riot of plants and bogs, mud and vines, nothing that indicated they should give it a second glance. Except—there, the outline of something in the night. Inorganic. Something that looked distinctly like a half-drowned X-wing.

Dirjo tugged fussily at his jacket. "Results," he snapped. "The Em-pire depends on us."

Maela hit a single button to delete the footage, erasing Dagobah from the Empire's vision. Then she moved on to the next eyes, seeing clearly at last.

HUNGER

Mark Oshiro

The ice cared for no one.

He knew that each time he left home, many suns and many, many moons could pass before he had enough to bring back, enough to feed them all. Especially now, as he swatted playfully at one of the cubs that darted between his legs then stood before his father and roared, a squeaking sound that did not inspire fear as it should. It was a start. With more practice, more food, more growth, this cub would soon be just as terrifying as his father.

The two of them made their way up the long passage from the central chamber of the cavern. Without the knowledge they possessed, it would be easy to get lost down here. It was why he and his den-mate had chosen this place so long ago. Someone had once lived here, and the strange things they had left behind were proof of that. Hard objects, not stone or bone or ice, that he had never seen before were strewn about the caves, along with the rotting remains of whatever these beasts consumed.

But this home was well guarded from the cold and from others. To find such a place . . . well, he knew even back then that this was something permanent, the kind of home that his kind sought most of their lives. The few predators that had ever tried to invade their territory in the time since had become hopelessly lost in the twisting tunnels, in the caverns that all looked so similar in the terrible darkness. They were easy to hunt down then, when they were weak and afraid.

And now he had a clan. Three cubs, their mother, a den-mate, all of them his family. They would not exist if this cavern had not been discovered.

It was time to leave, though.

The den-mate would look after the others while he was gone, but there was little comfort provided by this, only because . . . well, the hunt was the hunt. It took as long as it did, and there was no guarantee once you were out there. Days could blend together without a single spotting of prey.

But he had to go.

He had to keep his clan alive.

And so the need pulled him forth, and the mother who bore his children and his den-mate nuzzled him, their way of showing respect for what he was going to do. The cubs yapped and squealed and didn't really understand; they merely nipped at his feet. As he stepped out into the wind and the cold and the ice and the snow, one of them followed, swiping at his legs. He stopped and pushed her back, then growled. She understood. She remained in one spot to watch him

14

leave, and soon, he disappeared into the unending whiteness of the tundra.

The hunt had begun.

He walked. He crested the nearest range, and his instinct guided him toward a series of caves far in that direction. He had once found a pod of his favorite prey there: the beasts who stood upright, had those useless horns on the sides of their faces. They were easy pickings, at least if you focused on one of them at a time. As a group, they could be formidable, but it was easier to separate one, to chase it down, to prey on its fear that it no longer had the others to protect it.

He feasted on smaller creatures to keep his energy up and slept rarely; he knew he was most vulnerable then. He rested just long enough to keep going.

And the hunt continued.

The sun passed overhead. Again and again and again. The moons, each with their own color and shape, appeared as daylight vanished, as night took over, as the terrible chill threatened to take him away. But he continued. He sought refuge from a particularly nasty wind, one that seemed to cut through his fur, by hiding under a cliff face until the sun came up again.

He did all of this for *them*.

He found the prey on the southern ridge of a crag, and it was easy to trap them in the valley below. Once he took out the largest of them as it swiped at him with those stunted horns it had, the others were easier to track down. He feasted on the smallest, devouring every part of it, so that he would have stamina for the long trek back. There would be no stopping nor sleeping; it was too big a risk with the carcasses he dragged behind him.

So he walked.

He did not note how many suns and moons passed overhead.

He did not care how frigid it felt as he crunched through ice and snow.

He did not let the exhaustion in his bones and muscles bring him to the ground.

He just kept going, one thing in mind.

Return.

He crested the last hill, and for a brief moment, he thought the light of the sun was playing tricks on him. It could be blinding, reflecting off the sheets of ice, but he dropped the carcasses. He stared. He brought his body low.

They poured out over the ice near an enormous structure: little things, walking upright on their hind legs, dark shapes against the snow. Some of them rode on top of the very same kind of creature he had just killed; others guided herdbeasts forward, screaming and shouting at them.

This would delay him, but it would not stop his return.

He made for the entrance to the caverns on the far side of the ridge, wondering if these new arrivals would make the hunt all the more challenging. Would they bother his den? Would they invade it?

The anger boiled in him. This was his *home*.

He thought of his clan as he sneaked down into the valley, down toward the cavern. There was another entrance—smaller, less effective—he could use. All the while, he watched these creatures. They did not seem to have packs, but there were so many of them. No matter. He could crush them with a simple swipe of the paw.

He squeezed into the opening in one of the rear caverns, falling to the ground of the tunnel and clamping his paws to his ears. There was an awful sound echoing throughout: something high, repetitive, and it pierced his ears, sent nausea in waves through his body.

This seemed impossible; he was so far from those creatures. Had they somehow broken through? Were they not even aware of who had been here first?

He left the carcasses there and ventured forth through his den. When he reached the far side of it, the impossible was true: There, burned into the wall of ice, was a massive gap, and the sounds that echoed out of it filled him with a terrible pain.

But he pressed on. He *had* to. He had to find them.

He searched. In the area where they buried their waste. (Empty.) In one of the caves where they fed. (Now occupied by swarms of the terrible things.) He was low to the ground when it came upon him, walking out of one of the small caves deep within the cavern. (Out of *his* home.) After just a glance, the creature screamed at him. Did it mean to frighten him? Or was it so afraid that it made the sound as an instinct? Sometimes they did that before they died. It could not be helped.

He roared and prepared to crush it to death.

The thing raised its arm up, and there was something dark in its paw, and then a blaze of light burst forth, traveled the distance between them impossibly fast, like the streaks he often saw in the sky at night.

He had never felt a pain as searing as this; it seemed to plunge deep beneath his coat and skin, stabbing into the muscles of his leg, and his roar this time was of his *own* pain.

And then he gave himself over to rage.

He had no idea how many he maimed or killed in those moments, but he struck anything that moved. He could not find them. Where were they? Where were his den-mates? Where were his *children*? He stumbled into the greatest cave of them all, saw the countless beings scattering about, screaming and yelling, and he roared again.

He could only smell the remnants of his family, only a faint wisp of what they once were. Where were they? What had these creatures done to them?

17

There was more of that piercing light, but none of it struck him. He scrambled out of his home, out of the entrance, smearing blood on the snow and ice as he stumbled forth, as these creatures shouted unknown sounds at him, and he made himself disappear into the hills above.

It was only when he was safe that he knew he had failed them. Surely his den-mate protected the others. Perhaps they had fled elsewhere?

He packed snow onto his wound, forced it to go numb so that he could travel.

Then he walked.

He did not find them in the caverns on the other end of the range, in the place they had made their home. Perhaps his den-mate had taken them to where they'd lived before.

But he did not find them in the home they had inhabited before this one.

He did not find them anywhere.

Something filled him. He had never sensed this before. There was now a cavern in him, one that ate at his gut, that seemed to grow bigger and bigger with each passing of the sun overhead. He tried to fill it with food, picking off prey here and here. But while his hunger was sated, the other sensation bloomed. He was empty without his clan.

He waited. He watched. He despaired.

More and more of these creatures came to his home. They came and went, sometimes venturing out onto the ice on the backs of other creatures, but always together. There were so many of them. How could they do this? What did they want? Were they hunters like him, too?

He hungered. He watched. He waited.

A small pack left the cavern one morning, all riding astride the upright, horned beasts. His instinct took over: He could deal with a group this small. Eventually, all living creatures lost to his kind. And

18

with another upon its back, the horned beast could not maintain its normal speed.

Meaning it could not escape.

It would be too easy.

But the challenge did not matter to him. He followed the pack, watched them split up and spread out over the ice. He remained distant and quiet as he always did. He wanted the last thing his prey saw to be the whiteness of his fur, his ferocious maw cracked open, his sharp claws slicing at the softness of their neck.

He wanted that not for hunger. Not to satiate his need to feast.

No.

He needed to fill the cavern in his body.

And only blood would do that.

He chose one. There was no need to focus on the entire pack. It was the scrawny creature, the smallest of them all, that would be easiest to take down.

Would this reunite him with his clan? Would it reveal their fate to him?

No.

But it was a start.

He moved closer to the plateau, aware that there was not much cover, but there was only *this* chance. He stilled and observed. Watched the thing bury something in the snow.

He waited. The gangly creature climbed atop the other, and they moved forth.

Stopped.

He rushed forward then, keeping his body tucked in tight, and he closed the distance between them.

The horned beast twisted its head back, and he froze. It raised its snout in the air, sniffed a few times, and he was sure it could sense him, that the chase was about to begin.

It turned back. It remained unmoving.

He continued moving, his body hovering just above the snow, his breath even and steady.

Crash!

He stayed close to the ground, but he could not help turning his head to see the flash of fire and smoke off in the distance. It was not uncommon here; things plummeted from the sky all the time. One had once killed a packmate of his when he was a cub.

But the moment had arrived: the perfect distraction.

He glided over the ice. The creature aboard the other was making noise. Fear? Concern? Communication? He did not know. He just crept ever closer, stilling only when the beast cried out. This was it. If they spotted him, a chase would certainly follow. He would surely catch them, but he didn't want a chase.

He wanted *blood.*

He rushed forward.

His massive arm was in the air, and he swung it down and roared as loudly as possible, so as to strike fear into their hearts, to freeze them in place. The smaller one's body thumped on the snow after one slash, and then he grabbed the horned beast by the neck, snapped it with one powerful squeeze.

Neither creature moved.

And he would feast tonight.

But first, the preparation. He grabbed each of the creatures by a leg and dragged them back to the empty cavern he was now using. It was a long trek, and normally he would worry about other clans taking advantage of him. But many of them were gone as well, most likely frightened away by these strange beasts and the strange thing they had constructed out of the snow, that burst up into the sky.

He was alone out here in the ice and snow. He had been for some time.

He knew he would preserve the tiny one and consume the other. He needed the energy, and it would help him with what came next.

This would not be a lone act.

No, he would seek out the others. Pick them off one by one. Each time he took one of their lives, he would be closer to getting his home back. His den-mate. The cubs. The mother of his children.

He would get them all back.

And he had all the time in the world.

He strung the carcass in the rear of the cavern and focused on the other, the one that was still living. He examined its head. It only possessed a small tuft of hair there. He sniffed. It was wearing the fur of *others*. A strange thing. How did they survive in the cold of this world?

Well, this one would not survive a moon or two. He lifted it by its legs and used his breath to melt the ice at the top of the cavern. He licked the odd material at the end of its legs, spread as much saliva as he could over it, and then held it against the wetness above.

A small object fell from its body and landed in the snow piled on the ground. He thought nothing of it. Moments later, his prey hung solidly from the ice.

He studied it again. Its breath was shallow. It was built to be so frail, so useless. He did not comprehend how this thing had managed to survive; it did not appear to be a cub. Its arms were not suited for striking their prey, and it possessed no claws. Its legs were too short to run quickly across ice or snow.

He peered into its face. Did it have a family, too? A home? Did it know that it had taken everything from him? What did it think about? Did it hate his kind like he hated its kind? Was that why they had stolen his home?

It did not matter.

He would get back what was owed to him.

He ate. He tore at the flesh of the horned beast, devoured it quickly, then focused on the fatty insides. He wished that it was still fresh; there were few things more satisfying than warm blood in the throat.

He ripped at the sinews and muscles in one of the legs, lost in the sheer thrill of the feast, and the frenzy was what kept him from noticing it sooner.

He froze.

Heard a grunt.

A small crack.

He looked up at the creature, and it strained against the ice, stretched its arm out, and the rage filled him again. Did this *thing* believe it could escape? That it could fight *back*? That it could conquer *him*? He roared, loud enough that the cavern seemed to shake, loud enough that the creature's eyes went wide after it plunged to the ground. It stood and faced him and then—

A light. A beam of it. *Again.*

His kind never forgot. Their memories were what helped them track down prey, to remember which ranges give way to treacherous, deadly gorges. He remembered. His home. The scream. The flash of light that hurt so terribly, the blood, the chaos.

But this was different. Somehow. The beam was not moving toward him. It did not move at all, like the two of them in that tiny space.

This being could *hold* the light.

No.

It seemed to be *wielding* it.

He sniffed and caught a scent of the same sharp odor of the debris scattered around his former home. Was that what this creature held?

But he was not afraid. He couldn't be. The anger rushed up and out of him.

He would not let this happen *again.*

He charged forward, certain that he would crush this awful thing with one blow, and then the beam cut through the air, and there was no pain at first, and then *it* crushed *him,* filled his every thought, and he had never heard a sound like that, of flesh being severed so quickly, had never looked down and seen his own arm resting before him.

He roared again.

No.

He *screamed.*

The creature escaped out into the snowy unknown. It would surely die soon; it could not possibly survive the ice and wind like that. But he could not think of it anymore as the pain raced through his body. He packed his stump with ice, much as he had done that day long ago, and it stopped the bleeding. His mind drifted, first to the pain, then his den-mates, then to the cubs he might not ever see again.

He slept.

He hurt.

The pain did not subside for many moons. There were times when he felt his arm was still there, as if he could tear at the flesh of another with claws he could not see. He continued to hunt alone—more poorly than he had before—until his strength came back. Until he believed he was ready.

He finally ventured down into the valley when he was strong enough, when he had adapted to his new reality. He had feasted recently, and his hunger was now for retribution. Perhaps this would be fruitless; not every hunt was a success, and he knew he might fail, that this might be the day it all came to an end. Still, he *had* to try.

But when he crested the ridgeline, his body curled in anticipation, he found himself relaxing, unfurling.

He saw no strange objects on the ground.

No strange creatures fluttering about near the caverns.

He still descended slowly, assuming that at any moment, those *things* could ambush him with their beams of light and drive him back. But he heard nothing. Saw nothing. There was no stench of their sweat or odor. He sniffed again.

Something had recently been burning.

There was more debris at the mouth of the caverns: twisted pieces of something hard and sharp. A smear of frozen blood. Charred remains of what was once here, what came *after* his clan.

He crept into the entrance, his body low, but there was no torrent of sound, no clinking or clanking, nothing that pierced his ears as it had before. It was not long before his wandering was not cautious. He had risen upright and slunk from one cavern to the next, all of them empty, abandoned, forgotten.

There were many more nooks he needed to search, more places to examine, but standing in what was once the home for him and his clan, he knew that this place had been returned to him.

And that cavern within him shrank, replaced by something new.

Hope.

Hope that a reunion was possible.

With his clan.

With his den-mate.

With his cubs.

With what they stole.

His *home*.

ION CONTROL

Emily Skrutskie

Toryn Farr was certain she knew a lost cause when she saw one, so when the controllers had started the betting pool, there was no question where her credits were going.

"Even if he takes the shot, the princess will shut him down," she'd declared as she jotted down her wager on the datapad being handed around. It had already circulated through most of the rest of the room, and the odds weren't looking great for Captain Solo.

Then again, Toryn considered as the smuggler strode into the command center and every person whose name was on that ledger straightened with sudden awareness, *Solo's the type to gamble on long odds.*

She tried—she really tried—to keep her focus on the readouts she was supposed to be monitoring for anomalies. They'd picked up a signature that looked suspiciously like a Star Destroyer a day ago, and while it had cruised by Hoth without deviating from its flight path, the anxiety of the moment had left them all rattled and unsure. But Toryn couldn't help slipping her focus clear through the transparency in her charts to where Princess Leia was perched next to Captain Serper's station.

The princess's eyes were fixed warily on Solo. Behind her, Toryn caught the pause of his footsteps—and then, surprisingly, the moment he moved not to Leia but to General Rieekan, who was fidgeting with a comm array in the back corner of the command center. She felt the tension in her team loosen. Seemed no one was winning any bets today.

Toryn tuned back to her work, her eyes skimming with practiced precision over the asteroids flirting with Hoth's orbit. The cover they provided made Hoth an ideal place for a hidden base. The Empire's sensors would be hard-pressed to pick out a rebel ship from the more metallic of their number.

Unfortunately, the reverse was also true.

But before she could sink into the tedium of it, her ears latched onto the tail end of Solo's words to the general. *Did he say "I can't stay anymore"?*

A glance over at Corporal Sunsbringer, who was desperately trying to catch her eye, confirmed Toryn hadn't misheard. The corporal widened her eyes and flexed a hand, a motion that read as, *Seriously?*

Toryn was just as startled. The captain had been bumming along with the Rebel Alliance for *years*. Ever since the Battle of Yavin. Now he was claiming he had a price on his head set by Jabba the Hutt— which sounded like a convenient excuse to get off this freezing rock. Toryn wouldn't have begrudged him trading the desolate, icy world for the sands of Tatooine—except it ruined the best entertainment the base had seen since they'd touched down on Hoth.

And speaking of entertainment, Solo had just shaken hands with General Rieekan, turned, and fixed his eyes on Leia. "Well, Your Highness. Guess this is it," the captain said, sauntering up to her.

With the bank of controllers positioned on a shelf of ice above the main floor, the princess had a rare height advantage over the captain, one she lorded with the easy grace of royalty. "That's right," Leia replied coolly.

Toryn's grip on her stylus tightened as Solo's face contorted through a complicated emotion that convinced her of two things: Han Solo wasn't just leaving over some bounty, and she was about to come into some serious money. So she nearly groaned and dropped her head into her hands when Solo blurted, "Don't get all mushy on me. So long, Princess," and bolted for the door of the command center.

Leia was off like a shot on his heels, all sense of duty to whatever she'd been helping Serper with forgotten as she stormed out into the corridor shouting, "Han!"

The moment the doors closed behind her, the thin veneer of subtlety that had fallen over the command center dissolved. "Someone has to go after them," Sunsbringer declared over the mutters. When Toryn threw her junior a warning look, the corporal shrugged. "We *have* to know what happens—this is my Boonta Eve Classic, ma'am."

"Make those readouts your Boonta Eve Classic," she said firmly. "The barracks gossip will be there when you're *back in the barracks*."

It earned her an approving nod from General Rieekan, which Toryn returned with a wry look. She'd seen his name scrawled in a neat hand next to a modest wager on that ledger—one of the few pulling for Solo. "Settle down, folks. Back to work," Rieekan intoned, and the command center quieted under his order.

Toryn returned to the drudgery of her charts, the tension settling back into her shoulders like the fit of a trim dress uniform. It had been years since the Death Star, but every day had passed with a shadow hanging over it. The wasp-worm nest had been kicked. By luck, a miraculous engineering flaw, and a crack shot from a rookie pilot, the Rebel Alliance had taken down the monstrous battle station, but Toryn knew—had come to realize, over the years of running—that they didn't have the resources to hold out against the Empire's retaliation.

Bouts of entertainment like the Solo ledger were nothing but desperate attempts to stave off the creeping dread of the inevitable. Hoth could very well be the Rebellion's last stand.

Toryn had hated it on sight. She understood the necessity of hiding in a place that was remote, undesirable, and cloaked by a dense asteroid belt, but everything about the planet made her ache for the rolling green hills of her homeworld, Chandrila. Her only consolation was having her sister to commiserate with in the mess during the fleeting moments their schedules aligned. Samoc Farr, three years her junior, had a more optimistic view of the planet, though that was owing to the fact that she'd seen far more of it than Toryn ever would.

"It's beautiful, in an austere kind of way," Samoc would tell her through a mouthful of tough, oversalted cave lichen. "When it's just you, your patrol route, and all that ice. It's quiet. We haven't had quiet in a while, y'know?"

Toryn wished for something as simple as quiet. Her days were filled with the urgent chatter of the command center and the comm transmissions pumped through her headset, her nights with the worrisome creaking of the ice they'd dug out to form Echo Base. But the worst noise was the one that only she heard—that gnawing voice in the back of her head that had started the moment the Death Star blew. She never let it anywhere near her speech, not even in the

28

hushed conversations she had with Samoc where they both admitted how tired they were, how long it had been since the two of them were bright-eyed teenagers vowing to stake their lives on Mon Mothma and her cause. Rebellions were built on hope; it was true.

And Toryn Farr feared that the seed of doubt she carried might bring the whole thing crumbling down once and for all.

She knew two moments were approaching with increasing inevitability: the moment her crisis of faith could no longer stay hidden, and the moment the Empire grabbed Echo Base by the scruff of its neck, tore it out of its icy warren, and held it up in the cruel light of day. Toryn tried to use Hoth's tedium as an opportunity to reckon with her doubts, to quell them with pure, firm conviction. She owed it to the brave people she fought alongside—to Samoc, to General Rieekan, to Princess Leia. She owed it to Mon Mothma not to cheapen her years of faithful service by falling apart when the Rebellion needed her most.

But she was so tired, and Hoth was so cold. It felt like stagnation. Like freezing in place, unable to go on anymore.

So the second moment came first, and when it did, Toryn felt the pit of dread inside her blow wide as a nexu's jaws.

In some ways, it was a mercy. There was no time for internal crisis with a fleet of Star Destroyers inbound, and so Toryn forced herself to boil away her doubts like vapor off a ship's hull in the outer atmosphere. General Rieekan had given the evacuation order, and Echo Base had dissolved into a familiar, functional chaos as once again the Rebel Alliance prepared to drop everything and run.

It all boiled down to a flowchart of procedure—yet another mercy, because at least the simple logic of it kept Toryn's anxiety down to a simmer. A fleet of capital ships dropping from hyperspace in Sector

Four? Bring up the energy shield to stave off any hope of them bombing the base from orbit. Energy shield blocking the exodus of rebel craft? Drop it for seconds at a time, allowing the GR-75s and their escorts to clear Hoth's orbit. Star Destroyers targeting the escaping transports?

Well, for that there was the ion cannon and Toryn Farr's steady command.

She'd prepared relentlessly for these moments. Taught herself to process the trigonometry of the cannon's targeting in an instant, to boil down the ion blast's rate of travel and the distance to target into a simple measure of time, to reduce everything to an instinct that would allow her to keep her eyes pinned on the orbital charts.

As long as she was clearheaded. As long as she didn't think too hard about how the Empire would never stop coming, about how this battle would cost them people, ships, and equipment they couldn't spare, about how a battle had already been fought in her head over whether this was all worth it and she still wasn't sure whether it had been won or lost.

She wouldn't know until she spoke, and she wouldn't speak until the precise moment it was needed—the moment she could feel prickling closer and closer as Lieutenant Navander called the approach of the Star Destroyer *Tyrant* and Corporal Sunsbringer announced that the *Quantum Storm,* the first GR-75 staged for evacuation, had finished its final checks. The transport bloomed to life in the bottom left corner of her readouts, and the mathematics of its frantic escape from Hoth's gravity followed in a scroll of data that poured across her station. Toryn kept her eyes on the ship. The math she already knew.

"Their primary target will be the power generators," Rieekan murmured. At his side stood Princess Leia, ready to assist the moment the strategy required a bifurcation of command. As the *Quantum Storm* threw itself toward the perimeter of Echo Base's defenses,

Rieekan turned his attention to operations and declared, "Prepare to open shield."

The trick was not to think too hard about what that order meant—but of course, every officer in the command center was thinking about it. The shield dropping was a moment of vulnerability, one the *Tyrant* was in the perfect position to exploit as it wheeled its guns toward Echo Base. The Star Destroyer had an opening for a shot that would take out the Rebellion's best defense, one they'd opened just to give a single transport and the two X-wings escorting it time to slip away.

Fortunately, the *Tyrant* was too focused on the prey streaking toward it to realize the opportunity it was wasting. Its main batteries targeted predictably on the *Quantum Storm*—Toryn wasn't crass enough to say *disappointingly,* but she did think it. It was classic Imperial officer thinking, prioritizing the cruel over the strategic. Shooting down the transport full of refugee rebels rather than taking out their military base's most critical defense.

Toryn rarely took joy in her command, but *this*?

This she might relish.

"Stand by, ion control," she said, and watched as the v-150 Planet Defender wheeled its targeting to paint a straight line between its massive round housing and the *Tyrant's* distant bulk. Toryn's brain sank into the calculation it presented, weighing it against the data she'd been pulling together since the *Quantum Storm* launched. The problem she posited had a single answer: the moment she'd open her mouth next.

She couldn't doubt that answer when she arrived at it. She'd trained for too long, fought for too many years to make such a rookie mistake. But even so, there was a moment—a moment she felt grab her by the throat and ask her who she thought she was, to make a call like this, to climb out of her sodden, frigid cave and spit in the face of fascist oppression.

31

Toryn Farr kept her eyes steady on the charts, and when she felt the moment slip into alignment, she announced, calm and clear, "Fire."

Her voice was the finger on the trigger, the techs operating the Planet Defender the chemical reaction, and the end result was two pairs of pulses fired at a six-second interval hurtling away from Hoth's ice as the aftershocks of the ion cannon's discharge sent rumbles and creaks through Echo Base. They tore past the energy shield's boundary half a second before it bloomed back into existence, skimmed by the *Quantum Storm* and its escort and—

Toryn knew by the collective breath the room inhaled that every eye was on her readouts. Every eye saw the data—the moment the first bolt struck the *Tyrant's* body and the second slammed into the bridge. Perfect timing, married to perfect targeting, and this was the glorious result: an entire Star Destroyer going dark as the ion pulses made mincemeat of its systems.

The *Quantum Storm* sailed cleanly past it, hyperdrives already warming as it cleared the fringes of Hoth's grasp.

"The first transport is away," Lieutenant Navander announced into the base intercom. It felt as though every soul on Hoth roared in reply, fists flung in the air, nearly drowning out the lieutenant as he repeated the announcement.

Toryn sank back in her seat and let the triumph wash over her. She hadn't faltered. Hadn't tipped over the delicate balance of the base's morale. She'd nailed the calculation, taken out a Destroyer, saved an entire GR-75 full of rebels.

And it hadn't been enough. She could feel the victorious moment ebbing, ripped away from her shoreline by the gravitational pull of her dread. One transport wouldn't save them. It wouldn't sustain them. One transport wasn't the answer to the question that had risen inside her, ravenous for an answer that wouldn't come. *Why are we fighting?* it railed. *There's no hope left for the Rebellion. The Empire has whittled us away into nothing. Even if every blow we strike strikes true, even if every shot we fire hits its target, they'll keep coming until we're dust beneath their boots.*

Toryn Farr set her jaw and inhaled deeply. There were too many people relying on her and her splintering foundations. All of them were doomed, but if that was the case, then the final thing she owed them was everything she had left. She'd throw herself into her command and hope that somewhere along the way, she'd figure out the reason that kept her fighting. "Settle down, people—we've got twenty-nine more transports to clear," she called to her team.

This time it was undeniable: The tremor had crept into her voice.

Toryn had gotten a good rhythm going—one that the ceiling collapse ruined.

She rolled to her knees, her skin smarting from the sudden drop in temperature, and coughed against the acrid stench of the laser blast that had brought the ice down on top of them. Her brain grappled hopelessly with the fact that her station was *gone*. Even more hopelessly with the fact that she'd thrown herself clear in time.

Not everyone was as lucky.

"Sound off," she choked, but all she got was confused groans and more crumbling from the hole that had been blasted in their ceiling. "Come on, who's not dead?"

In the clearing dust, she spotted the hunched form of Corporal Sunsbringer slumped over her station. Toryn lurched to her feet and laid a hand on the younger woman's snowsuit, relief coursing through her when her breathing hitched. Sunsbringer's head rolled back, revealing a worrisome line of blood trailing down one cheek and an unfocused look in her eyes. "Co . . . mmander."

"Shh," Toryn said, tucking her junior's flyaways back behind her ears. "You're done. Get to the bay. Can you stand?"

Sunsbringer braced herself against her station, and Toryn's gaze dropped to the controls beneath her hands. Against all odds, the thing was still operational.

So when Sunsbringer vacated her seat, Toryn took it.

Her junior hesitated, peering at her in a concussed daze. "Commander, we need to g—"

"You go," she snapped, fingers already flying over the buttons and switches. This station wasn't designed for the kind of work she needed to do, but she'd make it work or . . . well, die trying. "*Now*, Corporal."

Sunsbringer still hesitated, even when another controller threw one of her arms over his shoulder and started drawing her through the minefield of rubble toward the command center's door. She was a good kid. Deserved to make it out on a transport. And that meant Toryn had work to do.

But what *could* she do? The ion cannon had been taken out by the Imperial ground troops, the sensor array was in tatters, and the blockade had firmed up around Hoth. Sunsbringer's station was set up for communicating with the hangars, not laying out the gauntlet of capital ships the remaining transports would have to get past. She was fumbling blindfolded through her duty with one hand tied behind her back.

Toryn glanced over her shoulder and found, to her shock, that she wasn't the only one scrambling to salvage the machines. Trailed by her fussy protocol droid, Princess Leia was working her way down a bank of comm stations, dusting off the debris that had fallen onto them and checking to see if they were operational. Toryn bit back a laugh when the princess reeled back and kicked one in frustration.

"Shouldn't you be evacuated already?" she called.

Leia's head snapped up. "Shouldn't you?" she replied, but there was a wry archness to it. When their eyes locked, Toryn felt their sameness click into place. Both of them had handed over their lives to this Rebellion young. Neither of them would give up the fight now.

All that remained was to give all that remained.

"There are five transports left to clear," Toryn said, turning back to her station and slipping a headset over her ears. "Let's give them the best shot we can."

She knew there was no going back to the rhythm of before. Her resources had been cut out from under her, and every minute that ticked by saw another sensor knocked from her array by a shot from one of the Imperial walkers thundering closer and closer. Her voice was scraped raw with dust and ash. The chatter in the headset had gone from the calm, firm order of the Rebellion holding its ground to the scattered chaos of retreat.

But she tried—for the freedom of the galaxy, for Samoc in her snowspeeder somewhere over the ice fields, for whatever damn reason she could muster that would keep her from hyperventilating in her chair, Toryn Farr kept her post.

Until Captain Solo's voice tore through her concentration. "You all right?" the smuggler shouted, picking clumsily through the rubble.

"Why are you still here?" Leia fired back from over Toryn's shoulder.

"I heard the command center had been hit."

"You got your clearance to leave," the princess snapped. Solo's distracting presence used to be a welcome one in this room, but Toryn shared Leia's irritation now. The captain should have been long gone.

The fact that he wasn't was . . . well, maybe some bets were getting won today.

"Don't worry, I'll leave. First I'm going to get you to your ship."

C-3PO pounced on the opportunity to get more nagging in. "Your Highness, we must take this last transport. It's our only hope."

Leia let out a hiss. Toryn kept up her frantic flipping of switches as the princess staggered to the other side of the center, where Commander Chiffonage was using the only other operational comm station to coordinate what was left of the ground defenses. "Send all troops in Sector Twelve to the south slope to protect the fight—"

The devastating thunder of a blast tore away Leia's voice. Toryn bent low over her station, covering her head against the rain of new debris. With her cheek pressed against the buttons, she felt like an animal pinned in a snare, kicking frantically to get free.

"Imperial troops have entered the base. Imperial troops have entered the base."

Solo stepped up to the princess's side, catching her arm with far too much gentleness for the middle of a war zone. "Come on, that's it," he murmured.

Toryn felt the pause in her bones. The moment the princess weighed everything they could still do against how much it would buy them. It was the calculation Toryn had been ignoring ever since the roof collapsed, and when at last Leia turned to Chiffonage and declared, "Give the evacuation code signal," she felt as if all the air had been let out of her.

"And get to your transports!" Leia shouted as Solo all but dragged her from the room.

The first, wholly irrational thought that crossed Toryn's mind was that Corporal Sunsbringer would kill to have seen that interaction.

The second, far-too-rational thought that chased it was that she'd just have to get out and tell the kid herself.

Toryn had all but expected to die with her headset on. It felt like throwing off the burden of an entire moon to slip it from her ears. She rose on unsteady legs, aches throughout her body barking reminders of all the places she'd hit the ground when she'd dived clear of the ceiling collapse. There was one last transport staging for evac.

Toryn Farr ran for it.

She tore through the crumbling remains of Echo Base like a wind across the ice flats, carried not by faith or love or conviction but by a scrap of barracks gossip—and damnit, that was enough. The Rebellion was filled with grand ideals, but a person's mind wasn't built to hold on to something so enormous when everything was crumbling around them. All Toryn could do—all she *needed* to do—was let the small things carry her convictions in a relay through the moments when it all grew too big to grapple with. When she skidded out of the tunnels and into the hangar, she swore the armored shell of the GR-75 was the most beautiful sight Hoth had to offer.

That was, until she spotted a familiar scrap of Chandrilan luckcloth wound around the arm of a flight suit in the knot of injured pilots waiting to be loaded onto the transport.

Her muscles could argue later—Toryn broke into a sprint, sliding to her knees next to the stretcher. Samoc grinned up at her from beneath a worrisome burn that had already been slathered in bacta. "Rogue Six, reporting for duty," her sister croaked. "Orders, Echo Base?"

Toryn threw her arms around Samoc and knew she'd found the next thing to keep her going. "Let's get the hell off this rock." She sat back and glanced up at the GR-75, her eyes catching on the letters etched across its hull.

With a rueful shake of her head and a thin smile, Toryn Farr prepared to board the *Bright Hope.*

A GOOD KISS

C. B. Lee

Chase Wilsorr tugs on his clothes over his thermal layers, shivering in the cold morning air. Not that he can tell it's morning aside from the 0400 blinking at him from his datapad. The barracks are dark aside from the soft glow of the screen, and he's the only one unfortunately awake at this hour.

He claps his hands to his face, trying to slap some life into himself, and jumps up and down in place. It's a new day. Anything is possible. Today could be his last day on kitchen duty, he knows it.

"I am confident. I am strong. I'm a valuable member of the Rebel Alliance, and any minute now Major Derlin is going to give me a mission of my own."

Chase swipes through the pages he was reading before he went to bed, mouthing Raysi Anib's words to himself.

To first make your dreams come true, you must be open to the belief that they can. You must embody it. If you don't believe it to be true, how can anyone else?

The winning smile of the author grins at him from the cover of *Be Your Best Self* on his datapad. The Mirialan genius got him this far. Without this book he never would have left Takodana for Yavin 4 in the first place to fulfill his dreams about being a hero for the Rebel Alliance, so he owes it to Anib to keep trying.

"It's too early for your self-help shenanigans," mumbles a sleepy voice from the top bunk. "I don't have to report to the bridge until oh-nine-hundred. Please let me sleep."

The naysayers will try to get you to doubt yourself.

Chase ignores Joenn's critical voice and the way the cold seems to seep through his socks as he tugs on his boots and pads to the shared bathroom. "I am a strong, capable person with value," he intones to himself in the mirror.

"Shut up, kitchen boy. Hurry up and get out of here, I'm gonna want breakfast," Poras calls from a few bunks down.

His smile falters at the "kitchen boy" comment. The reality of who he is and what he does sinks in with absolute disappointment. Chase looks unacceptably plain, with *boring* written all over his features, nothing at all like the heroes whom epic spy stories and romances are written about.

Imagine who you want to be. Use that energy to direct your actions.

Chase gives his reflection a roguish wink, trying to project the aura of a confident, dashing hero.

Instead, he just looks like he has something in his eye.

A new notification flashes across the datapad, and Chase opens it eagerly.

To: Chase Wilsorr,

I have reviewed your appeal regarding Major Derlin's denial of your request for sentry duty at Echo Station 3-T-8. As per Major Monnon's report of your subpar work in the Alliance Corps of Engineers and his recommendation you be removed from duty, I regret to inform you that you do not meet the qualifications and encourage you to continue with your training before you take on advanced duties. Please report to Lieutenant Harlize Dana in the kitchens as per usual.

Your continued contributions and your commitment to the Rebel Alliance are appreciated.

General Carlist Rieekan

Ugh.

Chase hates Hoth. He hates Echo Base, he hates the freezing cold, how cramped the bunks are, how the gray-white sky melts into the endless ice fields outside, and most of all, he hates how it feels like LOSER has just been stamped across his forehead and there's no way to get rid of it.

It was so different on Yavin 4. Even though he'd failed basic training six times, Chase still felt hopeful. The days spent with the other young rebels, listening to stories of dashing spywork and bravery, imagining himself fighting back against the Empire. Running through the training fields, lush green fronds swaying in the humid jungle air—Yavin had felt like a wild adventure, and even working in the kitchens had been fun, cooking spicy woolamander stew and learning about different foods from Reynolds's and Khan's home planets, laughing about how they'd be heroes.

Kitchen duty on Hoth is always the same; there's little variation in the menu, nothing but the endless monotony of peeling and dicing in the same four walls. Chase has long since memorized the line of every pipe across the ceiling, the sound of every creak and sizzle from the power lines ahead, even the way the ice is curved under from where he sits everyday, a slight dip from where it melts and refreezes to his trousers.

Chase peels another purple tuber and tosses it into the pile.

X0-R3 beeps affirmatively at him, taking the completed pile and dicing it efficiently.

"You don't even need me," he says morosely to the droid. "This could all be automated."

Harlize ruffles his hair. "You're important, Chase, we all are." She sweeps her long blue hair into an efficient bun, tucking it into her hat before joining Chase at the pile of tubers. "C'mon, completely staffing the kitchens with droids is a luxury we can't afford. You're quick with a peeler and a kriffing good supply runner. Not all of us are cut out to be pilots. Doesn't mean we aren't valuable."

"Caf. Delivery. Datawork." Chase groans. "Some hero I am."

His old friends had both completed training on Yavin with flying colors; Marinna Reynolds just started flying with the Rogue Squadron, and Oriss Khan trains regularly with Alliance Special Forces when he isn't taking on grueling shifts of sentry duty.

Chase, meanwhile, is still stuck doing kitchen work.

He peels another tuber and starts a new pile.

Chase's first kitchen duty is over by 0700, and then he's on call for "essential delivery," which makes his job sound way more important than it actually is. He delivers caf and food to people who can't leave their shift, runs whatever boxes or supplies people need, and occasionally relays messages.

Chase knows all of these tunnels by heart—in fact, he helped make a good portion of them, before Major Monnon booted him out of the corps. Chase wasn't cut out to be an engineer, but he wanted to help, despite Monnon's claims that he was a danger to himself and others with the heat-tech. He shudders, thinking of that first week on Hoth when they'd carved out and melted tunnel after tunnel. Sure, he kept dropping the tools and he did sprain his ankle, but the ice flooring had been uneven! And using the heat-tech was far slower than Shara Bey's idea to use the ion cannons of the A-wings. It's not Chase's fault he didn't know what setting to use, but they ended up with a nice big briefing room, which worked out for the best, even though Major Monnon finally snapped at him to go help with the setup of the barracks instead of making the tunnels.

Chase still uses the makeshift tunnels they'd built during construction scattered above and below the main access tunnels. Most people don't know about them or avoid them, preferring the wider corridors that connect the main areas of the base, but Chase likes his shortcuts, likes how surprised people are when he seems to pop out of nowhere.

He saves his favorite caf run for last, before he has to head back to the kitchens for his second shift.

The bustle of mechanics and pilots and the hum of speeders and X-wings gives way to the soft bleating of the furry beasts as Chase approaches the tauntaun pens. There aren't enough tauntaun handlers for adequate rotation to allow for both sleep and the mess hall, so the food runs are necessary to keep the handlers going. On today's early shift, three handlers are on duty, a fact that Chase definitely did not factor into his schedule.

Baesoon and Murell take the caf and food gratefully as Chase makes his way through the ice-formed stables, the floor littered with tauntaun droppings still being swept up for compost.

Jordan Smythe, the newest handler, spots him walking down the aisle between the pens, his face breaking into a wide grin. "You're the best, Chase."

"Just doing my job," Chase says. "Apparently I'm not good enough to do anything else."

"Oh, come on, you're the best runner in Echo Base." Jordan smiles at him, taking the cup of freshly poured caf Chase had specially prepared just a moment before.

Chase blinks, distracted by the brief warmth of Jordan's fingers brushing against his. "You're just saying that," he says, embarrassed. He pulls his hand back, sticking it in his pocket hastily. Was that too fast? Jordan didn't notice, right?

Jordan takes another sip of caf before setting down the cup on top of the gate of Sunshine's pen.

A stray curl flops into Jordan's face as he heaves another stack of ice fungus into the pen from the hoverlift behind him.

Jordan flicks his hair out of his face effortlessly. Chase watches the lock of hair fall back into sideswept ebony curls, captivated by the movement, by Jordan himself, at the way his muscles are straining through his thin long-sleeved shirt.

"It's true," Jordan says, tossing another stack of the purple-blue fungus into the pen. "Nobody else would be able to bring me hot caf from the kitchens. That's on the complete other side of the base. *I* don't even know how to get there without getting lost."

"Oh, come on, that's easy. You just take tunnel 02-91 east and then 03-31 and then take a shortcut through the easternmost barracks and pop out at tunnel 04-21 and cut through the western mess hall and you're there. Fourteen minutes tops. Hoth can't freeze coffee that fast." Chase doesn't mention that he pours Jordan's coffee into his own insulated thermos and keeps it wrapped in his pack when he knows he's making a run past the tauntaun pens.

"That's amazing." Jordan gives Sunshine one last pat before shutting the gate to her pen. The tauntaun noses him affectionately on the shoulder. Chase tentatively reaches out his hand, but she snorts gruffly at him.

"You're just saying that because you're my friend."

"No, I'm saying it because it's true." Jordan shakes his head.

Chase sighs. He can barely even feel pleased at the compliment; he knows he makes deliveries quicker than anyone expects, but ultimately saving a few minutes here and there because he's memorized all the shortcuts doesn't mean anything. It's not like being a pilot or a spy or someone who actually matters to the Rebel Alliance.

"I want to do something important. I need more than just kitchen duty every day and delivering supplies, but Major Derlin says I cause too much trouble underfoot and he doesn't have time to train me." Chase thumbs through the multiple messages he's sent Major Derlin today. "I can too handle a blaster," he retorts.

Jordan laughs at him. "Oh, yeah? Show me." He unclips his holster and tosses his blaster at Chase.

Chase fumbles, the heavy weapon flipping at an awkward angle as he tries to catch it.

The tauntauns seem to be laughing at him, and Jordan is laughing, too. "Here, hold it like this." He readjusts Chase's grip, his callused hands warm against Chase's own.

Chase's throat goes dry.

"Jordan, quit flirting on duty!" Baesoon's annoyed tone breaks Chase out of his reverie. "Commander Skywalker is heading out and I need you to gear him up now."

Chase can feel his face light up with embarrassment. "I—"

Jordan squeezes his hands and gives him an apologetic smile before reholstering his blaster. "Gotta get back to work. I'll see you later?"

"Yeah," Chase says. He can't look away from the brightness of Jordan's smile, or from the sight of Jordan walking back toward the storage pen.

He turns around and bumps right into Sunshine, who just gives him a judgmental look.

"Do not start with me," Chase says, shaking his head.

Today's drop is new—the command center. Chase gulps as he pushes open the door. It's not a usual part of his routine, but it is now—apparently Joenn's mechanic skills keep her in demand enough in the hangar that she isn't doing running duties anymore.

"New holoprojector for you," Chase announces.

Toryn Farr turns as he sets down the heavy package. "Can you set it up? I'm expecting—" She snaps back to her comm station, intently listening through her headset.

Chase waits awkwardly until she relays a short series of commands back, fidgeting with his pack until Toryn finally notices he's still there.

"Was there something else?"

"Bantha milk, from your sister. She says remember to take breaks." Chase offers the bottle with a smile.

Toryn's gaze softens as she takes the bottle. "Wilsorr, right?" The chief communications officer smiles at him. "Thank you."

Chase beams proudly. Raysi Anib was right. People *do* value him when he values himself.

Oh. General Rieekan is right there.

If you don't ask the question, you'll never have the answer.

"General Rieekan? Would you like some caf? I was doing a run to the hangar and had some—"

"Thank you, that would be great." Blunt. Short. To the point. The general doesn't even look away from the plans he's poring over, but he gestures at his empty mug.

Chase pours caf out of his thermos. Now's his chance.

"General Rieekan, I hope you know that I—"

The hawk-eyed man turns his scrutinizing gaze toward Chase. "Who are you again?"

"Chase Wilsorr, sir. I requested sentry duty and was denied—"

"Oh, right, Lieutenant Dana's trainee." General Rieekan frowns.

"I hope that—"

"Listen, son, I'm very busy. I know you want to help, but the best thing for you right now is what you're suited for. Major Monnon explicitly said—"

"I know that I'm not good with weapons, sir. Or hand-eye coordination. Or fighting. Or any of that, really. But I could take shifts on sentry duty, I really—"

General Rieekan claps him on the shoulder. "That's the attitude and determination I like to see. I have a critical mission for you."

Chase's heart pounds with excitement. "Yes?"

Chase curses as he hefts another heavy supply crate through tunnel 05-92 to Echo Station 5-4 outside the base. He knocks on the durasteel doors and waits for them to slide open.

Rainn Poras smirks as he sets down the crate. "Hey, thanks for the *critical* delivery," he says with a sarcastic smile.

Chase rolls his eyes.

"These blasters need to be recharged—they're all in this crate here."

Chase grabs the other crate, his eyes stinging in the cold wind. He can't even enjoy being out here at the sentry point, being able to see the sky and the sunshine. Ice and snow stretch out into the endless horizon—nothing on the tundra, everything swaths of the same off-white, white and gray and blue unrelenting ice.

"Can you believe he applied three times to sentry duty?"

"Apparently Lieutenant Dana keeps running out of excuses to keep him busy."

"Is it true Wilsorr tripped over his own feet during weapons training and destroyed three barracks?"

Their voices carry as he makes his way back through the tunnel, and Chase grits his teeth as he shuffles forward. *I am important,* he reminds himself, even as he doesn't believe it anymore.

"Don't listen to them. I mean, I can see how the general was thinking—you didn't think your duties were critical before, and he's said they are, so—"

Chase plops down on the crate he's supposed to be delivering to the hangar, sighing. "Should I just stop trying?"

Jordan shrugs. "I think if you really want sentry duty, you could keep asking for it, but I also think you're great just the way you are."

Chase bites his lip, quickly looking away from the way Jordan's shoulders look in his thermal shirt. "How are you not cold?" Jordan's jacket is lying discarded next to the hoverlift stacked high with bales of fungus.

"Gets too hot throwing these around. This is nothing." Jordan grins at him, his warm brown eyes sparkling with mischief.

Chase likes the way words fit in Jordan's mouth, like they're round with delight, his deep accent making ordinary words sparkle with Jordan's quick-witted amusement. These moments with Jordan are always the best part of his day.

Jordan leans forward, placing his hands on Chase's shoulders, rubbing them with his palms. "You cold, Yavin baby?"

"N-no. Yes. I told you, I'm from Takodana! I mean. Cold. Uh, not anymore. I—"

Be open to possibility. Others won't know how you feel unless you tell them. Your most confident self is waiting for you to open the door.

Chase opens his mouth, and then closes it.

"I gotta go," Chase mutters, stumbling backward and grabbing his crate. He breaks into a quick jog. He's not running away from his crush. He's not. He's just . . . getting back to work.

Chase's breath billows in front of him in quick puffs as he leaves the tauntaun pens with the crate. Ugh, why didn't he stay? Was that flirting? Maybe he should have said something witty or suave. "I'm from Takodana!" Chase mutters to himself. Un-kriffing-believable.

Ugh. Hoth. He hates it so much.

Where was he going again?

Right, main hangar.

Chase makes a quick right into one of the main tunnels; other personnel walk quickly through, and the sounds of the command room echo through the wider corridor. Ahead of him are familiar voices.

"You want me to stay because of the way you feel about me!"

Chase can see Captain Solo striding ahead of Princess Leia Organa as she quickens her pace to match his. "Yes, you're a great help, a natural leader—"

Oh, not this again. Chase has seen them pretend to argue all over the base; in the mess halls, in corridors, in the hangar. Not that the argument against fickleberries baked on meatpies was without merit—Chase is clearly for combining savory and sweet and loves that Alderaanian custom—but honestly, to drag it out for an hour just to annoy the other person is too much. And now they're in his way. Can't they flirt somewhere else? He's got a job to do.

Captain Solo leans closer, and every centimeter of his handsome face annoys Chase to no end. Some people can't just sweep into the Rebellion with their own ship and accept actual critical missions from General Rieekan and banter with the princess all over Echo Base. Some people aren't handsome and don't have a presence like Han Solo. Some people are just ordinary people, okay?

Chase grips his crate tighter and steps right into the scant space between them and ignores the rising argument behind him.

"You could use a good kiss!" Captain Solo bellows. It echoes throughout the corridor.

The absolute nerve.

Chase bristles, his knuckles turning white as he picks up the pace. He's so tired of people like Solo. You know who's never been kissed? Chase Wilsorr, that's who. *He* could certainly use a good kiss. It offends him that Captain Solo and Princess Leia are just arguing about it, the way they've been dancing around each other since they've arrived on Hoth, clearly pretending to hate each other. Don't attractive people have anything better to do than to taunt everyone else on the base with their unresolved tension?

Chase is startled out of his normal kitchen duty the next day by a booming voice over the base's central communications system. "This is General Rieekan initiating the evacuation sequence. Imperial forces are approaching. All personnel must report to transport ships in the main hangar. Pilots, report to your X-wings . . ."

"Evacuation sequence!" Chase mutters. There had been a strange tension in the command center during his caf run yesterday, and then an increase in weapons distributions to the sentries. Chase always knew evacuation was a possibility, but he never thought it would come to this so quickly.

"We were trained to be able to go at a moment's notice," Harlize says. "Let's go—"

Chase follows Harlize out of the kitchens, and grabs her shoulder before she starts down the main corridor. "Come on, this way is faster!"

The main hangar is in chaos. Deck officers are rapidly directing crowds onto transport ships, crates and crates of supplies hastily being shuffled along the line as people hurry back and forth.

Chase tries not to gape; he's never seen the main blast doors just open like that, ships being deployed—in the distance, he can see the ominous angular shape of a ship he's only heard about in stories: a Star Destroyer.

"Imperial ground assault to the west! I need pilots with me, now!" Major Derlin shouts.

The ground rumbles. Something moves on the horizon, and another, and another—monstrously large vehicles stalking forward on legs. Explosions dot the landscape, and X-wings are escorting freighters. One freighter jumps to hyperspace and suddenly the evacuation is terrifyingly real. They're leaving the planet.

"Echo Base is not going to survive this," Harlize mutters. "Wilsorr, you boarding?"

"Yeah, I'm coming!" Chase scans the people in the loading bay, but he doesn't see Jordan anywhere. He types out a quick message on his datapad. *Come on, Jordan, where are you?*

"Has anyone seen Dr. Tristan Melthabi?" Major Derlin looks up from his datapad. The urgent question hangs in the air, concern drawn on the faces of everyone in the hangar.

"Cave-in on the access corridor to the medical facility," Deck Officer Serenity Meeks says, tapping her comm unit, bristling with anxious energy. "Dr. Melthabi is trapped, along with three other medtechs."

51

"I know another way!" Chase jumps off the loading ramp, waving his hands frantically as he runs up to Meeks.

"Quickly, we may not have much time." She nods at him. "Go!"

Chase nods, dashing off to the tunnels without thinking. He ignores the frantic thrum of his beating heart, the way his blood pounds in his ears, the laserfire in the distance. It's just another caf delivery. He can do this with his eyes closed and still bring that caf steaming hot to whoever needs it. Chase may not know how to fire a cannon or pilot any sort of ship, and maybe any weapon in his hands is a hazard, but he knows *how to run.*

Chase spots the opening to his eastern shortcut and ducks into the narrow tunnel, running as quickly as he can. Right, right, left. Cut through the barracks. Right. This should open up to the access corridor outside the medical facility. He pushes against the crushed ice and manages to clear a path wide enough to squeeze through. A quick glance at his datapad says he made it to the medical facility in 7.3 minutes, a personal record that he doesn't have time to preen about, but his shortcut takes him right behind the cave-in.

"Dr. Melthabi? Hello? The transport ships are all leaving, you have to evacuate!"

"The cave-in—"

Chase grabs the doctor by the sleeve and guides her and the other three medtechs to the hole he squeezed through next to the cave-in. "Down this tunnel, turn left, run right through the barracks—you should know because Poras's striped bedspread is really obvious— then right and two lefts and you'll be at the hangar."

"Thank you," the panicked doctor says breathlessly.

Wait, if this corridor collapsed, that means everyone behind it is trapped—

"Go ahead, Doctor! I'm going back this way to see if anyone else needs help."

Chase runs down the corridor, checking storage rooms and then each of the living quarters. He finds three foot soldiers and two communications officers and a whole group of refugees from Habassa II. Jordan *still* hasn't messaged him back yet. Where could he be?

Unless he doesn't have his datapad on him, which Jordan usually forgets if he's with the tauntauns—

"The *Bright Hope* is leaving in ten minutes. I repeat, ten minutes. This is the last transport ship for all evacuees." That's Toryn Farr's voice echoing throughout the base now.

"Go!"

Suddenly all the lights in the corridors go out. That's it. They've lost power.

"That's too many directions, I can't possibly remember that and in the dark!" Officer Sendak cries out.

"Just follow me," Chase says. He knows every tunnel here by feel, and even if he can't see, he knows how many paces it'll take to get to the next intersection—yes, turn here—another ten paces—another right—he checks to make sure everyone is with him, and they burst into the hangar just as another transport ship takes off.

Officer Meeks is gesturing people toward the *Bright Hope,* the launch door still open as people rush aboard.

"Good work, Wilsorr," Meeks says, looking up in relief as Chase approaches with everyone he's found. "Stormtroopers approaching. We don't have much time."

"Just give me a few minutes!" Chase says.

"You've got three."

Chase runs, ignoring the sounds of blasterfire and the base falling apart all around him. He makes it to the tauntaun pens, which are alarmingly silent—they must have all joined the fight.

Sunshine is still in her pen, and she clambers toward Chase when she sees him, snorting in distress.

To Chase's immense relief, Jordan is with her, trying to calm her down as she rears up.

"What are you still doing here?"

"Major Derlin said to stand by in case anyone else needed to gear up to fight!"

"Echo Base is lost. Come on, we have to evacuate!"

"I'm not leaving Sunshine!"

"I'm not leaving *you*! There's one ship left that's leaving"—Chase doesn't want to think about how much time they have left—"*now*! Let's go! We'll take her with us!"

"We'll have to ride."

Jordan throws a saddle onto Sunshine, who harrumphs but stands still as Chase approaches. He's always been afraid of the massive creatures, but he takes Jordan's outstretched hand and climbs up behind him.

"Which way do we go?"

Chase thinks quickly—they can't take his usual shortcut, it's too small for the tauntaun—they'll have to risk the main corridor.

"Take the eastern corridor, and then hang left!"

He shouts out directions as Jordan steers, and Sunshine gallops forward.

As Chase feared, there's a massive cave-in blocking the way to the hangar.

If there's one thing Chase can count on, it's his inexplicable certainty to mess up weapons. He grabs Jordan's blaster out of his holster, presses all the buttons at once in a slapdash sequence, and hurls it directly at the blockade.

"What are you—"

The blaster malfunctions and explodes, causing the ice to shatter just enough.

"Jump, Sunshine!" Chase shouts.

She clears the ice and they're free.

The doors to the *Bright Hope* are closing, and the engines are already lit.

"Wait for us, Meeks!"

"More personnel incoming!" she says, stalling the takeoff. "Come on!"

Sunshine dashes forward and clambers up the ramp just as it shuts. The ship's loading bay is full of people—many of whom Chase just guided through to safety.

The room explodes into whoops and claps.

"We've made it," Jordan exhales, as if he barely believes it.

They dismount, and Chase pats Sunshine distractedly as Dr. Melthabi claps him on the shoulder and Poras says, "Good work, Chase."

Chase grins, the words from *Be Your Best Self* echoing through him and for the first time feeling true. *You've always had this power in you.*

"Hey, Jordan?" Chase taps him on the shoulder.

55

"Yeah?" Jordan steps closer, close enough for Chase to see the flecks of gold and green in his eyes.

"You look like you could use a good kiss," he blurts out. For a second, Chase thinks it might be too much, but Jordan laughs and pulls him close.

"I thought you'd never ask."

Their lips meet, and Chase thinks maybe there's something to this confidence business after all.

SHE WILL KEEP THEM WARM

Delilah S. Dawson

A tauntaun's life has two rulers: warmth and cold. The first is a signal to wake with the sun, to hunt, to mate, to feed crop milk to squeaking taunlets, to run through the snow, nostrils huffing steam. The second is a signal to sleep, night's fall triggering a darkness so cold on the planet Hoth that even tauntauns can't survive it unless they huddle together, barely moving, their blood slowed to slurry. For Murra, matriarch of this herd of tauntauns, such natural rhythms have lost all meaning. She's been captured, corralled, tamed. She can smell the shift from day to night and back again but rarely sees the sun and moons. The odd, hot, buzzing things that provide false light in the pens among the caves are weak and cloying, and they never turn off.

She now has a third ruler: The strange two-footed creatures that control her.

They call themselves rebels.

For these captured tauntauns of Echo Base, part reptile and part mammal, the entire world has shrunken down to a few sections of a single cavern. Tauntauns can't count, but Murra knows she's with fewer animals than she once had under her care, when they lived free. Back then they often spent the night in caves like this one, sleeping so deep that nothing could wake them, their blood a heartbeat away from freezing as they piled together, their scents and bloodlines commingling. But when morning came, they crept out into the sparkling brightness, scenting the air for the reek of predatory wampas and, when finding none, snorting their pleasure and tossing snow with their horns to make sparkling rainbows against the white sky.

That's what Murra misses the most—freedom and high spirits, the ability to throw her head, butt horns, nudge a sister or daughter with her hip, sneak away with the bull of her choice, wiggle her tail to give the taunlets something to chase. When she leaves the caves now, she's bound with straps, head and body no longer capable of fully rejoicing in the fresh snow. The rebels turn her neck to tell her which way to go, nudge her ribs with hard boots, and shout things that have no meaning when she makes too much noise. She knows her name only because someone said it over and over again while feeding her ice scrabblers from a bucket, and now she knows that if she hears that sound and pads over, they'll have something else for her to eat, even if it's generally less appetizing.

This morning, she had a rare treat: She was taken out on patrol with her favorite daughter, Riba, and although they were both bound and saddled by the noisy rebels, they were still together in their element. The world was bright and full of smells and room to move, and they tossed their horns and bugled until the one riding Riba said,

"Wow, they're really excited today, huh, Han?" And the one on Murra's own back yanked on her head and muttered, "Only dumb animals could get excited about this much snow."

Not that Murra understood any of it.

Murra vastly prefers the female rebel with the soft voice, the one who stayed with her when she was throwing her most recent set of taunlet twins, confined to a stall, alone. It was a difficult birth—probably because tauntauns are meant to run out their labor, not to pace in a cramped corner—but the female rebel sat with her, stroking her face, murmuring comforting things, and when the two taunlets were finally out, that same rebel warned the male caretakers away, saying, "She's exhausted. Give us a little breathing room. Goodness knows we all need it."

Before she was captured, Murra would've spit in the rebel's face, but that night, weak from giving birth, she gently lipped clumps of fungus from her salty hands and didn't fight when the rebel stroked the fur down her neck. When Murra pushed her head against the rebel's shoulder, she was rewarded with a good scratch around her itchy horns.

"I know how you feel," the rebel said softly, right by her ear. "Always busy, always pushed this way and that. I think this is the first time I've been alone in months." A soft chuckle. "Not that I'm alone, with you and the babies." When the rebel reached down to caress the new, sleeping taunlets, Murra allowed it.

Those taunlets are sturdy and strong now, and the rebel female sometimes visits the pens in the quiet part of night, alone, when only Murra is half awake and keeping watch over her herd. Murra is always pleased to have her horns scratched, and the rebel seems glad to have someone to talk to.

So, yes, it was a good morning running with Riba, but their time together in the snow was all too brief. Now Murra is back in the caves and unsettled. She wouldn't usually fret over her strong daughter being outside where she belongs, but the air tells her it's going to be an unusually cold night, and Riba should be back by now. Riba is pregnant, although it's early, and these will be Murra's first granddaughters. She opens all her nostrils, scents the air, paces nervously.

There's no sign of Riba, but the female rebel is nearby. And even for one of her kind, she smells . . . disturbed. Anxious. Uneasy. Just like Murra feels. She wonders if perhaps the female rebel is worried about someone she cares for—maybe the male rebel riding Riba? Are rebels capable of such feelings? They certainly don't rub and touch and snort like tauntauns, and the way they wrap their own bodies completely in straps and smelly cloth suggests they're too primitive to read scents.

Murra is at the edge of the makeshift fence, watching the rebel and puzzling at the strangeness in the air, when an unwelcome odor makes her snort. She spins, head already down, presenting her horns.

Keelak faces her, horns ready, and squeals a challenge.

Murra softly sighs. Keelak is the sort of upstart cow she would've driven away from the herd, if they were outside, where they belong. Keelak has nerve but no wisdom, belligerence without care. Her taunlets are strong but poorly behaved. She is a leader for a wilder time, but here, in the caves, the tauntauns must show restraint, or else . . . they simply disappear.

The younger cow charges, and Murra is ready. She's weathered such threats before. Their horns crash with an intensity that jars Murra's old bones.

They both rear back, eyeing each other.

Keelak hit hard—harder than expected.

So this is real, then.

Keelak isn't playing, isn't testing her.

Keelak wants to usurp her and take control of the herd, and she's taken Murra's worry for weakness.

With a toss of her head to check the big open door one last time for any sign of Riba, Murra snorts her own rage, letting her affront and anger seep out her pores, drowning Keelak's scent. The older cow circles with her challenger, her senses taking in every minute sniff and sound that might help her best the younger, smaller, but more motivated beast.

Murra is the matriarch. She was the matriarch before this cave and she plans to be the matriarch long afterward, to midwife her granddaughters and great-granddaughters into the icy world outside without the strange, hot lights of the murmuring rebels and their scents of panic and fear. Keelak has no battle scars, has never made tough decisions to keep her herd safe; she only wants domination. Murra has never trusted her.

Normally, that lack of trust would be bad for the herd, because tauntauns are bound by smell and touch.

61

Now it's good because Murra has no qualms about destroying her rival. They share neither love nor blood.

Keelak throws back her head to bellow, and that's when Murra attacks, ramming her horns into the smaller cow's throat and throwing her onto her back. She saw that trick once when her own mother ruled, a bachelor challenging the lead bull, so perhaps Keelak didn't know to be careful. Horns are to be butted, but horns have other uses.

Twisting in the air, Keelak lands on the meat of her hip with a cry of pain and scrabbles awkwardly, trying to stand. The other tauntauns have all stepped back, forming a circle, watching the fight with intense curiosity. Their most sensitive language is one of odor, and Murra smells the crowd: concern, excitement, indignation, ferocity. Some would like to see her go; others pulse with their love for her and their need for her leadership. Empowered by their support—and enraged by those who would betray her—Murra bugles her superiority and runs for the struggling, vulnerable Keelak. Tauntauns don't do well on their backs, especially not on the slick floors of the warm cave, with no thick, soft snow to provide cushion and grip.

A spurt of rage emboldens her, and she lunges for the smaller cow's exposed belly, her strong, yellow teeth bared. But before her teeth can close on that blubbery skin, a hot splash of Keelak's saliva slashes across her eyes, blinding her. Murra paws at her face, but her claws can't quite reach her eyes. She knows that if she turns to wipe her eyes on her haunch, she'll leave her other side open for Keelak's attack, and she can't risk it. With a taunlet's mew of desperation, she blindly lumbers into the circle of her herd, begging for help. Pombo steps back uneasily, but then a warm body swings toward her, offering fur that no longer carries the scent of snow but still smells like home. Her old friend Tova. Murra gratefully rubs her face against the familiar flank until the saliva is gone, gives a purring nuzzle of appreciation, and spins to charge Keelak, snaking her head to avoid another wad of spit.

"Hey, now. What's this? Murra, you've got more sense than that."

Her favorite female rebel is there, ducking under the makeshift fence as if she's completely forgotten she's surrounded by an entire herd of huge, upset beasts, any of whom could easily snap her in half with one hard thwack of a tail. The rebel hurries up to Murra, who's gone still at the sound of her name. There could be food involved.

"Keelak, cut that out. Ugh, what a smell. I swear, what is it that gets into you tauntauns? Lieutenant, put a halter on Keelak and put her in a private pen, would you? She looks like she wants to spit."

The female rebel has her useless little paws up, and Murra snuffles at them, hoping for some hidden tidbit. She sighs to find them empty, but then they're rubbing her long neck, scratching around her horns and ears. It's calming, like a mother's barbed tongue, and Murra's earlier rage melts at the touch. Keelak is led away, and the tension breaks, the tauntaun herd milling around as if they've forgotten they nearly watched a fight to the death.

"Are you worried, big girl? Your daughter is out there with Luke. He'll keep her safe. And she'll keep him safe, won't she? Riba is just like you. Strong. Capable. Careful."

Murra lowers her head for more scratches. She doesn't know what the language means, but there's something pleasant about it, something comforting. Her name and her daughter's name, murmured together like the wind's song. She purrs, deep in her throat, and delicately rubs her head against the rebel's fingers. The rebel leans in, head down, her voice soft, a secret just between them.

"Oh, Murra. Luke's taking too long, and Han is leaving. Why can't they both be in the same place at the same time, where I can keep an eye on them?" The rebel looks around at the other tauntauns and smiles. "I wonder if that's how you feel when Arno and Boz are out. Like your taunlets are full-grown and you trust them, but you'd feel a lot better if you were personally watching over them?"

Murra snorts; something caught in her second set of nostrils. The rebel keeps talking.

"I'm worried about Luke. It's not like him to be careless. It's *exactly* like Han, but at least Han's still here and safe. I know he's about to leave, but . . ." The rebel trails off, uncertain, and sighs. . . . "They're kind of impossible, aren't they? Or maybe just Han is. Or maybe I am." She slings her arm around Murra's neck and looks at the open door along with the tauntaun, wisps of snow curling in as the sun begins to set. "I sent Threepio to ask Han about going out to find Luke. I hope he doesn't botch it up. Six million forms of communication and that droid still gets the wording exactly wrong half the time."

Hearing the word *Threepio*, Murra's tail tip twitches in disgust. The shiny thing smells wretched, and it once tried and failed to com-

municate with her using a loud, grating squawk she didn't conde-
scend to return.

"Princess?"

It's another rebel, some random male, and he's carrying a bridle.

Her rebel, the female, the leader, looks up. She smells annoyed
now, as if she's been interrupted in the midst of something very important. Murra knows that feeling.

"Yes?"

"Captain Solo is gearing up . . ."

The female unhooks her arm from Murra's neck, a sensation the
tauntaun immediately misses. But then she takes the bridle and slips
it over Murra's head, buckling it gently. "You'll bring him home, won't
you, girl?" she whispers into a furry ear. "You're a tough old broad."

Murra twitches her ear back toward her rebel, listening.

"Princess, wouldn't you rather send out one of the younger, stronger animals?"

The female leads Murra over to the smaller corral where they keep
the saddles, and for once, Murra eagerly follows. Not because there's
food involved, but because the saddle means she's going outside, and
that's where her daughter Riba has been for far too long.

"There's no stronger tauntaun than this old battle-ax," her rebel
says, patting her neck. "She was here before us, and she'll be here long
after us. For some reason . . . I trust her."

The female rebel leaves as the male begins the lengthy saddling
process, but then she returns with a handful of fungus, which Murra
daintily nibbles from her open hand, following it with a wide lick of
thanks.

"I'm counting on you, girl. Bring them back safe."

And then the female rebel leaves, a scent of hope mixed with
worry trailing in her wake.

The male rebel grooms Murra with a currycomb—it would be enjoyable if she weren't so anxious to leave—and saddles her, pulling the strap a little more tightly than she'd prefer and making her snort in surprise. She knows this dance, she's ready for it, and when the noisy male rebel finally arrives, she can smell him, too—he's angry, but more than that, he's scared. And he carries the faintest whiff of her female rebel, a tender but lingering scent of affection.

The noisy one doesn't seem to like what the other rebels are telling him, and he climbs up into her saddle with purpose, thrumming with energy that resonates in Murra herself.

He wants something very much, and she does, too.

She can feel it in her blood, in every muscle.

She needs to run outside, needs to open all her nostrils and hunt for her daughter. She is the matriarch of her herd, and this is her greatest responsibility—keeping those she loves safe, no matter what.

"Your tauntaun will freeze before you reach the first marker," the male on the ground says, but *tauntaun* is the only word that means anything to Murra.

"Then I'll see you in hell!" the noisy rebel shouts back.

Murra doesn't know what that means, either, but it feels an awful lot like the bellow of rage she unleashed on Keelak earlier, and she wants to bugle along with him, to share in his determination. But the sound she wants to make belongs outside, just like she does. She can wait a few moments longer.

The noisy rebel nudges her forward, and Murra gladly runs out the open door, nostrils wide open, scenting the icy air for any sign of her daughter. She takes in a deep breath, and her body lights up, incandescent. Here, she is an animal again, she is herself, she feels the snow underneath her feet and her tail swinging fully in the freezing air. It is exhilarating and right and beautiful, and for just a moment, before he jerks her reins and sets her course, Murra remembers what it was to be free.

She throws back her head and calls for her daughter, and for once the noisy rebel lets her, doesn't yank the reins to quiet her.

"You can say that again, sister. Now do me a favor and find my friend."

Murra runs, nostrils open, searching, hunting, fully herself for the briefest of moments.

There—the faintest scent.

It's the younger rebel male, the one Riba carried this morning.

The trail is old and faint, but it is enough. If she can find him, perhaps she will find her daughter, and when the temperature falls, they can huddle together and share their warmth. It's the only way to survive a night this cold on Hoth, and she is determined to live to morning.

She runs like the wind as the sun begins to set.

She will find her daughter and protect her, protect the next generation of taunlets in her daughter's belly. She is driven by blood and love. She will protect those that she loves.

She will keep them warm.

HEROES OF THE REBELLION

Amy Ratcliffe

Corwi Selgrothe imagined herself at home—wrapped in her beloved bantha-fur blanket and comfortably reviewing footage for new recruitment holos. Instead she was still on Hoth. This was not how the trip was supposed to go.

She adjusted her gloves to make sure they were tucked inside her sleeves. Being inside Echo Base's shield doors was far superior to being outside in the unforgiving elements, but she wouldn't go so far as to call it warm. Corwi let loose a frustrated breath, forcibly enough to make a tauntaun dozing nearby give her what she could only describe as a rude look.

"Hey, believe me, I'm not thrilled about this situation, either," Corwi told the tauntaun.

She leaned back against the pen keeping the conscripted creatures from roaming at will. Corwi needed to collect her thoughts, and this was one of the few places of respite she'd found in the base. She should have been interviewing Luke Skywalker, the most well-known hero of the Rebellion. Time had passed since his triumph against the Death Star, but the name Skywalker still inspired potential recruits—had them with stars in their eyes, dreaming of fighting the Empire and restoring good to the galaxy. Corwi had leveraged the rebels' victory above Yavin 4 to great effect, releasing numerous holos about the mission to counteract the Empire's "terrorist attack" lies.

And this trip to Hoth should have given Corwi material for months. Maybe even the next year of the Galactic Civil War! Besides Skywalker, she was going to talk with Han Solo and Princess Leia Organa. Sure the locale was rough, even by rebel standards, but all three of them were in the same place at the same time. Given what she'd heard about one or more of them frequently dashing around the galaxy on missions, this was a rare gift. Corwi knew she could extract stories about their service to the Rebellion and that she'd find stirring quotes in them—quotes that would make others see the promise of the Rebel Alliance. Lines like, "Rebellions are built on hope."

Capturing Jyn Erso's moving words before she took off to Scarif with the doomed Rogue One group was one of Corwi's greatest achievements as a rebel propagandist. And Corwi intended to find similar success on Hoth. She'd certainly lobbied to be sent here, this top-secret location on a frozen rock. She'd made a professional case directly to Mon Mothma about why she should come to this mysterious base—she'd heard rumors that the heroes of the Rebellion were all headed there, and she wouldn't be foolish enough to try any live broadcasts, or transfer data, or send a message to anyone offworld. She'd save all the glorious interviews she'd get for review after the rebels left Hoth; she didn't want to give them away. In fact, she told

Mon Mothma, she would stay embedded with her fellow rebels for the near future to document day-to-day life. It's the kind of thing potential recruits were curious about.

Corwi didn't quite sell the poised, confident leader on the latter idea, but she secured permission to travel to Echo Base. She'd be on Hoth for as long as the Rebellion stayed there, so she'd go ahead and chronicle everything she saw. Corwi liked to think her passion for sharing the Rebellion's story with the galaxy in the hope of attracting always-needed recruits came across as enthusiastic to Mon Mothma. She knew she asked for a lot, but Corwi believed in the Alliance's mission to restore justice to the galaxy. She put her all into her work to increase the numbers, because she knew the more people stood against the Empire, the better off the galaxy would be. Corwi balanced any pleading edge in her voice with recruitment data and anecdotes.

Her arguments worked. Corwi arrived on Hoth dressed in layers of vests, shirts, and wraps, her recording gear carefully wrapped in a large pack. She wasn't one to waste time "settling in." Particularly not in this sort of location. It all had a *we'll make do with what we have* feel, which was very much the Alliance way. Roughly carved walls met a stark floor with supplies strewn in a haphazard fashion here and there. Maybe she could find some hot broth, but as far as creature comforts went that was about it. She made holos to inspire, but Corwi tried to temper her material with realism. She knew she couldn't win the Rebellion interest or respect by pretending every day in this war was a noble parade.

Corwi had to be honest when she made holos to galvanize others to stand by the Rebellion. Honest and hopeful. She knew quotes from Luke, Leia, and maybe even Han would be exactly what she needed. Others in the Alliance uttered the trio's names in a kind of awed tone; they put the heroes on pedestals. Her sources reported that even some backwater planets were beginning to recognize these names and trade stories about them. This was the time to put together new holos, to work with her artist friend Janray on new propaganda posters with any—or all—of the three heroes. They would be the fulcrum for this next, wide wave of recruitment.

But Corwi had to find time with these heroes first. She had no way of knowing if she'd be expected. Her trip came together quickly, and she understood communications to and from the secret base were on an as-needed basis. They'd expect this final shuttle carrying supplies to make the base optimally operational but maybe not so much the propagandist who had tucked herself into a tight space between crates of rations and blankets for the ride.

She reported in to a General Bygar. He was hurried and clearly had other matters to attend to, but he welcomed Corwi nonetheless. Bygar passed her off to a communications officer, who gave her a brief overview of Echo Base. Where to find the caf, the medical bay, the basics. Comms Officer Farr outlined the evacuation plan quickly, with the weary voice of someone who had clearly been through it a million times. When she finished, Corwi inquired about speaking with Princess Organa. Surprise flickered on Farr's face. She all but laughed at Corwi's request. The princess, she informed Corwi, was working in the command center, an area limited to essential personnel only. Corwi had no chance of speaking with her.

Corwi filed that information for later; she wasn't going to give up that easily. So she asked after Luke Skywalker. Farr described Luke as affable; he'd probably be happy to talk with her, but he was on patrol outside. That left Han Solo. Corwi had heard the smuggler and informal rebel could be taciturn; she wasn't thrilled about having Han as her only option, but she had to try. And despite his reputation as a scoundrel—or maybe because of it—he had to have interesting stories to tell. Farr took Corwi to the *Millennium Falcon,* where Han stood with a frustrated look on his face. Normally Corwi wouldn't bother with someone who was scowling, but her choices were limited. Han actually rolled his eyes when Corwi introduced herself and muttered something about not being the kind of role model the Rebellion should put forth for recruitment. Determined to get something—anything—Corwi quickly set up her equipment. She asked Han why he flew into the battle above Yavin 4, what the Rebellion meant to him.

"Listen sweetheart, I'm no hero. I saw a fight and pointed my ship at it," Han barked.

She tried to pose a softer follow-up question; he brushed her off.

Then Han gestured at his Wookiee companion. "You know what? Chewie would be happy to answer your questions," he said with a patronizing smile on his face.

The resolute feeling she had when she approached faded. Corwi didn't think she'd ever interacted with someone so unpolished, so brash. She'd been wrong about him. Corwi probably would have received more useful answers from Chewbacca. He was a hero of Yavin, too, she recalled, and there had to be a protocol droid somewhere around here to translate. Maybe she would try to talk with Chewbacca later—only when Han wasn't grumbling nearby.

She stowed her gear and asked the nearest officer about Luke. He was still on patrol. As evening crept closer, word traveled around the base that Luke Skywalker hadn't reported in and no one knew where he was. Han apparently left on a tauntaun to search for him. Corwi noted the tension in the air when she dined in the mess hall. When she wandered back to the hangar deck out of curiosity, she saw Leia looking outside into the unfriendly mass of white and blue, distress rolling off her. Corwi took a step toward Leia and paused. Leia looked . . . scared. Corwi struggled to process the thought because she'd never witnessed Leia show vulnerability. If the princess was this concerned, the situation was more dire than Corwi first thought. It wasn't the time to pepper Leia with questions, especially as it looked like they were going to have to close the shield doors to block Hoth's fatally cold nighttime temperatures with Luke and Han still missing.

The next morning Corwi was relieved to learn that Han had discovered Luke, and they'd both returned to the base. The Rebellion needed them. Their friends needed them. Corwi wanted to give them time to thaw and recover before she checked in again. But according to a conversation she overheard in a corridor, a vicious creature had attacked Luke. He wasn't in critical condition or anything, but he did require medical attention. That could actually work for Corwi—a holo featuring a hero in the medbay, injured in his service to the Rebellion but still bright-eyed about his purpose and belief in the Alliance. It could be perfect. And though Corwi dashed to the nearby medical bay, Luke was in a bacta tank when she arrived. That wouldn't do.

72

So here she was, bonding with the tauntauns and waiting on word of Luke being in a less compromising position. She needed to formulate a new plan. Tauntauns' garbling, rustling noises weren't really recruitment material. To have to tell Mon Mothma she didn't get anything would be embarrassing after all her pleading—she didn't want to consider the option. Mothma gave Corwi a way out of the Imperial Press Corps all those years ago. The Empire had pulled Corwi in with other holojournalists after the fall of the Republic. At first, Corwi was naïve about the Empire's intent. She thought she'd continue reporting the truth of events around the galaxy, as she'd been doing for years. Instead, the Imperial Press Corps was a propaganda machine for the Empire. Broadcasters were fed stories that were either outright lies or a heavy manipulation of the truth twisted to put the Empire in a flattering light. Though the extent of the Emperor's ambitions weren't clear in the early days, Corwi felt the oily sense of wrongness in her bones. It wasn't only being made to tell lies, it was that it became obvious the Empire was in the business of oppression. Where their forces went, a certain bleakness followed. She didn't last long before quietly leaving one day and going into hiding.

In her new life, traveling from planet to planet, she listened from the corners where no one looked. She heard whispers of rebellion. Seeing clearly fictitious reports from her onetime colleagues, like Alton Kastle, further pushed her to seek out the Rebel Alliance. The Empire's influence and control were spreading. She wanted to push back against the Emperor in any way she could, to do her part to bring life back to the corners of the galaxy the Empire had drained until they became a dull gray. When Mon Mothma resigned from the Senate and announced her intent to restore the Republic, Corwi knew how she could help. She realized the Rebellion was in need of their own version of the Imperial Press Corps. People to craft and release recruitment holos to raise awareness and bring more allies to their cause. It would still mean putting a certain spin on events, yes, but Corwi knew this would be for the good of the galaxy. She held herself to a code; she wouldn't twist the truth. She'd only bolster it. Corwi believed it to be an acceptable compromise. It took a while to get in front of rebels who would listen and pass her ideas on to the new leadership.

But eventually, she stood in front of Mon Mothma and earned herself a place. A place that made a difference. A place she would use today to speak to Commander Skywalker.

Corwi stood straight. She removed the holorecorder from her pack, slung the bag over one shoulder, and cut a focused path toward the medical bay. She spotted a medical droid.

"Excuse me. Have you seen—"

An overhead announcement cut Corwi off. She couldn't make out the words, but beings started moving in every direction—not with panic, but with purpose. The base flipped from brisk business as usual to a hub of overlapping activities in an instant. Something was happening. She'd been adjacent to combat before; that experience didn't stop the heavy weight suddenly pressing on her chest. Corwi tried to capture the attention of someone in a pilot's uniform without getting in their way.

"What's happening?"

"The Empire found us," the pilot replied in an unnervingly calm voice.

He ran off before Corwi could ask follow-ups. She let raw emotion course through her veins for exactly ten seconds, a calming method she'd discovered in her days in the press corps. She could allow herself to worry but only because she knew she could control her reactions. With a clearer head, Corwi tried to recall the evacuation instructions. When she drew a complete blank on what she was supposed to do and where she should be going, Corwi turned her holorecorder on almost reflexively and raised it to eye level—she may as well use the circumstances to get shots she could insert into holos that needed some dynamic action—and raced in the direction of the hangar deck. That's where the ships were, that's where she'd find a way off Hoth. She hoped. That feeling of desperation, of wanting to survive another day, started to creep in like a haze around her thoughts. She had to keep moving.

A sense of urgency saturated the air of the hangar. Corwi sidestepped droids rolling into action, technicians scrambling to fighters. She rooted herself to a clear area and slowly rotated in a circle, capturing the oddly delicate motions around her. She could almost pretend she was watching a choreographed scene, planned and blocked to the last detail with everyone moving in harmony. Unlike her,

Corwi noted, they evidently knew the procedures backward and forward. She watched these soldiers operating in a remote, uncomfortable location preparing to confront a threat without a second thought. Everyone had an important role. Everyone was ready to risk their—

A sharp voice interrupted Corwi's musings. "All troop carriers will assemble at the north entrance. The heavy transport ships will leave as soon as they're loaded."

She recognized it as belonging to Leia. Corwi saw her just ahead, gathering the pilots for a briefing. She stepped to the side and spun her holorecorder in the princess's direction. Finally! She was catching a rebel hero in action. Corwi felt a brief second of joy despite her surroundings. She already envisioned folding Leia's words into a holo targeted at pilots. Even if Leia didn't give the most eloquent of speeches here, the visual would stand on its own. Potential recruits would see Leia, survivor of Alderaan and leader of the Rebel Alliance, leading from the front lines, caring about those who serve. And she clearly did care; Corwi wouldn't be stretching for that angle. It was just what she needed.

But it wouldn't matter if she didn't get on a transport. The recordings she'd gathered had to leave physically with her or not at all.

Corwi may have been caught up in her work, but she heard a pilot mention a Star Destroyer. The Empire had arrived in force. Corwi watched the pilots scramble to their ships while she got her bearings. She had a vague idea about where she actually should have gone and that was enough. Worst case, Corwi figured, she'd just move in the same direction as everyone else. No, the worst case was that she would get lost and killed or captured by the Empire. She couldn't allow that. As she turned to what was probably the escape route, she saw a familiar face cross in front of her. Luke Skywalker! Even the briefest moment of Luke preparing to head into battle would be invaluable.

"Commander Skywalker!" Corwi shouted.

He didn't hear her. Corwi scrunched her face, annoyed that she was so close and yet not close at all. She fully understood the unfortunate timing, but she felt compelled to keep trying. She just needed to stretch over a tangle of wires to get a little closer. Corwi leaned back to give herself momentum to take a big step, but she slammed squarely into a solid mass.

The rebel soldier skidded to a stop. "Karabast! Keep an eye out, won't you?"

Corwi picked up the bag he'd dropped. "I'm sorry. I'm just trying—"

"To what? If you're not part of the battle, you need to get out of here," he grunted. "Do you know which carrier you're assigned to?"

"I didn't know there were assignments," Corwi admitted, upset with herself for not paying closer attention to Farr. "I'm not even sure how to get to the transport ships. I thought they would be here."

"Follow me. We'll figure it out when we get there," the soldier shouted.

Corwi looked around him to see Luke clambering into a fighter, like everyone else—a hero of the Rebellion yes, but also just a pilot trying to do his part. Several other pilots surrounded her, their dedication no less remarkable for not being Luke Skywalker. Then her whole world narrowed to the soldier ahead of her and the rugged hallway they soon rushed through. The sounds of the ground assault rang outside, the walls of the base shaking from the attack. Small chunks of debris fell from the ceiling. Corwi put her left hand up as if it could alone stop a cave-in; with her other hand, she folded her holorecorder in near her body protectively. She wanted to preserve her life, but she'd rather not lose her work if she could help it. Her job was to get the word out for recruitment. It was important, and she couldn't do it if she didn't survive this.

Finally, Corwi and the soldier emerged from a compact hallway into a wide transport bay. She spotted bulky transport ships in every direction she turned. She'd thought the hangar deck was chaotic; that was nothing compared with this. She registered the columns of evacuees as a blob of white and gray. Again, rebels moved with a seeming order, but to Corwi, it was overwhelming. She wasn't ashamed to put her hand on the soldier's arm so as not to lose track of him in the crowd. If he was irked with having an unexpected charge, he didn't show it. He helped her weave through the crowd and deposited her in a line boarding a personnel carrier.

"They'll take care of you, I promise," he said.

"What's your name, soldier?" Corwi asked.

"L'cayo Llem."

"Thank you, L'cayo. I won't forget this." Corwi brought her holorecorder up in front of her and tilted her head toward it. L'cayo nodded. She didn't know exactly why, but she felt compelled to capture an image of the soldier—she wouldn't be in a position to escape without him. Gratitude emanated from her every pore.

Covered in sweat and breathing heavily, Corwi glanced around her as she waited to board the carrier. Rebels waved others onto ships, urging their comrades on with encouraging, if stressed, shouts. Everyone looking out for one another. Everyone who volunteered to join the Rebel Alliance and defy the Empire. Everyone who stepped up to save the galaxy from oppression.

A waving hand motioned her to board the carrier. Corwi wasted no time filing in and sitting where instructed. Beings rushed aboard, but the atmosphere was eerily quiet. She followed the example of those around her and strapped in. The space around her filled with bodies. They were still on Hoth, so they were still in danger. In the stillness, Corwi could hear snippets of frantic comm chatter, but she couldn't make out the words. She tried not to give in to spiraling fear.

Tried not to think about all she still wanted to do. She redirected her focus to how she got on this carrier and to those around her who had committed their lives to this kind of existence—the kind of existence that can be upended in mere minutes once the enemy arrives.

Corwi closed her eyes and took a deep breath. She thought about how she'd chased the heroes of the Rebellion around Echo Base. But it wasn't only about them. Not at all. The pilot of this carrier, the defensive fighters waiting to escort and protect them, L'cayo who led her to this seat of safety—heroes. Every one of them. Maybe their names weren't uttered in cantinas around the galaxy. Maybe the galaxy didn't know about their heroic deeds. It didn't make the efforts of the dozens of beings around her any less significant. Everyone was a hero.

The sound of the ramp closing rattled through the ship. The engines groaned. Corwi felt the ship move out of the transport bay and swiftly into the air. She released a deep breath she hadn't realized she was holding. It was one step closer to safety, but they were far from celebrating a successful escape. She surveyed those around her and absorbed a range of emotions from the other evacuees: a single tear running down a cheek tense with fear across from her, white-knuckled hands clenched on top of a bowed head in a seeming plea for help near the front of the transport, multiple unfocused anxious stares. She heard someone nervously tapping their foot. Corwi strained to listen to the comms, to the rumbling of the ship—whatever might give her a clue about whether they would survive. She recalled Leia mentioning that each ship had only two fighter escorts and wished she had forgotten that detail. Two fighter escorts against a Star Destroyer? Corwi blinked the scenario out of her mind and pictured an entire squadron just beyond the ship's hull protecting them as they leapt into hyperspace.

A blast buffeted the ship's hull. She gasped. Was that . . . was that the Empire shooting at them? Corwi squinched her eyes so forcibly she saw lights dance at the edge of her vision. She heard a sharp sob far away and a chorus of ragged breathing. Her own knuckles turned white as she gripped the seat underneath her and braced for an explosion. Another light movement. More intense breathing. And then the light sound of comm chatter. The pilot shouting, "We're away! Repeat: We're away!"

Those words, those precious few words, hung in the air as despair turned into elation. A few individuals looked numb, as if their hearts couldn't take the emotional whiplash and the revelation of survival. Grim mouths turned to broad smiles. Hands relaxed from worried grips to pound friends, perhaps strangers even, on the back in triumph. Loud cheers replaced the terror-infused breaths. Corwi cried from relief; she slumped in her seat as every bone-crushing worry lifted and tears streamed down her face. They were safe. She was safe. A feeling of hope settled back into her mind.

"Hope," she whispered to herself. "Hope."

Jyn Erso's words came to mind. "Rebellions are built on hope." Corwi had equated hope with heroic deeds like Jyn's sacrifice or Luke destroying the Death Star. She'd believed those huge moments and the heroes who carried them out were key to inspiring more beings to join the Rebellion. That wasn't true at all. Hope wasn't limited to only a handful of names. That's not who made up the ranks of the Alliance. Hope was about people—ordinary people that made a choice to join the fight and to stay in it.

Hope was the rebel soldier who guided a lost propagandist to safety, who recognized the value of a single life and did what he could to protect it. Hope was all around her in the now reassured faces of the evacuees. People who had decided to band together against the Empire and didn't waver even in the face of annihilation.

Every person in the Rebellion was a hero. But it wasn't only that. They all represented hope. And that was the way forward for the Rebellion. Not to focus only on the big, sweeping heroic deeds. No, it was to create more hope. And they would do that by honoring and championing the heroism people exhibited every day. Hope.

An energized Corwi flipped her holorecorder on. She turned to the person next to her and took in his weary, cheerful demeanor. Corwi gave him a warm smile and asked, "Why do you fight the Empire? Tell me your story."

"Why me?" he asked.

"Your story is going to save the galaxy."

ROGUE TWO

Gary Whitta

Zev Senesca hated the cold. He hated the snow and ice, so cold it burned, hated the freezing wind that whipped at your face until you could no longer feel it. He hated this entire Maker-forsaken planet—if you could even call it a planet. Hoth was more like a giant frozen rock floating in space, as uninviting a place in the galaxy as could be imagined.

But maybe that was the point. The Empire had the Rebellion on the run after discovering their former base on Yavin 4 and forcing a hurried evacuation, and since then had made it near impossible for them to find a new home, having issued a galaxy-wide declaration that any civilized world offering safe harbor or passage to the Alliance would be subject to crippling sanctions and Imperial occupation. So in finding a location for a new base, all the rebels had left to choose from were the most remote and least suitable sanctuaries: the deserted, barren planets and moons to be found in the far reaches of space. But as desperate as the Empire knew the Rebellion was, they likely never considered they'd be so desperate as to hole up in a place like this, a planet so cold it was barely capable of sustaining any kind of life save a handful of indigenous creatures, most of which lived deep beneath the surface, closer to the planet's still-warm core. So maybe it was smart of leadership, in a way, to hide here, one of the last places the Empire would ever think to look.

Still, that didn't take the sting out of the day-to-day hardships of living in a place like this. Carving out the hangars and tunnels for the base itself had been hard enough, a brutally laborious job that had taken weeks and come at the cost of several lives, mostly to the cold or to cave-ins during construction. But now here they were, as comfortable as they could be under the circumstances. The techs had even managed to pipe heating throughout the base, and everyone had cheered when they first turned on the generators and they actually worked, allowing them all to strip down to fewer than six warm layers for the first time since they'd arrived.

But that had been just the beginning. Even with a functioning base to shelter inside, Hoth threw up one problem after another. The snowstorms and atmospheric interference were often so severe there were only limited windows in which Echo Base's sensor operators could conduct scans for any signs of Imperial presence in the system—although that one at least cut both ways, the harsh weather also obscuring any rebel emanations from the surface that a passing Imperial ship might otherwise detect. They were often blind here on Hoth, but at least they were often invisible, too.

A bigger problem concerned the surface speeders the rebels had brought with them from Yavin 4. Zev and the other pilots of Rogue Squadron loved to fly them; they were fast, maneuverable, and responsive, and though they had limited range they were perfectly suited to scouting Hoth's otherwise inhospitable landscape. But they had been designed to operate in temperate climates and their engines immediately froze up here, rendering them grounded and useless until they could be adapted to the cold—if that was even possible. Last Zev heard, the engineers reckoned that was a fifty-fifty prospect at best. That left the rebels grateful for any small break they could get, and one had come in the form of the tauntauns, the only native surface-dwelling species they had so far encountered. They were ugly and they smelled terrible and they were headstrong beasts, not easy to break, but patience had paid off and now the base had a small paddock of the animals, strong and fast, that could be saddled and ridden. Having been satisfied with the progress of the hastily improvised program, and in the hope that it would only be a stopgap measure until the speeders could be brought online, General Rieekan had given the go-ahead for regular tauntaun patrols, restricted to a limited radius around the base's perimeter. That had given the rebels some degree of short-range reconnaissance capability, at least.

83

But one thing Zev had learned was that for everything Hoth gave, it took twice as much away. There had been unconfirmed reports— little more than rumors, really—about giant creatures spotted lumbering around in the frozen wastes. Roughly the shape of a man but easily twice a man's size, those who claimed to have seen one had said. But they couldn't be sure; the weather on Hoth often made visibility severely limited, and it was easy to mistake a rock or other natural form for something else even from just a few meters out. And after only a few months in this wasteland, some of the men and women stationed here were showing the first signs of struggling to cope with the suffocating isolation. It didn't surprise Zev at all that some might start claiming to have seen things that weren't really there, their minds playing tricks on them. And that's all he believed it was, people seeing things that weren't there. But Rieekan, still counting the lives of those already lost establishing this base, wanted to be sure. And after the general gave the order to conduct sweeps of the area and place sensors capable of picking up any life readings, it was of course Commander Skywalker who insisted on leading the first patrol. Always unwilling to let any of his Rogue Squadron pilots undertake a risk he wasn't willing to volunteer for himself, he had taken a tauntaun and gone out into the great white waste.

Captain Solo had insisted on joining him, arguing that the job would go faster if the two of them split up and shared the sensor-placement area—but doing so always with one eye on the princess, Leia, standing nearby. Trying to impress her as usual. If Solo wanted to keep his feelings for her a secret, he had done a spectacularly poor job of it. Everyone in Echo Base knew about it. Gossip was a key weapon in the fight against boredom in a place as desolate as this, and Solo's painfully obvious attempts to impress the princess provided plenty of fodder for it. Zev had even secretly started a squadron betting pool, and every pilot had a wager placed on what day she would finally tire of his schoolboy attempts to show off and tell him exactly where he could shove them.

Reluctantly, Leia had allowed both Solo and Skywalker to go, while imploring them to stay within the authorized search radius—and with a particular instruction to Solo that any heroics he might try to pull out there would only succeed in doing the exact opposite of impressing her. Solo had assured her that he would play things by the book, then as he often liked to do added a cocky wink to undermine everything he had just said. And so Leia had stood by the north entrance's shield door and watched as the two men headed out until they were swallowed up by that great blanket of white.

That was this morning. And now Commander Skywalker was missing.

The news moved through Echo Base like a howling gale, chilling everyone it touched. Within minutes of Skywalker being declared overdue, every being stationed there was fearing the worst. They knew Hoth was a pitiless world that would kill you the moment you let your guard down. The commander was not the kind of man to do that, but then Hoth had other tricks up its sleeve, too, ways to kill even the most vigilant and prepared. Maybe even someone protected by the Force, as Skywalker was rumored to be, ever since he had become a legend by firing the shot that destroyed the dreaded Death Star and saved the Rebellion. That was another popular subject of base gossip—was he or wasn't he? Zev, who was old enough to remember the tales of the Jedi from his childhood, was ambivalent about it, not willing to rule it out but deciding it was more likely that the kid was simply one hell of a pilot.

Not just one hell of a pilot but one hell of a man. After Skywalker's incredible feat at the Battle of Yavin, Leia had rewarded him with the rank of commander and permission to form his own squadron. As the squadron's founder he had the task of naming it, and though there were many delightful color choices available Skywalker had decided instead to dedicate his new outfit to some fellow heroes of the Rebellion. He had heard the story—as everyone had—of the heroic sacrifice made by Jyn Erso, Cassian Andor, and dozens of other valiant rebels in stealing the closely guarded Imperial plans that revealed the Death Star's critical hidden flaw and giving the Alliance a fighting chance at survival. Rogue Squadron it was, then. But Luke went one step further. The specific Rogue One designation that Erso and her crew had given themselves was to be forever retired with honor in the annals of rebel heroism. He would be Rogue Leader, but the next pilot in the roster would be given the call sign Rogue Two instead of One. That call sign fell to Zev Senesca, and he considered it a badge of pride. He would never tire of telling others how he got that designation, because it was an opportunity to regale those who might still be unfamiliar with the Erso story, a tale that summed up rebel courage and determination in the face of overwhelming odds better than any other he knew.

More than anything, though, Zev was proud to serve under the commander. Though Skywalker enjoyed revered status among the rank and file, he never traded on it or even seemed to enjoy it. Quite the opposite: He seemed to hate the idea that he was special or any better than the men and women who served under him, and he went to great pains to make that point. He wasn't like other commanders Zev had served under. When he asked you how you were doing, he actually listened to you. He seemed genuinely interested in the lives of those around him, cared about every soul he had been entrusted with. *I'm just a kid from a moisture farm on a planet no one's ever heard of,* he had told the assembled Rogue Squadron pilots when he first brought them together. *So try to go easy on me when I screw up, okay?* That brought a laugh, the first of many the Rogue Squadron pilots would enjoy as they grew together under the commander's humble but firm leadership. Everybody liked him. And now he was gone.

Two things happened immediately. The first was that the rebel mechanics assigned the task of adapting the speeders to the cold started working round-the-clock shifts. Those speeders were the best chance, maybe the only chance, of finding the commander before he froze to death or succumbed to whatever other fate had befallen him out there. So now they didn't take breaks, didn't eat, but instead devoted themselves to laboring constantly until they found a workaround for the coolant problem that was keeping the speeders grounded. When Zev first heard that Hoth was so damn cold it was even freezing engine coolant, he thought it was funny. It didn't seem so funny now.

The second thing that happened was that Captain Solo insisted on going back out and looking for the commander. Even though there were no ships available, even though the temperature was dropping rapidly as the day's light waned, he had taken a tauntaun and gone out alone. He hadn't asked Rieekan for permission, of course, because he knew he would never have gotten it. He just went. That was Solo's way—act now, think later. The former smuggler had a mixed reputation among Rogue Squadron; pilots are by nature a cocksure bunch, so many admired his pluck and his seemingly limitless ability to speak his mind, no matter how ill-advised it might be to do so. Others—like Zev—saw him as a blowhard who had been blessed with more luck than talent and who liked to talk way too much about that piece-of-junk freighter of his. But the fact that Solo had left the safety of Echo Base and gone out into that frozen wilderness alone and without consulting his superiors told Zev something else about him—this time at least, the man's damn-fool heroics weren't about impressing the princess. This time he was genuinely concerned about his friend.

Zev knew how that felt. The thought of the commander somewhere out there, lost and helpless and alone as the cold bit deeper and deeper into him, felt like a ball of ice in the pit of his stomach. Worse still was the feeling of helplessness—Solo's one-man rescue mission may have been foolhardy but at least he was *doing* something. All Zev and the other Rogue Squadron pilots could do was sit and wait and try not to go out of their minds with worry as the hours ticked by, waiting for any news. But the only news that had trickled in so far had been grim: The base had now lost contact with Captain Solo, and the shield doors had been closed for the night, meaning there could be no further attempts to locate him or the commander until first light tomorrow.

Zev was squadron leader in the commander's absence, so the morale of the other pilots was now his sole responsibility. He could see how anxious they all were, how on edge, and tried to think of some way to distract them or relieve the tension. Every squadron had its own betting pool—it was often said that rebel pilots loved to play the odds because they gambled with their lives every time they strapped into a cockpit—and Zev was the guy who ran Rogue Squadron's. Since their founding he'd run a number of popular pools, including betting on what would be the most awful thing about the location of their new base (Dak Ralter had won that one by betting on "too damn cold"), and the current one centered around Solo's clumsy attempts to impress the princess. Now he had an idea for a new one.

He entered the pilot barracks and marched over to the board where the Solo bets were placed. Some of the other pilots jumped up in protest as he wiped all the bets off the board and started writing up a new one.

"Listen up," said Zev. "Today we start a new pool. Everyone antes up one week's flight pay. First pilot to find the commander wins the pot. Who's in?"

At first there was hesitance. Then Dak, the youngster whom everyone knew idolized Skywalker more than most, stepped up to the board and wrote his name. Then Wedge Antilles, Rogue Three, stood and did the same. Then another, and another. The rest were still hesitant.

"Kinda morbid, ain't it?" asked Hobbie, Rogue Four. "Betting on the commander's life?"

Zev was about to respond when another voice came from the barracks entrance at the far end of the room.

"Morbid? Not at all."

Everyone who wasn't already standing jumped up and stood to attention immediately. It was Leia.

"As you were," she added as she stepped inside the barracks. The pilots relaxed a little but remained standing. Leia's very presence commanded attention and respect. She had been through hell—imprisonment, torture, the destruction of her homeworld and loss of her beloved parents—and still she kept fighting. She was the embodiment of grace under fire, and the Rogue Squadron pilots admired her as much as they did the commander. Perhaps more.

Leia leaned against one of the pilot bunks and looked at the men assembled before her. "You're not betting on Commander Skywalker's life," she told them. "You're betting on his survival. Every bet you place on that board is a vote of confidence that it'll be a matter of *when* you find him, not if. It's an expression of hope. And as a great rebel once said, rebellions are built on hope. In fact, I'd like to place a wager of my own."

She stepped up to the board and took the marker from Zev's hand. She then wrote the names, first and last, of every single pilot in Rogue Squadron onto the board. She didn't have to consult a roster or ask anyone; she knew the names of every pilot from memory. When she had finished writing the list of names she signed her own at the bottom.

"I'm betting on every pilot here," she said. "That's what General Rieekan and I and the other Alliance leaders do every day—we bet on each and every one of you to keep us all alive, keep us fighting. And I have no doubt in my mind, none, that one of you will find Commander Skywalker and Captain Solo. I don't like to lose, so I place this bet knowing that I'm not going to."

And with that she gave Zev back his marker and headed to the exit, every eye in the room on her. She stopped at the door and looked back. "May the Force be with all of you," she said. And then she was gone.

After she left, Hobbie and the other pilots who hadn't yet placed their bets stepped up and wrote their names on the board.

The next morning Zev and the other pilots woke early to the news that the techs, having worked all through the night, had finally figured out the coolant problem and gotten the speeders running. There were a dozen of them in the air within the hour, Rogue Squadron splitting into groups of four to cover the search grid with maximum efficiency. Zev led the search across the western sector, and for most of the morning they had flown across the frozen tundra scanning for any signs of life without success. The storm that had battered Echo Base throughout the night had at last abated, and now that the sun was up visibility was the best it had been in weeks, meaning there was a greater chance of eyeballing something even if the commander wasn't able to respond to comm messages or his lifesigns were weak. But so far all Zev had seen was endless rolling white.

Some had tried to make the best of it here on Hoth by talking about the natural grandeur of the place, the majesty of its vast ice plains and glaciers. Zev thought all that was a load of bantha fodder; he would have happily traded in all the natural grandeur in the galaxy for a toilet that didn't freeze your ass off when you sat on it. But the one thing he wanted right now, more than anything, was a hit on his scanner, some sign that the commander was still out there, somewhere, alive. He knew the chances of anyone surviving after being caught overnight in a merciless Hoth blizzard were remote, but still Leia's words rang in his ears. *Rebellions are built on hope. Rebellions are—*

A sensor ping on his cockpit display brought Zev out of his reverie. He reset the scanner to make sure it wasn't malfunctioning in the cold, and the ping was still there. Weak, but there. It wasn't much, but it wasn't nothing, either, and right now he'd take anything he could get.

"Echo Base, I've got something," he said into his helmet mike. "Not much, but it could be a life-form."

He piloted his speeder across a snowcapped ridgeline, closing in on the sensor blip, which was getting gradually stronger as he approached.

"Commander Skywalker, do you copy?" Zev said. "This is Rogue Two. This is Rogue Two. Captain Solo, do you copy?"

There was still nothing but endless wastes of snow and ice visible beyond Zev's cockpit, no visual sign of life. But the sensor blip was still there, drawing him closer.

"Commander Skywalker, do you copy? This is Rogue Two."

His comm system crackled to life.

"Good morning! Nice of you guys to drop by!" Zev knew the voice instantly. It was Solo, and the wiseass tone could only mean one thing—the commander was alive, too. Zev's face broke out in a broad grin.

"Echo Base, this is Rogue Two," he said, smiling the whole time. "I've found them. Repeat, I've found them."

He saw Solo in the distance, a tiny figure amid a vast blanket of sunlit white, waving at him. As Zev's speeder flew overhead, he felt the relief wash over him like a wave. Hoth might have been the coldest place in the galaxy, but in that moment he felt warmer than he had since arriving here. Luke Skywalker was alive and soon he would be back in charge of the squadron. And with him leading them, they were ready to face whatever the Empire could throw at them.

In the meantime, Zev thought, all that extra flight pay he just won wouldn't be so bad, either.

KENDAL

Charles Yu

Ozzel had a few regrets. Not only because he was, at that moment, getting Force-choked by the big guy himself. Although that was certainly part of it.

No doubt Veers, the weasel, was enjoying this. And the rest of them, sniveling yes-men, were all doing their best to hide their obvious relief at not being the target of Lord Vader's wrath. Ozzel didn't blame them. It wasn't long ago when it was Tagge being held up, dangled like a rag doll for everyone to see. Ozzel remembered the secret thrill he felt watching it. The admixture of feelings, the unsettling combination of *at least it's not me* and *at least it's over for that guy*.

Because if he was finally going to be honest with himself (and there's nothing like being seconds from death for some real introspection), Ozzel had to admit that although excruciating, being in Vader's grip was in some ways preferable to a regular day on the bridge. The constant tension. The helmet breathing. The awkward silence. *What does he want me to say? What did I do wrong this time?* Always second-guessing yourself. Always on pins and needles. The dread of knowing it was just a matter of time before the next eruption. Not if but when. For the choking to finally be here was, in a way, cathartic even if blindingly painful.

Granted, what he did wrong this time had been pretty bad. So the rebels *had* been on Hoth. Honest mistake. That was the nature of war. Making decisions with incomplete information. Even if it wasn't the right call, at least he had made the call. He hadn't risen all the way to admiral by being a sycophant. The boss had enough flunkies and, despite Vader's not-so-great track record as a manager of people, the Sith Lord did depend on (if not respect) the acumen of his senior advisers. How else would he, a kid from Carida, have made it this far? Atop the Imperial Navy. Commanding officer of an *Executor*-class Dreadnought.

So yeah, he'd screwed up. On top of that, coming out of lightspeed right above the planet was not great. Big oops, actually. Although was it really grounds for death? No. No way. Even Vader had more heart than that. No, this was humiliation. All the more so because it was being done telekinetically. To be Force-choked in person is at least somewhat honorable. Doing it by holoconference was just sad. This had to be Lord Vader's way of teaching Ozzel a lesson. And Ozzel was okay with that. Appreciative, even. This was his wake-up call. Surely any moment now the grip would loosen and he'd slip to the floor, bruised and chastened.

Except it didn't. Get looser. It got tighter. This wasn't the moment where his life turned around. This was the moment it ended.

He struggled at first. By instinct. The lower brain kicking into gear. Live. Survive. Endure. No matter who it is doing this. You want to live. His heart still beating. Getting weaker. Blood flow decreasing now. Each beat of his heart pumping less oxygen to his brain.

There was a boy.

On Carida.

What was his name?

A boy from the same small mountain city. Barely a city. A village. They were the same age.

The memory escaping him. Vader fading, Veers fading, Hoth fading. The battle might be lost, the war might still be won, but all of it fading.

It felt almost silly now, to think of how much he'd cared about military strategy. About pleasing his superiors. About his reputation, or lack of it. They'd mocked him, even as he surpassed them all. Even as he ascended to his current rank, the whispers never stopped. Was it some kind of joke? Vader wanting someone weak and non-threatening? Or even: Was Ozzel a rebel sympathizer, and Vader playing mind games with the resistance, promoting Ozzel, manipulating the flow of information? Just moments ago, he had been thinking of how this would go down in the history data banks. How Admiral Ozzel lost the Battle of Hoth for the Empire by making a key tactical mistake. How Piett would capitalize on it for his own career advancement.

Those thoughts slipped from him. Turned liquid and dripped away now. Colors, light, blurring together.

His hearing went.

A silent movie played out. The other officers scurrying about, trying to avoid Ozzel's fate. The buzz of activity. On the surface of the planet below, a battle. In front of him, the blackness of space. The stars. Around one of them, his homeworld. Memories flooded, all picture and no sound.

He and the boy, running up the mountain. The rocky, blasted landscape of Carida a comfort to him. He remembered racing up the hillside, sure-footed, running toward his mother.

What had happened to that boy? What was his name?

Ozzel remembered he had once been young, idealistic. There had been a choice. His fiancée. They were to be married on Carida, in front of his family and friends. A good, simple life. They could have had it.

But then, under cover of darkness, she whispered something to him. She kissed him, tender. He remembered the smell of her hair. She whispered and the first time he pretended not to hear it, did not want to acknowledge what she'd said. Wanted to imagine he had misheard it, to imagine she might just let it go if he ignored it. Knowing that it would change everything. It had already changed. History was here. Already, on their small planet. Had found them, as it would find every distant part of the galaxy. History was sweeping both of them up. *Join the rebel forces.* She said it again, and this time there was no denying. He did not say no. But he didn't need to. She knew what his answer was. Ozzel remembered how they had cried the whole night together. Holding each other. And then in the morning, they said goodbye forever. Ozzel had chosen his course: the Empire. That was years ago, or moments. Color and light had turned liquid, and now time had as well.

His decades-long career. Decorated, promoted, derided. How had he missed it? How had he not seen until it was too late whom he had pledged his allegiance to? He was not alone in his complicity, but that did not excuse it, either. He was not the first nor would he be the last to go down this particular slippery slope. Authoritarians do not announce themselves and knock down your door. They are invited in. This one promised order. This one promised stability. Ozzel had the fleeting regret now: If only he had been a spy, as some had suspected. If only he had done one thing. One single solitary thing to resist.

And then his sight went.

He was blind and deaf now. The pain had surpassed all thresholds and was all-encompassing and in that he no longer felt it. The only sense he had left was smell.

There was a kind of euphoria, now. From the lack of oxygen. These were his final moments. Watching Darth Vader on a screen, reaching across space and time to touch him. His last contact with another human.

He smelled his dinner.

He and the boy running up the hill in tandem, matching strides. This mysterious boy. His oldest memory. They couldn't have been more than six. Maybe younger. Was the boy his brother? How could he have forgotten that. It would have been in the records. No, the boy must have been his friend. His closest childhood friend. If he could just remember that boy's name, hold it in his head. That would be the way to go. Not an act of resistance. It was too late for that. He had lived his life in the service of the dark side. Killed innocents. Given the commands to destroy peoples, families, cultures. Worst of all, he had been a tool, an instrument. Admiral Ozzel. The vanity of it. The high rank nothing now. He was a foot soldier, a body, just another stormtrooper marching in lockstep. Marching for the Empire. Decades from now, when the war had been fought and the histories had been written about it, no one would remember Ozzel. They would only remember the fruits of his work, the contributions he had made to consolidating Vader's power and control. So much of the vast galactic story written across the sky, chronicled and told and retold, hardening into myth. And hidden in this grand narrative of good and evil, millions, billions of lost histories, personal histories, details that would rot away leaving only the shell.

They had taken everything from him: his youth, his middle age, his fiancée. All the possible lives he could have led. He had not been to his home in how long. They took his whole life. He gave it; they took it.

But there was one thing they couldn't take. This memory of the boy. Dinner, the rich perfume of stew, of meat and vegetables, eaten in the thin, cold air on the side of a mountain, looking at the double twilight of the twin stars of Carida. Two suns setting, he and the boy running together.

Spooning the last bits of their meal, savoring it. Sharing a cup of warm water, later. Under cover of darkness, something whispered.

He remembered the smell of her hair.

Whose hair? The boy's hair?

Join the rebel forces.

The time line confused now. Just moments, scattered everywhere. His fiancée, the boy. His mother's stew.

Again: the whisper. The choice. His silence. History sweeping up Ozzel, carrying him along. History already here, in this moment, always there.

He remembered the whispers. Remembered crying the whole night together. Holding each other. Him and his fiancée. No. Him and the boy. No. His mother, holding him. No.

All of it. The boy, what was his name? Running stride for stride up the hill, his name. Before Vader finished his work, before he thought his last thought, if Ozzel could remember the name of the boy.

Kendal.

His name.

There was no boy. No twin. No brother. No friend. No choice.

There was just Kendal Ozzel, six or maybe seven, running up a mountain on Carida. The smell of his mother's stew. The smell of her hair as she held him to sleep. The boy he was before he put on the uniform. Before he joined the Empire. Before the stormtroopers and the Star Destroyers and Veers and Piett and rebel forces. Before he ever knew who Darth Vader was, ever feared him. Before he did any of this, he was that boy.

AGAINST ALL ODDS

R. F. Kuang

The rebels have practiced an evacuation like this before. In case of an imminent attack, troop carriers escape first out the north entrance, escorted by two fighter craft each. Ground troops and snowspeeder units stay behind to buy them time. They've known this was coming; they knew the Empire was searching for them in every corner of the galaxy. They knew they couldn't hide forever, but damned if they're getting caught. The hangar explodes into chaos as pilots and gunners run to their ships, but it's chaos with a purpose—everyone knows where they're meant to be and where they need to go.

Still, a palpable fear thrums through the air. This isn't a drill. The rebel base at Hoth is under attack, there's a fleet of Star Destroyers coming out of hyperspace to blow them into oblivion, and somehow Dak Ralter feels more alive than he's ever been.

Dak understands the bleak hopelessness of rebellion.

He was born into a family of rebels—merchant traders and loyalists to the Republic who refused to bow when Emperor Palpatine assumed power; who were caught smuggling Jedi Knights to sanctuary on their transport ships and sentenced to a lifetime in prison.

At least his parents knew a free world before it was shattered. Dak was born in chains.

You've no idea what the Empire is capable of. The older Alliance pilots are always telling him this like it's a lesson he needs to learn; as if someone has to check his boundless enthusiasm.

But Dak knows very well what the Empire is capable of.

Dak was born and raised in the Scargon region of Kalist VI, a penal colony in the dregs of the Deep Core where the Empire sends its political prisoners to rot. Kalist VI is a part of the criminal justice system in name only—there are no judges, juries, or courts on that rocky, barren place. On Kalist VI, there are only life sentences.

Dak understands cruelty. He knows what the Empire does to its enemies—the ones it doesn't obliterate from a distance. In many ways, he thinks, that instant death is kinder compared with what he's seen Imperial guards do—not with lasers but with conventional, glinting steel—to prisoners they suspect of knowing things.

Dak's parents knew things.

On Kalist VI, the guards make prisoners serve on the firing squads. They think it's funny. They like to watch the doomed inmates begging their friends and family not to shoot, knowing full well that the firing squads have blasters aimed at their own heads.

Dak happens to be a very good shot—uncannily good, for a gunner as young as he is. He'll never tell a living soul why.

Rogue Squadron is suiting up to fly out. Dak and Luke's snowspeeder is parked in the far end of the hangar, right where they'd left it after the last time Dak took it out.

Luke's not there yet. He wasn't at Princess Leia's briefing, either. Dak shakes off a niggling sense of worry—Luke's likely just running behind—and focuses on double-checking his controls. It's hardly necessary. Every flip and switch is set to right where it should be. The harpoons are loaded, the guns are calibrated. All he's missing is his pilot.

Dak leans back in his seat, takes a deep breath, and places his hands on the triggers. The cool metal feels smooth and familiar under his skin. When he's firing, the guns feel like an extension of his body. He doesn't look at his hands when he's shooting. He looks at his target. The rest is not a sequence of mechanics, but an act of will.

Dak isn't a Jedi. Dak can't manipulate the Force. He can't make objects shake without touching them and detect things his eyes can't see like Luke can. But sometimes, when he's pulling the trigger—when he blasts his targets with such precision it feels as if his mind is guiding his laser blasts to their destination—he wonders if this is how it feels.

He's always acutely aware, whenever they gear up to fly out, how stark the military asymmetry is between the Rebel Alliance and the Empire. The Imperial fleet is outfitted with thousands of sleek, state-of-the-art Star Destroyers, each carrying hundreds more TIE fighters. The rebel fleet is a hodgepodge assortment of ships of every make and build, most of them outdated, scrounged together from a combination of charity and theft.

The fleets, seen side by side, are laughable. The disparity is so stark it's absurd. It means that to have a shot at victory, the rebels must plan better and fly better. It means they always need sheer, dumb luck on their side.

To Dak, it's thrilling.

Dak knows hopelessness. He knows the Empire as insurmountable steel walls, unbreakable shackles, and guards in helmets stationed around every corner with their fingers on their triggers. He knows it as a ubiquitous net of surveillance that makes you feel like you can't speak, can't breathe, can't even *think,* without the Empire's knowledge. He knows it as the source of all the screams.

He knows how it feels to perceive the overwhelming presence of evil on a daily basis; to see its control permeate and dictate every facet of your life; for it to wear you down so thoroughly you become convinced there is no possible recourse but a pathetic attempt at continued survival; to believe that all you can hope for, all you are allowed, is to scrape by from day to day solely for the prospect of swallowing down the next ration of clumpy, gray gruel.

Dak has seen the very worst of the Empire. He doesn't need an education in reality. He knows the nature of their enemy.

But to Dak, it's outrageous enough that he's *here.* That he's still alive; that he got out of those quarries to fly with living legends across the galaxy. How much more outrageous could it be to take down the Empire?

Kalist VI never broke him, because Dak learned early on what it meant to hope—to hope when freedom was such a distant possibility it seemed laughable; when the enemy was so overwhelmingly, soul-crushingly powerful it seemed eternal; when the only thing you had going for you was the fact that your thoughts remained free and your heart was still beating.

As long as you're alive, Dak has learned, you hope. As long as you haven't yet lost, there's still the possibility, no matter how faint, that you might win.

The other rebels see Hoth as a miserable, barren hellhole of endless snow and howling winds. Dak looks at Echo Base, that defiant hunk of metal on a terrain where it shouldn't exist, and sees starlight.

Dak still can't believe he's Luke's gunner—that he flies with *Commander Luke Skywalker*, the nobody from Tatooine turned hero of the Rebellion; the floppy-haired farmboy who turned up out of nowhere, rescued the princess, and proceeded to obliterate the Death Star.

To Dak, he's the hope of the rebellion incarnate. Princess Leia is courage and perseverance against tragedy; General Rieekan is weary, experienced competence. But in Luke, Dak finds faith in the impossible.

"Heard a lot about you," Luke said with a grin when they were introduced on Hoth, pilot-to-gunner, two of the newly formed Rogue Squadron's best. "Heard you're a great shot."

"I do my best." Dak grins back. "I won't let you down, sir."

103

Being assigned as Luke's gunner is an honor Dak doesn't take lightly. He's worked hard to live up to the job—since they started flying together, they've been the best pilot–gunner pair in Rogue Squadron by far. They decimate simulation exercises like they're telepathically linked not just to each other but to the machines themselves. Luke maneuvers them through flight patterns that snowspeeders weren't designed to take, and Dak manages long-distance shots that technically, physically, shouldn't be possible.

Luke has never doubted Dak. He's never asked why he didn't take a shot when he could have; never criticized him for waiting a few seconds to get a better lock on a crucial target that they could have taken from a distance. Luke trusts Dak to keep them safe, and so does

Dak—he's never doubted Commander Skywalker for a second, not even that time on their lone snowspeeder test flight when Luke took them on hairpin twists that brought Dak's breakfast roiling in the back of his throat, or when they skimmed so close over icy peaks that Dak could have sworn paint was chipping off the snowspeeder's belly.

They've only been flying together for a few weeks, but Dak feels like they've been flying together for a lifetime.

The night that Luke didn't report back, the night he stayed out to check out a meteorite, Dak couldn't sleep. When Han Solo brought him back, barely kicking but alive, Dak went weak-kneed with relief.

But, he tells himself, he was never really worried. Luke's got the Force. Luke would never let him down.

They've gotten one transport out. The rebels have temporarily disabled a Star Destroyer with an ion cannon that the Empire doesn't know they have, freeing space for one ship carrying some of the rebels stationed on Hoth to flee into hyperspace. There's cheering throughout the hangar, but the celebration is brief—the Imperial assault has barely started, and there are still twenty-nine transports grounded on Hoth.

They won the opening salvos. Now the real battle begins.

Dak's seated in his snowspeeder, and he's just starting to get antsy when he spots a figure in orange darting in his direction. He feels a small wave of relief—he'd gotten word that Luke had recovered from his night out in the snow, but he hasn't seen him in person until now.

"Feeling all right, sir?"

"Just like new, Dak," Luke says. "How about you?"

Luke can't see him, but Dak beams. "Right now I feel like I could take on the whole Empire myself."

Luke gives a low chuckle. "I know what you mean."

Dak grins and yanks the cockpit roof down over their heads.

"Echo Station Five-Seven," Luke says over the comm. "We're on our way."

Rogue Squadron is racing over the snow, smoothly dodging laser-fire from Imperial walkers like it's child's play.

"All right, boys," Luke says calmly, as if they're not skirting through air thick with energy blasts that could decimate their engines in a split second. "Keep in tight now."

Everyone in Rogue Squadron knows what that means—he's going in for the kill.

"Luke, I have no approach vector," Dak urges. He can't see how he's supposed to fire from this angle—he's nowhere close to the walker's weak spots. "I'm not set."

"Steady, Dak. Attack pattern delta." Luke's speaking so casually, he could be telling them what he wants for lunch. "Go now!"

So Dak throws his reservations to the wind and clutches the triggers, waiting for his shot.

Even though they're arcing through the air at a perpendicular angle that makes his stomach roil, and even though they're darting so close to the walker Dak could swear they nicked its leg, Dak doesn't doubt for one second that Luke's guiding them to exactly where they need to be.

If Luke's in the cockpit, then they're immortal.

Dak's flying with a Jedi. He's flying with someone who navigates not just with his eyes but with the *Force;* who dodged death a dozen times over during the Battle of Yavin because he could perceive everything around him even without the automatic navigator; even with his eyes closed.

So Dak doesn't feel a sliver of fear. Not when the engine of the snowspeeder at their right bursts into fire. Not when Luke realizes

105

the walker's armor is too strong for lasers to penetrate, which means they'll have to get in terrifyingly close to wrap harpoon cords around their legs.

Imperial blasts fill the air around them, but there's no way, Dak thinks—no way they'll ever land.

It happens so quickly Dak doesn't have time to hurt.

There's a split second when he's not focused on the walker—he's distracted by a sudden malfunction in fire control, and then he's scrambling for the tow cable release because there's no time to worry about the malfunction—then there's a flash of bright light, a noise like a firecracker, and a searing, astonishing heat.

Oh, he thinks, stunned more than anything, and then a little bewildered that he can't move his hands. He blinks, but his eyes won't clear. He can't see the walkers—just a haze of white, and pulsing red clouds in the middle.

"Dak?"

He hears Luke's voice but it's muffled, as if Luke is yelling through a wall. Dak's fingers have gone numb. Black keeps creeping into the edges of his vision. He feels like he's falling backward through a tunnel, away from his body.

He struggles to come back to himself—he needs to get his hands on the controls, needs to release that tow cable, needs to shoot *something,* because Luke's counting on him, Luke needs him to—

"*Dak!*"

He can't.

He can't feel his hands. He can't feel anything. *I've been hit,* he realizes belatedly. *That was a hit just now. I'm hit.*

It's too late. Luke's not getting him out of this.

He couldn't save you, whispers a little voice, but it's immediately crowded out by a more urgent panic—this can't be the end, he can't—

he's let Luke down, he's let the Alliance down, he must fire that tow cable, he *must*—

He can't.

"Rogue Three," he hears Luke say. "Wedge, I've lost my gunner. You'll have to make this shot."

Luke says something else, but it's all fuzz to Dak now; his hearing is fading with his sight.

Dak fights like hell against the dark, but his body's too far gone. Dak doesn't even know where he's been hit. His wounds are so severe there is no singular point of agony. Instead it's a shroud, a total numbness that pulls him further and further into the looming dark. And Dak is *trying* to lift his head, to move his hands, but he can't, he can't, he can't—

Somewhere, as if from a very great distance, he hears a great crash. He feels the speeder twist around, arcing back through the air. Seconds later there's a great explosion; a series of booms that rattles the speeder and vibrates through his bones.

That had to be the walker.

The harpoon, he realizes. *They did it.* They've downed an Imperial walker with nothing but a cable.

Incredible.

He feels the speeder twisting around again, darting back for another shot.

That's when he knows, with as much certainty as he's ever known anything—they've got this. They don't need him. He's just one soldier. But Luke, Wedge, and Janson; the rest of Rogue Squadron, the rest of the Rebel Alliance—they'll finish the job.

He doesn't have to fight anymore.

He can let go.

Calm sweeps across him. Suddenly the numb isn't so bad. The panic's gone. Nothing hurts.

It's all right, he thinks. *It's all right.*

He's falling through the tunnel; he's left his body and the speeder behind.

He's left Luke behind.

But Luke's going to be fine. The rebels will get off Hoth. They'll escape the Imperial fleet; they'll find another hideout and build another base. And if that base is attacked, they'll escape again—they always do—and start again somewhere else. Over and over, until one day they get in another lucky shot.

The Rebellion will survive him. It'll beat the odds like Luke once beat the odds; like Dak once beat the odds.

Soldiers die all the time. It's the occupational hazard of rebellion, the obvious likelihood of demise.

But that's the funny thing about hope, Dak's learned—you only have to get lucky once.

BEYOND HOPE

Michael Moreci

Crimson particle bolts screamed through the air just over Private Emon Kref's head; the enemy fire found its home in the turret at Emon's back. Shards of metal, charred and scored black, rained down on Emon's and his squad's heads, reminding them just how feeble they were in the face of the Empire's AT-AT walkers.

And the Battle of Hoth had only just begun.

Emon took cover behind the trench's frozen wall and shook the bits of turret debris off his goggles.

"Still glad you joined the Alliance?" Andry Ked yelled. He and

Emon were shoulder to shoulder, huddled against each other just as much as they were huddled against the wall. More crimson bolts sizzled overhead; explosions echoed and reverberated up and down the trench until it sounded like one big eruption.

"I was never glad!" Emon shouted back. Which, in a way, was true. It'd been a few short weeks since the Empire scorched Koshaga, ending a war that'd been waged on Emon's homeworld for as long as anyone could remember. Emon had been born into that war; his father was a general in the Koshagan People's Movement; he'd battled arm in arm with his own people against the tyranny of the ruling class and those who supported it. That fight was Emon's life.

But then the Empire came.

In one single, swift operation, the war was over. The Empire swarmed Koshaga, and with its machines of death and its phalanx of stormtroopers, it smothered the planet's Lowlands. Lines of defense were shattered; leaders—Emon's father included—were taken prisoner. The will of the Koshagan people, once so strong and so proud, withered before Emon's eyes.

A week later, a rebel recruiter who'd gotten wind of the Koshagan uprising quietly arrived on Emon's home planet. When the recruiter's ship left a day later, Emon was on it, a full-fledged member of the Rebel Alliance. Still in a state of grief and shock, he couldn't conceive how anyone could topple the Empire. But war was all Emon knew, and the Rebellion was offering him just that. So he took the secret transport off Koshaga and, in no time at all, Emon was given a uniform and a blaster. The officer aboard his transport told him that they were going to win back the galaxy, one system at a time.

"Whatever you say," Emon had replied.

Andry, who was in his early forties and thus a senior citizen among the grunts, poked Emon in his ribs, snapping him out of his reverie. "Come on, you're going to need more enthusiasm than that, Kref!" he yelled in his gruff voice. "Rebellions are built on hope—hasn't anyone told you that?"

Emon groaned. "No, Andry, you're the first," he yelled back, certain to convey his sarcasm. "When we get out of this trench—*if* we get out of this trench—you'll have to tell me more!"

Andry laughed. "You'll get it—one day, kid. You'll get it."

Overhead, a squad of snowspeeders howled past the trench, racing toward the walkers. Emon breathed a sigh of relief. *Good,* he thought. *At least that'll distract those damn things.*

He and Andry—and all the other infantry grunts lining the trench—popped back up and steadied their weapons back on the trench's frozen shelf. Walker fire still assaulted Emon's position, but at least now there was less of it.

"Focus all fire on those walkers!" Sergeant Trey Callum shouted across the trench. "Keep them back!"

Emon steadied his A295 blaster rifle and checked that its energy pack was in place. While on patrol a week ago, the pack had fallen out of Emon's rifle, and all the Alliance could offer Emon was a cord and a strip of tape to help keep it in place. On Koshaga, Emon would have been deeply offended by such an unsatisfying response. But this wasn't the People's Movement, and Emon wasn't the only one equipped with a weapon that had the potential to fall apart in the heat of battle. Cally Pon's A280 was always overheating; Su Torka's rifle jammed as much as it fired; and Andry's scope was so misaligned there was little sense even using it. And none of those problems had been addressed any better than Emon's.

That was the Rebellion, though. Elastic bands and good intentions.

Sometimes, Emon wondered what the hell he'd gotten himself into.

Emon followed the orders he'd received and fired his blaster at the

111

approaching walkers. Up and down the trench, the rebel infantry sprayed a steady assault of blaster bolts; the turrets, which were dug into the snow and provided heavier firepower, unleashed concentrated blasts. Bolt after bolt landed true, striking the AT-ATs in concert with the snowspeeders' assault.

And not a single strike managed to leave so much as a scorch mark on the Empire's armored machines.

"Maybe when they get closer we'll be able to do some damage!" Andry shouted.

"You really want to get closer to these things?"

Emon continued to fire. At least his energy pack was holding, though the bitter irony was not lost on him.

Ahead, Emon watched as a snowspeeder took a direct hit; flames erupted out of its rear—maybe its power generator had been penetrated, but Emon couldn't be sure—and the vehicle careened through the air before pounding into the frozen ground. It was more flaming wreckage than ship by the time it crashed.

The walkers kept coming. Emon's ears began to ring. Explosions continued to rip through the trench, one after another after another; the crunch of the AT-AT's metal hooves thundered across the expanse separating the only line of rebel defense from the unstoppable enemy. To Emon, though, it all seemed so distant. Someone was shouting, and their voice sounded like it was coming from the far end of a long, dark tunnel—too far for the words to reach Emon.

Emon continued to fire. His bolts joined all the others, bringing flashes of color to the bleached landscape, but they still had no effect. The shouting continued. A hand gripped Emon's shoulder, hard. It pulled at him, but Emon squeezed the trigger on his A295, unabated. Smoke wafted from a fire burning somewhere nearby, and it filled Emon's nostrils.

It tasted like the ashes of Koshaga, hot and dry on his lips.

Emon blinked as memories of his homeworld flashed across his mind. He remembered the swarm of stormtroopers—their white armor practically glowing against the night's darkness—overwhelming the Lowlands with their endless numbers. He remembered following his brothers and sisters into an unthinkable retreat, only to encounter more of the enemy everywhere they turned. Emon's home, infiltrated and ravaged, had been twisted into a maze, and every turn seemed to lead him back into the enemy's crosshairs. He remembered the Empire's monstrous machines obliterating everything in sight, sending a clear message: They'd rather see this world burn than see it resist.

And Emon remembered running, leading his people—so very few of them—to safety as, indeed, Koshaga burned.

Emon gasped, startled by the hand that was wrapped around the sleeve of his coat. He was on Hoth, not Koshaga, and Andry was at his side, screaming in his ear.

"You gone deaf, Emon?" he howled. "Sarge says to get down!"

The world came rushing back. Alongside Andry, Emon slid to the ground and, again, took cover against the trench. The wall quaked at Emon's back; it—and everything around Emon—felt on the brink of collapse.

Emon looked at Andry, who was covering his head as chunks of ice blasted off the trench's opposite shelf and came hurtling forward. Emon didn't know much about him, other than his home planet was Alderaan, and if any system was worse off than Koshaga, Alderaan was it. Up and down the line, Emon identified squadmates that he thought he'd understood—they were people like him, like Andry, who came to the Alliance because they had nowhere else to go. Maybe they were motivated by revenge, maybe by justice, maybe by plain old rage. Regardless, they were the losers, and they were taking up arms against a proven superior force.

And yet—armed with insufficient weaponry and outnumbered to an unfathomable degree—they still fought. Soldiers returned to their feet; they pushed their blasters back down into Hoth's frozen surface, and they fired back at an enemy they knew they couldn't stop.

Emon couldn't understand *why*.

"What are we doing?" Emon asked, grabbing hold of Andry just as he, too, was standing back up. "We don't stand a chance—we have to get out of here!"

Amid the panic and the fear, Andry turned to Emon, and he smiled. "You don't understand what we're doing here, do you, kid?"

Emon could only shake his head, because he *didn't* understand. On Koshaga, they had had better weapons, better resources, and an infantry that dwarfed the Alliance's. And still, they were annihilated. What could the Alliance possibly hope to achieve against the Empire's might?

114

"You know," Andry continued, "I've heard some people say that the Empire is a dark shadow spreading across the galaxy. But you know what? Shadows pass. The Empire's darkness pushes down on you relentlessly; it smothers you until darkness is all that's left. Think about Koshaga, Kref. Now picture what happened to your home happening everywhere."

Emon didn't have to think hard.

"None of us want this war, Kref," Andry said. "We want what comes after the war."

Emon paused. *After.* It seemed so strange, but he'd never really considered an after to the conflict on Koshaga. The war always was, and everyone assumed it always would be. They didn't fight to win, Emon realized—they fought not to lose.

Alongside Andry, Emon got back into position. The moment he

did, a profound rumbling shot across the battlefield. Emon caught sight of a downed AT-AT, its face buried in the snow, just before a pair of snowspeeders raced by, dousing the machine in blasterfire. The Empire's mobile weapon of destruction exploded, bits of it bursting across Hoth's surface.

The trench, galvanized from one end to the other, sounded with cheers. Emon's own voice blended with the celebratory cacophony, though he didn't realize when he'd joined in.

As the exultation died down, Sergeant Callum marched up and down the narrow space, pulling his troops near.

"Word from our scouts is we've got stormtroopers approaching our position," Callum said, his commanding voice heard sharply over the din of battle. "We cannot let them get inside the base. You understand me? The enemy will not pass this trench."

"Yes, sir!" Emon and his squadmates assented.

Still, Emon realized as he turned back to the battlefield, even with one walker down, the battle was far from over. With Andry at his side, Emon joined his squad in resuming fire against the enemy. Andry's theory was proven false—proximity to the walkers didn't make them any more vulnerable. Another snowspeeder was blown out of the sky and, just a few meters away, a P-Tower took a direct hit; the heat of its flames warmed Emon's face, yet still he kept firing—until Cally Pon yelled "Troopers!" and Emon and the rest of his squad shifted their focus to the western edge of the trench. There, barely visible against the bleary white landscape and through the haze of smoke, was a line of snowtroopers, rushing their position.

Emon was almost relieved to see an enemy he stood a chance against.

"Fan out!" Callum yelled. "Press the attack!"

Emon followed Andry up and out of the trench. They charged forward, though Emon's legs felt weak and tired, like he'd been holding his position in the trench for days on end. He fired his A295, and his first bolt struck a trooper square in the chest. The trooper crumpled to the ground, and others soon followed. As the enemy's numbers diminished and Emon's squad remained, Emon couldn't help but feel like there was something shared between himself and the beings he fought alongside.

On Koshaga, Emon fought because that's what he was born into. And the Empire's troopers, they fought because that was what they were ordered to do. Emon had heard stories of how they were conscripted from the worlds the Empire plundered—and here they were, obediently fighting for the very enemy that had brought ruination to their homes. The thought chilled Emon deeper than the frigid air. That could have been him.

The Alliance was different. The conflict wasn't some grim destiny passed down across generations. These people from all over the galaxy chose to be here, in this Alliance, on the frozen plains of Hoth, fighting against a nearly insurmountable enemy. And that choice gave them strength.

It gave them the power to hope, and Emon was beginning to feel what that meant. He was coming to understand the power of *after*.

But just as Emon felt like the rebels could win, that they could do the impossible, the sound of an explosion penetrated his ears and rocked Hoth's surface with such power it nearly brought him to his knees. Emon turned to see the Alliance's shield generators burning in the distance; black smoke billowed into the sky, and Emon knew—

The defense of Hoth was over. Now survival was all that mattered.

And in what seemed like a flash, everything was chaos.

Emon had no idea where the orders came from, or if there were any orders at all, but the whole of the Rebel Alliance infantry was retreating toward the South Ridge. Soldiers scrambled across the ice, pursued by walkers and stormtroopers. Emon's heart sank as he witnessed rebel fighters being cut down before they could make it to the rendezvous point. Their bodies buckled as blaster bolts drove into their backs. They'd tumble ahead a few more steps—haunting steps, Emon shuddered to think, as they were dead people walking—before collapsing into the snow.

Emon turned to Andry.

"Come on, we have to—"

A blaster bolt split the air just in front of Emon and buried itself into Andry's body. Andry growled; Emon tried to grab his friend, but he fell out of his reach too quickly.

Emon turned and spotted a trooper just ten meters away. He had his blaster raised, nearly pressed against the hood that covered his face. Emon dropped; he felt the heat of the trooper's blaster bolt as it raced by, just missing him. Prone on the ground, he lifted his own weapon, took aim, and fired.

His shot landed directly in the trooper's torso and propelled him off his feet.

Emon crawled to Andry, who was on his back, his complexion already a shade lighter. Emon knew that was never a good sign.

"Get out of here," Andry said, breathlessly. "Get to the transport."

Emon ignored him. He braced his arm beneath Andry's shoulder and lifted. Andry grimaced, but at least his upper half was off the frozen ground.

"Can you walk?" Emon asked.

Andry nodded. "Might need some help, but—"

Emon had helped Andry get to one knee, but then he stopped. He looked at Andry, and expected to find him in intense pain. Maybe Emon had pulled too hard, too fast. But it wasn't pain on Andry's face; it was horror. Eyes wide, mouth agape, Andry's gaze was trained upward and kept rising. Emon couldn't bring himself to say a word. He screwed his head back over his shoulder and felt his breath catch in his throat.

An AT-AT stood over them, mere steps away. Its size, from this close, was almost incomprehensible to Emon. It was monstrous, and it was created with the sole purpose of delivering death wherever it went. A single cannon blast, from this range, would reduce both him and Andry to nothing but ash.

Emon relinquished his grip on Andry and left him propped on his one knee. He turned to the walker, which was firing one volley after another, driving—Emon was certain—more rebel troops to the ground.

"What are you doing?" Andry asked. "Run, get out of here while you still—"

Emon couldn't run. He'd fled on Koshaga, and it took hardly any time at all to be back where he'd started. Andry was right: The Empire's darkness was inescapable. There was no running from it, no hiding. You either fought back, or you lived in the obsidian of its clenched fist.

There was no choice at all. Emon lifted his blaster, training it squarely on the underside of the walker's head. He wrapped his finger around the trigger and pulled.

And nothing happened.

Emon pulled again, and again. His weapon didn't discharge a single shot.

The energy pack. Emon closed his eyes; he heard his breath, sharp and clear, and he brought his hand along his blaster to where the pack should have been. It was unnecessary, because Emon knew. It was gone, lost somewhere in the snow.

Above him, the walker's head screeched and groaned as the gears that controlled it shifted. Emon imagined it adjusting slightly downward, and he imagined what would happen then.

Emon braced himself, but he didn't despair. He was a rebel, and that meant he was more than his weapon, his uniform, or his rank. He was an idea, and ideas couldn't be snuffed out, not even on the desolate, frozen plains of Hoth.

As Emon stared down the walker, steeling himself against the inevitability pressing down on him, he was distracted by the sound of something shrieking through the sky—shrieking and approaching fast. Emon turned. A snowspeeder, engulfed in flames, was hurtling directly toward the walker. Emon barely had time to leap back as far as he could, knocking Andry to the ground with him. Over their heads, the speeder crashed directly into the walker's cockpit. The machine's head burst into a million pieces, reduced to fragments that came tumbling across the snow and ice. A cloud of smoke poured from the walker's body, and then it crumpled beneath its own weight and crashed to the ground.

Emon stared at Andry. Neither had any words for what just happened, but they knew what to do—

With Andry's good arm wrapped around Emon's shoulders for support, they got to their feet, ran as well as they could—finding coordination eventually—and joined their fellow rebels in the retreat.

On the transport ship, medical droids attended to Andry's wound. Emon was told that while Andry had lost a lot of blood, he'd make a full recovery.

In the moments after takeoff, a hush settled over the ship. The rebels had lost their base on Hoth. Alliance leadership was scattered, and no one knew where they were going next. But while Emon saw trepidation and exhaustion on the faces of the beings around him, something told him that, despite how grim things may seem, they'd be okay.

Rebellions may be built on hope, Emon considered, *but they end in a better galaxy.*

119

THE TRUEST DUTY

Christie Golden

General Maximilian Veers strode briskly down the corridors of the *Executor*, his boots ringing on the hard metal flooring. His posture was perfectly upright, his hands clasped behind his back, every movement executed with controlled precision. Years of service in the Empire's military had shaped and claimed him, body and soul. Decades of strategizing and combat in a variety of climates and situations had schooled his mien to appear composed and cool at all times. Had carved his body into lean, feline fitness, which he maintained even as he slipped into what for others were "middle years." Had honed his mind to the sharpness of a well-crafted and -cared-for blade.

The Emperor's right hand was the fearsome Darth Vader, the Dark

Lord of the Sith; he of the unseen face, black armor, brilliant mind, and swift discipline. If the elite troopers aboard Vader's flagship, the *Executor,* were known as Vader's Fist, then Veers liked to think of himself as Vader's Dagger: silent, elegant, and lethal.

Veers would be the first to admit that serving aboard the *Executor* brought unique challenges, but it also brought unparalleled rewards. And for Veers, it brought an honor that could never be eclipsed in this lifetime.

At this moment, Veers was bringing unwelcome news to his master, but that did not trouble him. The amount of . . . attrition . . . at both higher and lower levels on the ship was troubling to some, terrifying to others. Fear had been beaten out of Veers quite some time ago, and he had no patience for it. It confounded him that others failed to grasp that the secret to promotion, respect, power, and a long life was very clear:

Don't fail Vader.

Maximilian Veers never had. Because who would ever want to fail Lord Vader? And who could live with themselves if they did?

Lord Vader's obsession, one that fueled and frustrated him in equal measure, was obliterating the Rebellion against the Empire. So many had died aboard the Death Star. A terrifying symbol of the power of the Empire, it was the darling of the late Grand Moff Wilhuff Tarkin. It was where Veers had first met Lord Vader. He had admired them both, but he had privately wondered if the moff might, one day, meet his death at Lord Vader's hands. The question was moot, as in the end, it was Tarkin's own overweening arrogance that had doomed him and everyone who had the misfortune to be on the Death Star. In his own mind, Veers felt that Tarkin had failed to give Lord Vader the respect he was due.

Veers himself had served on the Death Star for a time. It had loomed so large, a seemingly invincible construct, both space station and weapon, and yet it had been destroyed by a mere youth—the rebel pilot known as Skywalker. Now the *Executor* and its commander were on a search to discover, and obliterate, every last rebel, especially the troublesome boy. This was the task of all who served aboard the *Executor;* their unwavering focus all day, every day, from the moment of waking until the quietness of sleep descended. And even then, the singular duty haunted one's dreams. All had a part to play.

In Veers's mind, there were those who led, and those who followed. Sometimes a person was one, sometimes the other. It was important, Veers had learned, to excel in either role.

All powerful beings relied upon the obedience and willing service of others equally remarkable.

So Veers watched and observed. He took great care to align himself with strong leaders, and treated the troops he led with care and support. This mutually beneficial relationship had existed since the dawn of time, and would not go away anytime soon. Not so long as there existed powerful leaders like Lord Vader, and devoted, unfailingly loyal followers like himself.

Earlier, the general had been walking alongside Admiral Kendal Ozzel, both heading to speak with Lord Vader. Ozzel was older than Veers, less spit-and-polish, and softer, physically at least; his mind and strategies were still sound. He was genial, so long as he was agreed with, and like Grand Moff Tarkin quite sure of himself. Captain Firmus Piett, a sharp-featured man with an eye toward rising in the ranks, had called Ozzel over; the younger man thought he had a lead on the rebels' location.

Ozzel scoffed, Piett insisted . . . and then, suddenly, Darth Vader was there.

In his career, Veers had met many diplomats, leaders, generals, and royalty. Many were impressive; some intimidating. But no one

123

had a presence like Lord Vader. He was a massive figure swathed in darkness; the very energy around him seeming to change upon his entrance: charged, elevated. And, always, the sound. Rhythmic, constant, it terrified those who were the object of the Dark Lord's displeasure. Those ill-fated fools knew that sound would likely be the last thing they heard. Veers, however, found it calming. Steady. As unfaltering as Vader was, as he, Maximilian Veers, was. The Dark Lord was many things to Veers, but he was not a threat. Because Veers never failed him.

Vader was certain the rebels were at the site Piett had discovered, and that the most highly desired object of all—Skywalker—was among them.

That should have been the end of it. Veers knew it, Piett knew it . . . but somehow Ozzel did not. He implied that Darth Vader, Lord of the Sith, was wrong. That was a mistake, and it was not Ozzel's last.

124

Veers came to a precise halt in front of Lord Vader's meditation chamber and waited.

Veers was perfectly well aware that Darth Vader was not a god. On more than one occasion, while reporting to the Dark Lord when he was in his meditation chamber, Veers had caught a glimpse of Lord Vader donning his helm. There was only a man in there; one who had suffered horribly, whose skin was nothing but angry red scar tissue. He had bled, had burned; had felt agonizing pain. And he had endured. Veers did not know the man Darth Vader had been, before the helm and armor and glowing red lightsaber, but it did not matter to him. Darth Vader was who had been born from that unimaginable suffering. He was no stranger to violence or malice. And all Lord Vader demanded of those who served was respect, obedience, and success.

It was so simple. And it was because of that simplicity that Veers had never failed him.

There was the pneumatic hiss of the chamber, looking like the jaws of a sleek, black beast with an almost too-bright, white interior.

"What is it, General?" The deep, rich voice, smooth and calm save when it was even deeper with rage. Such a tone had never been directed toward Veers.

Veers used no extraneous words, nor did he fail to provide the particulars his lord needed to know. He informed Vader that the *Executor* had dropped out of lightspeed and that com-scan had detected an energy field on the sixth planet of the Hoth system; one powerful enough to deflect even the *Executor's* bombardment.

"The rebels have detected our presence," Vader said, calmly, as if he were musing about trivialities. Veers knew what was coming. "Admiral Ozzel came out of lightspeed too close to the system."

And there it was. Ozzel's loyalty had never been questioned, but the man suffered from the same malady Grand Moff Tarkin had— arrogance. Veers suspected that, like Tarkin, Ozzel would find the disease fatal. Even so, Veers felt moved to attempt to explain the admiral's decision. "He-he felt surprise was wiser—"

"He is as clumsy as he is stupid," Vader said, annoyance creeping into the booming voice. Veers's heartbeat remained steady. The anger was not for him. "General . . . prepare your troops for a surface attack."

"Yes, my lord," Veers replied, bowing his head, then turning smartly on his heel.

He slowed as he approached the door, though. He knew what was about to unfold. But despite his flaws, Admiral Kendal Ozzel deserved to be witnessed here, at the last, by at least one who respected him.

125

While Veers rarely displayed emotions, he certainly possessed them. He was a human, not a droid, and he cared deeply about winning battles for his lord, the soldiers under his command, and the technology that all their lives relied upon. He had a special fondness for the All Terrain Armored Transport, or AT-AT, as it was nicknamed. AT-ATs weren't swift or flashy. They were steady, slow, and got the job done. Veers had spent so many hours in them that the languid, rhythmic movements of the transport, akin to riding a great beast, felt as normal to him as walking. Nothing had stronger armor than an AT-AT, and often the mere sight of one of the behemoths striding toward ground fighters was enough to psychologically rattle them without a shot being fired.

The unit Veers commanded was Blizzard Force, so named because the AT-ATs were specifically designed to function well in cold-weather operations. Veers had personally selected each and every soldier who served in this unit. His AT-AT was, of course, Blizzard One. He did not believe in sentimental nicknames, although he often oversaw repairs, and everything inside was to his exact specifications. Forty armed and armored troops were ensconced within the transport's belly, and stationed along with Veers in the front-facing command center were TK-5187 and TK-7834, the finest gunner and pilot Veers could find.

The mission of Blizzard Force was clear and attainable. Bring down the generator powering the defensive energy field that stood between Lord Vader and his ultimate goal: the Rebellion's destruction.

The rebels were already proving that they would not give up without a fight. They were smart, too; Veers would give them that. They had to be, against something as enormous, as deadly, as the AT-ATs. The rebels could not attack directly, so they targeted the weakest parts—the neck, the joints. And a particularly clever one realized that if the transports could be tripped, they would topple, and began to wind cables around the legs.

Blizzard Force was taking more casualties than expected, and this troubled Veers. They were his soldiers. His unit. They trusted him to lead. But he had also trusted them to follow. Follow, obey orders, die for the Empire if need be. For Lord Vader.

There would be time to mourn the fallen later, when those still living had achieved what they had died for.

The pilot was smooth, the gunner relentless and accurate. And then . . . there it was: the main generator. The goal. Veers had not wavered; his heart rate had never risen. Worry was uncalled for. He knew he would not fail.

There was a humming sound, and a holographic figure no larger than Veers's hand appeared. It was Lord Vader in miniature; the small image only served to remind Veers how tall the Dark Lord was in person.

"Is victory imminent, General Veers?"

"Yes, Lord Vader. I've reached the main power generator. The shield will be down in moments. You may start your landing."

Veers pressed a button. "TS-4068, report to me immediately." The captain of the squad was always prompt, and shortly stood beside his commander, silently awaiting orders. Snowtrooper armor, like that of most troopers, was white plastoid, but—the "snowies," as they liked to call themselves, had unique adjustments ensuring they would be as effective in a harsh frigid environment as their stormtrooper brethren were. The most unique visual aspects of their armor were helms that seemed to flow over their heads rather than enclose them. It made for a disquieting image, this ghostly figure in the snow, if one was a rebel. Veers, like his lord, understood how powerful a weapon fear could be.

"All troops will debark for ground assault," ordered Veers. The captain nodded and hastened to notify his men. Now the moment had come. Veers stood behind the gunner and pilot. His features were still composed, but he couldn't resist a hint of a smile. He could see it clearly with the naked eye, now, jutting up from the snow.

"Prepare to target the main generator."

Out of the corner of his eye, Veers caught a flash of green. He turned in time to see an AT-AT explode, first its belly, then the command center. It toppled like the great, headless creature it now resembled. Did his soldiers debark? Or had the attack slain forty good troopers? Veers deliberately looked away from the smoking hulk of the AT-AT. The goal was the only thing that mattered. He could not fail Lord Vader.

Below and in front of him, he could see the snowtroopers racing toward the rebels. And beyond them . . . the generators.

"Distance to power generators?" he inquired, his voice calm. Steady.

"One-seven-decimal-two-eight."

"Target. Maximum power!" Veers barked. The gunner fired. Seconds later the generators were gone, transformed into a pulsing yellow cloud of fire. Veers gazed at the scene, quietly satisfied. Now Vader and his stormtroopers could enter the rebel base. Now Vader would find this Skywalker, who had so vexed him, and the Rebellion would crumble.

At this moment, having delivered his lord's greatest desire, Veers had not failed Lord Vader. Far from it.

"I am sure Lord Vader is very pleased, sir," TK-7834 said.

"That is the goal, is it not?" Veers replied, brushing off the compliment. "This is merely how everyone in the Empire should behave. Obey. And excel."

At that moment, at the edge of his vision, Veers caught movement. His head snapped to the left, and his eyes widened as a smoking rebel snowspeeder careened toward them.

Thump. Thump. Thump.

Fast, so fast. Sounds, dreamy, muffled, distorted. Water. Swimming in water. Weightless, at ease, warm. Ready to drift away. But no, no. That wasn't right . . .

The thumping grew faster, faster. Fear crept in, tendrils of darkness, wrapping around, squeezing—*no, no, please*—

And then came the sound. Rhythmic, almost soothing, calming. Steady. As unfaltering as Lord Vader himself.

Veers tried to say, *My lord,* then realized that the labored breathing he heard was his own. And as if the knowing of this suddenly made it real, pain such as he had never felt raced through him. The armor had protected him—hadn't it? He opened his eyes—*ah! bright, too bright*—and where there had been darkness and softness and warmth and comfort, now there were colors and chaos and agony, so intense and powerful it was almost . . . pure. And cold. So, so cold . . .

The strange sounds formed themselves into known things: words, his own heartbeat.

". . . pretty bad . . . Still alive . . . where are the medics . . ."

Snow. *I remember* . . .

"He's awake!" It was TK-78 . . . he could not remember the number. It was Lastok. He had removed his helm, against regulations. His face was bloody, but the trooper looked more worried about Veers. Why? Veers tried to ask, but no words came out.

"General . . . General Veers! Sir, you've got to listen to me. Hang on, all right?" Lastok glanced away, looking around, then shouted, "Medic! It's the general!" He waved, flagging someone down, then returned his attention to Veers.

"Stay with us, sir. You're going to be all right!"

But Veers had heard fear and hope warring in a soldier's voice before. He was not at all sure he was going to be all right. He was sufficiently aware to notice that the cold stopped at his midsection. His legs . . . were they just too cold for him to feel? Or . . .

His armor should have shielded him from the cold, but he could not stop shivering. Could he move? Legs, arms . . . anything?

"No, no. You can't die, General!" Veers knew what Lastok was doing: trying to keep him from drifting away into a place where no medic would be able to help. He closed his eyes again. The softness, the comfort was calling to him again. Veers listened.

". . . Lord Vader!"

The gibberish had once again formed into words Veers knew. Words that gripped him, dragged him back into this place of life, of anguish.

Tears stung his eyes at the thought of how close he had come. Lastok was right to have reminded him of his truest duty.

No. I must not fail Lord Vader.

He stopped resisting the pain and welcomed it instead. As Vader would. As Vader must have once. His mind flashed to the glimpses of the man inside the helm. His lord had not just survived unbearable torment but used it to reshape himself. Become the stronger for the suffering.

Each labored gulp of air sent excruciating stabs through his chest. He endured them. He heard the medics rush up, and knew it was safe to let go; they would catch him now. All was well.

No, my lord. I shall never fail you.

Ever.

A NATURALIST ON HOTH

Hank Green

"The Empire is here." My commander's voice was resigned, not as strong as he probably would have liked. "Your evac slots have been assigned." I looked around the room; we were a bunch of scientists and mechanics, not military personnel. We knew we were in harm's way, but our job was not to fight and kill. Nonetheless, in war, sometimes it is your job to die.

"There's a good chance that you'll make it out of here alive, but if you have any final messages you'd like to send, now's the time. We'll encrypt them and then distribute them through the entire fleet, so if anyone gets out, your message will."

That made the situation seem more real. I had had my chances to leave this assignment a dozen times, and yet I never had. When they told me I could go, I just found that—I couldn't. Of all of the things to fall in love with, this hostile, bitter rock was not the one I expected.

"It has been a pleasure to serve with each of you." I could see the tears filming his eyes, but his voice showed no sign of them. "And wherever we go on this day, may the Force be with us."

I wasn't born to fight. I never ached to feel like a blaster was an extension of my body. And while my friends went to the Incom/Subpro air shows, I was only ever annoyed by the screeching of X-wings or Headhunters ripping open the sky. That doesn't mean that I don't know the difference between a Z-95 AF4 and a Z-95 AF4-H. I still lived in an Incom company town, and even if you weren't interested in starfighters, they were still the basis of our economy and our culture.

132

I understand that I'm the weird one. It would make sense, growing up surrounded by both classics and fresh-off-the-line starfighters and speeders, that you would imagine yourself becoming a pilot. The problem was, when I surveyed my homeworld, starfighters looked clumsy and brutish compared with even the ugliest, lumbering sand slug or the most garish, invasive mynock. The complexity of nature far surpasses the most marvelous of human engineering. An ecosystem leaning on itself into a structure so magnificent that it can never be fully understood is a force so great that it both tears and lifts me.

This is the only thing I've ever been able to imagine when I heard stories of the Force. I've never felt it, but I can see all of the folds and crevices where it must hide.

Growing up, my classmates thought the only thing a mynock could possibly be good for was eating . . . if you'd already eaten all the sand slugs. But the first time I watched an organic animal actually *suckling electricity* from a landspeeder, I ran to my teachers and asked every one I could if a living animal could actually sustain itself on electricity.

The good news was, even in an Incom company town, there was a need for all kinds of folks, and a kid with exceptional interests got exceptional attention. If I was just another kid jockeying to be a pilot, I'd've had to compete with nearly everyone else. Studying biology and ecology, on the other hand—I knew more than most of my teachers by the time I was fifteen. That wasn't saying much, as our schools focused almost entirely on engineering, tactics, and galactic history.

I actually managed to not be mocked for my enthusiasms, though I am aware that this was entirely because of my parents, who were both high-level executives at Incom. Every kid in my school was told to kiss up to me because every one of their parents wanted a promotion. And my parents didn't mind my interests, either. The instability of the Clone Wars had been good for Incom, but bad for pilots, and if I didn't show interest in dying in a cockpit, they weren't going to push me.

Somehow I managed to get into a Core world university, on Corellia, actually. I was immediately out of my depth, but in a beautiful way. There was so much to know, and now I was among people who actually wanted to know it. I expected to be treated well, so people treated me well. I never stopped being disoriented by big cities, but this was less about the people and more about how hard it was to get back someplace that felt real and not manufactured.

The Republic dissolved when I was a teen, and the Empire—well, it seemed bad. But I told myself that, regardless of who was in power, the world needed people studying sand slug physiology because they were far better at absorbing and retaining water than any system devised by even the most innovative moisture farmers.

Yes, occasionally I'd hear rumblings that a mining colony was simply wiped out because the laborers tried to organize, or that the Empire was supporting slavers operating on the Outer Rim. But I had a bench full of slugs that needed watching, and every day I was discovering things that literally no one had ever known before. It was exciting, and I was proud of my work.

And then . . . Alderaan. No one could equivocate or lie or cover up Alderaan. There's a moment when you can't sit back and watch anymore, and if it wasn't Alderaan, it was never. It broke me. I could no longer work, I could no longer think.

There were many days in my life when you could say I became an adult, but that was the day I grew up.

I was on the next transport back to the Rim.

NOTES ON THE DESERT SAND SLUG

134

There isn't much that makes less sense to the average naturalist than the desert-dwelling sand slug. This little beast, striped dark and light blue, almost like a tropical flower, is covered in wet, sticky mucus. But why? Why would any organism in the desert be so cavalier with its water use as to literally keep it evaporating on its skin? More important, where did this water come from?

Possibly unsurprisingly, not many people had cared to spend much time observing these creatures. They are beautiful, if slugs can be beautiful, and I believe they can. But more beautiful than their striking appearance is their mere existence. And I wanted to get to the bottom of it.

So, armed with nothing more than a stick and a tank, I did what any young naturalist would. I snagged one and put it in a terrarium. I was not prepared for what I found next.

At twelve hours, the slug had dug beneath the surface of the sand, hardened, and lost all color, appearing to be nothing more than a dark brown pebble.

This was nothing compared with the next transformation.

The little seed of the slug then began to extend tendrils out from its body—thin, hairlike filaments that stretched, by thirty-six hours, up to fifteen centimeters away from the slug. At seventy-two hours, these filaments spidered through the entire tank, and the seed of the slug had shrunk from three centimeters across to a mere fifty millimeters! The slug's body was almost entirely in those filaments!

On a whim, I then poured a cup of water onto the bare sand of my terrarium. Over the course of only three hours, the filaments had retracted, and the slug was happily slugging over the once-more-parched sand.

I never wondered what good I might be to the Rebellion, because I never questioned the worth of my work. I couldn't shoot a bantha from five paces, but if you wanted to exist anywhere outside of deep space, you needed to understand the organisms you'd be living alongside. You needed to understand them because they could help you and also because they could kill you.

My homeworld was, by this point, full of rebel contacts sourcing parts for their secondhand snubfighters, so it wasn't hard to say a few words to the right people before my potential utility was recognized.

In a matter of months, I was having my first briefing.

Every briefing was done in a small group. A geologist, an ecologist (me), a meteorologist, two soldiers, and a commander.

Somehow, no one groaned when General Jan Dodonna told us about our candidate planet in his confident, no-nonsense voice.

"Candidate Nineteen Point Two is an iceball planet in an actively forming solar system. It's treacherous. Constant meteorite impacts create thermal signatures that would make it easier to hide. However, it will be difficult to survive. It is frozen from equator to pole, with glaciers covering the majority of the surface of the planet."

Ryssle, the meteorologist, spoke then. "Water glaciers?"

"Yes," the general replied.

"But that would mean snow, which would mean water was evaporating somewhere," she told him.

"I am not a scientist, I'm telling you what we know. Your job is to solve exactly that kind of mystery. The other thing we suspect is that there are predators, big ones." This took me aback. There was no way an iceball planet would have the ecology necessary to support an apex predator. I wasn't going to mention it to the general, but my interest in this mission had gone from *Well, maybe I'll get to see some interesting lichen,* to *I need to get to this planet right now.*

NOTES ON THE ECOSYSTEM OF HOTH

Anyone who looks at Hoth from above would be forgiven for thinking it a mostly dead ball of ice. But mostly dead would not be a problem for us. My research and exploration team arrived on what we were then calling Candidate 19.2 with enough supplies to keep us warm and fed for a year.

Within two weeks, and over the objections of several team members, Tev, the team geologist, and I had convinced our commander that we had to track a tauntaun over the open surface or we would never uncover the secrets of the planet. We understood why other members of the party were not interested in this, and so we offered to make the trek with just the two of us. Tev's compact frame and fur made him the most well suited to the planet of our group, and my ecological knowledge was most necessary to the mission. Commander Habria, of course, refused to split the party, and so everyone was dragged along on our hunt.

Our working theory was that the planet could not house a rebel base on the surface. Temperatures during the night were simply too low, and any base would be visible as a massive source of heat. But the planet was geologically active, and so we hypothesized that the ecology of the planet was based on that energy, and that the large organisms must exist in subterranean ecosystems.

We packed for a ten-day excursion, and then one of the team's troopers fired a tracking dart into the flank of a tauntaun. It soon became obvious that the conditions of the planet limited the range of the tracker, so we had to stay within three kilometers of the beast.

That, combined with the indisputable reality that we could not travel at night, soon became a clear problem. By evening the tauntaun had led us nowhere except into the middle of a glacier. I had been steadfastly ignoring the complaints of our two troopers and the milder but more worrying anxieties of Ryssle, our meteorologist, all day. But as the temperature dropped, the concern escalated.

Eventually Commander Habria called for us to make camp. I argued strongly that we would lose the tauntaun if we stopped and thus had to follow for at least another half hour. My arguments were not well received by anyone in the party, not even Tev, and so I, resigned, took one last look at the tracking screen.

There I found my deliverance . . . the tauntaun had stopped.

Commander Habria put together a three-person party to go and examine the tauntaun while the rest of the team made camp. The team was Anita, one of the troopers; Habria herself; and me. The other trooper's tone changed then, from gentle but friendly complaints to legitimate worry. It was then that everyone realized that the two troopers, Xaime and Anita, had, in the short time we'd been on-planet, become a pair, and he was worried for her safety. It was touching, but also worrying. Any strong emotions could make a mission like this more deadly.

When Anita, Habria, and I arrived at the tauntaun, I was immediately distraught, though I tried not to show it. Anita, however, came right out to say it, and asked, "Is it dead?"

It certainly seemed so. The animal had simply lain down in the snow, which was now drifting on one side of it. I approached cautiously, pulling my glove off, and placed my bare hand against its unfurred muzzle. It was the temperature of ice. I said a word under my breath, only remembering that we were on an open comm when Habria chastised me for my language.

It did not make sense to me that the animal was dead. Why would this native animal be less able to survive than us? There were only three possibilities. First, that it was ill and dying when we started tracking it, which seemed extremely unlikely. Second, that it knew we were following and ran from us past exhaustion. Third, that it was not actually dead.

138

Now, it turned out to be true that it knew we were following it, though I would not know for some time of the extreme infrared radiation sensitivity of tauntauns. But on this night, I made a guess and then, against my instincts as a scientist and a member of my squad, I proclaimed it as if it were definitely true.

"It's just playing dead" I said, confidently. "It will wake in the morning, when the threat has past." No air was exiting its nostrils, no warmth was radiating from its body, but there was no one who was qualified to argue with me.

And then we went back to camp and I lay awake, knowing that, if the tauntaun did not get up in the morning, I would have to tell my commander and the rest of the team that I had lied to them and we had risked our lives in the snow for my pride.

I did my best not to show how pleased I was when the dot began to move the next morning. And in less than half an hour, we were back on the trail.

It was that second day that the animal turned sharply down a valley and then, suddenly again, into a glacial ravine.

And then the signal disappeared.

The area the signal disappeared in was treacherous, with sudden jagged slants of broken ice that were only visible from a few feet away, but finally we found a crack from which warm air was rising.

This was how we found our first tauntaun family group, and the future location of Echo Base.

A keystone species is one that isn't just part of an ecosystem, but helps create it and holds it together. Like the sapphire ice worm on Hoth. These worms can burrow through miles of glacier in search of food, and they leave behind small channels, smaller than the width of my finger. But as warm air rushes up and out after being heated by the interior of the planet, these tiny tunnels widen. Over decades, or even centuries, they become massive. They become a home for the entire subterranean ecosystem of Hoth. They build their world and have no idea that they do it.

This is how I felt. I came to Hoth to study this world's life, and while I did it, a base formed around me. I had found a way to do what I loved while also helping the Rebellion, but that didn't make me a soldier. In fact, despite my efforts, I feel a quiet contempt for those reckless souls who are here only to kill and be killed.

Not long ago, I watched such a man hop on a tauntaun as dusk rushed over the base. I turned to my commander and said, "He'll need to closely monitor the animal's vitals if they both want to make it back alive." My commander then repeated my concern to him, louder, and abbreviated, "Your tauntaun'll freeze before you reach the first marker." The man had nothing kind to say in reply, but that didn't stop him from saying something. When the man returned, and I discovered how he'd made it through the night, I felt sick. Had he even noticed the warning signs as the creature froze to death? Had he even cared? The tauntaun was another casualty, a natural creature conscripted to be a soldier in a war it couldn't understand. At least he had saved his friend, but the Rebellion's lack of respect for this planet still had me quietly seething.

We all have our blind spots and our indulgent ignorances. None of us can know everything, and that is more true of me than anyone. I do not know how to win a war, but I find myself also no longer able to care. Alderaan tore a hole in me. I didn't just lose faith in the Empire; to some extent, I lost faith in my species. That was not a thing done by evil, it was a thing done by us, and I will never forgive us. I will never be able to see my own face in the mirror the same way. And so maybe I have stopped looking. As this base formed around me, I became less and less a part of the Rebellion—not because I don't feel like their mission is worthwhile, but because I feel less and less like a part of the human species.

Only now am I finally accepting what I've known since the moment we found out the Empire was coming.

When we found out General Dodonna had been killed, I stayed on Hoth. I stayed after Ryssle disappeared from our camp one night and never came back. When the Rebellion reassigned my team to a new planet, I convinced them I had more work to do here. And just now, when my evac shuttle assignment was called, I stayed. I am sick with this knowledge, but I cannot stop knowing it.

I am not going anywhere.

I know these tunnels like no one else on the planet. I know this planet like no one else in the galaxy. Yet still, I know almost nothing of what there is to know. I cannot leave these mysteries behind. The sum of what I have learned, I have attached in the form of field notes in the hope that they will be of use or interest to someone in the future. I apologize that they are not well organized; I did not have much time to prepare.

And to my family. Mom, Dad, I hope you get this. I'm fine. The Empire will not find me, and neither will the wampas. When the war is over, send someone for me. I'll be in the worm caves with the tauntauns. It's where I belong.

—Kell Tolkani, Base Naturalist, Echo Station, Hoth

THE DRAGONSNAKE SAVES R2

Katie Cook

FOR THE LAST TIME

Beth Revis

One breath.

Admiral Firmus Piett allowed himself one breath as the door closed behind him, sealing him in Lord Vader's private chamber aboard the *Executor*.

One breath, to remind himself that he *could* breathe.

Unlike Admiral Ozzel.

In the space of that one breath, Piett felt the soft thud of Admiral Ozzel's body hitting the floor at his feet. He felt the still-twitching hand clutching at the hem of his immaculate uniform, wrinkling it, which was, frankly, unnecessarily rude even in the throes of death. He felt the surge of adrenaline as he realized just what Lord Vader could do, and just what it meant to him.

He heard Lord Vader tell Ozzel with cold efficiency, *You have failed me for the last time.*

Lord Vader had killed Ozzel without even being in the same room as him, with merely a thought.

And in one breath, Captain Piett had become Admiral Piett.

Piett squared his shoulders, straightened his spine. He deserved this position. Ozzel had not. It had been an unfortunate—but not unwelcome—side effect that Ozzel's demotion had come in the form of his own choking death.

There were two types of men, just as there were two types of power. It was one of the first lessons Piett had learned as a junior officer serving under Grand Moff Tarkin himself: People are ruled either through fear or through a false sense of security. The men who had been given their power like a piece of candy to an obedient child—those men thought they were secure.

But the men who took their power knew how to make a fist.

Those who believed themselves safe were weak. Those who lived in fear were strong. It was natural, the difference between the hunter and the prey. Prey had the luxury of ignorance, oblivious to threat, but a hunter knew the terror of starvation if the prey was not killed.

And so Piett had watched and waited, as patiently as a lyxine watching a bouf rat. A good hunter knew when to leverage power for a kill-strike. In any given situation, he knew, there were men who believed they were in charge, and there were men who truly were.

Admiral Ozzel had walked across the bridge of the *Executor* as if it were his right.

But Lord Vader strode over the black enamel as if he would burn it from the sky before he let anyone take it from him.

And that was the man who truly had the power.

Ozzel deserved nothing because he had taken nothing. He had only ever been handed things in his life—positions, power, prestige.

Everything Piett had, he had taken. He had long suspected the same was true of Lord Vader.

Even though Lord Vader had been the first to call Piett "Admiral," it had been Piett himself who'd positioned each piece on the holo-chess board to make that title happen. He had waited to call attention to Hoth—which he knew, thanks to his private resources, likely housed the rebels—until Lord Vader was on the bridge. He had planted the seeds to make Ozzel dismiss Hoth, thanks to an influx of dead ends piling up on his desk from Piett's own subordinates. He had moved those holo-chess pieces.

And he had waited.

Until Lord Vader made a fist, just as Piett had known, eventually, he would. And Piett took the title that he deserved.

Piett did not have a false sense of security. Even before Ozzel's body had fallen at his feet, he had known the game was dangerous, that the hunt continued. The moment Piett showed weakness—as Ozzel had through his own arrogance—that would be the same moment it was Piett's body twitching on the floor, gasping.

Piett also knew, though, that a man who seized power was a man who knew never to let it go.

So he didn't.

Piett strode down the three steps into Lord Vader's chamber, ready to give him a report on the rebels. Other Imperial officers avoided this whole floor, much less the room, fearing to get too close to the volatile Vader.

Piett was no fool. He saw the bodies; he saw Lord Vader's fist clenched. He knew to be afraid. But what set him apart was the way Piett relished the fear.

Fear made him strong.

If he was not afraid, after all, he would be complacent. He would be weak.

Lost in thought, Piett did not realize at first that Lord Vader was not fully prepared for his arrival. His steps slowed from efficiently measured to hesitating. Curiosity made him peer closer, leaning in to see better as the electronic hiss of shifting mechanics filled the chamber.

Piett had known, logically, that beneath the mask of Lord Vader was a human.

He had not known how *broken* a human, though.

The shiny black helmet descended over Lord Vader's head . . . or what remained of it. Raw, wrinkled skin was streaked with red veins and painful-looking welts. A tall neckpiece seemed to do the work of Lord Vader's spine, supporting the bulbous mass of flesh stretched over the patchwork skull. Piett's calculating mind counted more than a dozen electrode-bolts screwed into the neckpiece, connecting to Lord Vader's nerves, before he had the wherewithal to look down, swallowing the bitter bile rising in his throat.

It was only a few moments. Seconds, really.

But more than enough to see just how horrific it was beneath the mask.

He's a walking corpse, Piett thought, and the words reminded him of Ozzel, his body writhing at his feet, eyes bulging, tongue lolling, trying to gasp out words but unable to form a single sound other than that weird, sputtering choking noise that sometimes woke Piett at night.

Piett allowed himself one breath.

Then he looked up.

With a hiss and a metallic click of the connectors locking into place, the helmet was sealed over Lord Vader's bare skull. Piett could imagine the darkness inside the all-black helmet, the light sensors that must communicate to the eyes—*Does he have eyes?* Piett wondered, the thought making his blood cold. Had he seen Lord Vader's mangled face, would nothing but gaping black holes stare back at him? There must be nerve endings, surely, but they could connect to optic sensors, and . . .

Piett was used to being ruled—and ruling—by fear.

But this was different.

This was . . .

What turns a man into such a monster? What makes a man choose *this* over death? Death seemed easy. Ozzel had made it appear so. But this way of living . . . Why would Lord Vader choose such pain?

Lord Vader's seat turned in a slow circle. Piett should feel the power and intimidation from him, but when he saw the black suit, all he felt was . . .

Pity.

It took so long for Piett to recognize the emotion that he almost could not name it. Pity. Prior to this, Piett had never seen anything but the black of Lord Vader—the black helmet, the black cape, the black gloves curled into a fist. Lord Vader was a commander, a near-god with his power over life and death, cloaked in the universe's darkness.

149

But the pale white flesh with a waxy sheen, so much like a rotting cadaver . . .

That had made Lord Vader a man.

Mortal.

Pitiable.

Weak.

Lord Vader's seat was fully turned, and the commander—the man—looked through the dark eyepieces of his helmet toward Admiral Piett.

"Yes, Admiral?" Lord Vader said, his voice even, emotionless.

Piett almost wished that Lord Vader had allowed his rage to leak into his voice. His eyes darted to Lord Vader's hands—fingers relaxed against the rests of his chair, palms open.

If Piett wanted to sit beside Emperor Palpatine, now was the time to realize that he no longer feared Lord Vader, and without that fear, Lord Vader had lost some of his power against him.

It was not courage that destroyed fear. It was pity.

But Piett had what he wanted—the *Executor.* The admiralship.

And if being beside the Emperor meant being behind a mask, he did not want that.

Suddenly Piett heard, as clearly as he had a few days before, Lord Vader's voice: *You have failed me for the last time.*

Ah.

There it was.

The fear was back.

Fear was power.

Piett forced the breath from his body, and with it, the image of the man. Lord Vader was no man. Piett would not allow him to be. He imagined that weak, feeble *thing* he had seen under the mask. And he killed it in his mind's eye.

He put that corpse beside Ozzel's in the graveyard of his memory.

Lord Vader was only the mask. Piett would never again allow himself to think of Lord Vader as anything but the black fist, clenched, choking away the life of anyone who did not properly fear him.

There was something calming in that idea. Piett had not liked those moments when Vader had been more man than mask.

"Our ships have sighted the *Millennium Falcon,* my lord," Piett reported without a quiver in his voice. Fear, after all, gave him strength.

But even though he bowed his head, even though he accepted the command that followed, even though his heart surged at Lord Vader's reprimand after he informed him of the situation, Piett could not quite keep the pity that lingered out of his eyes.

Much as he wished to erase the moment, he *had* seen past Vader's mask.

And that had cracked his own.

RENDEZVOUS POINT

Jason Fry

Wedge Antilles had always wanted to fly.

When he was a kid on Corellia, he'd finish watching an episode of a somber documentary about starfighters (*Zero Hour: The Tentraxis Campaign*), then dive into a breathlessly written memoir written by a retired ace. (*Fly Fast and Die Young!*)

Those digi-dramas and holonovels had been heavy on descriptions of high-g maneuvers and defiance shouted over comms, but light on other parts of life as a starfighter pilot.

For instance, none of them mentioned that you couldn't sleep for more than a few minutes while in a cockpit. Pilots talked about sitting in the "easy chair," but "torture rack" struck Wedge as a better description. The restraints cut off your circulation, but release them and you'd wake with a start when you nodded off and smacked your helmet into the control panel.

Nor had he learned that you sweated profusely during combat and emerged from battle drenched and rank. Which was fine if you had a shower waiting, but not if you had to stay crammed in a cockpit for hours. When a starfighter canopy opened after a long mission, flight crews stepped back to avoid getting a noseful of funk.

And Wedge had never heard about a starfighter ace heroically donning "maximum absorbency undergarments" before soaring off on an extended mission. Which, he had to admit, was probably for the best.

After the evacuation of Echo Base, Wedge had switched from a T-47 snowspeeder to a T-65 X-wing, but he'd been stuck in his cold-weather flight suit, and his X-wing's heater was stuck on FULL. He'd reported that problem weeks ago, but every technician on Hoth had been working to get the T-47s adapted to the planet's brutal cold. And a broken heater counted as an up gripe—meaning the fighter was operational—rather than a down gripe that would have left him grounded.

He'd been relieved at the time, but now he was sweaty and parched.

"I've made some terrible life choices," he muttered to himself.

He winced as his astromech, R5-G8, beeped a question. Or more accurately, *screeched* a question. Something was wrong with the droid's acoustic signaler, leaving it sounding like an agitated mynock.

"Just talking to myself," Wedge said, grimacing at another fusillade of whistles. "Yes, people do that. No, I don't need a diagnostic check once we reach the rendezvous point. No, do *not* log this exchange for a medical droid to review. Yes, I'm sure."

R5-G8's personality quirks had developed personality quirks of their own: Wedge had never worked with an astromech more prone to citing regulations. That up gripe would get fixed, he vowed—if not with a memory wipe, then with a wrench.

More piercing squeals. Wedge eyed the readout's translation, ready to tell the astromech to shut himself off, Alliance flight-operations regulations notwithstanding.

But his anger leaked away when he read the droid's question.

"I know," he said. "We had a lot of losses at Hoth, Arfive. Too many losses."

The first Rogue Squadron pilots to die had been Zev Senesca and Kit Valent, killed when their T-47 was shot down by an Imperial walker. That had been the start of a numbing parade, culminating with the loss Wedge could barely bring himself to think about: Derek Klivian, killed along with his gunner when he plowed his damaged T-47 into an AT-AT's head.

Derek Klivian. Who'd hated being called Derek, insisting that his friends use his childhood nickname, the one Wedge had thought ridiculous for a grown-up or anyone trying to become one.

Hobbie.

They'd met as Imperial cadets at Skystrike Academy, playing endless hands of sabacc in the barracks. They'd defected to the Alliance together, fleeing Montross with the rebel agent Sabine Wren. They'd battled the Empire together at Atollon, Perimako Major, Distilon, and a dozen other worlds.

It was Hobbie who'd tried to comfort Wedge—in the awkward, emotionally stunted way of starfighter pilots—after he'd been left off the duty roster for the raid on Scarif. Days later, it was Wedge who'd tried to comfort Hobbie after he'd been grounded for the Battle of Yavin.

Now his friend was dead, and a galaxy without Hobbie struck Wedge as impossibly cold and cruel.

Another squawk from R5-G8.

"We'll have to see," he said. "I'm sure there will be a briefing once we reach the rendezvous point."

They flew in silence for a while, surrounded by the endless churn of hyperspace. Then R5-G8 squealed a different question, one that actually made Wedge smile.

"Yes, I'm sure Artoo-Detoo will be there—and that he'll have brought Commander Skywalker with him."

But Wedge was wrong.

After the latest briefing, he wiped sweat from his brow and returned to the pilots' ready room aboard *Home One,* known as the Hub. He got a slice of Kommerken steak—the Hub had a surprisingly good chef—and plopped into a chair across from Wes Janson, an old friend who'd served as his gunner on Hoth.

"How you holding up, Wes?"

"Oh, splendid, Lieutenant Commander," Janson said, stroking his stubbled chin. "Filling up on grub but sweating it all off, thanks to our hosts building military vessels that double as saunas."

"Well, it *is* their ship," Wedge pointed out.

Not that he disagreed. Conditions humans and many other species considered comfortable struck Mon Calamari as borderline arctic and arid, leading to constant negotiations.

"Double-M have anything to say?" Janson asked. That was a nickname in the ranks for Mon Mothma, the Alliance leader.

"We're waiting for more personnel to reach the rendezvous. But remaining on high alert."

"Hurry up and wait, in other words. Any word from Skywalker? Or the princess?"

"No. But critical personnel often have to use the full scatter protocol. Ackbar probably has them making extra hyperspace jumps for security."

154

Janson scowled and looked down at something in his hand.

"Sure, but then they'd be hours late. It's been what, three days?"

Wedge had to think about that for a moment—time had become a smear of anxiety and waiting for news that didn't come.

"I heard the princess told her transport to take off without her," he said. "She was going to hitch a ride aboard the *Falcon*."

"So maybe Solo's junk heap finally disintegrated in hyperspace," Janson said, shaking his head. Wedge saw that the object he was holding was a small metal cylinder.

"What is that thing you keep playing with?"

His friend looked startled, then embarrassed.

"It's a miniature aerosol dispenser. One of the techs back at Echo Base made it for me."

"I'm not following."

"Double-tap this little doohickey here and twist it to the right, it starts a timer. Two hours later, the contents disperse as a mist. Twist it back to the left, it shuts off. Pretty simple."

"And the contents?"

"Tauntaun bull musk. Actually, it's even worse than whatever you're thinking, Lieutenant Commander. None of the stable hands would help me, so I had to express the scent glands myself. I used gloves, but my hands smelled so bad that I scrubbed them like thirty times. First with water, like a smart person. Then with solvent, like a stupid one. Took the top layer of skin right off."

"You're certifiable, Janson," Wedge said. "You do know that, right? What in the name of every Corellian hell could you possibly need that for?"

"It was a surprise for Hobbie. He was next to pull recon duty—a three-day hop."

Ah. Now Wedge could fill in the rest. Janson and Hobbie had been inseparable companions despite being apparent opposites: Janson could crack a joke during a hair-raising firefight, while Hobbie never failed to ponder the worst that could happen. How many of Janson's pranks had Hobbie endured? A dozen? A hundred?

"I'm pretty sure that would have counted as a war crime," Wedge said.

Janson laughed—but it wasn't the easy laugh Wedge was used to. It was more of a harsh bark.

"I know, right?" Janson said. "He would have been *so mad*. I was going to make sure I was right there in the hangar when he got back—so I could see his face before I started running. Oh, it would have been *amazing*."

"He would have killed you. And the court-martial would have ruled it justifiable homicide."

"Probably," Janson said, still staring down at the little device. "I keep finding this dumb thing in my pocket. Hobbie's gone, but I can't bring myself to get rid of it. Isn't that strange?"

It wasn't strange at all, Wedge thought, groping for a way to reassure his friend.

156

Before he could find it, a protocol droid clanked up to their table. Its plating was a brilliant blue, and some bored rebel had taken an inordinate amount of time adorning its torso with a gold Alliance starbird.

"I have no idea how our undercover agents keep getting discovered," Janson said.

"Espionage work is not part of my programming," the droid said primly, then turned to Wedge. "Lieutenant Commander Antilles? Ess-fiveveethree, at your service. Your presence is requested in the chancellor's office."

Wedge looked quizzically from the droid to Janson, who shrugged.

"What does the chancellor want with me? I'm just a starfighter pilot."

"I am not at liberty to disclose the purpose of the meeting," S-5V3 said.

Wedge scooted his chair back. Janson was still gawking at the droid's gaudy paint scheme.

"But if you *were* programmed for espionage . . . wouldn't that same programming keep you from admitting it?" he asked, tapping his temple.

"Ignore Wes," Wedge told the baffled droid. "It's the only way to stay sane."

"I will update my personnel-interaction database accordingly," S-5V3 said.

To Wedge's surprise, the person waiting for him in the chancellor's office wasn't Mon Mothma but a dark-eyed woman wearing a flight suit, her black hair pulled back in a tight bun.

"Lieutenant Commander Antilles," she said briskly. "You can call me the Contessa."

"What?"

157

The Contessa sighed. "I dislike when people say 'what' when it's perfectly obvious they heard the words. What you actually mean is, 'I don't understand what you said, could you please explain it to me?'"

Wedge regarded her for a moment.

"I don't understand what you said. Could you please explain it to me?"

"Eventually. Provided you're still alive, and provided you've earned it. Sit."

Wedge sat. The Contessa picked up a datapad and flicked her finger across its surface, her eyes moving rapidly. She scrolled down again, then a third time. Wedge couldn't tell if she was reading quickly or had no interest in what she saw. Then she set the datapad down and regarded him above her steepled fingers.

"You were born on Corellia."

"That's right."

"The Empire hasn't been kind to your homeworld. And yet you joined them. Why?"

"Because I was young. I was flying bulk cargo out of Corellia—produce and spare parts, mostly—and it was boring. So when the Empire recruited me, I said yes."

"And is that why you defected from Skystrike Academy? Because you got bored again?"

Wedge said nothing, his thoughts going back to the day he wished he could forget. The day he'd learned he'd lost people he loved, and that the Empire had been responsible. But he wasn't going to tell this strange, rude person about that. If it wasn't in his file, it wasn't her business.

"No," he said instead. "That's not why."

He remembered reaching for his TIE helmet and realizing his hands were shaking. The idea of flying an Imperial fighter suddenly struck him as obscene. The Empire kept order, but that order was a product of terror. And it was training him to become an agent of that terror. That was the moment Wedge had vowed—first only to himself, then later to Hobbie—not to let that happen.

The Contessa was waiting for an answer.

"I'll explain it eventually," Wedge said. "Provided you earn it."

He folded his arms across his chest, wondering if she'd throw him out of the office and not particularly caring if she did.

Instead she smiled. "So there's a little Corellian in you after all."

"When I need it. What's this about, Contessa?"

"Rebuilding your squadron."

Hope flared in Wedge. "The fleet's reuniting?"

"No," the Contessa said, and that hope guttered out as quickly as it had kindled. "There are . . . complications. We're maintaining our position for now."

"We're down too many pilots," Wedge said. "Starting with our commander."

"Skywalker hasn't returned," the Contessa said. "We have to accept that he may not."

"He's Luke Skywalker. He destroyed the Death Star and saved the Alliance."

"Even heroes die, Lieutenant Commander. In fact, they die all the time. For whatever reason, we don't have Skywalker. But we do have *you*. Wedge Antilles, who was first in his class at Skystrike. Who flew with Phoenix Squadron, and was one of two survivors of Red Squadron at Yavin."

"Because I bailed out of the Death Star trench," Wedge said. It was a memory that still made his insides knot with shame.

"Spare me. You had six kills above that battle station despite flying a T-65 the techs feared wouldn't make orbit. You blew your hydraulics and couldn't maneuver, so you got clear rather than endanger your fellow pilot. Once clear, you recharged your auxiliaries and tried to go back into that trench. Which would have killed you within seconds, but you did it anyway."

159

"I was Luke's wing and I left him. That's the bottom line."

"I doubt Skywalker sees it that way. We need your squadron, Antilles. And we need it now."

Wedge thought about the faces he'd seen in the Hub and the duty rosters he'd scanned. There were enough experienced pilots for two flights of three T-65s each. But that was only half a squadron.

"If we're staying put, why the urgency?" he asked. "Our capital ships can repel anything short of an Imperial task force."

The Contessa tapped on her datapad, then passed it over.

"We've been using civilian cargo ships to resupply. Over the last thirty-six hours, two of them have failed to arrive. Turns out a pirate band's stumbled onto our supply line."

Wedge scanned the intel in dismay.

"I know we don't have enough experienced pilots," the Contessa said. "You're going to create a few. You're promoted to commander."

"Luke is our—"

"We've covered that. I know you don't think you're ready, Antilles, but I need you to be. And the pilots you're going to lead? They'll need that a lot more. We can't let a bunch of pirates starve us out or sell our location to the Empire. Before they can do either, you're going to destroy them. As squadron leader."

"Heck of a way to start a squadron," Janson said.

The Hub was a little too public, so Wedge and Janson had retreated to one of the observation blisters that dotted *Home One*'s hull. That gave them privacy, but at the expense of comfort—they kept knocking knees as they sat facing each other, datapads on their laps.

"Seriously, how do two Mon Cals even fit in here?" Janson asked.

"Schooling instinct. You've noticed the way they maneuver in tandem, right?"

"No, I've never . . . wait. You made that up."

"Possibly," Wedge said.

"Did Wedge Antilles just make a joke? Wedge Antilles, the Great Stone Face of the Spaceways?"

"I make jokes."

"Every six months?"

"You've usually got it covered. Now come on. You go first, then I go. We alternate till we've got a squadron."

Janson blew out his breath in frustration. "There aren't many candidates, boss. Even with this Contessa of yours giving us all the personnel records. And why can't she fly with us?"

"The chancellor needs her to coordinate our overall starfighter defenses. And she's got her own squadron to put back together."

"Well, that makes the pickings even slimmer. I'd take Aron Polstak in a heartbeat, but Double-M's got him on special assignment. At least there's Will Scotian. He's flown with us, which makes him a definite."

"Scotian was my first choice, too. Done. I want Bela Elar."

"Twi'lek pilot, right? I didn't know she was here."

"She just got towed in. Her T-65 blew its alluvial dampers, and she had to go extravehicular to fix them in deep space."

Janson whistled. "So with your first pick you've found us a competent pilot *and* an engineering department. Guess that's why you're squadron leader and I'm general skytrash."

Squadron leader. It still sounded wrong to Wedge. But he supposed he better get used to it.

"You're not general skytrash, you're my newly appointed executive officer," he said.

"You say Princess Lay-a, I say Princess Lee-a. And I say Keyser Salm. He's Horton's little brother. I've flown recon with him. Green but teachable."

"Done."

Janson smiled. "Well. This is gonna be easy. Your turn, Commander."

"Barlon Hightower," Wedge said.

"On my list, too. Though he's so green he makes Keyser look like an ace. My turn: Cinda Tarheel."

"She's got a temper like a scalded rancor. General Rieekan grounded her on Hoth because we all feared she'd fly her T-47 into the side of a mountain. Remember?"

"All too well," Janson said. "Still, she can fly. We can teach her anger isn't a superpower."

Wedge sighed. "If she lives long enough to listen. But you're right, she can fly."

"You're up, Commander."

"Sila Kott."

"I don't know who that is."

"That's because she flies troop transports. Commander Narra found her back when he made every pilot do simulator runs. He tried to recruit her for a squadron but she refused."

Janson frowned. "She can fly but she doesn't want to. Isn't that disqualifying?"

"Normally, yes. But this isn't normally. I'll ask again. And if her answer is no, I know someone who won't ask."

"Fair enough. Ix Ixstra."

Wedge scanned his datapad. "She spent two weeks at Echo Base in the brig for fighting."

"Admirable combat spirit," Janson said.

"She hit a Pathfinder over the head with a meal tray."

"Experienced at ambush tactics."

"A Pathfinder twice her size."

"So her threat recognition needs some work. But if we start passing on the Ix Ixstras of the fleet, we're going to be asking Double-M herself to climb into a cockpit."

"Not how I want to go down in Alliance history. All right, fine. Grizz Frix."

Janson sighed. "Another hothead. Still, he never brained a fellow rebel with a tray. And with that ringing endorsement, he's part of the squadron. That's ten pilots. My final pick is Penn Zowlie."

"I have no flight record for him," Wedge said.

"That's because he's never even simmed. He's a med-droid assistant who kept pestering me back on Hoth, from some asteroid cluster on the edge of Wild Space. Spent his childhood jumping hoversleds and vac-skims from rock to rock."

Wedge raised an eyebrow.

Janson grinned. "Bush pilot from the back of beyond? Big dreams, runs off to join the Alliance? I just found the next Luke Skywalker."

"Or the forty millionth kid to get vaped on his first mission. But fine, we'll hope you're right. Because you're really not going to like my last pick. Tomer Darpen. Don't give me that look—he can fly."

"Yeah, he'll fly off to sell his T-65 for a crate of spice. How many times did we spot him doing shady stuff back in the day?"

"Daily. He can fly."

"Within five years he'll be a spicerunner or a pirate."

"Then he'll be someone else's problem. He can fly."

"All right, all right. But when the moment we both know is coming arrives, I get to stun him."

"Agreed. So we're done?"

"We're done, Commander. Rogue Group is reborn. Or at least the name is."

Wedge shook his head. "I think we should ground that name for a while. Too many losses."

Janson's eyes turned flinty. "So the Empire gets to take that from us, too?"

"It's not that," Wedge said. "It's that there are call signs I'm not sure I could say in battle right now."

Janson's face fell and he stared out at the stars surrounding the observation blister.

"We'll go back to Red Squadron," Wedge suggested. "Maybe that name will motivate our new pilots."

"Or we could go with reverse psychology and call ourselves Reject Squadron."

Wedge sighed. "When we're heroes, let's remember to pretty this story up for the Alliance historians."

"Absolutely. 'Why, we had dozens of decorated pilots to choose from. Impossible decisions! Fortunately, we made our choices in a lavishly appointed conference room, assisted by fancy Alliance dignitaries. Oh, and when we got peckish, there was a fine repast.'"

"Is *peckish* even a word?"

"It's what fancy Alliance dignitaries say when they mean 'hungry.' Which I am. Hub grub, Commander? Hey, that's fun to say."

"You sound like one of those stuffed toys with a comm chip."

"Exactly the effect I was looking for. Hub grub, Commander. Hub grub."

To Wedge's surprise, things moved at a decidedly unbureaucratic pace. The Contessa approved his roster within an hour, and all the pilots agreed to his request—though he suspected they'd been told it wasn't really a request.

But when he asked for a week of simulator time for the new Red Squadron, the Contessa shook her head even before the sentence was out of his mouth. He had two days.

Fortunately, *Home One* had a full suite of sim tanks, allowing all twelve members of the newborn squadron to fly at once.

Unfortunately, that first run-through showed Wedge how much his newborn squadron had to learn.

Scotian and Elar were solid pilots, and all of the newcomers were basically sound—even Zowlie, who as far as Wedge knew had never so much as simmed an X-wing's controls.

The exception was Sila Kott, who could barely fly a simulated kilometer without accidentally lowering her shields or overcharging her acceleration compensators. That was bizarre, given her service record as a pilot, and Wedge spent the last hour of the first sim wondering why.

The exercise ended and the pilots emerged from their tanks, sweaty and shielding their eyes from the tactical suite's bright lights.

"That was awesome!" crowed Zowlie. "You were flying fangs out, Lieutenant Janson! How many bandits did you splash?"

Janson put Zowlie in a headlock.

"Here's your first demerit, kid—only one bit of pilot slang per conversation. More than that gives Uncle Wes a headache."

"Okay, settle down," Wedge said. "Red Group, that was a good first exercise. We're back here at twenty-one hundred, so go get some Hub grub. Kott, stick around a minute."

Kott was tall and thin, her hair cut short and ragged with what struck Wedge as almost deliberate indifference, and she had an odd habit of ducking her head against her shoulder, as if she wanted to appear smaller than she was.

"I figured you'd want to see me, Commander," she said when they were alone. "I'm sorry."

She looked embarrassed but also relieved. Wedge made himself count to five, then leapt.

"Don't be sorry," he said. "Just tell me why you deliberately sabotaged the exercise."

"What? I didn't . . . I've never flown a T-65 before, Commander, and . . . I don't know why you'd . . ."

"You're an experienced pilot. You know how not to lower your own shields, or any of the other inexplicably dumb things you did. And the rest of the time you were flying that bird like a natural. So what's going on?"

Kott's shoulders sagged.

"I don't want to fly a starfighter. I never have."

"Why not?"

Wedge watched her try to find the words. Then they all came spilling out.

"I've been in this Rebellion for years, but I've never killed anybody. It's bad enough flying a transport, feeling like all those soldiers' lives are in your hands. But taking someone's life? I can't do it. I won't."

"Walk with me, Sila," Wedge said. "I was still just a kid when I made my first kill, flying an old starfighter I'd borrowed. The target was a gunboat, crewed by pirates. They'd . . . they'd taken people from me."

"I'm sorry," Kott said.

"I punched a hole in their aft deflector shields, settled in behind them at zero angle, and took the shot," Wedge said, raising one hand and pantomiming the gesture. "A second later that gunboat was a cloud of vapor. When I flew through it, it felt good. For a few seconds. Then I didn't feel anything. And that night I couldn't stop throwing up."

Kott's face was unreadable.

"That was a lot of kills ago," Wedge said. "I should know how many, but I don't. But every time I pull the trigger, I hope it's the last time. And I pray that I'm helping create a galaxy where no one has to do it. But that galaxy doesn't exist yet, Sila. And it won't exist without our help. Which means killing people. We find different words for it, but that's what it means. You made it through years of service letting someone else do that killing, but your time's run out. I need you. The Alliance needs you. And all the people in the galaxy who can't protect themselves and their loved ones? They need you most of all."

Two mornings later, the Contessa summoned him to the chancellor's office.

"They're not ready," Wedge said before she asked. "And you're going to tell me that doesn't matter."

"Two for two, Commander. But tell me *how* they aren't ready. Even if it's only for a minute, I'd like to imagine assembling this squadron the way it's supposed to be assembled."

Wedge looked at her curiously. Had that been a bit of humanity—vulnerability, even—breaking through the Contessa's flinty exterior?

So he told her how Salm and Zowlie were having trouble flying in formation, and how Ixstra and Frix could do that but kept breaking formation to chase down targets. He left out how Kott was a natural pilot but had frozen and lost three kills, or how Janson was certain Darpen was running a smuggling ring from his simulator. They had troubles enough as it was.

"Given the lack of capable pilots, you're in better shape than I expected," the Contessa said. "Assuming you're being honest and these are really all the problems we need to solve."

Had any squadron commander ever been completely honest with a superior officer? Wedge doubted it.

"The real problem is you can't sim adrenaline," he said instead. "Once they're actually out in vacuum and their hearts start pumping, all these issues will get magnified."

"You're right. Which means you also know the only solution is to fly them. The good ones will learn how to make the adrenaline an ally instead of an enemy."

"And the bad ones will die."

"I know."

That exchange hung between them for a moment. Then the Contessa leaned forward.

"The chancellor fears our location has been compromised. She thinks we need to abandon the rendezvous point."

"Without Skywalker and the princess?"

"She's worried they've been captured or are dead."

Wedge tried to imagine what the absence of Luke Skywalker would mean to the Alliance—and to himself. Luke was a galactic hero who commanded a power Wedge could barely understand, yet he was also a farm kid from Tatooine who'd become Wedge's friend over dozens of missions.

It was impossible—just as it was impossible to think of the Rebellion without Leia Organa, the leader who embodied the reason they fought. But perhaps Hoth had been the border between the possible and the impossible. Perhaps they were now across it, in a strange un-discovered country, but had yet to realize that.

Still, it felt wrong.

"If the Empire had Organa, it'd be all over the HoloNet by now," Wedge said. "Which means she's out there somewhere, and trying to reach us. And if she finally arrives and we're gone . . ."

"She has the encrypted protocols for the backup muster point," the Contessa said.

"Which might be no safer than this one. There's nothing in the galaxy that could keep Leia Organa from her duty, or Luke Skywalker from his friends. We need to give them more time."

"All right. And are *you* ready, Red Leader?"

"Yes," Wedge said, without thinking. And to his surprise, he found he meant it.

"We're doing fine, Arfive," Wedge said for the sixth time in the last hour, or maybe it was the seventh. "Just keep scanning."

His X-wing was moving straight as an arrow through streamers of ionized gas, high above a scree of ice and rock, stellar debris that had failed to gain enough mass to coalesce into a sphere. At least it was pretty—the ionized gases were an unlikely combination of magenta and blue, shot through with ribbons of silver and gold.

He was too far away to spot the pirates' base or their ships, but the sensor gear attached to his starfighter saw them plain as day and was busy collating data. An hour after he returned to *Home One*, it would have a detailed picture of the enemy forces.

Assuming they didn't spot him, of course. If that happened, the best-case scenario was that he'd escape after shedding the sensor gear and discarding most of that carefully collected intel. And the worst-case scenario? No more Wedge Antilles.

"Almost done with the sweep," Wedge told his droid, blinking sweat out of his eyes. "Then two hours back to *Home One*. Open a private channel to Red Eleven."

He winced at R5-G8's answering squeal—apparently his request for a recalibrated signaler was still on some to-do list, along with fixing his T-65's overenthusiastic heater.

"Janson? Time to go home. How are they flying?"

"Well, nobody's crashed into anything, which isn't bad for a first hop. By the way, my mission chrono's acting flaky, Red Leader. It's telling me we've been out here for an hour fifty-three. What's yours say?"

Wedge glanced at his console. "Hour fifty-eight."

"Ah. See you at home, then."

Wedge wondered why Janson sounded amused. Two minutes later, he sniffed the air in the cockpit curiously. Then he sniffed himself.

"Nothing, Arfive. Smells bad in here is all. Almost like . . . oh no. No no no."

That was tauntaun musk he smelled, and it was getting worse. Wedge fumbled under the console, searching for Janson's little device, the one intended for Hobbie's X-wing.

R5-G8 squealed in alarm.

"Yes, it's a contaminant. No, it isn't dangerous. *No, Arfive.* Do *not* open the cockpit to vacuum. *Yes*, I am sure. In fact, this is the least ambiguous order I have ever issued."

Wedge suspected the two hours back to the rebel fleet might be the longest of his life. On the other hand, when they were over, he'd get to throttle Wes Janson.

But his anger drained away when he climbed down from his cockpit to find all eleven pilots waiting for him—variously applauding, holding their noses, or grimacing comically. They were all there, brought together courtesy of the twisted mind of Wes Janson.

Kott was the only one who didn't seem amused. As the group broke up, Wedge inclined his head for her to follow him.

"What's wrong, Red Three?" he asked, reaching into his pocket to touch the dispenser he'd found affixed to the underside of his flight console.

"Why play pranks?" Kott asked. "They endanger the mission."

"When going into combat, sure. And if Janson did that, I'd throw him in the brig. But he wouldn't have. He knew the operational phase of the mission would be complete by the time his little present unwrapped itself."

"But something can always go wrong. Why introduce a new risk?"

"Because there are other risks. Such as falling into a routine. You get used to being behind the stick, so you get complacent, and then you get killed. Pranks force you to look over your shoulder, and that might be the thing that keeps you alive. Make sense?"

"Maybe. I need to think about it."

"Fair enough. But I'm giving you a demerit for making me defend Wes while I smell like I came out of a garbage masher."

"Demerit accepted," Kott said, and actually smiled.

"Looks like they're using an old asteroid mining station as a base," the Contessa said.

"That's what I thought, too," Wedge said, looking down at the intel from his recon mission. "I count six fighters and gunboats on the ground."

"There might be others," the Contessa pointed out. "See this shadow and scarring? Could be an interior hangar, doubling as a ready room."

"We'll rig proton torpedoes. If visual scanning confirms, we hit it. I'm more worried about all these craft IDs. Besides the bandits on the asteroid, I counted fifteen ships in the area. That's a lot for a brand-new squadron, and we don't know what else they might have."

"So what do you propose?"

"I dropped sensor buoys. I'd say give them two days to record comings and goings, so we can get a better confidence interval on the enemy's strength. But you're going to tell me I don't have two days."

"None of us do," a woman said.

Mon Mothma was standing in the doorway. As always, the Alliance chancellor looked calm, and her white robes were clean and crisp. But he also saw the hollows below her eyes.

"Madame Chancellor," he said, coming to attention and wondering if that was the proper form of address. And was he supposed to salute?

"No need for all that," Mothma said. "What have you found?"

Wedge stepped back so she could look down at the datapad, listening as the Contessa went over what they'd discovered.

"Any hyperspace wakes?" Mothma asked. "Where are these pirates coming from and where are they going?"

Wedge called up the relevant parsecs of space.

"Their origin is probably the Vosch Cluster, here. They've blazed a hyperspace lane to the trade worlds around Caldra Prime and Caldra Tertius. We're right here in the middle."

Mothma nodded. "The Vosch worlds were always poor, and then their economies were hammered by the Clone Wars. I helped craft a relief bill in the Republic, but it got voted down—and of course the Emperor never cared. Little wonder they've turned to piracy. If our scouts had spotted the pirate traffic, we would have chosen a different rendezvous point. Bad luck, when we didn't exactly have a shortage. What do you think, Commander Antilles? Can your squadron destroy them?"

"Yes," Wedge said after a moment, but Mothma had heard the hesitation in his voice. "It would be a straightforward mission for an experienced squadron. But we're not an experienced squadron. A lot could go wrong. And even if it doesn't, we'll lose pilots."

"Because your squadron isn't ready." Mothma said. "That's a statement of fact, Commander, not a criticism. 'Miracle worker' isn't part of your job classification."

"No, they're not," Wedge admitted.

"Then we should jump," Mothma said, her lips a tight, thin line.

"Chancellor, don't give that order," Wedge said. "Luke will find us. The princess will find us. I'd never bet against either of them."

"The risk is too great," Mothma said, and Wedge could hear the pain in her voice.

"This entire rebellion is a risk that's too great, yet here we are. One day. Give me just one day."

"And how will one day make a difference?"

"It'll give us sensor data from the buoys, and an attack plan to test in the simulator. If my squadron can't destroy the pirate nest tomorrow, we jump."

"But you'll still lose pilots," Mothma said.

"I will. But my pilots knew that the day they signed on, Chancellor. It didn't stop them. It can't stop us."

Mothma looked from Wedge to the Contessa, then nodded gravely. "Then may the Force be with you, Commander."

Few pilots liked simulator training, considering it a criticism of their flying abilities. But Red Squadron assembled on time, with minimal grumbling. Even the rookies guessed that the frantic pace of preparations meant imminent action.

"At ease," Wedge said. "The pirates have compromised our security at a time when we're still waiting for high-value Alliance personnel to arrive. That gives us two alternatives. The first is we jump to the backup muster point and hope the missing can find us. The second is we destroy the pirates."

Zowlie was staring at him eagerly, while Frix and Tarheel had their arms crossed. Kott was chewing her fingernails, eyes wide.

"We've chosen to destroy them," he said, to nods and murmurs of approval. "Tomorrow at oh-eight-hundred."

Elar and Scotian exchanged a quick glance.

"These mission parameters aren't ideal," he said. "But nothing is right now. It's our job to give the chancellor some breathing room so she can fix that."

He paused, giving the pilots a chance for objections. But they stayed quiet.

"We're going to sim a pincer maneuver," he said. "Two flights of three birds coming from each direction, converging on their base. Our mission objective is straightforward: total destruction."

When the Contessa found Wedge, the weary members of Red Squadron had departed for their quarters, leaving the tactical suite empty— except for one tank tumbling wildly on its gimbals, from which muffled yells could be heard.

"I thought the exercise was over," the Contessa said.

"I asked Janson to run a quick additional sim."

"With what mission objective?"

"The parameters changed mid-exercise," Wedge said. "Now the goal is to see if Wes can locate and deactivate an aerosol dispenser emitting tauntaun musk while experiencing heavy g forces."

The Contessa just blinked at him before turning away.

"Pilots," she muttered.

"Anyway, let's leave Wes to it," Wedge said. "You were watching the exercise?"

"I was. You've picked good flight leaders, and your plan is sound. My advice? Talk a lot. Keep the rookies listening to you and watching what's around them. Once the blood starts pumping, they'll lose situational awareness, and tunnel vision will kill them."

Wedge nodded. "I will. Thank you."

"You're welcome. And you've earned something else, Red Leader." Wedge cocked his head at her.

"I come from a world you've never heard of," the Contessa said. "My family ruled it for centuries. I'd like to think we were benevolent rulers, but our word was still law. When the Empire sent an ambassador, we refused her and thought that would be the end of it. Five years later everyone in my family was dead and our subjects who'd greeted the Empire as liberators were enslaved. I no longer use my birth name, but I still call myself the Contessa. It's to remind me of everything I thought would protect me and didn't."

She put her hand on Wedge's shoulder. "We all have something like that, Commander. Remember it's no better than a charm around your neck, or crossing your fingers. Protect your people, pick your targets wisely, and hit them hard. It's all you can do."

174

Wedge's X-wing came out of hyperspace with a bump and a squeal from R5-G8. A moment later the starfighters flown by Sila Kott and Tomer Darpen arrived to port and starboard—in perfect formation, he noted.

"All wings report in," Wedge said.

The pilots ran through their call signs, from Keyser Salm (Red Two) to Cinda Tarheel (Red Twelve). Zowlie was breathing so hard that his words dissolved into static.

"Red Nine, take five deep breaths," Wedge said. "Better. Now stick with your flight leader."

"Copy that, Red Leader. Deep breaths!"

"Red Eight, we'll make the target run," Wedge told Scotian. "Cover us."

That was the plan they'd simmed—his flight and Janson's would hit the targets on the landing field, with Scotian's and Elar's flights running interference. But he knew plans only survived until the first laser blast.

"Ix, Cinda, tighten up," said Scotian. "Keep them off Red Leader's back."

"Landing field's locked in," Wedge said. "Watch your vectors—Wes's and Bela's flights will be coming in at twelve o'clock. Stay out of their flight path."

An alert buzzed in his ears.

"Commander," said Kott. "Three bandits at point two-seven. Looks like Z-95 Headhunters."

"I see them—stay on target. Scotian? Engage."

Laserfire flashed around him, the brightness making him blink before his viewport dimmed to compensate. Kott's X-wing bucked and swerved to port.

175

"Stay with me, Sila," Wedge said. "Red Eleven, any signs of a hangar on the landing field?"

"Too far out to tell," Janson replied. "But torpedoes are armed."

"Red Leader, multiple bandits incoming from below," Scotian warned.

A Z-95 shot past Wedge's bow, followed by an ungainly fighter cobbled together from patchwork parts. Wedge banked smoothly away from them, peppering the pirates with laserfire to keep them honest, then swung back onto his approach vector.

"Stick with your wings," he said. "Engage, but don't get lured away. Sila, Tomer, on me."

Within another minute the engagement had devolved into a

brawl, with pilots talking over one another and space lit up with explosions. Wedge tried to make sense of the alerts and shouted warnings, then gave up—as with any dogfight, there was too much to track. All he could do was talk to his own wings and rely on the other flight leaders to do the same.

His screen flared crimson, warning of a weapons lock. Wedge rolled to starboard, throttled back his engines, and then snapped his fighter back to port. The pirate who'd been chasing Wedge found himself dead in his sights instead, and a moment later Wedge flew through the bright cloud that was all that remained of him.

"I got one, I got one!" yelled Zowlie. "Gonna take out his buddy!"

"Penn, maintain formation," warned Elar. "Get back here *now*."

"Almost there," Zowlie said, and Wedge could hear his excitement. "Oh! Wait—"

"We lost Penn," Elar said. "Grizz, do *not* engage. Stay with me."

"Stay focused," Wedge said. "Wes, time to target?"

"Thirty seconds," said Janson, and Wedge heard the strain in his voice. "We lost Red Ten."

"Red Six KIA," Scotian said grimly.

Red Ten was Barlon Hightower. Red Six was Ix Ixstra. Wedge forced himself not to think of their faces.

Flashes dotted the asteroids. Wedge spun his X-wing through a corkscrew turn, throwing off a bandit's aged interceptor. A moment later Darpen's laser cannons reduced the pirate to scrap.

"Nice shooting, Red Seven," Wedge said.

"Red Leader, positive ID on the hangar—and lots of scurrying around on that landing field," said Janson. "Torpedoes locked. Watch my six, Salm—it's a lot of demerits if you get your flight leader killed."

"I've got you, boss," said Salm.

"Sila, down!" Wedge yelled.

Wedge spun out of the path of an onrushing Nighthawk fighter, juking to port and then catching the craft amidships with a barrage of laserfire. He could hear Kott's breaths coming short and fast over the comm.

"You're okay, Red Three," he said. "We're almost there. Wes?"

"Torpedoes away," Janson said. "Bela, get me a damage assessment."

"Hangar's a crater. But looks like one bandit got out. Some kind of modified freighter—and her engines are hot."

"We can't let that bandit jump," Wedge said. "Sila, Tomer—full throttle and follow me."

Acceleration pressed him back into the pilot's seat, briefly dimming his vision as his X-wing shot forward. He kept his hand steady on the control yoke, knowing his body would adjust and the disorientation would pass. Kott's and Darpen's X-wings hurtled along behind his.

R5-G8 shrilled an alert—a minute to target.

Wedge's eyes flicked to his sensors. The pirate mothership was definitely some kind of modified freighter. His lasers would take it apart—provided it didn't have a course locked in that allowed it to make a quick jump to hyperspace.

"Commander, incoming," Darpen warned, and a moment later Wedge's X-wing was kicked sideways by an impact. Two starfighters streaked past in front of him, R5-G8 squealed in indignation, and red lights lit up across the console.

"Arfive, patch the starboard deflectors," he ordered.

Thirty seconds to target.

Darpen had barrel-rolled his X-wing to chase down one of the fighters, but where was the other one?

An alarm wailed—it was behind him, in the kill zone.

Wedge juked the X-wing left, right, and then left again, lasers sizzling past his cockpit.

"Sila?"

"On it, Commander," Kott said, but her voice quavered.

Wedge kept dodging and weaving, but he had to stick close to his trajectory or risk missing his shot at the freighter. Another hit rattled his starfighter.

Ten seconds.

"Sila! Take the shot!"

Five seconds.

Wedge forced himself to keep the X-wing steady. The starfighter's sensors blared a warning—his pursuer had a lock. Wedge felt the hair rise on the back of his neck.

His targeting computer flashed red and he mashed down the trigger, sending bolts of destructive energy hurtling toward the pirate mothership. At the same moment his X-wing bucked and he heard a roar in his ears.

Then all was still.

Was he dead? He closed his eyes experimentally. It felt about the same.

"Great shooting, Red Leader," said Janson. "You too, Kott."

Wedge opened his eyes and saw nothing but stars ahead of him. His targeting indicator blinked—the freighter had been destroyed.

"Still with us, Commander?" asked Kott.

"Thanks to you," Wedge said, then switched to a private channel. "You all right, Sila?"

"No," Kott said. "But I will be."

Which struck Wedge as both halves of the right answer.

Nine X-wings returned to *Home One*. The Contessa was waiting in the hangar, next to the chancellor. When the pilots recognized the slim figure in white, they stopped chattering and got into line, without Wedge or Janson having to give an order.

"We will mourn those we've lost," said Mothma. "I will always be grateful to them for their sacrifice, as I will always be grateful to you. Your bravery has given us something precious in wartime—time. To gather those who have yet to find us. To recoup our strength. And to ensure that those we've lost will not have died in vain."

Mothma walked among the pilots, taking a moment with each of them. She spoke quietly with Kott, who listened intently and then nodded repeatedly, and reached Wedge and Janson last.

"You and your pilots have done far more than anyone could have fairly asked of you. Thank you. And now please get some rest."

Wedge had been trying to think of something to say, but found himself too tired to form words. Janson had no such difficulties, though.

"In addition to my other talents, Double . . . um . . . ma'am, I am a highly decorated napper," he said. "Maybe you could drop us off at a beach planet for the next month or so?"

"I'd like nothing more," Mothma said, while the Contessa made a face at Wedge. "But I'm afraid the Alliance will have to give you a raincheck. Because I suspect we'll need your squadron sooner than that."

She smiled and moved off alongside the Contessa.

"Highly decorated napper?" Wedge asked Janson. "Really?"

"Just making conversation."

"Making a mess, you mean. Wait, shh."

Mothma had bent her head close to the Contessa's, and Wedge was able to just catch the end of her question.

". . . but why do they both smell like they've been in a barnyard?"

The Contessa offered a whispered explanation, and the Alliance leader looked at her curiously. Mothma shook her head, sighed, and then Wedge saw her smile.

"Pilots," she said, and Wedge wondered if that was admiration or exasperation in her voice.

He suspected it was a little bit of both.

THE FINAL ORDER

Seth Dickinson

"In time of peace, the Imperial Star Destroyer will disburse the Emperor's peace and justice, and by its presence deter disorder, both material and ideological."

His new XO paused here for breath. Captain Canonhaus wondered if they'd trained her when to breathe on Carida. You may take the initiative, Cadet Tian; you may even take unscheduled breaths. The Imperial Naval Academy on Carida produced superb officers, officers like Kendal Ozzel, who had taken the initiative and would never again take a breath, scheduled or otherwise.

Certainly Tian was also superb. She had excellent marks, except in Tabor Seitaron's history class. Seitaron always downgraded students who missed his hints about what had really happened. *No special in-*

sight, he'd written on Canonhaus's own file, when he was Canonhaus's captain. *Officer must seek this insight through experience.* Fine, old man, give us poor marks for regurgitating official history—but COMPNOR will give us good ones. The Commission for the Preservation of the New Order approves of those who know the *official* truth.

Look what had happened to Seitaron, after all. Disappeared. Proscribed.

Her name was Tian Karmiya, Commander Tian to him, and with her prime marks from Carida and her fine service on *Enigma* and *Victory at Batonn,* she must have expected to serve under Commodore Rae Sloane here on the *Ultimatum.* But Sloane was indisposed. So Canonhaus had received *Ultimatum,* and this bright young plaque of New Order excellence as his XO.

She was calm, cheerful, occasionally quite droll at the captain's table. "An officer's love life," she would say, "operates under the same rules as old religions: two sides, and they must never meet." When he laughed at her quips, Canonhaus felt his dry scabs crack, and some of the old blood, the old love for the work, welled up to stain his thoughts.

Bad luck for both of them.

Full of breath, Tian now said:

"In time of war the Imperial Star Destroyer will seek out the enemy's principal force and close, by means of superior speed and protection, to destroy the enemy with massed fighter strikes and the fires of the main battery; and, if the enemy is planetbound, by the deployment of the embarked legion."

"Very good. And in which element of the doctrine are we now engaged?"

She sometimes had a sly way of looking, this Tian. Just a little flash of teeth. "Pursuing an escaped transport falls under disbursing peace and justice and deterring disorder."

"The *Emperor's* peace and justice, Commander."

"Yes, sir. It goes without saying, sir. As there is no other source of true peace or justice."

They stood side by side, hands clasped at their backs, before the incredible panorama of *Ultimatum's* bridge. Ahead, the endless chaotic detonation, the swarming scatter of the Hoth system's fragmentation-cascade asteroid field. They had sent fighters in after an escaping rebel ship. None had returned.

"And the need to pursue one small transport with all our forces, rather than attempting to vector the other rebels?"

"As we said on Iloh, better to catch the fish at hand than to cast at shadows, sir."

"Quite. Very good. Very good."

Canonhaus tapped his foot. The lieutenant running the crew pit to his left glanced up to see if the captain wanted his attention. You had to train a new crew to understand your mannerisms. One tap meant "conversation over, I'm thinking." Two taps signaled "get on with it." Shooting his cuffs meant "I'm about to give an order." Back on *Majestic* his officers understood this, all four watches.

Old Seitaron had once told him, in the wardroom, that it was important to know your crew. Read their files, learn their failures and talents. Canonhaus had tried that, on *Majestic*. He had been a good captain, or at least a good mayor of a town of ten thousand, which was the real trick to command. Anyone could say *full speed, open fire* or *hold the range, deploy the fighters* or *send in a team to make a scan.* The unbelievably difficult part of the job was not fighting a Star Destroyer in combat, but keeping the beast fed and fueled and trained, and in communication with the rest of the fleet and with your own local network of informants and contacts, so that the ship could turn up where and when it was needed.

He could do that. He could do it better than most, he'd thought.

But after Alderaan and Helix, they took *Majestic* away from him,

183

moved him from sector fleet duty to Death Squadron on account of his "excellent reliability." And he had to start all over, learning the names and faces of the nearly ten thousand people aboard *Ultimatum*. It was impossible. Only the roles were familiar, like the cards in a sabacc deck. First and second weapons officers, first and second defense officers, three sensor watch officers; communications, operations, engineering with its reactor and engine substations; navigation, helm and hyperdrive and the constant plot of objects in the narrow and chaotic jump-collision hazard radius; bay and flight officers; flasks and sabers, air and darkness, staves and coins. All the cards slotted into their stations in the crew pits below the gleaming black walkways, which were as polished and satisfying as boot leather.

On *Majestic,* all his officers knew what he'd done with the refugees. An ugly piece of work, they all agreed. Hard work. But it had to be done.

He tasted acid and coughed.

"Commander Tian," he said.

She had begun to turn away, to go check with the helm officer about their formation. She was a stickler about formations. The idea that *Executor* itself was tracking her must be very exciting. A chance to show her talent at staying in her slot.

Now she turned back. The *youth* in her bright eyes, her clear dark skin; how could she already be a commander? They got younger every year. And hungrier.

At Carida, gossip said, she had reported two cadets with better marks for selling their exam answers. They had been expelled, and she'd made it into a merit society in their place. A snitch.

"Sir?"

"What do you think of Admiral Ozzel's recent decisions?"

She flinched like he'd pulled a weapon. A flash of fear, like the light of a blaster reflected from wide white human eyes in the jungle night on Haruun Kal. The place where he had learned to fear blasters more than anything else.

That was all it took. The flashbacks came on him unpredictably, for no reason at all, for a reason as simple as Tian's frightened eyes.

And he was there again. Is there again. Will always be.

He is a lieutenant, a liaison to the stormtroopers aboard the *Quasar Fire*-class cruiser-carrier *Swoop*. They call him Footoo. They like him, because he tells them honestly what the navy expects, but don't trust him, because he hasn't seen combat.

There is an insurrection smoldering on Haruun Kal, in the highland jungles. Something left from the Clone Wars.

He goes down with the Sentinel assault shuttles to land in the "smoke circles" where orbital fire burns back the jungle. The air smells of burnt pollen and sulfur, and he has to borrow a stormtrooper helmet to breathe outside. In two days, fungus grounds the shuttles and all the speeders forever. Only the wheeled Juggernauts still work. Their weapons are only saved by obsessive cleaning.

The CO orders a foot advance toward a lake thirty kilometers away. It is not a very good decision, tactically, but the CO has fever wasp larvae growing in her brain. By the time anyone realizes, the wasps are crawling out of her tear ducts and they are all lost in the deep jungle.

The Korun natives attack from the trees at night. Their crude slugthrowers can't pierce stormtrooper armor, but their bombs can. At first, *Swoop*'s stormtroopers return fire coolly and accurately. Later, they take to mowing the jungle with the squad E-Webs.

Canonhaus takes it upon himself to confirm their kills. He thinks it will help morale.

He sees everything a blaster can do to a body. The primary wound, a crater of red and white, where galvened plasma flash-boils skin and detonates bone. Seams of black char where fat burns like buried coal. Heads are full of fluid, all of which expands when hit: stormtroopers call this kind of hit a "detonator," call those who are hit deep enough to burn from the inside out "dry bones." By the time you see the remains of a dry-bone, a wretched pile of skeleton and hair, your lungs are already coated in a thin layer of burnt *them*—

"Sir?"

Canonhaus blinked. "What?"

Tian was at his side, watching him. "You seemed not to hear me, sir."

"I was thinking of Haruun Kal." Why had he said that? Because he wanted a reason to pour out his bile and regret, to corrode her as he had been corroded.

"A glorious victory, sir."

"Oh, yes. One of the battles that gave the Imperial Navy its dread reputation."

"Did you help conduct the bombardment, sir?"

"Yes," he lied. His unit had sheltered in the lake while the fleet exercised Base Gamma One. The lake boiled off in the firestorm. Their Juggernauts couldn't cool the air fast enough. At first it was dry, and thus survivable; but when the air filled with their sweat, their sweat could no longer cool them, and people began to go into convulsions. As he stripped down, Canonhaus found a dead fever wasp in his uniform. Perhaps the heat had killed its eggs. Perhaps he was just lucky.

"Yes," he repeated, unsteadily. "Yes, now—now *that* was an example of a bombardment well handled. But what do you think about Ozzel's approach?"

"Yes, sir. His decision to drop out of hyperspace inside detection range was a good one. Violence of action would have caught the rebels unprepared, and if they hadn't been forewarned, he would've caught them all in the initial bombardment. He made no mistake."

"Mm. So why do you think Lord Vader executed him?"

"Perhaps because he failed to account for the possibility the rebels had been forewarned by a spy, sir. Or by the probe droid that discovered their base."

"So you believe Vader acted correctly?"

She hesitated, looked away. In profile, her full nose echoed the uniform cap, echoed the perfect prow of the Star Destroyer, the ideal shape for a warship, all its broadside weapons capable of bearing forward. He wondered if she had been born with black hair, or if she dyed her usual Ilohian green to match the uniform. What did such young people think about? Did they do the exact same things he had done, say all the things he had said, to get that perfect COMPNOR reliability score—but *believe* it all, too?

187

"Permission to speak freely, sir?"

He blinked in surprise. "Granted?"

She addressed the open windows, the red light of *Executor*'s titanic engine array. "Ozzel was lucky. He knew everyone on Hoth was a rebel. He didn't have to flush one of their cells out of a loyal population. Or make a punitive attack on collaborators. Or choose a settlement for a demonstration strike. His only decision was one of tactics. Whether to close in aggressively, or to make a cautious approach."

"And yet I sense an objection . . . ?"

"He failed to consider the political aspect of his choice. He should have anticipated that Vader would prefer prisoners. An aggressive posture and rapid bombardment would leave none. Therefore, he should have taken a cautious approach."

Ah. So she would rationalize his execution: snitch thought. What a fool Ozzel had been to plan an attack from orbit! Hoth was one of the major rebel command cells, and therefore, given prisoners, an opportunity to roll up every other rebel in the galaxy. Ozzel's idiocy had nearly wasted that chance. Therefore it was not just Vader's right but Vader's duty, as a direct representative of the Emperor, as a black hand wiping away corruption and cronyism in the ranks, to execute Kendal Ozzel on the spot!

Before Alderaan, Canonhaus would've told himself exactly the same thing.

No, that was a lie. He would've rationalized it to himself even *after* the refugee mission. He had rationalized everything. Doubt grew much slower than fever wasps.

He said, "You talk about easy choices. Do you think of Death Squadron as an easy post?"

"Not easy, sir. But I *was* very excited to be posted here. Direct pursuit of the rebel military is what I want. Not . . ." She paused, performing inner politics, composing something that would look nice in a COMPNOR transcript. "Not the painstaking and difficult work, which our colleagues perform so well, required to separate rebels and collaborators from loyal citizens. Of course, loyal citizens must take on some of the burden of battling insurrection, including the emotional duty of assigning blame for any collateral damage to the rebels. But my own personal strengths, I feel, are in direct tactical warfare against the rebels, rather than counterinsurgency."

"You feel that Death Squadron's mission is cleaner, then. Compared with that of, say, ISB or the Ubiqtorate agencies. Or a stormtrooper legion."

"Yes, sir. The Imperial Navy's mission, in general, I find more morally direct."

"Mm." He thought, of course, of Helix. Was he ever not thinking of Helix? "Did you grow up admiring the navy?"

"Yes, sir, in my adolescence."

"You had model fighters? Miniature legions? Snappy uniform-style fashions? Sub-adult group membership?"

"Yes, sir. I was a patriotic child."

"Hm," he grunted.

"I think you should file a protest over Admiral Ozzel's execution, sir."

He was so shocked that he thought the code cylinders would pop from his uniform. "Against *Vader*?"

"Yes, sir. Obviously the protest will not be sustained. However, it would be appropriate to place a summary execution under review, in the same way that a captain who loses a ship always stands to court-martial. This way, Vader's correct decisions can be fully documented and entered in the record for future officers to appreciate."

Oh, child.

He took his XO by the shoulder. "Listen to me. There is no 'protest' against Vader. Vader can do anything he wants. He could strangle you and me and everyone on this bridge and face no censure.

"The New Order does not exist to bring order to anything. It is not the bright strong energy that lifted us from the Clone Wars and the Republic's corruption. It's not the maker and the organizer and the fixer that you thought it was when you buttoned on your junior-officer uniform.

"You liked to learn the names of stormtrooper legions, didn't you? You liked to read staff notes, memorize the weapon loadouts of our starships, and debate tactical theory on the HoloNet. You think *those* things are the Empire. But all the sharp outfits, all the insignia and code cylinders, all the protocols and monuments . . . they are all burrs. Things that attach themselves to the Empire's real purpose.

"The real purpose of the Empire is to give people like Vader the power to do anything they want. The bureaucracy, the ideology, the gleaming *system* we so admire—it accretes around that central core of cruelty solely because a bureaucracy allows us, the followers, to rationalize our participation through laws and protocols. If there is a cruelty the Emperor wishes to commit, a reason will appear for it. If there is an atrocity Vader perpetrates, a bureau or a directorate or a fleet or a squadron or a legion or a special sort of stormtrooper will be created to carry it forward as necessary for the security of the galaxy.

"There is no restraint or principle at the center of the New Order. And that is why people admire it. The Empire does all the things that people secretly believe should be done with power."

He did not say any of that. And of course he did not take her shoulder.

Instead, he clasped his hands behind his back and said, "You know, I was recently detached to support a special task for Lord Vader. We were in a support role—perimeter control, navigational interdiction, logistics. Other forces carried out the primary mission."

She shifted from foot to foot. Nervous or excited. "What was that mission, sir?"

"The destruction of a convoy."

"And how many rebels did you bag, sir?"

"Not rebels. Alderaanian refugees."

Her bright eyes took on the cold, sharp, dead aspect of a security droid. "A very difficult mission. But you are known for your perfect reliability, Captain."

"Yes. I am." He sniffed, and missed the faint burnt-dust smell of *Majestic*'s old filters. Something tickled in his sinuses. Surely not the beginning of a cold. "After it was all over, I was given charge of the legal follow-up. I filed all the documents to establish that what we'd done was lawful, necessary, and fully in accord with Imperial law. No HoloNet transmissions—everything was couriered directly to Coruscant by stealth shuttle. I didn't even keep my own copies."

She nodded rapidly. "Very good, sir. I'm sure there was no problem."

"No problem at all." What was he doing? Was he really going to say this? Yes, he was, he was, because he was overflowing with bitterness, because he wanted to fling that bitterness at her, even at the cost of his own post. "Despite the fact that I misfiled every single report."

"Beg pardon, sir?"

"I did everything wrong. The wrong codes. The wrong clearances. The wrong order of events. I dated our receipt of initial orders later than the actual mission reports. I listed Lord Vader as a spacecraft in our order of battle, and our targets as accountants from a Neimoidian purse world. I said that we were attempting to erase all records of Emperor Palpatine's old gambling debts."

She blinked at him, twice, trying to divine what in the galaxy he was trying to say. "As a test, sir?"

"Of course it was a test."

"To be sure that someone was reading the reports, and holding the Imperial Navy accountable."

"Of course. My duty."

"And . . . ?"

"No one made any protest. I suppose the forms went into a vault somewhere. Some airless place tended by droids. But no one read them."

She swallowed, as if digesting. "And if we made a complaint about Admiral Ozzel's death, sir?"

"I think we both know what would happen, Commander."

They stood side by side in silence. A long-derelict faculty stirred in Canonhaus, and to his surprise it did not give up and slink away. It was curiosity about what was happening inside someone else's head. He glanced aside to watch her, in this moment of crisis when she could do many things, depending on which of many people she might be. She could write him up to COMPNOR, or save this fraction of the bridge logs for future blackmail. Or arrive at a silent, shared understanding that they both recognized a problem.

But she would be making her own interior calculation about who *he* was, and about whether he was trying to confide in her. Or whether this was reliable old Canonhaus laying out bait for the disloyal.

He did not know the answer himself.

He supposed that in this place, surrounded by the black corridors and white armor of *Ultimatum,* surrounded by all the uniforms and guns and systems of technology and personhood she had worshipped since childhood, she could really only make one choice.

Her shoulders squared. "The destruction of Alderaanian refugees does proceed directly from the Tarkin Doctrine, sir. Terror is an instrument of the state's power. So it must flow from the state, not from the stories of confused refugees who lack the context to understand their own situation. Arbitrarily allowing some Alderaanians to live while others die would negate the lawfulness of Alderaan's sanctioned execution. Either all are guilty, or none are."

"Oh, precisely, Commander. Precisely." It burst out of him: "And what would you have done in my situation? Given that you prefer direct tactical action against the rebels to . . . harder duty."

"I would carry out my orders completely and enthusiastically, because I believe that the Empire is larger and smarter than me, and that I cannot possibly determine the right thing to do as well as my superiors."

That was not what she said. That was what *he* had said when questioned about his ability to carry out his mission.

"I don't know, sir," she said.

"You don't *know*?"

She touched the back of her cap in agitation. "Sir, I don't wish to give a poor impression. But it would be arrogance on my part to assume I would rise to the challenge as well as you did. I only hope I can learn from your example."

He flinched.

A mouse droid whirred up with a hard copy of the watch report. She retrieved it, passed it to him, their gloves skimming with a sound like the first whine of a migraine. He fussed over his datapad. The report was full of routine traffic, administrative matters, totally unrelated to the operation around Hoth.

"Changes to the uniform standard again," he sighed. "New regulations for the display of recognition flash and skill tabs. The new header on personnel files accidentally corrupted dental records, and it has been judged faster for all officers to receive a new checkup than to restore from the archives, so we are encouraged to get our teeth cleaned at soonest opportunity. New orders from KDY on the safe use of pilots and tugs while in harborage . . . power system updates to defeat ion weapon attack, we could've used *those* today . . ."

She said, stiffly, "What do *you* think I would do, sir?"

"Eh?"

"If ordered to support a mission to eliminate Alderaanian refugees."

"I suppose you'd do what everyone does."

"What's that, sir?"

He coughed into his glove. "Well, you do the work. Hard work. Awful work. But no one hesitates, really."

"No one at all?"

"No. It's a job, and the job is to carry out orders as efficiently as possible. That's what you worry about—that you'll screw up, let your end down, make things harder for the others. And if it gets to you afterward"—which it had, nightly—"well, ultimately you're not the one who pulled the trigger. Or if you are, you're not the one who gave the order. Or if you are, well, you're not the one who made the whole mess necessary. You get to discussing it with the other officers, very coolly, very civilly, over caf in the wardroom. And you find there's always someone else to blame. Someone who did something *cruel,* whereas you were simply merciful. Very well-designed system, all in all. A testament to the rational efficiency of the New Order."

"I see, sir," she said, with a kind of warmth. Did she pity him? Did she respect him? Was that the warmth? Had she just come to understand that Canonhaus truly was a person with a heart?

Or was she grateful to discover that reliable Canonhaus was in fact weak, and old, and unfit for command?

Perhaps his own eyes betrayed his vicious fear. Tian recoiled, turned sharply, paced away to consult with a lieutenant commander taking a report in the crew pit.

He tried to find a calm, authoritative stance to hold. Thinking of that mission always slashed him up inside, a long knife working at his guts like the underbrush on Haruun Kal. Where he had tweezed little wasps from his CO's pores as she died, where he would always be, in the wet darkness of that jungle—

"Sir?"

He started. She'd crept around his other side. "Yes?"

"Orders from the flag. We're to take *Executor*'s port station and screen her against asteroid impacts as we move into the field."

"We're going *in there*?" *Ultimatum* would happily have transited a normal asteroid field, but the Hoth field was young and dense, the cascading result of an interplanetary collision. Gravity drew the rocks back together into dense nodes where they shattered one another— and anything else in the way. "This is a capital warship, not a pursuit craft! We have squadrons for a reason!"

"We could file a protest, sir."

Was she taunting him? "No, no. Asteroids must not concern us. Take up station on *Executor*'s port. Rig the ship for close defense."

The old growl of power came up through the deck, engines battling compensators, swaying them both. Tian jostled against him: the hazards of standing with your hands clasped behind your back.

"Sorry," he said, and coughed. His throat itched now. He *was* getting a cold, wasn't he? The weaknesses of flesh.

"Sorry, sir. My fault."

"You get used to it quickly enough. The acceleration. It's not like on the smaller ships, you know. The big KDY engines take a while to fight through the compensators. They'll catch you by surprise."

"I imagine they will, sir. May I ask, sir, how long you've been on navy ships?"

He had to do the math in his head. "Thirty years, I think. Since I was a midshipman with the old . . . the prior regime."

"And if I may also ask, sir, where do you see yourself in another thirty years?"

Eighty years old. In a white place with polished black floors, in dry air that made him sneeze, in a uniform with a cap that hurt his head.

In the jungle.

"In command of a sector fleet, I suppose. Or a staff position." He smiled, and coughed again. "Or writing my memoirs."

"And the New Order, sir? The navy? Still chasing rebels?"

"Oh, the Rebellion will be long over. I suppose we'll be . . ."

He trailed off. He simply could not imagine what the New Order would do once the Rebellion was crushed. Would the Tarkin Doctrine have achieved a full galactic peace? Omnipresent fear becoming omnipresent respect and obedience?

She was watching him closely. She would pore through the bridge records and select any sedition on his part to put in her file of old Canonhaus's mistakes. He could not show any doubt.

But no matter how he twisted himself around, he could not imagine what general orders the navy might operate under except to crush insurrection and bring worlds into the Empire's control. In twenty years, the inner emptiness of the New Order would become outer; the logic of loyalty and rebellion would be accelerated until everyone who was not aroused to the highest state of loyalty would be marked as a traitor and denounced; professionalism would become fanaticism, temporary measures would become permanent, the conditions those measures had been meant to avert would become routine; old loyalties would become grounds for suspicion and purge; the New Order would become newer and newer, constantly revised and updated, containing less and less of substance and more and more of reaction, each new day's ideology ready to denounce the last day's thought as regressive backsliding. Until at last the New Order was newer than all other things, the first thought, the first principle, from which all else proceeded, even truth itself. It would not be about anything, intend anything, *mean* anything. It would simply exist for the sake of power, absolute and unlimited, without constraint.

That was the eating core of the Empire. And in time it would chew through all the shells of bureaucracy, all the Kuat Drive Yards contracts and orders of battle and armor patterns and TIE acronyms and XX-9 turbolasers and uniform tab codes. In the end, the Empire would not be about tactics and procedures and logic. It would be about the empty cruelty of men like Vader. It would be fear for fear's sake, power without purpose, symbol without meaning, nothingness, nonsense. A man in a mask, like the Hendanyn death masks that had given him nightmares as a child. But when you took off the mask, there was no man.

"Sir," Tian said, "you're *shivering.*"

"Ah. Yes. I kept the bridge a little warmer on *Majestic.* And I'm—" He shook his head. If he admitted he felt ill, she would offer to relieve him. She would take the ship into the asteroid field herself.

Maybe that was good! Maybe *she* could face the danger on the command tower while he was safe in the armored hull! But what a craven, cowardly thought that was; what an unworthy and conniving act it would be . . .

"Would you like some caf, sir?" she asked.

"No, thank you, Commander. Your talents are wasted on an ensign's work."

"I *do* look forward to commanding my own watches, sir."

Oh, she did want the bridge, didn't she? Make way for Tian's ambition. "On second thought," he said, "do fetch that caf."

She stiffened, sensing the closure of a door she hadn't known was open. "Yes, sir."

He sighed. "Wait."

"Sir?"

"Never mind the caf. One of us should transfer down to auxiliary control, in case the bridge tower is hit."

The *Imperial*-class kept its helm and weapons functions tightly centralized, to ensure "reliability." Transferring command to the auxiliary was not an easy process—a measure meant to prevent trickery and hijacking. At Scarif there had been serious, if brief, fears of a boarding action. "If there is an impact, we'll need to be ready to clear the field and make repairs."

She eyed him carefully. "Yes, sir. As senior officer, perhaps you should take the better-protected station . . . ?"

"No, no. My place is here. The bridge deflectors should be enough to stop anything that gets past the batteries and tractor beams." And asteroids, unlike rebels, were not likely to make runs under the shields with proton torpedoes. At least the Separatist droids had been civilized enough to stand off and trade broadsides.

"Still, sir, you'd be much safer below."

Ah, she was afraid that he was manipulating her into seeming cowardly. Maybe she thought he would report that she'd fled her post. Or was it the opposite? Maybe she wanted to command the bridge in combat, and claim *he'd* fled below . . .

Maybe she was the empty avarice of the New Order, waiting to eat him. As she'd eaten her two peers at Carida.

Or maybe she was honest, principled, funny, the hope of a new

197

generation of better officers. He didn't trust himself to tell the difference.

One of them had to go below. One of them had to stay here and risk death.

What would a decent man do? Impossible for him to know. But he could pretend he'd never heard of Helix Squadron. Never come around a lammas tree in the croaking jungle dark to find a Korun boy, drinking from a tap hammered through the gray bark. Never seen that final instant of white reflection from the boy's terrified eyes. He could pretend.

What would the man who had never known these things do now?

"Go below," he ordered. "Stand by in auxiliary control to take over if the bridge drops out. If that does happen, your orders are to clear the field and save the ship. On *my* authority."

She looked up into his eyes. Wondering, perhaps, if he was trying to save her, or if he wanted all the glory for himself. Wondering who he was.

"You're sure, sir?"

"I gave you an order, Commander. Go below."

"Yes, sir." She saluted. "Don't forget the command conference with Lord Vader. I've configured the holo pickup and set it to the proper channel. You can take it right here."

"I do not intend to displease Lord Vader by forgetting anything, Commander."

"Yes, sir. Good luck, sir." She turned smartly and headed for the lifts.

Canonhaus turned, settled back into the clasped-hands posture of cool consideration, and (when no one could see) screwed up his face to sneeze.

It wouldn't come.

The maelstrom of the Hoth field whirled and pulverized itself ahead. *Ultimatum*'s sensors and tractor projectors reached out, plotting the turbulent courses, prioritizing larger fragments for deflection or destruction. The odds of anything getting through were—well, he was no droid, but they were acceptably low. Nothing would get through.

"None shall pass," he murmured. He had vague pre-Imperial childhood memories of a show he'd loved, hazy, taboo, something COMPNOR would certainly not approve of. He remembered it as if from another reality. It was called *Laser Masters*. In one of the later episodes, a Laser Master defended the Senate chamber from an army of monsters. Those were the Laser Master's last words before his final stand. *None shall pass.* He had loved that show. How many years since he'd thought of it?

"None shall pass," he repeated. Something a hero would say.

The lieutenant commander running the crew pit to his left looked up in confusion. Canonhaus ignored him.

He looked back to be sure Commander Tian had gone below. No sign of her. He felt an unaccountable sadness, like an alien growing in him, fever wasps crawling out his tear ducts. And a sense of something rushing toward him from the dark, coming closer, wanting nothing, needing nothing, destroying whatever it touched. His brooding on the New Order had clearly set him badly off-kilter.

If something did go wrong—if the ship *was* hit, and they looked over the logs at his posthumous court-martial—they would find his final order was to send Commander Tian below. That thought comforted him, though he did not know if it should. A hero's order. Standing the watch himself. None shall pass.

He sneezed.

AMARA KEL'S RULES FOR TIE PILOT SURVIVAL (PROBABLY)

Django Wexler

Please note I said *probably*. Nothing is guaranteed in this galaxy except taxes and the navy post losing your mail.

Rule number one: Don't get attached.

Not to anything, not to anyone.

Don't get attached to your fighter. I know some pilots get cute, tuning the tolerances and controls. Then they get killed when their precious machine is in maintenance during a combat scramble, and they're not used to stock. TIEs are meant to be mass-produced, disposable.

Like us.

Don't get attached to your officers. All the good ones will move on as soon as they possibly can. The bad ones will stick around killing people with their stupidity. High turnover among officers is a good thing.

Don't get attached to your squadmates. Eat with them, drink with them, play sabacc with them, sleep with them if it suits your fancy. But don't get attached, because then one day they'll do something stupid, and then *you'll* do something stupid, and then it's a couple of fireballs and some Imperial morale officer sending your family a plastoid medal and a heartfelt note. And it probably gets lost in the mail.

You want to be the one still sitting on your bunk when they bring in the next round of new recruits. Those of us who've made it past one tour call them "cloudflies," the kind that only live for a day. It helps us remember rule number one.

Until proven otherwise, you're a cloudfly.

One shift ends. Sleepwell pills; supposed to pack a whole night's rest into a quick nap, but all they ever give me is bad dreams. Shower. Two precious hours in the rack. Next shift begins. Alarm goes off, pop a stim, the motion of opening the bottle so automatic I could do it in total darkness. Feel my heart slam against my ribs, limbs shaky with nervous, chemical energy. Roll out of bed half naked, climb straight into my flight suit. One of the cloudflies stares like he's never seen a girl before I zip up. Maybe he hasn't. Lot of weird planets in the Outer Rim.

This shift's assignment glows red on a wall screen, but I don't bother reading it. It's the same as the shift before, and the shift before that. Patrol the edge of the asteroid field by half flights, make sure nothing gets out.

Down the gangway, slide down a ladder, moving by feel and memory, the Star Destroyer *Avenger*'s blueprints now a part of my blood and bones. Grab my helmet from the rack in the ready room, round the corner to the hangar, swing myself into the nearest docking tube.

A cockpit so tight the only way in is to hang from the hatch rail and lower yourself into the seat. Foam cradles me as I settle in, my hands moving in more automatic reflexes—air hose slots into the back of my suit, restraint straps click in beside it. My fingers flick switches, powering up comms, navigation, flight control, glowing lights rippling around me in cascades of red and green. Displays come to life with a rising hum.

The TIE/ln. Home, sweet home.

Rule number two: Don't be a hero.

When you join up, you get a speech about how we are the true defenders of the Empire, the real front line, where durasteel meets vacuum, and that means upholding the proud traditions of blah blah blah. A lot of cloudflies take this speech very seriously, I guess. Or else they're just so happy to be off whatever dirtball gave birth to them that the *sheer exuberance* drives them to push the limits, cut the corners, and end up a thin carbonized smear on some tumbling rock.

You know what the leading cause of exploding cloudflies is? Definitely not rebel blasters. It's running into things, or else running into one another. It makes sense, when you think about it. There aren't that many rebels, but there's a whole galaxy full of stuff to smash into.

They must tell them this in basic training. They certainly told *me*. But there are always some who think they're going to make that turn, beat that blast door closed, dodge that rock, and then, well. Crunch, boom, plastoid medal, the Emperor thanks you for your sacrifice, citizen.

Don't fly slow. That just gets you a different kind of dead. But fly *careful*. And never be the one in front.

"Attention Theta Squadron." Lieutenant Obrax's voice in my ear. "Prepare to receive a message from Captain Needa."

A tiny holo appears above my controls, blue and flickering. I've never met the captain of the *Avenger* in person, but he's familiar from a hundred announcements like this one. Arch and aristocratic, like so many of the Empire's elite. He glares like he's disappointed with me in particular.

"Lord Vader has impressed on me that this mission continues to be one of the utmost importance to the Empire," he says. "It demands constant vigilance and attention to duty. If I discover any pilots returning after failing to complete their assigned patrol, I will personally escort them out the nearest air lock. I hope that's sufficiently clear."

The holo cuts out. Motivational speaking, Imperial Navy style.

My comm lights up with a private channel from Howl.

"And then I will *personally* piss into the air lock," she intones, mocking Needa's Core accent. "And then I will *personally* fly the ship into a sun before pushing you out, because that's *just how angry I will be*. Do I *make* myself *clear*?"

I make sure I'm not on the general channel before snickering, another old instinct.

"You should put together a show," I tell her. "We could sell tickets."

"Wait till you hear my Vader." She mimes heavy, raspy breathing.

Lieutenant Obrax comes on again. "You heard the captain," he says. "No excuses. Lock down and prep for launch."

I put my helmet on, hear the click of the latch and the hiss as ozone-scented air fills my nose. Flip another few switches and my machine rumbles to life, twin ion engines projecting a familiar buzz

I can feel in my teeth. Test the controls, stick, foot pedals, exterior thrusters twisting in response. I glance at the diagnostics, see green lights. Flip on the comm.

"Theta Four, go for launch." Among ourselves, we go by our chosen nicknames—mine is "Shadow"—but only elite hotshots can get away with using them when command is listening.

"Theta Seven, go for launch." That's Howl, only moments behind me.

The other four pilots in my half flight are cloudflies. Fresh recruits. The best of them has only been with us four months. The worst came in a week ago, just before we deployed to Hoth. Hell of a time to start your tour.

"Theta Eleven, go for launch."

"Theta Thirteen, go for launch."

"Theta Eighteen, go for launch."

"Theta Twenty-Two, go for launch."

Clipper and Dawn, Flameskull and Shockwave. The latter are good examples of why you shouldn't let recruits pick their own nicknames.

"Theta Squadron, launch," Obrax says. "Glory to the Empire!"

The docking clamp extends out into the cargo bay with a whine of hydraulics, then lets go. My TIE drops through the insubstantial blue of the atmo shield and out into the black.

Rule number three: Don't go at them head-on.

I know, it's not what the tactics manual says. Listen, though.

If you manage to keep from crashing into things for long enough, eventually you're going to find yourself going up against an actual enemy starfighter. It's what we're here for, after all. For the last few years, that's usually meant rebels.

The tactics manual says that a TIE squadron, twenty-four ships

205

strong, should endeavor to go directly at enemy starfighters, maximizing the number of guns on target. The Academy geniuses who wrote this calculate thusly: maximum firepower, maximum casualties on both sides. Some of ours go down, some of theirs go down. We have more pilots and fighters than they do, because we're the Empire, so we win. Glory to the Empire!

As a bonus, recommending this approach means you don't need to spend that much time prepping your pilots, because any half-trained womp rat can fly straight at the bad guys and hold down the FIRE button until he gets blown into flaming dust, right?

Right. So. *A couple of things.*

It's easy to feel invincible in a TIE, if you haven't taken one into battle before. It seems big and solid, and the practice targets blow in a satisfying way when you hit them with the rapid-fire lasers.

It's easy to *forget* that the rebels fly X-wings, A-wings, B-wings, Y-wings. They seem to have a lot of credits and not a lot of pilots (easier to find people willing to support the Cause with a few credits than actually jump in the cockpit and die for it, I guess), so they fly ships with little amenities like "shields" and "armor" and "hyperdrives" and "repair astromechs." The ship that *we* fly, on the other hand, was meticulously designed by the brains at Sienar Fleet Systems to be the absolute cheapest platform that can carry a laser cannon a few thousand kilometers.

So you go in head-on. Pew pew pew! And the X-wing's shields barely flicker, and it starts to fire back, and you realize *very briefly* that it has twice your firepower *plus* a rack of proton torpedoes, and then, you know. Thank you for your service, et cetera.

Thank you very much for the tactics manual, Academy geniuses. It's all well and good saying that we can trade two for one with the enemy and come out ahead, but I'm not volunteering to be part of the two, and neither should you, if you can help it.

We skirt the edge of the asteroid field, engines building up to their endless shriek as we head to our patrol zone.

That *sound*, like a cross between an angry beast and a groundcar skidding on wet asphalt. They say it drives some pilots crazy, but I love it. It's ugly and angry, perfect for the TIE. When we swoop in on the enemy it's like the machines themselves are screaming with rage.

Not that there's any enemy here, of course. Just space, lots of empty space, a three-dimensional zone encompassing one side of the asteroid field where we fly the prescribed search pattern, an ever-expanding spiral. What we're in for, probably, is four hours of hot nothing, then back to the ship for a recharge and out again for four more. It's fine with me. In my book, it's a good day when nobody's shooting at you.

Shockwave disagrees. (However stupid the nickname, it's easier than memorizing a new cloudfly's designator every time one dies.) "If I have to fly past these scum-sucking rocks one more time . . ."

"It's a different zone than yesterday," Howl says. "So these are new and unfamiliar rocks."

"Could be worse," Flameskull says. "The bomber squadrons actually have to go into the mess. They've been blasting, trying to spook the bastards into moving."

"What, exactly, are we supposed to be tracking down out here?" Dawn's the longest-lived of our cloudflies. She seems nice enough. But. Rule number one.

"A modified YT-1300 light freighter." This from Clipper. Clipper is an Academy boy. That means he *chose* to be here, unlike the rest of us, who just tested high in the right categories on the conscript intake exams. Academy boys all want to get promoted out of the TIE/ln squadrons as soon as they can, get themselves at least an interceptor, start climbing the ranks, maybe shoot for the Imperial Guards. Never trust Academy boys. Maybe I should make that a rule.

"Yeah, I read the mission brief," Dawn says. "But why have we got half the fleet chasing after one busted old freighter?"

It's a reasonable question. But this is the Imperial Navy, we don't do reasonable questions.

"Ask Lord Vader," Howl says. "But be ready for a real short conversation."

The spiral expands outward. The rocks tumble and wheel in the light of the distant sun. My mind goes blank, as though my fighter is disappearing around me, and I'm the one flying through hard vacuum. The smallest twitch of my fingers pulses the thrusters, sends me into a gentle turn, easy as thought.

Rule number four: Learn to love your machine.

This one might surprise you, given that I spent the last rule crapping all over the TIE/ln. But. *But.*

They built this thing, this ugly piece-of-junk made-by-the-lowest-bidder mass-production death trap, and somehow—presumably by accident—they made something beautiful. It turns out, when you take away the shields and the armor and the hyperdrive and all the rest, when you strip a starfighter down to the absolute bare minimum, what you're left with flies like a damn dream.

There's no excess weight on it anywhere, because excess weight might cost money. It has power to spare, and it twists and curves like an exotic dancer. You can pull moves that, if Joe Rebel tried it in his X-wing, he'd find it coming apart around him. Only the A-wing comes close, but the A-wing is a creature of straight lines and raw force, all thrust and no finesse.

TIEs are all about finesse. Fly it long enough, and you learn when to tickle the thrusters with a light touch, when to jam the throttle in and push the stick hard over, how to spin and roll and come out right behind some meathead, guns blazing.

I knew a guy who got the promotion every TIE pilot dreams of, up to driving a Lambda shuttle. A nice, safe bus with plenty of shields to protect the brass. After a month, he gave it up, transferred back to the line squadrons. He said he missed the rush.

At the time, I didn't understand it. It wasn't until I saw Howl fly that I really grasped how you could fall in love with this machine.

Howl transferred to the *Avenger* about six months before Hoth. Two years since Yavin and things were still hot, rebel cells flaring up and Imperial command determined to crack down, show that the loss of the Death Star had only been a minor setback. We were way under-strength, and basic training could barely crank out cloudflies fast enough.

But Howl wasn't a cloudfly. She'd been flying nearly as long as I had, already on her third tour. That she was still in a line squadron after so long told me that she either had no ambition (like me) or was a terminal screwup (also like me, depending on who you ask). So I was interested enough to look up when she reported to the squad in the middle of mess, and I had to admit I liked what I saw. Hair dark as space, just a little longer than regulation, lips the color of a fresh bruise quirked with a hint of sarcastic smile. Not everyone can pull off the Imperial dress uniform—I look like a ten-year-old boy—but she managed.

In a mess full of teenage cloudflies, I wasn't the only one looking, of course. I think five boys and two girls offered to bunk with her that first night, and she sent them all down in flames. Canny operator that I am, I held back for a while.

Okay, I was just chicken. I'm better in a cockpit than I am with people. "Amara Kel's Rules for Getting Laid Aboard a Star Destroyer" would be a really short book.

As luck would have it, though, Howl and I got put on patrol together, so we had a lot of time to get to know each other out in the black. On one of our first shifts, I asked her what a Howlrunner was.

"It's a canid native to Kamar," she told me as our TIEs screamed through the big empty. "Massive, nasty-looking thing with a skull for a face. Hunts humans, if it gets the chance."

"Is that where you're from?" I asked. "Kamar?"

She laughed. "Kamar's a desert full of talking bugs. I just saw a holo and thought it sounded cool. Plus everyone else in basic was picking names like 'Stormsmasher' and 'Foe-Render' so I didn't want to get left out."

I laughed out loud. What I'd learned on these patrols was that under her polished exterior, Howl was something of a goofball. The combination did warm squishy things to my insides, and I had to breathe and remind myself to remember rule number one.

"So why Shadow?" she said, a little while later. We were far enough out that command wasn't going to be listening in.

"Dunno," I mumbled. Nobody had ever asked me that before. "Nobody notices a shadow, right?"

About a week later, things got hot again, thanks to Imperial Intelligence. Now, any TIE pilot—any navy officer, really—can tell you all kinds of stories about Imperial Intelligence and the thrilling works of fiction they produce, safe behind their keypads. This was actually one of their better moments, considering. The rebel supply base was right where they said it would be, in a derelict Clone Wars–era deep-space installation. Only they'd missed the little detail that the rebels had been there awhile, so they'd repaired the defenses and upgunned the place into something closer to a battle station. When the *Avenger* dropped out of hyperspace at close range, it took only a few broadsides before Captain Needa decided he didn't like the way things were going. He backed off and told the bombers to work the place over a bit to make it more digestible, and we went along as escort. The rebels had anticipated this, naturally, and some X-wings and A-wings came out to join the party.

Some days, you can tell things are junked right from the start. We didn't have anything like the numbers we needed—maybe sixty TIEs against two dozen rebels, and most of ours were cloudflies going into their first engagement. Our lieutenant tried to keep our squad together, blazing away as five X-wings came right down our throat, which worked as well as it usually does. I clipped one of the rebels, sending it spinning off into the black, but the lieutenant went boom along with four others, and the cloudflies panicked and scattered. Then it was down to a mess of little dogfights, which tends to favor the side with ships that don't explode at the drop of a hat.

I did what I could, sliding in behind a flight of three A-wings smooth as you could ask for, raking one with fire until its shields flared out and the ship broke apart. The remaining two split up, one of them punching in full thrust while the other threw itself into a tight turn to get on my tail. Apparently nobody taught the pilot not to get into an ass-kicking contest with a Maxilian megapede, though, because a TIE/ln will out-turn any starfighter ever built. I twisted the stick, jammed the pedals, and screamed through an arc so tight that the force coming past the inertial compensator was enough to squeeze my eyeballs. It worked, though, and the A-wing lost me completely. Soon as it evened out, I was on it, and I watched the starfighter spin into the side of the station and go up in a fireball.

That bought me time to take a leisurely turn and look out at the battle. We were losing, bad. Someone screamed over the comm. Sounded like Drake, which would be a pain. She owed me thirty credits.

Rule number one, right?

"Theta Four!" Howl's voice in my ear. "I'm on the leader! Could use some help!"

I found her on my scopes, twisting and dodging with a red-painted X-wing. The rebel was *good,* a veteran for sure, lasers spitting just aft of Howl's gyrating ship. I could dive in, take a pass at him, but X-wings are sturdier than A-wings and it would probably just make him mad. Any minute now we were going to get the order to pull out—

I snarled a word that would have drawn a rebuke from the lieutenant, if he weren't a red mist already. "I'll try to tag him, get ready to break—"

"Just come in bearing three-twenty-six by ten and go into a left skid," Howl said. "I'll handle the rest."

"But—"

"Trust me!"

I shouldn't have. But, well. You know.

My TIE screamed as it sliced downward, not directly at the rebel but above and to one side of him. On Howl's mark, I tweaked the thrusters, sending the fighter into a hard spin to the left, not a great idea if you want to see where you're going—

But it gave me a front-row seat as Howl put her machine through some kind of mutant upside-down Koiogran, crossed with a twist I don't even have a name for. The rebel hotshot tried to follow her through it, but the X-wing wasn't made for that kind of tight maneuver, and he lost control and ended up sliding after her, *right* in front of my guns. I barely even had to aim, just held down the trigger until their shield flared and the ship went up, stupid little astromech's head popping off like a pull-tab on a can.

Howl had *known.* Where she would go, how he would follow, where I would need to be to make the shot. I'd never seen anything like it. Still haven't. Vader himself couldn't have pulled that move.

"Thanks!" she said, cheerful and unfazed, as though she hadn't just given me a divine-level master class in combat flying.

"N . . . no problem." My voice shook only a little.

Five minutes later, we got the recall order. Fifteen minutes after that, I plugged my TIE into the docking clamp and lifted myself out of it with shaking hands. Five minutes after *that*, I was in the shower with Howl, kissing her as frantically as I've ever kissed anyone, and finding to my shocked delight that she was kissing me back just as thoroughly.

I blink, and swear. Daydreaming. Don't daydream while flying, no matter how pleasant the memory. Maybe that should be a rule.

"I've got something on my scope," says Clipper. "Down in the rocks."

"That's not in our brief," I tell him. "We're on watch in case they make a run for it."

"It's right there," he says. "Just on the edge."

"I see it, too," Dawn says. "Grid two fourteen by forty-five."

I poke my scanners. There's . . . something. A lump of metal. Could be a ship, could be a rock with an ore deposit. No way to know from here.

"Stay on course, follow orders," I tell them.

"Lord Vader himself wants this freighter," Clipper says. "If we're the ones who bring it in, do you have any idea what he'll give us?"

"I have a pretty good idea what he'll do to you if you mess up your patrol route," Howl says. "Theta Four is right. Stay on course."

"The Empire's glory isn't achieved without risk," Clipper says. It sounds like some dumb slogan they teach at the Academy. I consider telling him about the rules, but I doubt he'd be interested. "I'm going to check it out."

"Theta Four has seniority here," Howl says, "so that's *her* call, not yours—"

Clipper's TIE is already veering off. Scum-sucking Academy boys.

Not surprisingly, Flameskull and Shockwave go after him. After a moment, Dawn turns off as well. I thought she had better sense.

That leaves Howl and me, flying our patrol pattern.

"The lieutenant is going to *love* this," I mutter.

"Assuming anyone tells him," Howl says. Which is fair, because I certainly won't. Getting one up on a cloudfly like Clipper isn't worth getting tagged with a rep for ratting people out to the officers.

"Let's just hope the rebels don't come blasting out anytime soon," I say, "because you and I probably aren't going to be able to stop a YT-1300 on our own."

"Speak for yourself," Howl says, teasing. "Did I ever tell you about the time—"

Someone screams over the comms. Dawn.

"Theta Seven," I say, warningly. "Don't."

"They're not far in."

"*Howl.* They broke formation!"

"There's something there. Scan won't resolve. But—"

"*Howl!*"

Her fighter veers off, heading into the asteroid field.

I thumb the comm off and turn the cockpit air blue with every bad word I can think of.

Rule number one. Cloudflies are cloudflies. Chat with them, sleep with them, but don't get attached . . .

Kissing Howl in the shower, skin slick and water scalding.

Rule number two. Don't be a hero. Never be a hero, heroes end up dead.

That smile. Like she's got one up on the universe, and she knows it.

The rules—

I keep up the barrage of profanity as I jam the stick hard over and lean on the pedals, torquing the TIE into a hard turn, diving among the rocks.

It doesn't take me long to find Dawn and the others, or to figure out what the problem is. The problem is a hundred-meter worm that emerged from a burrow in one of the larger asteroids, maw gaping, studded with teeth the size of our fighters.

The asteroids are *dense*, like flying through a moving mountain range. Clipper and Flameskull are circling one of the spinning boulders. No sign of Shockwave. And Dawn's fighter is in a hundred tiny pieces, but she's still screaming into my ear, so she must have ejected.

Speaking of—

Rule number five: Never eject.

I mean, if you're in an atmosphere or something, fine, go nuts. But out in deep space, in the middle of a battle? You're almost guaranteed to be safer *in* your TIE than out of it, until it actually explodes. Thing is, while the TIE/ln doesn't have *much* armor, it's still a lot more than your flight suit. A battle tends to produce a lot of debris, which means a lot of little fragments pinging around that will bounce right off your canopy but would happily zip through your suit and your guts and come out the other side. Not to mention the hard radiation from weapons fire and ships going up. Three guesses how much rad protection is built into our flight suits.

Plus, the navy isn't always scrupulous at picking everybody up after the action is over. There's always somewhere else to be, some other rebellion to crush. Stay with your ship, eventually a salvage crew will come along. You may be asphyxiated by then, but at least someone will find your body! That's something!

It's not. But still. Never eject.

I'm not going to put too much blame on Dawn, though, given the state of her fighter, and the fact that giant space worms aren't exactly in the handbook.

"What in the name of the Emperor is that?" Clipper said.

"Giant space worm," I snap, "obviously. Now shut up and let me get a location fix."

"It's gonna eat me it's gonna eat me it's gonna eat me—" Dawn moans.

"What happened to Theta Twenty-Two?" Howl says.

"He turned the other way," Flameskull says. "Lost track of him."

Probably halfway home by now. Smart kid. My scanners finally pinpoint Dawn, floating in her ejector seat near the surface of the rock. Spectacular.

"Right," I say, dropping protocol. "Howl, you and me will make a firing run, get its attention. Clipper, you and Flameskull go for Dawn, tag her with a utility line, get out of here. Got it?"

"Got it," Clipper says, and the others echo it.

"On my mark—"

But Clipper is already powering in, so I just shout "Go!" and throttle up. The worm twists toward us and shifts ponderously in our direction. But it's not agile enough to catch a TIE, not by half. Howl skates by above it, her stuttering laser cannons leaving a line of scorched craters across the thing's skin. I go for the base, guns tracking a spray of shattered rock and space-worm hide. As it swings toward me, I cut to the left, ready to make my escape—

—and find Clipper coming right at me, about to commit an egregious violation of rule two, subsection one: Don't run into each other.

In the quarter second before we pancake, I yank the stick the other way and stand on the thrusters. Acceleration shoves me sideways, the TIE slews, and I go into a spin, missing Clipper by the space of a fingernail. Unfortunately, that leaves me whirling the wrong way, and I fight the suddenly overloaded stick to get the spin under control.

Not fast enough. One panel tip slams right into the space worm with a *crunch* I can hear through the hull, shearing entirely away. The engine on that side screams, and I slam the control for a hard shutdown before feedback blows the reactor. And *that* leaves me dead in space, no weapons, drifting slowly in front of a giant space worm, which opens its jaws wide as a cavern.

Why? I wonder. How much of a mouthful could I make for it?

(The giant exogorth, it turns out, is a silicon-based life-form that tunnels through the asteroids eating ore. It doesn't give a damn about squishy organics, but our fighters, dense with refined alloys and radioisotopes, must look like candy)

I close my eyes and try to draw an appropriate lesson.

Rule six. Don't go chasing after your girlfriend no matter how much you like her.

Rule six. Asteroid fields are bad news.

Rule six. Don't get eaten by a giant space worm.

Rule—

"Shadow! Hang tight!"

Howl's fighter screams past me, into the worm's gaping maw, cannons spitting green fire. The thing rears up as her lasers scorch its insides, and its mouth starts to close. Howl, halfway down its throat, spins her TIE in a neat pirouette and punches forward at full power. The ship is fast, but not *that* fast, nothing is, and the last I see of her is a glimpse between the interlocking teeth of the worm as its jaw closes—

"*Howl!*" No no no no no, not her. I *taught* her rule number one, not for me—

A stutter of green light. The worm's tooth shatters, fragments blowing outward, and Howl's TIE sneaks through the gap in the thing's smile, the fit so tight it scrapes the paint on her side panels. Then she's free, drive flaring, and the giant worm has had enough for one day, slipping back down into its tunnels.

There's a *clunk* as a utility line hits my hull, magnetic grapple catching.

"You all right, Shadow?"

"I'm still here." I gasp for breath, tears beading inside my helmet where I can't wipe them away. "Palpatine's withered *nuts*, Howl—"

"Let's get you back to the *Avenger*." The cable goes taut, and the rocks slide gently around us.

"You're supposed to finish your route," I say when I can trust my voice. "Otherwise Captain Needa might throw you out an air lock."

"Let *me* worry about Captain Needa," Howl says, and I can hear her grin.

Rule number six: If you are going to get attached to somebody, make sure it's to a girl who flies like an ash angel hopped up on death sticks.

Clipper, I later learned, had grabbed Dawn, and Shockwave wandered in eventually. Even cloudflies sometimes get lucky.

And we didn't even get in trouble! Turns out Vader had strangled Needa just before we finally got back. All's well that end's well, Imperial Navy style.

THE FIRST LESSON

Jim Zub

Harmony, we seek.

The swaying stream of existence brings shifting tides of chaos and order in measures that can never be fully understood, only recognized and confirmed.

Reality, we accept.

A patient agreement with existence does not mean one cannot influence or improve one's position in the universe. Acknowledgment does not equal passivity.

The future, we behold.

Meditation is not a body at rest or a stagnant state of selfishness. It is the diffusion of self, a desire to reach further than the physical bounds that anchor us so we may attempt to experience the wider patterns at play.

This moment of oneness paints itself upon an infinite canvas. It is a fleeting concordance between the physical world and spiritual senses that look beyond.

These thoughts and many others echoed through the energy that surrounds and binds the being known as Yoda.

A name. An identity. A shell of crude matter housing a form set upon this sharpened point of time and all the points preceding it.

The nine-hundred-year-old Jedi Master had come to Dagobah for rest and reflection. Living here was a way to carry out the fleeting time he had left before joining the spirits of his enlightened predecessors in the Force.

In the past Yoda may have occasionally used his cane to trick students into believing he was frail, but now it had become a necessary tool to keep his footing in weaker moments. His fighting form, long behind him, replaced with even greater inner strength, enlightenment, and acceptance.

Acceptance of his past mistakes and foolish assumptions. An acknowledgment of the swaying stream and his place within it.

Yet there would always be more to learn.

Feel the Force and go beyond.

Sitting outside his meager hut, introspective and silent, Yoda let his awareness swirl out in all directions, connecting him to the diverse biome that was Dagobah. He had carried out this mental exercise countless times throughout his years spent in exile, yet each time experiencing it felt engaging and new.

The ground was soft and damp. The air thick and hazy.

The seasons were in transition on this planet of marshy mist. In this moment he felt each new sprout and rotting root.

A cacophony of sounds near and far signaled a menagerie of creatures carrying out the delicate arrangement of their unfettered instincts.

A spade-headed smooka dragged its snout through mud in search of food. Yoda smelled the thick soil as it shifted to and fro beneath his nose.

A skittering nharpira built a loamy nest to keep its impending young well hidden. Yoda felt soft clumps of cool soil in his hands.

A ferocious dragonsnake hunted for a meal worthy of its grand gullet. Yoda heard the rumbling growl within his own throat.

Yoda perceived these beasts and more in ever-widening waves of awareness. He knew he was not at the center of this ethereal experience. He was just one link in an eternal and immeasurable web built and broken among the stars.

Broken?

Why broken?

That vile thought dropped into the stillness of the self, a jagged uneven thing with a strange gravity of its own that drew in tiny motes of fear and anger, disturbing the stream . . .

. . . A flash of darkness . . .

. . . A *disturbance* in the Force.

Yoda could not remember the last time something had broken his concentration in such a manner. Was it a sign of inner doubt or an old fear he'd managed to keep hidden within?

No. This was an outside presence.

A presence he had not felt in many years.

Potent and prophetic. Foreign, yet familiar.

A *Skywalker.*

Obi-Wan's spirit had contacted Yoda years earlier. His old friend spoke of Anakin's child and hope for the future of the Jedi, but the old Master assumed he meant Leia. Yoda relished the chance to help her find her place in the universe and potential within the Force. But this was another.

Luke, the brash.

Luke, the reckless.

Luke, the echo of his father's yearning need to control that which he could not understand.

And Luke was now on Dagobah.

The boy arrived in a ship ill suited for a lengthy stay, carrying barely enough equipment to sustain him for a month or more. It was a perfect microcosm of his shortsighted approach to life and danger, proof he would not have the restraint required to fulfill the arduous training of a Jedi.

Courageous, but foolhardy.

Resolute, but woefully unprepared.

Yoda could already sense Luke's mind was a jumble of excitement and anticipation. The boy's thoughts raced with assumptions about who he would encounter on this strange planet.

A Jedi Master.

A warrior.

A being of great stature and even greater power.

Most amusing, this first lesson shall be.

With a sigh, the old Master stood up, returning his awareness solely to the frail form that housed it. He could already sense the discord Luke brought in his wake, unsettling the swaying stream and all its inhabitants.

The smooka fled its feeding ground.

The nharpira abandoned its new lair.

The dragonsnake attempted to eat the boy's astromech companion but, upon finding it a poor fit for digestion, furiously vomited the droid out of the water and into the trees.

Carefully moving through the swamp while staying hidden beneath the fog, Yoda soon spotted the boy and his droid unpacking their supplies. Even though the droid was caked with algae, dirt, and stomach fluid, its appearance and familiar blips were still quite recognizable.

R2-D2.

Of course the boy had Anakin's old droid with him. Such cycles of fate no longer surprised the nine-hundred-year-old Jedi.

Yoda watched Luke's gaze wander as he inspected the marshy environment while cracking open a metal container filled with travel rations. At the same time, he absentmindedly chatted aloud to R2, voicing his concerns.

"It's really a strange place to find a Jedi Master . . ."

R2-D2 responded with high-pitched whistles and warbles of reassurance.

"This place gives me the creeps."

He hesitated.

"Still . . . There's something familiar about this place."

Place, place, place . . . Repetition and small-mindedness. The boy saw only the surface of things. His perception of reality still so limited. He was less than a Padawan regardless of his age.

R2-D2 tried to comfort Luke with more chirping sounds even

while his sensors failed to notice as Yoda quietly perched on the root of a nearby gnarltree.

"I don't know . . . I feel like—"

It was time for the first lesson to begin.

"Feel like what?"

Luke turned with a start and swiftly drew his blaster, leveling it at the frail-looking creature in robes sitting in front of him.

"Like we're being *watched*."

This would be a test for the boy. A way to see how he reacted to the unknown and unusual.

"Away put your weapon! I mean you no harm!"

Luke hesitated as Yoda continued.

"I am wondering, why are you here?"

Luke slowly lowered his blaster but kept his gaze locked on Yoda.

"I'm looking for someone."

"Looking? Found someone you have I would say ~hrmmm!"

A shrill cackle escaped from the old Master's throat, and Luke smirked as the amusing sound pierced the dull muffle of the marsh. The boy didn't seem predisposed to violence, in any case.

"Right."

"Help you I can, yes ~hrmmm!"

Luke looked unimpressed. Assumptions guided all his actions.

"I don't think so. I'm looking for a great warrior."

"Oh! Great warrior! W'ohhh~!"

Yoda cackled again as he pulled himself down from the root to get a closer look at his impetuous and immature new student.

"Wars not make one great."

The boy did not have the hotheaded anger and confusion that poured forth from Anakin the Fallen. Nor did he have the calm and resolute countenance of his mother, Padmé Amidala.

Luke Skywalker's form had yet to be set in one mold or another. His glory or downfall were yet to be defined.

Would the boy come to understand harmony, reality, and the future?

Could he bring balance to the Force?

Yoda would try to show him a way toward the light.

The old Master hesitated, realizing his own momentary doubt.

No, he would *not* try.

There is no try.

DISTURBANCE

Mike Chen

Emperor Palpatine felt a great disturbance in the Force.

It erupted, clear as a ship emerging from hyperspace, sending shock waves through the dark and the light, the cold and the flame. He closed his eyes, and despite being physically surrounded by pitch black, doing so gave him sight.

He was no longer seated in the cold lightless chamber hidden far below the former Jedi Temple, a place he used to deepen his mastery over the dark side. Instead he felt the sheer violence of the Force, the rise and fall of its infinite currents, something only a true Sith Lord would dare to invite in.

The Jedi, in their ancient foolish ways, had wasted their lives, even their Order, concerned with their *connection* to the Force. Symbiosis. Flow. Such primitive idealism.

That was why they went extinct. The Force was never elegant or luminous, at least not for those that saw the entire scope of possibilities. The Jedi, with their myopic commitment to *life* of all things, only experienced a sliver of it. But the dark side demanded more. It worked amid the chaotic ocean of the Force, the very embodiment of life and death, past and future, everything and nothing. There was no symbiosis to it, only a never-ending battle for control over both the shadow and the light. Only then was it possible to bend it to one's will, to exploit its potential into the most powerful path.

But when a strong enough disturbance roared from the turbulence, the Force shook free. For only a second, perhaps a mere flash. Some might have felt a shadow of fear upon recognizing the disturbance, but Palpatine knew better than to *ever* give in to something as trivial as emotions. Those types of risks were shed long ago, in another lifetime. All he cared about was the source of the disturbance. Because when the dark side loosened its grip, only one thing had to be done:

To fight back.

To tame it. And conquer it.

Some time had passed since a disturbance erupted with this magnitude, when a spike in the Force let the galaxy slip from Palpatine's oversight. It was a tiny blink, the slightest movements of one being's finger. But in that instance, the finger pulled the trigger at a very specific time, flying at a very specific velocity and altitude, thus allowing proton torpedoes to launch and hurl through a small exhaust port.

One moment of precision. *How* that spike came to be, Palpatine remained unsure. Only vague certainties appeared despite his efforts. There was a pilot. One in the Rebellion. One that flew an X-wing during that battle. One that pulled that trigger.

But that pilot's connection to the Force? It remained a mystery, even up until moments ago.

Then everything changed.

Because as Palpatine felt the great disturbance, he gave in to the chaos, riding through the Force's crashing waves and underlying slip-streams until the source revealed itself. An energy rippled outward, a frequency that answered one question and created another.

This was indeed connected to that rebel pilot from three years ago. And yet there was more.

The Force surged, something gathering defenses around the disturbance, pushing all who dared approach away. But Palpatine fought back, clawing his way to the eye of the storm, step by step. The current retaliated, shielding itself like a sun-dragon guarding its treasures with all the might of an exploding star.

But the dark side was too strong.

Palpatine was too strong.

Sheer will powered Palpatine through as it always did, fending off the determination of someone or some*thing* wanting to hide this, a secret held so tightly that the very desire to protect it gave itself away, if only for a blink.

229

Much as the Force spoke to the rebel pilot pulling the trigger, it revealed itself to Palpatine here. Not by guiding the launch of torpedoes, but with a vision.

What Palpatine saw in the Force should have frightened him.

On the floor of his office in the Imperial capital lay the bodies of two Royal Guards, their severed red helmets tossed across the space. And next to them, a figure stood.

Stoic. Intimidating. Cold.

Just as the Sith of legend, with power emanating from its very breath.

The Sith, after all, always attempted a coup. It was the way of things.

This figure remained at attention, the crimson glow of a drawn lightsaber reflecting off panoramic transparisteel. Shadows cast over the figure's hooded face, a brief glance enough to show that it was a young man; not an old wizard like Dooku, not covered in demonic tattoos like Maul, and not a lumbering clash of organic and mechanical like Vader.

Only, it seemed, a boy.

Draped in black, his cloak hid any other identifying details. He walked calmly, circling the floor until he came within range of the large chair at the end of the space.

Palpatine watched, his perspective stuck near the office's entry as the vision unfolded. From the far chair rose another hooded figure, one that he recognized clearly as his own doppelgänger. The mystery assailant raised his lightsaber, holding it in a ready position as the Emperor approached his attacker.

The Sith of lore always contested in an endless battle of Master and apprentice. Palpatine himself had experienced these visions when visiting Moraband, Malachor, and other places steeped in the dark side. Always the hooded apprentice wielding a lightsaber. Always the arrogant walk up to the intended target.

Sometimes the Master fell. Mostly the apprentice fell, a victim of their own naïveté and hubris. Either way, it played out as the familiar dance under the Rule of Two.

This encounter felt different. This felt *more*. Each step the boy in the hood took echoed and rippled outward, not just in the vision but through the undertow of the Force. He paused, his lightsaber going silent, the red blade slinking back into its hilt. His other hand raised, fingers pushing down against nothing.

A choke.

Palpatine watched the Emperor retaliate. Lightning burst forth from his fingers, but the power of the choke stymied his assault; the electricity spidered outward, grazing the boy but dancing all over the room, shattering vases and catching nearby curtains on fire. The lightning ceased, and instead a subtle *click* sound came from a back chamber, soon followed by the whirl of a lightsaber handle whipping through the air, heading toward the Emperor's open palm.

But it never arrived.

Instead, the hooded figure turned his head, a simple look pausing the lightsaber hilt in midflight. The boy nodded, and a red blade of energy emerged from the floating lightsaber, tip inching toward the Emperor.

Palpatine could practically feel the Emperor retaliate with dark side energy, causing the room to rattle. Fixtures tore off walls, launching toward the boy. Despite their speed and trajectory, none of the projectiles reached him, lamps and statue pieces and other furniture-turned-weapons dropping to the floor with dull thuds.

The Emperor was being completely overpowered. And Palpatine was intrigued.

Against the brilliant cityscape of Imperial City, the Emperor fell to his knees. His arms collapsed, and though Palpatine's perspective remained fixed at the office's entrance, such a distance from the battle couldn't hide the Emperor's tremble.

Not with fear. Not with *any* emotion.

But from sheer pain.

The room reverberated as the boy pressed onward, commanding the Force's invisible tendrils to choke his elder.

"Do it," a new voice whispered, seemingly from nowhere.

The floating lightsaber suddenly thrust forward, its red blade piercing through the Emperor.

Around the room, the rattling stopped. The floating lightsaber's deep-red blade withdrew into the hilt, which then dropped to the floor. The air itself seemed to exhale despite the transparisteel sealing the space. And the Emperor's body collapsed sideways, a cold shell of weight and flesh no longer capable of a single breath. Silence crept into the room, broken only by the swish of the boy's cloak as he turned.

Palpatine *should* have found the vision frightening, perhaps even threatening. And yet only mild curiosity arose. Of course another ambitious would-be conqueror existed. Such delusions were admirable; it was the way of the Sith. To *not* expect someone, somewhere dreaming of this was naïve in its own right. It seemed entirely possible that a disciple of the dark side trained away in the Unknown Regions with the goal of sneaking into the Core Worlds, to the heart of the Empire itself, deluded enough to have this very vision as a goal.

The boy approached, as if he could see Palpatine. As he came near, something struck Palpatine, as if another layer existed to this mystery. Nearly face-to-face, the boy knelt, then looked up and removed his hood to reveal pursed lips over a cleft chin, striking blue eyes, and unkempt blond hair that had seen too many days in the sun.

"You have done well," the new voice said, its location now confirmed. It was coming from the very spot Palpatine experienced the vision.

As if he was the dreamer.

No. *Because* he was the dreamer. Or tapping into the dreamer's vision.

A great disturbance in the Force.

And the voice: It finally registered in Palpatine's mind. A strong, low timbre that he hadn't heard in decades.

Anakin Skywalker.

It didn't surprise Palpatine to discover that Lord Vader dreamed of overthrowing him. All Sith did. But mere dreams weren't usually powerful enough to cause a disturbance in the Force, even ones that carried some level of potential prophecy. Something else was behind this. Something this powerful needed passion, *desire* behind it.

This boy, what was the connection?

And why was Lord Vader so focused on protecting him?

The vision screamed and shifted, nearly pushing Palpatine back into the vacuum of his meditation chamber, but he clung on, the dark side pulsing through to anchor him. His own murder was only the first step, and though Palpatine sensed something trying to control, perhaps even protect, the details, he held his ground, using all his will to channel the dark side. The chaos abated like dust blowing away as the vision evolved. The boy, this anonymous apprentice, now stood on a veranda beneath a blanket of stars.

No. Not stars.

Star Destroyers.

Bright pulses of hovering engines lighting up the sky, a fleet so dense that the natural sun was blocked out, hovering ion drives as the source of illumination over the Imperial City on Coruscant. Line after line of ships caused the entire city-planet horizon to vanish, their collective hum almost powerful enough to tilt its axis. Below these ships, the boy waited without a cloak or hood, simply a black tunic with a lightsaber on his belt.

The vision began to move—no, Lord Vader began to move. He walked with methodical purpose, yet something seemed different.

No respirator.

Through Vader's eyes, the vision continued, and as he was set to cross the threshold, his gaze turned, breaking focus from the awaiting boy for a second to catch a flash in the window.

A reflection.

And with that image came a realization: This was not a vision. This was a delusion, a *hope* or a wish or a desperate dream. It was everything Vader wanted—or maybe it was everything taken from him.

Palpatine had always ensured that those were one and the same.

There Vader stood, not a hulking tank of black armor, but a man, whole. The familiar face of Anakin Skywalker peered back from the reflection, a face that hadn't existed in more than twenty years. He looked as he'd last lived, the vertical scar over his right eye partially hidden behind rugged dark locks of hair, strong chin framed by an intensely focused stare. He remained clothed in dark-brown Jedi robes crossed over broad shoulders, and the only difference between the man in the reflection and the general who'd graced the HoloNet news so many times as the Hero with No Fear was the red-bladed Sith lightsaber on his belt.

Before moving onward toward the boy, Vader turned, focusing on a figure crossing the interior of what looked to be an elaborate rooftop apartment. Was that . . .

Of course.

If this was Vader's delusion, then only one thing would make it complete.

The familiar figure of Padmé Amidala paused in her movements, making eye contact first with Vader, then the boy on the veranda, her presentation so ornate she may as well have been giving one of her familiar impassioned senatorial speeches. She smiled at him, her radiance fully restored. Together they strode out under the sea of Star Destroyers.

The boy watched, his composure shifting slightly. And then he spoke, his voice tinted with soft affection.

"Father." The boy looked at Padmé. "Mother."

And suddenly Palpatine saw things for what they truly were. The disturbance. The fierce defense of the vision within the ethereal chaos. The desire, the *need* for secrecy, not just a strategic endeavor but an explosion of emotion that ripped through the Force itself.

How long had Vader known?

"Luke," Vader said. "You have done well." A gloved hand rose, gesturing to the thousands of ships in the sky. "Behold, my son, the most powerful fleet in the galaxy." This person, the soul of Darth Vader within the still-whole body of Anakin Skywalker, looked up, staring above his son as countless ion drives came to life, the twinkling blue-white globes suddenly bursting with intensity before wave after wave launched into hyperspace.

Within the vision, the ground shook, and what had merely been the rumble of launching vessels turned into catastrophic shaking, so powerful it was physically impossible on an artificially regulated planet like Coruscant. From afar, the Imperial cityscape evaporated into white. The veranda, so meticulously re-created in this vision, began to absorb the white, turning durasteel curves into an empty canvas. The white bled into every physical corner of the space, swallowing the apartment and even the shadow of Senator Amidala. The ground-shattering sound dropped away, leaving only the quiet breath of father and son.

All that remained was Darth Vader and this Luke.

Luke *Skywalker*.

"Yes, Father," Luke said. "*Our* fleet."

Through the Force, a guttural scream washed over Palpatine, pushing him away from the vision. But this time, Palpatine let it.

He had seen enough.

For some time, Vader had covered the galaxy in his search for rebel leadership, insisting that every lead go through him. Informants, bounty hunters, spies, probe droids, Vader's search had bordered on obsessive, though Palpatine allowed it; his efficiency and ruthlessness had always been assets. Now that Palpatine understood, the truth behind Vader's devotion unfolded quickly. Hoth, Hoth must have been the answer. Once Vader knew his son was there, it seemed he simply could not fully shield his anticipation. Thoughts, desires, *dreams* must have consumed him during the journey to Hoth.

Vader's lack of control over his feelings caused them to be his very undoing. Again.

This surge, the culmination of Vader's relentless nature and his inability to free himself from his past, was simply too powerful to fully hide from the dark side. Just as he couldn't contain his own impulses when facing Kenobi on Mustafar, he now exposed the secret he held most dear.

Still the fool.

But who was this Luke Skywalker? Palpatine would uncover that answer in time, but one thing was certain: He was a blank slate waiting for a Master to unlock his potential.

Any Sith would covet such an opportunity. As Vader did. If he wanted to find his son, then Palpatine would let him. In fact, Palpatine would do everything in his power to accommodate that. An entire armada, the unlimited capital of the Empire, all of those would be at Vader's disposal. He would search. All while Palpatine would plan.

Then Vader would eventually make a mistake. He always did.

And Palpatine would step in and exploit it. He would be the one to propel Luke to the true potential of his bloodline—over his father's final rasping breath.

That was how the Sith handled disturbances in the Force.

Now seated in his Imperial City office, the very same one as in Vader's delusion, Palpatine dived into the Force's chaos, eyes closed in meditation as he explored the currents for possibilities. He exerted his will over the Force, demanding insight into this unexpected variable until a singular path forward presented itself, a staggering power loaded into two simple questions:

How much did Vader know?

And how far had he gone to hide his betrayal?

Palpatine would soon discover the truth.

He tapped a button on the arm of his chair. A tinny beep chirped, then a voice spoke. "Yes, my lord."

"Commander," he said, his tone neutral and curt. "Summon Lord Vader. We have matters to discuss."

For the first time in the longest time, Palpatine decided to let a feeling come through. Unlike Vader, he retained all mastery over the chaos that ran around and through him. But it was a real emotion fueled by his own amusement—not because it propelled the Empire to greater conquest or was a display to twist the knife in his apprentice; simply a flash of satisfaction that came and went.

In that moment, Palpatine smiled.

Several minutes passed before holographic lines came together to display the kneeling form of Darth Vader.

"What is thy bidding, my Master?" Vader remained still, and through the Force, Palpatine could feel the battle within him, the struggle to contain his desires. Despite the armor and machinery, Vader's heart still beat with the fire of Anakin Skywalker.

A fire that Palpatine would put to the test.

"There is a great disturbance in the Force."

THIS IS NO CAVE

Catherynne M. Valente

It was born on the thin breathless edge of the galaxy where light and warmth are legends told to frighten children.

Space is so much quieter out there. Safer. There are stretches of dark on the Rim where even something as vast and vulnerable as its father-and-mother could pass unnoticed.

Its birth-cluster ruptured in the secure shadow of a black dwarf star. Dead as any fallen tree in a forest, prickling with radiation instead of mushrooms.

This was its first feast. The memory of sunlight a quadrillion years gone still clinging to the last lump of an iron core, the ghost of a star that once nurtured planets, systems, wonders. This will be its last gift:

to become hot, invisible, crackling milk slurped up by a weak and naked creature, poor eyeless child, nosing instinctually in the blackness for the first desperate drink of life.

When it had finally slurped its fill, it rolled backward in the vacuum in satisfied delight. It sealed its mouth and did not open it again for centuries. It grew. It learned to hum, the long, slow, closed-jaw song-language of its kind, a collective vibratory echolocation that was also a poem without beginning or end. Its father-and-mother loved it, after a slow, stony fashion, protected it, taught it the meaning of being as it understood such things, gave it a name.

Sy-O. In the Hum, it meant *the color of unloneliness.*

The digestive gases in Sy-O's silicon stomach expanded, propagated, equalized, turning that first exquisite ancient meal into a stable, pressurized atmosphere flowing throughout its fragile body, enrobing the massive density of its crystalline-metallic heart.

Outside, the empty fury of space. Inside, a world.

And though Sy-O turned its ponderous head then toward the Galactic Core, a pulsing source it can sense, can smell, all the way out here, the way flowers turn toward the afternoon sun, it will remember this nameless, dimensionless place forever after. It will remember it the way a little girl with arms and legs remembers the smells and sounds and secret pockets of the neighborhood where she grew up, where she first knew about things. Where she first realized there existed things to know about, and that knowing was a magic trick she could perform anytime she liked. In its time, Sy-O will return here, or somewhere very like it, seeking another black, dull feasting star to sustain its own young.

In the space between, Sy-O traveled. It accreted, particle by particle, fragment by fragment, dust by dust. A shell to protect its flesh, for it *is* flesh, pierceable, burnable, tender. The first line Sy-O added to the Hum was this: *How unsorrowed the galaxy is to see me! It hur-*

tles beautiful debris into my skull at the unchanging velocity of love, and gives me the gift of my skin. Sy-O retreated comfortably inside its accretion sphere, an interstellar snail, carrying its house on its back down the Road of All Moons.

The Road of All Moons. The great rhythm of life: the infinitely repeating journey toward the Galactic Core and away again, out to the Rim, then back to the churning stew of life and energy, then the long sail into emptiness once more. At sublight speed, the Road was long, but Sy-O did not mind. Not on its first circuit. There was so much to witness. So much to experience. Empires and apocalypses, golden ages and eons of suffering swarming over planets as it passed them by. Wars that consumed systems, peaces that devoured time. Sometimes the soldiers wore masks, sometimes they did not. Sometimes they all bore the same face; sometimes they were children. Sometimes they used ships; sometimes they snuffed out their enemies with a thought. All of it interested Sy-O, even the things that horrified it. It watched the Sith and the Jedi before they invented those names for themselves, and then it watched them swell and diminish and swell again like tides of light and darkness. It added mournings and jubilations for them to the Hum and swept on through the stars.

Sy-O wept for the dead. Sy-O marveled at the living.

It was a billion years old.

It was nothing but a baby.

It was so alone.

Sy-O was still a child when the tenor of the Hum changed. A musician would say it shifted into a minor key. A painter would say it turned blue. Neither of those would be true, but neither would be false. It did not matter. Sy-O understood immediately.

The time of the Clew had come.

All of Sy-O's kind, wherever they floated on the Road of All Moons, would come to a point in time and space to congregate, to exchange, to mate, to hum, to celebrate, to debate, to exhibit the fruits of their experiences, and to part again. In their slow, imperturbable lives, the Clews were almost fast, almost bright. Holidays. The closest thing they could know to a thrill.

Sy-O had never experienced one before. The opposite of alone. The opposite of travel: a destination. It had butterflies in its stomach. It would bring them to the Clew, and everyone would see that Sy-O had grown up good and strong enough to contain butterflies and keep them happy.

It had found them in a ship graveyard in the Ryloth system. By then Sy-O's aloneness had grown sharper and colder than planetary rings. It yearned, but could not comprehend its own yearning. It yearned for *others*. By the time Sy-O emerged from the background blackness, whatever battle had been so important to those ships had ended. They floated in space, inert, blast scars blistering their hulls, broken guts orbiting breached engine cores. And like carrion birds on a temperate world, the butterflies had come to feast on the dead.

Sy-O trilled into the Hum, too enraptured to form proper phrases. They were so pretty, so full of energy, so delicate and radiant! Their leathery wings, their translucent proboscises, their musical screaming like symphonies of hunger and satiation! Sy-O adored them. Sy-O wanted nothing more than to be their friend.

So Sy-O ate them.

Carefully.

And now they were together forever. Now they were born and grew up and had gorgeous butterfly children and suckled at the organs of Sy-O for sustenance and aged and died, all in the great world within Sy-O. That was what love meant. Love meant togetherness. It meant containing and sustaining another living being. It meant making sure they were unsorrowed, for all time. It meant no longer being *I,* but *Us.*

Sy-O would bring its butterflies to the Clew. They would all bring the worlds they carried to the meeting place. Some of them would have butterflies, like Sy-O. Some of them would have three-eyed rays or squid-whales or other, wilder things. What you could carry, what you could sustain, was the only status among their people. At the Clew, they would preen, they would strut, they would show off the life they could nurture. It was their art, an art of centuries and vast interior space.

To any other being, the Clew would look like nothing more than an asteroid field. Ten thousand dead rocks that were in truth ten thousand snails in their stony shells, drifting in nothingness. But any other being could not hear the Hum, the great conversation passing from rock to rock, from the creatures within those rocks to their kin.

These are my butterflies! Sy-O hummed with pride. *They are wonderful and unhated of my heart!*

The Hum snickered. And flickered. And answered: *Those are mynocks, silly child. They are nothing. You know nothing. Look at the acidic Unark worms inside Si-Yy or the star-colored pylat birds in To-X. They evolved on* planets. *Now they live within the exogorth. That is accomplishment. Mynocks evolved from space vermin to become space vermin. Do not speak again.*

They are beautiful, Sy-O whispered into the Hum. *They are uncruel. They can Hum a little. I have taught them. They are not like their brethren now.*

The Hum became a laugh.

And when the mating spirals began, no one would come near, for Sy-O stank of butterflies and youth. It was as alone as it had always been.

It slept.

It tried to dream.

The ship surprised it.

It had eaten ships before. Countless in number, infinitely varied in design. But none had fed themselves to it so eagerly.

Sy-O wanted everything, the whole cosmos. No one had ever wanted Sy-O before. The galaxy did hurtle its gifts, it *did*. Sy-O felt them in its upper digestive tract. It bore down and adjusted pressurization slightly for their comfort. It would take some time to craft air they could breathe. Sy-O would do it. With such care.

It could not see what they were exactly, butterflies or starlight-colored birds or lizards. No one can see well inside their own stomach. But Sy-O could taste and smell them. It could *feel* them. And more important than any sense, it knew they were together, at last, together forever, the great worm and these tiny flames, so alive, and so bright. So hot. So quick. Talking! With their mouths! Back and forth at a speed that made Sy-O feel slightly ill.

One screamed like a beast, covered in long hair whose every strand carried the musk of other worlds. One spoke always as though he was mocking, but was not. And some of them were not carbon or even flesh, but silicon, like Sy-O. Not quite like. These tasted like metal, where Sy-O was stone. But they crackled with life all the same.

And something else. One of them, the female, burned with another light all her own. A light Sy-O had sometimes felt in its long travelings, a force that bound the planets and the space between them and everything on them, too. A wave that carried the exogorths through the galaxy, but also splashed on each lonely shore of each lonely world. Almost like the Hum, but without sound or vibration, without a dislike of butterflies, without border or boundary.

One of the beings inside Sy-O glowed incandescent with it, as steady as her own heartbeat. And so, in those moments as dear as darkness, Sy-O glowed, too.

They were very busy, Sy-O's new friends. They didn't have to be. They constantly ran from here to there on their little ship, yelling instead of humming, whispering urgently. Sy-O tried with its excretions and gaseous emanations to indicate that they could rest now. They had reached the end of their small, insignificant journey and joined a far more important one, joined the Road of All Moons, joined the great circuit. They could let their burdens fall and become unsorrowed here.

But they could not stop *moving,* these new citizens of planet Sy-O. It seemed to be a kind of compulsion. They even left their ship and walked on the raw flesh of its insides. What a strange sensation! So heavy, so purposeful! Nothing like the pretty flutterings of the mynocks. What pain and pleasure! Sy-O felt deep honor that its new friends wished such intimacy with it already, and hurried to send them butterflies so that they would know how passionately they were welcome, to introduce them to their new nation.

245

Sy-O instructed the butterflies to Hum: *I am your home now. I love you.*

The newcomers screamed and ran. But perhaps they were screams of delight! Of recognition and gratitude! Yes, Sy-O was certain of it.

But they were not always loud. They did not always fill their hours to the brim with running and banging and arguing. Sy-O could feel their every breath and pulse of blood the same way it could feel the Galactic Core singing to it off in the far great distance. It could hear their talk, if it could not always understand their strange, limited language. It could feel their feelings—they were so bright, after all, so urgent.

Two of them whispered. They made a quiet place between themselves. A Clew, but not a Clew. There were only two of them, not many, not enough. But enough for their needs, perhaps. When they looked at each other, the color of their feelings was the color of un-loneliness. A new kind of stellar radiation, with a warmth that made Sy-O shiver.

Sy-O heard words echoing in its bones that it did not understand. But it loved the sound of them all the same, because they made those sounds with their tiny alien high-speed bodies hurtling toward one another.

Worship. Trembling. Afraid. Scoundrel.

Yes, Sy-O thought with half-frozen stony joy, *come together. Pursue life. Be present. How happy will be your children safe and unharmable inside Sy-O, protected from the terrible background radiation of the universe, the crackling heat and noise of conflict, of temptation, of ambition. I witnessed the rising and falling of this searing energy on so many worlds, only to see it eat them all at last. It will not touch your babies here. It will not even once so much as crease their skin. I will keep them soft and kind. I will be the black star that shields and feeds them, and no child of the glowing woman and the man with the mocking voice will ever know pain but always peace and ungrief. Are you not glad we met?*

And the creatures did come together, butterflies or starlight-colored birds, whichever they were, it hardly mattered, and Sy-O quietly added their names to the Hum.

It seemed to Sy-O that it slept in contentment, but it could not have dreamed long.

The beautiful animals inside it were angry. They were hurting it. They made fires and stoked them hot, so hot the delicate membranes of its body recoiled and shrank back. The Hum in its mind became a shriek of agony.

What was happening? Why would they do this? What had Sy-O done wrong? How had it angered its new friends? The belly of Sy-O lurched and quailed. Perhaps they had guessed what the other ex-ogorths knew: Sy-O was silly and stupid. It had no real art. It thought mynocks were butterflies and it loved them. They had found out Sy-O was a child and decided they could not love it, no one could.

They were leaving.

No, cried the Hum of ancient, infant Sy-O. *You can't. Please. Don't leave me.*

Their ship, containing them as Sy-O contained their ship, the ship that was worthy as Sy-O was not, roared through its digestive system, into its throat cavity, no care or quarter, scorching its flesh with every centimeter of progress. Scorching its butterflies, whose tiny cries went unheard in the thunder of engines. Sy-O tried to close its mouth, to keep them in, to keep them loved, to keep them tucked away from that dreadful rhythm of rising and falling worlds that could do no good for anyone. *Stay. I am all you need. Stay with me, friends. I will make the butterflies go, if you do not like them. They are nothing, as the elders said. I was silly. I was young. I know better now. Please. I do not want to be alone again.*

It could hear the tenseness in their voices even through the hull of their ship. The metal could not hide it. Sy-O felt the sounds of them bracing for impact, their circulatory systems working in overdrive to compensate for their fear.

Fear? But why? Everything was going so well.

More words it does not understand. Sy-O wails in sorrow.

The cave is collapsing!

This is no cave.

The little ship bursts out of Sy-O's immense mouth, blackening its teeth with its afterburn.

No, Sy-O Hums pitifully. *No, no, no! Come back! Come back! I will be better! I will be good! I am almost finished making air for you! You will miss it! Please don't go! I need you! Who will I love when you are gone?*

247

But they are gone. Nothing remains of them but scars. Blisters already freezing on its exposed flesh. It left the shell. Made itself ridiculous for them. And they are still gone.

Sy-O and the butterflies are left alone. It is quiet. It is quiet except for the great worm weeping. The Clew will soon disperse. The Road of All Moons will begin again, its slow silver thread through the maze of the galaxy.

Perhaps that was them, Sy-O thinks to itself. The fairy tales. The beings that do not walk the Road but live and die quick, glittering, incandescent, never to know what it is to contain worlds or glimpse what lies at the center or the edge of all that is.

But that is not possible.

Such beings do not exist.

Sy-O curled into its rocky shell and mourned in the Hum. It missed them. It will miss them forever. When the suns that fed their homeworlds have burned to black eggs with just enough life left to nurse a newborn exogorth, when their names are either forgotten in the sand of a blasted barren planet or writ in letters of starfire across the heavens, when their descendants' descendants do not even know the color of their eyes. Sy-O will still miss the scoundrel, and the metal ones, and the screaming beast, and the glowing woman. Its organs will hold on to their memories like blood and nutrients.

It is not possible. Such beings do not exist.

Such beings do not exist.

Such beings—

A century later, the thought begun in the asteroid field of the Clew finishes. Sy-O exhales the breath taken as the beings left its gullet in their ship of pain. The slow flapping of the butterflies' wings are the punctuation of this thought. They have long since forgiven it for calling them nothing. They do not hold on to hurt. Hurt is a photon; it grows dimmer as it travels away from its source.

It is not possible. Such beings do not exist. They can never exist. Everything in the galaxy traveled the Road of All Moons. Even if they did not know what those words meant. Even if they could not understand that they *did* move in the great caravan. They moved nonetheless. The slow entropic expansion of matter into void moved every being together. In their tiniest cells, in their planets and systems and meta-systems. Exogorths moved faster, that was all. With more purpose. The others took the long way.

But everyone traveled, all together. Always. That was a small part of what the incandescence the woman carried meant. There was another word for it, a word those beings used. But Sy-O could not recall. A small word, for small mouths. But it meant something so big.

Sy-O would meet its beloveds again. It would meet the atoms that had once been them, which was no different. In the incandescence it had sensed reverberating through the woman, it would find them again and they would laugh at these ancient times long past, these griefs that once seemed so important. They would understand then the love Sy-O meant when it sealed its mouth and altered its internal pressure and instructed its respiratory system to begin the manufacture of oxygen. Sy-O would understand in turn what urgency drove them so hard toward unsafety. It would know the other beings they knew, it would grasp what kept them so hot and quick. What had made them afraid. And in that glow, they would all move as one outward, toward the known and unknown.

One day. They would find each other again, and no one would be alone.

Goodbye, Sy-O thinks a century afterward. *How unsorrowed I will be to see you, my friends. One day soon. On the longer path.*

249

LORD VADER WILL SEE YOU NOW

John Jackson Miller

"**W**hy does Lord Vader keep stormtroopers stationed on his bridge?"
"To carry out the bodies."

It was a silly joke in the ranks when Rae Sloane was just a junior officer—but it wasn't funny for long, and no one had dared to utter it in years. It was too real, had touched too many.

Unbidden, that joke popped into Sloane's head as she led the stormtroopers down the corridor. *That*, she knew, was the only way to think about an activity she'd done thousands of times before. If she looked behind her even once, she might see that this time was different: that the troopers' weapons were pointed at her, and that she wasn't a commodore, but a captive. But she did not look back, and as long as she didn't, she remained in command—in her own mind, if nowhere else.

As much as Sloane despised self-deception in others, it made sense here. She had never visited the Super Star Destroyer before, but fellow officers had told her that the *Executor* seemed designed to strike terror not just in those it opposed, but in those it carried. With every step taking her deeper into the metal warren, she understood what they meant.

"This is it," the trooper behind her said as a pair of doors parted to admit her. "Step forward."

She did—alone.

The chamber was at once large and claustrophobic, bright and in shadow. A large cylindrical black structure towered at its center. A massive containment unit, perhaps, or a giant torpedo? She thought she knew every part to an Imperial capital ship, but this was new. She decided to assume it was ordnance of some kind—but why would it be here, so deep in the ship?

Seeing nobody before her, she spoke to the air. "I . . . was told to report to Lord Vader."

"Keep your voice down," rasped out a voice from behind her. She looked back to see a uniformed figure standing near the bulkhead, to the right of the doors she'd entered through. Piett spoke in a tone both low and urgent. "Step here!"

"Of course—*Admiral.*"

She caught her breath as she joined him. She'd nearly said *Captain.* Firmus Piett was a nonentity, a rank plebe when she first knew him; now he commanded Death Squadron—and her. She thought to congratulate the bland-faced officer, before remembering it wasn't the kind of promotion one celebrated. He was just in the right place when it was the wrong time for someone else: Admiral Ozzel.

Things changed fast in the Imperial Navy. Especially depending on who else was aboard.

"You will deliver your report to me," Piett said at the wall.

She looked around again. Was Vader making him wait, too? And if so, why in such a strange place? "I'm sorry, Admiral, but my orders—"

"Orders? You're here because you've *ignored* orders." Piett glanced anxiously at the room and its looming cylindrical centerpiece. "Lord Vader will know what is said here. Speak, but understand: He already knows what you did. It is only in respect for your services to the Emperor that you are receiving this chance to justify your actions."

"My actions, Admiral?"

"Don't play games. You were recalled from your temporary assignment soon after the action at Hoth began. You should have been back long before now—but instead, you remained away, making no communication. All while your command burned." His whisper grew louder. "Lord Vader is not interested in your excuses or apologies, and neither am I!"

She steeled herself. "I make no excuses—and I never apologize."

But she did explain.

253

She'd missed it.

Carefully traversing the Anoat asteroid belt in the *Lambda*-class shuttle *Bastinade,* Commodore Sloane reread her orders to return—and about the events that had prompted them.

The discovery of the hidden rebel base. The colossal ground battle that followed. A chance to tangle with Luke Skywalker, the destroyer of the Death Star and murderer of her old commanding officer, Grand Moff Tarkin. And the rebels' hurried evacuation of said base.

She'd missed it all.

She'd missed it because she was on the other side of the galaxy, leaving *Ultimatum* with a substitute captain as she went on a weeks-long inspection tour of new shuttle technology. She'd missed it, one might argue, because she knew her stuff. No officer in the Imperial Navy had a better handle on the operational capabilities of the fleet, and how to improve them.

But there was no putting a good face on it. The greatest ground battle of her lifetime—not just a career maker, but a possible career pinnacle—had taken place while she was fiddling around at the shipyards at Fondor, trying to tell the engineers which so-called upgrades her shuttle, *Bastinade,* didn't need, even as they made them anyway. The call from Piett—*Admiral* Piett!—to return to Death Squadron and retake command of *Ultimatum* had been a blessing.

There was just one problem. After the battle, the *Millennium Falcon,* likely carrying members of the rebel leadership, had fled into the asteroid field, and it was proving an excellent place to hide. So excellent that, hours after entering the field, she still couldn't find where *Ultimatum*—or the rest of the fleet it was traveling with—was. Rocks, rocks, and more rocks filled the broad expanse in the viewport before Sloane.

"Looks like the Alderaan Welcome Center out there," Kanna Deltic said as she entered the cockpit, hydrospanner in hand. Sloane's precocious lieutenant, simultaneously her most able scientist and her least favorite person in the galaxy, had been her sole companion these last weeks during the detachment.

But Deltic was right about the mess before them—an immense obstacle course whose hazards had already inflicted damage on *Bastinade*'s transmitter. "Still can't get a clear transmission in or out," Sloane said, rechecking her instruments. "You've tried rerouting the power feed?"

"You tried it first," Deltic said, rubbing grease from her face. "Didn't work then, isn't working now." She clambered beneath the starboard console and called out, "The debris's fouled up the scanner array something awful, too."

Sloane had another idea. "Try to—"

"Trying."

The commodore let out a breath. She had to get back before it was too late, before she missed anything else—but as she sat back from the controls, she contemplated that it may already have been too late for her.

That's why I keep getting sent off on these damn fool errands, right? She'd actually made vice admiral years earlier, only to be busted down barely a heartbeat later for letting the rebel Kanan Jarrus slip through her fingers on the planet Lahn. She'd have lost command of *Ultimatum* back then, had it not been for her patron in the aristocracy. But Baron Danthe had fallen out of the Emperor's favor, and in the years since, Sloane had gotten every mundane assignment there was. Tasks, not task forces.

So the Fondor junket was really just another boondoggle in a series, taking her farther from where she had wanted to go. Farther from advancement, from adventure—and from the eyes of people like Grand Moff Tarkin and, yes, even Vader, both of whom had rewarded her in the past.

Tarkin was gone now, and she'd rarely seen Vader at all. And while Piett's elevation suggested that proximity to the latter might not be such a good thing, the truth was that in the Imperial Navy, you needed to be seen—and you needed to be seen *on your ship*. She knew that better than most, because *Ultimatum* was never supposed to be her command in the first place. She'd served as a substitute while its intended captain was away; perseverance had made it hers permanently.

It was a danger to be away from one's post for any time at all—especially when her relief was someone as experienced and capable as Canonhaus. She had to get him off of *Ultimatum*'s bridge before he stole her command altogether.

If only she could find it.

"These readings are gibberish." Sloane looked back out onto the asteroid field and frowned. "The whole squadron's somewhere in here. I refuse to believe we can't find it."

"I refuse to believe in reincarnation, but I'm pretty sure Count Vidian came back as this new computer system," Deltic said, emerging from beneath. "The autonavigator keeps trying to send us into asteroids. The reactor interface thinks we want to play pazaak with it. And as for the shields—"

"Enough." Sloane rolled her eyes. Deltic had always been a bit too familiar—and much too peculiar—but the reference to a former nemesis of theirs was apt. Sloane had chosen *Bastinade* for the refit as it was the last survivor of the original complement of *Ultimatum*'s shuttles; the first two had long ago been destroyed in her first encounter with Jarrus. But just about every "advance" the engineers at the testing station had installed had failed since they'd entered the asteroid belt.

She began punching controls. "Shut it all off. I'm going to manual."

Deltic reluctantly took the copilot's chair. "My instructors always said I'd grow up to be part of a debris field."

Control stick in hand, Sloane looked at the boulders tumbling in space before her. She pointed above Deltic. "Activate the near-range scanner—the one for docking operations."

"It won't help us avoid the big rocks."

"It'll tell me where the small ones are. Do it!"

Sloane had been trained to fly the most colossal ships in existence; she knew something about avoiding collisions with the very large. She'd kept current on her other pilot ratings as well, if only to be able to demonstrate to her underlings that she understood every job.

Still, the asteroid belt the rebels had chosen to flee into was like no other she'd seen. Hours passed, with no proof that *Bastinade* was any closer to exiting the field.

Her hands sweating, Sloane had escaped what felt like a hundred close calls when far ahead to starboard, she spotted a flash. "There. On that big one."

Deltic checked it out on the scope. "It's TIE bombers, pounding the hell out of the asteroids."

"Looking for the rebels. Signal them."

"It's not going to work."

"Do it anyway. At the very least, we can follow them home." *Or we can try.* Sloane banked the shuttle and gave pursuit.

She'd closed almost half the distance when a hammer blow aft disabused her of that idea. An errant stone struck one of the sublight engines, and while it did not result in an explosion, it did reduce their top speed dramatically.

"Forget talking to the TIEs," Deltic said. "They're not hearing us."

"See if we can at least listen to them."

Through static, they caught part of a transmission—and as she listened, Sloane's heart sank:

"*—repeating, bomber squadron, this is bomber leader, relaying change of plan. Return to* Devastator, *not* Ultimatum. *Repeat, do not return to* Ultimatum." A pause. "Ultimatum *destroyed.*"

Sloane released the throttle and stared at the console. The message repeated, this time more broken as the TIEs shrank in the distance ahead. It was clear that an asteroid had taken out *Ultimatum*'s bridge and main reactor, leaving a blazing wreck.

There was also something about how the bombing campaign had rooted out no rebels at all—but Sloane barely heard it.

Ultimatum—*her* starship—was gone.

She closed her eyes for a moment—which was as long as she dared, in that environment. She thought about those aboard who had served her long, if not always well. She shook her head and looked to Deltic. The woman's eyes were wide; her lips moving as if calculating.

After several moments of silence, the science officer said, "I guess I don't have to worry about that money I owe Ensign Cauley."

"Shut up, Lieutenant." Sloane squinted hard. She hadn't cried since childhood, and wouldn't do it now over this—and certainly not before Deltic. But she knew she had to go, while there might be time to get anyone off what remained of the vessel. If she could just get some useful information from any of these damn systems—

"*Wait.* What's that?"

Deltic looked down at the monitor. "Near-range system's picked up a cluster of objects. Two meters long." She looked more closely. "Odd shapes."

"Those aren't rocks." She grabbed the control yoke again and banked *Bastinade,* urging it ahead as best she could.

"The crazy readings are into this system, too." Deltic stood and stared outside. "It says those are *organic*!"

"Bodies."

"Maybe we got lucky and the rebels jumped ship?"

"That usually doesn't mean jumping out the air lock." But as *Bastinade* eased closer, she could tell the scanning system was right, at least about this one thing: The contacts were organic. They just weren't humans.

"Are those—?"

"Yes. You remember the mission we had in the asteroid field near Taris? What we found there?" Sloane's jaw set. "It could be why the TIE bombers aren't having any luck. We've got to inform the squadron."

"That could be a problem." Deltic gestured at the transmitter—as dead as it had been. "We'll have to do this in person. But at the rate we're going—"

Sloane's eyes narrowed. "You're right. We may have time for something else. Do we still have that new forward cargo collector mounted under the cockpit. . . ?"

"You did *what*?"

For some reason, Admiral Piett had not wanted either of them to raise their voices during her explanation, despite no one else being in the room. But he seemed to care less about that now.

"It's as I explained," Sloane said. "We found the first corpse, and noticed another." Arms crossed behind her back, she stood straighter. "A whole trail of them in space. *Mynocks*."

Piett's pallor grew a shade redder. "Why would you care about finding mynocks? They're common to the space lanes."

"But not to asteroid fields—not unless there's food. And that means ships, with power cables to dine on."

"They could have fallen off any of ours. And how could they be dead? Mynocks are immune to the hazards of space."

"Begging the admiral's pardon, but we know these didn't come from our ships—and we know how they died. They were in an exogorth."

"An exogorth?" Piett looked at her as if she were mad. "A space slug?"

"That's the common term. I encountered them during one of my industrial support missions."

Piett was flustered. "There are no space slugs in the Anoat field."

"I thought that, too—most of the asteroids are poor candidates on the Vandrayk Scale. But there must be some, because that's where the mynocks came from."

Piett looked to the ceiling. "Panic. Panic and guilt have taken your senses."

Sloane kept going. "The environment inside the mouth of a slug is warm and moist. Not breathable, but an atmosphere. When a slug wakes and emerges, a few mynocks are invariably expelled from its oral cavity. An observer would hardly notice the small creatures—but the abrupt transition is often fatal to them. We call it mawshock."

"I call it nonsense."

"And if there are space slugs, that means there are tunnels deep enough that our scans can't reach them—and we already know our scans can't penetrate the beasts' hides. Our bombers wouldn't have been able to succeed."

Piett rubbed his head and let out a deep breath. "I'm going to cut to the end of this story to save what remains of your dignity. They say when you arrived, most of your shuttle was missing."

"That's correct. After we made our first collections, we were struck by another asteroid. I executed an emergency separation and used the cockpit's sublight thrusters to continue. The best we could manage was a crawl, I regret to say."

"I'm sure. Wait—you said first collections?"

"That's correct. The slower pace gave us the chance to find more mynocks on our route. We indexed the nearest large asteroids so we'd know where they came from—which ones were slug-infested, providing possible havens." She decided to skip past the other hardships of the long journey. "Finally, today, we located the fleet."

"You did not make for your ship, to see what had become of your crew?"

"I saw the wreck," Sloane said, looking down for a moment. "But I also saw that *Executor* was returning to the fleet. I determined that it would be better to make for the command ship."

"Would it interest you to know there were no survivors aboard *Ultimatum*?"

"It does interest me." She pursed her lips. She'd suspected as much—but she'd also had time to come to terms with it out in the asteroid field. Then she looked up. "I made the right decision. I had information for Lord Vader."

"This foolishness about exogorths?"

"That, and something to see."

"He sees *you*, I guarantee it! And he will see someone derelict in her duty. Who feared exactly the fate that befell *Ultimatum*, and who deliberately took her time returning." Piett stepped back from her and snorted with derision. "Hiding with space slugs! The idea is laughable. The *Millennium Falcon* was almost certainly destroyed, just as your own ship was." He threw up his hands. "This interview is over. A summary court-martial would be ordered, if it were solely my decision."

Sloane inhaled. "I take it that it's not."

"Sadly for you." He looked over to the ebon cylinder—and tugged at his collar. "What you do not know is that Lord Vader—"

The doors to the room opened. Piett looked over, startled. "What now?"

Lieutenant Deltic entered pushing a hovercart. On its bed was something covered by a tarp. "I found it, Commodore!"

"What's the meaning of this?" Piett stormed toward her. "Those doors are sealed. Who told you to enter here?"

"Lord Vader did. He sent the order to the guards moments ago."

"But how did—" Piett stopped.

Vader sees all, Sloane thought. She stepped toward Deltic. "Is this what I think it is, Lieutenant?"

Deltic smiled and knelt beside her cargo. She yanked the tarp back. "Meet Smiley!"

Piett looked down at the sprawled form of a massive winged beast: a mynock. He winced, covering his face with the back of his hand. "How dare you bring this here? It—"

"Yeah, it's pretty rank. It's been thawing since we got it out of the collector."

Sloane covered her own nose and nodded. "During the trials at the nebular station, *Bastinade* was outfitted with gear to scoop up samples for later analysis. We'd first just wanted to confirm they'd died of mawshock. But when this one got close to the ship, we noticed something else."

With a heave, she and Deltic tipped the bed of the hovercart upward, causing the now oozing mynock to roll off it and onto the deck. It landed with a sickening squish.

Sloane stepped around to it and knelt. "You see, Admiral, *this* creature's death had nothing to do with exogorths." She pointed. "It was killed with a hand blaster."

Piett gawked at the blackened scorch mark on the creature's carapace. "Are—are you sure?"

"Your forensic analysis tools down below confirmed it," Deltic said. "It's a score mark from a medium-weight blaster pistol. Not a ship turret—a hand weapon. A shot fired very recently, I might add." She looked to Sloane. "Just as you suspected when you saw it in space, Commodore."

Sloane nodded. *Thank you for saying the right thing just this once.* She stood. "Dismissed, Lieutenant."

The scientist looked over at the black cylinder. "Ooh, look at that thing. What is it?"

"*Dismissed,*" Sloane and Piett said in unison. Deltic and the troopers quickly exited.

Sloane paced around the dripping carcass. "Someone was clearing mynocks off a starship with a blaster, Admiral. Whether they were on EVA in space or hidden inside an exogorth, there's only one conclusion."

"The *Millennium Falcon* was not destroyed. It remained in the asteroid field," boomed a voice from behind. Sloane's whole body spun as she saw the black cylinder crack open. With a whoosh, two interlocking metal blossoms separated—and the upper half rose into the overhead, revealing an occupant in the lower portion. A seat mechanically rotated, revealing its occupant, who had been there all the time: Darth Vader.

His voice boomed. "It seems your 'thorough' search was anything but, Admiral!"

Piett flinched. Sloane stared, for a moment, bewildered. Vader had taken note of her once as a cadet, but she'd learned little about him beyond the rumors—and had no idea why he would have ensconced himself in such a chamber. The very sound of the man's voice, his mechanical breathing, made her want to take a step back.

But she controlled her emotions—and answered for Piett. "I was in the right place at the right time, my lord. We were all engaged in the same pursuit: finding the rebels. I just found something different." *The right thing,* she did not say.

The admiral broke from Vader's gaze long enough to glance at the mynock. "It does tell us they were still here recently, my lord."

"Clearly your methods are insufficient," Vader said. "Summon bounty hunters."

Piett blanched. "My lord?"

"The fleet cannot remain in the asteroid field indefinitely, but individual searchers may succeed—*if you fail again.*"

Piett audibly gulped. "It will be done, my lord."

Vader's chair began to turn.

Sloane spoke up. "And *me,* my lord?"

She didn't know why she'd opened her mouth. It was wrong to say anything, she knew. And yet she had gone unseen for so many years that now, here, with her command in ruins, she wanted to hear— something definitive. Anything. Even an end.

Vader's chair stopped, but he did not turn to face her.

She took a breath.

"Report to the Kuat Drive Yards to take command of *Vigilance.*" His chair resumed its rotation, and the chamber's shell slammed tight around him.

"*Vigilance,*" Piett repeated, taken aback. "But . . . that was to be my nephew's command."

"Things change quickly . . . *Admiral.*" Sloane smiled pleasantly. "And I'll need a shuttle. Any functional one will do, sir."

Piett smoldered. "Dismissed."

She turned and walked toward the exit. The doors opened before her, and the stormtroopers stationed there turned. She pointed her thumb behind her. "You two—in there. There's a body to carry out."

At her words, the troopers took half a step backward.

"Relax," she said, smirk barely visible. "It's just the mynock." She walked past them and headed up the hall, alone.

VERGENCE

Tracy Deonn

There have been many of them. So many that the number is not worth counting. This I know.

What I did not know, even after a millennium of their minds in mine, and mine in theirs, is why they approached me with thoughts of light and dark. These words were never enough. Why did they matter, here? Here there are the deep greens of moss, the silken silver of slow mist, the dim blue of steam rising through the ever-twilight. Inside me are the twisting gray shadows of desire and the bright crimson flare of wrath.

And yet, the dark ones called me dark, too, so dark is my color.

They used to arrive in their ships. The harsh, piercing whine of engines—that artificial, lifeless sound—jarred every living thing within my stone walls and without.

It took scores of them before I knew that I . . . was. That I had been. That I am. That some few of them had created stairs to make my entrance easier to manage. Before that, I existed, but did not know so. I absorbed awareness from these visitors, these *Force*-users, until I gained my own first understanding.

Time.

Just as the beings had a beginning and birth, so did I. Before, all had been dreadfully present. But with their awareness of life, death, growth, I saw that time moves as a stream, and there is a *before* for these beings, a *present* that they ignore, and a *future* toward which they are always turning, minds busy with life unlived.

They were disruptive creatures. They'd come climbing through the woods with their minds so loud that my second understanding came quickly.

Thoughts.

Some thoughts were sharp, fresh, and brandished before them like a shield. Some were worn like tumbled stone on the bottom of the bog, thoughts rolled around in a mind, then buried. Thinking themselves alone, many would broadcast their curiosity. Their needs. Their questions.

I could always feel them coming. At the edges of the swamp shore, their boots either slowed with care or quickened with pride. But when they reached the gnarltree, they'd pause at my cold and dread. Always.

This threshold is where they made a decision. Oh, certainly a decision had been made to bring the beings here. Decisions were made to avoid the dragonsnake, duck the bogwings, trek through the swamp. But lying in wait at my gnarltree are the questions of unknown sacrifice. The hesitation before shapeless risk. *Am I ready?* their minds asked. *What will I find inside? What will I see? What if? What if?* And most would proceed forward, ducking beneath the gnarltree's roots, finding purchase on soil long since smoothed over by previous supplicants.

Once they entered my realm, they were mine. I seized upon the shields. Slithered like a vine snake around their mental barriers. Exhumed the stone. I sought their thoughts no matter how buried, how polished. No matter where their secrets hid, I'd find them. Past their hopes, I struck like a scrange to the source of their pain.

Their minds carried images and words. It took many more of them to give name to what I experienced. My third understanding:

Memories.

I consumed these memories until they flooded me, a fuel so rich as to bring a kind of life to stone and slime and rot like me. While the visitors pursued *themselves* within my walls, I fed from *them.* Full lives on other planets across the galaxy. Dry planets. Gas planets. Ice planets. Worlds teeming with species. I saw beings that looked like them. Beings that birthed them. Faces bending at the mouth, lip edges turned up or down. Written records called books. Transparent speaking records called holos. Languages that I could never utter, and yet I became fluent. Great battles. Power at their fingertips.

I fed until I became sentient, almost as alive as the bogwings, the pythons, the prowling and stomping elephoths.

Then, the fourth understanding. The one I value most of all.

Fear.

I learned how to parse through their memories (times past) their thoughts (words, names, action), and their fears. Eventually, such an assortment of visitors had landed on the surface that I could offer more than a space to gather power and strength, to meditate and plan. Instead of simply reflecting what they brought, I could manipulate.

267

This is when the hunger began. Every twist of their emotions, warp of their thoughts, produced more fear. Enough to sustain my evolution and enough to make me stronger. Just as there is no morning, no night in my forest, but an endless twilight, there is no waxing and waning of my ravenous hunger. And, I learned, there is no limit to what I can devour.

Terror comes in many flavors. Threaded through it most often is anger at being mistreated or wronged. There is a layer of arrogance, because if one is not lofty, then one is lowly. Many times I taste envy at being left without, then a desperate sort of doubt at what being left behind might mean of their value. But the base note of all of these emotions is raw, animalistic fear. Always fear.

Visitors seek my offerings, perhaps even claim to desire them. But none truly desire what I show them. None hold them close when they exit. None carry them out willingly. No. They leave in a rush, already shedding what I've given, pressing my images down and away and pushing them out of their young minds as quickly as possible. They leave seeking the vast emptiness of space or the faces of comrades or the life that does not ask them to face the fears that I relish.

And so, for millennia, there was only one kind of entrant. Those who seek me, resist, and flee. I watched them run with my belly full.

Then one day, a new type of visitor arrived.

A small, green being. Accompanied by another whose body did not manifest—Qui-Gon, returning to Dagobah. Unusual in and of itself. I felt the green one's arrival, but as he approached, there was silence. Nothing.

No, not nothing.

A well so deep I could not take its measure. *His* measure. Not until Qui-Gon guided him closer to my threshold.

Then. Then! A flood greater than any who had come before me.

Time. He'd lived hundreds of years. Not rivaling my own age, but more than any other living thing I'd encountered. Eight centuries. No, nearly *nine*.

Thoughts. Weighted. Curious. Measured.

Memories. So very many. More than I could ever sift through in a single visit.

Fear. At the surface, there was none for himself, but much for others. Fear *only* for others.

This fear tasted sweeter than any I'd fed on before. The agony of loss so rich I could barely stand it. But such fodder. Such material to work with.

For this small being who felt fear for his Order, I showed loss on a scale beyond imagining. Bright blades of blue and green. One of purple. Clashing, sparking, and thrust through flesh.

For this ancient being, whose fear held dread, I showed a hooded, faceless lord so great that I wished I had form so as to fall servant at his feet. *Sidious. Sidious. Sidious.*

And then he was gone.

Until he came back. *He came back!* No offworld visitor had ever returned to Dagobah and chosen a life in its swamps, so close to my domain. He made a home far from my reach so that I could not find his thoughts in the dark and damp, but that did not mean he intended to stay away.

No offworld visitor had ever come to *me* a second time. And yet this one did.

And then a third.

A fourth.

A fifth.

His name is Yoda.

He visits me once every few orbits, and our dance continues.

Today Yoda approaches slowly, and I wonder what fear he desires to see. His body is not as spry as it once was. I feel his anxiety before he reaches my tree.

He pauses. Looks up at the worn roots of my gnarltree, at the canopy that blocks the light. Then he stares into my chamber, a strange look on his wrinkled features. It has been several orbits since he last came to see me, and I am surprised at the intention I feel in his mind, even at this distance.

"A crucial visit, this will be."

Crucial? What has changed for him? What has happened? No one has arrived. No ships have landed. And yet I sense a new purpose in his mood. Anticipation.

"Begin, shall we?" he asks, hobbling forward one small step at a time, his three-pronged foot sinking into the soil in heavy slow steps.

And so we begin.

The images in Yoda's mind are new to me, recent to him:

A shimmering, near-translucent older human man sitting near him in his small, warm hut.

No fear. Yet.

Yoda speaking, "I am old, Master Kenobi."

A ripple of emotion. Slight. Yoda *is* old. Though not as old as I.

"Master, I want you to take on a new Padawan."

Something new, now. Not a feeling others have brought to me. The shape of this emotion is strange. I can't place it. Yoda is always surprising me.

He gives me the word even as I grasp for it. "Pleasure, that is."

I rankle. I've heard this word. A multitude of minds, thousands of years of envy all say the same thing: that *pleasure* is for others to wield over our heads. Mocking laughter fills the cave, regurgitated from entrants who were once hunted, berated, harmed to the tune of others' *pleasure.*

Yoda frowns, shakes his head. Disappointment.

The new memory continues.

"Master, I want you to train Luke."

Who is Luke? There are no images of this Luke.

Older memories. Flashes of a scowling, furious young man with light hair and blue—no, yellow—eyes. A woman in distress. A birthing chamber. An infant. Two. Yoda murmurs words from the then, in the now. "To Tatooine, to his family send him."

Luke. The boy child. But what does—

To the ghostly man in Yoda's hut, Yoda had replied. *"And if I try to teach this rash, this impatient, this mindless boy the ways of the Force and fail, what then?"*

271

There! Fear. Sour and bright and mine!

I do not let Yoda's thoughts continue, instead I show him exactly what he fears, and why it will happen again.

Around the old Master swells the black mist of memory and the spoiled green of regret.

I create Dooku, his former Padawan, face twisted in corrupt passion. Yoda's failure to steer him away from the dark.

I generate near-identical men in white armor, flowing in waves upon waves away from Yoda, under his feet. Marching to follow Yoda's orders. Yoda failing them as living beings, the lives he claimed to so honor.

The young one rises from the dirt floor in a swirl of orange smoke and blue and white. Ahsoka. Turning away from the Council that

Yoda led with arrogance. Yoda's failure to her bright light in the galaxy, ego and overconfidence leading the way.

The now familiar shape of Anakin swells up from fire and smoke. His anger brewing for years and growing under Sidious. Yoda's failure to stop his training before it started, failure to detect his corruption as it happened. Yoda's failure to save him before he rose as a specter even the old Master had not faced.

Yoda's breath comes in short pants and he leans heavily on his cane. With an outstretched hand, he walks through my apparitions until he reaches the other entrance tucked between long roots. Behind him, the phantoms of his past roar as one, rising up into a whirlwind. Where he goes, I will follow, I will send his ghosts—

He turns abruptly. *Smiling.*

"Old fears are these. Stubborn. But see them, I must." Yoda stands against his tormentors, nodding not at them but at me. "My thanks, you have."

And then the old Master leaves my shadows.

I am still angry when Luke arrives. No one thanks me. I am in no one's *service.*

He is young and rash, just as Yoda had predicted. Against his Master's warning, he takes his weapons within my walls, the fool. A blaster and a lightsaber are no match against the phantoms from *this* boy's mind.

Luke's fear produces a black specter. The boy gives him shape and sound. A menacing cape, darkness embodied. Mechanical breaths like the many starships that have landed on my surface. Luke's mind supplies a name:

Vader.

This Vader is walking death.

If I could laugh, I would. The boy makes it easy. I do not need to amplify the fear that this lord instills. Luke's doubt overwhelms even me, but I use it, expand it until the light in him has grown small. Smaller. So that his own terrifying visions can grow.

The boy brought his lightsaber, didn't he? And now he creates a reason to use it.

Luke floods *his* Vader with all of the prowess that he fears the real one possesses. Calls into existence the red weapon of those who call themselves dark against the blue of those who claim the light. One blow. A second. A third.

I press his dread down, and shape it into panic. Luke swings.

Nothing feeds me better than the ones who think they know their true fear.

The black specter's helmet rolls—and reveals the boy's own face.

The disgust and horror that spill out of him is enough to feed me for a year.

273

Later, when Luke readies his ship, even I can hear Yoda's protests. The boy wishes to leave and face Vader, his fear in both flesh and machinery. Let him.

Then: "The cave. Remember your failure at the cave!"

The cave is me. Yoda means *me*. Luke's *failure*?

But I am not a test. I am not a lesson. I am mist sweeping aside to show weakness. The trap beneath the leaves of blackvine. I am a mirror. A revelation.

Luke shouts back, "But I've learned so much since then!"

And the shimmering man speaks, too. The three of them argue about Luke hurrying to face Vader, caution him against temptation toward the dark.

But on my side of the swamps, smoke spins within me and without as I search for answers. *How?* How have I shown Luke a future he could *learn* from? How have *I* provided a warning against danger that, paired with Yoda's teachings, could prevent that future from coming to pass?

As Luke's ship powers up and the droid trills and beeps, I answer my own question.

I remember Yoda's willingness to pass my threshold, these many years, and grow denser and colder with realization.

Over time, we had both sought dark apparitions, had we not? Yoda always worked to confront his inner darkness, while I always worked to show it . . . because we both desire the manifestation of fear. Different methods, for the same ends. Alongside, *not against.*

A dance. A push and pull.

And Yoda knew all of this when Luke came to me. He knew his teachings and he knew my methods. He'd *relied* on my darkness. I had been alone, but with the old Master—

As Luke's ship rises and he rushes to his friends, a fifth understanding dawns in the light. A word that is both emotion and fact. One that acknowledges the past, the future, and the present. One that means hope and sacrifice. This word, this understanding, is one I cannot mimic or shape into terror, no matter how hard I try. It is . . .

Alliance.

TOOTH AND CLAW

Michael Kogge

Bossk scraped his tongue across his teeth, tasting blood. His trap had worked.

Though the gunship that had emerged from hyperspace on the asteroid belt's edge didn't appear on the *Hound's Tooth*'s scopes, he wasn't troubled. He had visual confirmation through his cockpit canopy and could even make out the ship's curved prow and tubular fuselage. Only a Wookiee would helm a ship shaped to resemble that most antiquated weapon, the bowcaster. And a Wookiee ship meant this had to be his long-sought quarry. This had to be Chainbreaker.

Bossk engaged the timer on his wrist chronometer, sealed his vac helmet, and hastened to the air lock, grabbing his Relby mortar rifle on the way. He'd already suited up in preparation for the next phase of his plan, since every second was precious. The Imperial flight itinerary he had altered to lure his target here afforded him approximately nine standard minutes until a dungeon ship full of Wookiee prisoners was scheduled to pass through the Rycep belt. But Bossk gauged he had even less time than that. The famed liberator known only as Chainbreaker hadn't freed thousands of Wookiees from captivity without knowing when to run. If there were any signs that the dungeon ship was a ruse, Chainbreaker would assuredly skip to lightspeed, and Bossk doubted he'd be able to trap his prize again. For this reason, he'd deliberately chosen a more furtive approach to boarding the gunship than ambushing it in the *Hound's Tooth*.

As Bossk entered the air lock, a chime alerted him to the reception of a high-level communication. It was probably another candidate holo-ad for the upcoming guild elections—he'd been swamped with those recently—so he ignored it. He was about to press the EGRESS button when he noticed on the air lock viewscreen that the communication wasn't from the guild, but from an Imperial address. He played the message.

"This is for the bounty hunter Bossk of Trandosha," said the pale-skinned human male in a black Imperial uniform, his hands behind his back. "I am Lieutenant Masil Veit, communications officer on the Star Destroyer *Executor,* and am contacting you based on the recommendation of your guild. My commander will pay a significant bounty for the capture of a Corellian freighter called the *Millennium Falcon.*"

Bossk drooled at the mention of the *Falcon*. Its pilot, the renegade known as Chewbacca, not only rivaled Chainbreaker as the most wanted Wookiee in the Empire, but was also the one being Bossk detested more than his own father.

"Lord Vader will receive you on his flagship for further instructions," Veit said. "The rendezvous coordinates are—"

The human's image became distorted and disappeared. Bossk prodded the viewscreen controls to continue, but there was nothing more to play. Perhaps the ionic winds that occasionally swept through the belt had interfered with the transmission, though oddly the *Hound's Tooth* hadn't picked up any since landing on the asteroid to hide. Veit's comm address was also garbled, so Bossk couldn't request that the coordinates be re-sent, and he didn't dare relay his interest through the guild. Notice of a bounty offered by Darth Vader, the second most powerful being in the Empire, would attract other hunters in the guild, like bug-eyed Zuckuss or that crosswired protocol droid 4-L-something, if they didn't know about it already. Truth be told, Bossk stood a better chance of trying to reconstruct the message with the new military-grade transceiver he'd installed. But that would take time, and his chrono presently read eight minutes, eleven seconds.

He hit the EGRESS button.

Launched into space with the pressurized air, Bossk initiated a quick burn of his jetpack to stop his spin and propel him on a path toward the Wookiee gunship. The energy emitted wouldn't register on sensors as anything more than a blip, equivalent to the tiny collisions that were commonplace across the belt.

He navigated the outer ring of asteroids without incident and entered empty space on a trajectory that would take him to the gunship in less than three minutes. For that duration he tried to relax into semi-estivation so as to reduce his body temperature and make himself virtually undetectable. Normally, he could self-regulate without much effort, but right now he was utterly distracted.

Bossk couldn't get his mind off Chewbacca.

The notorious Wookiee renegade had been one of the first Imperial bounties Bossk had collected more than a decade ago, when he was part of a posse of Trandoshan hunters. But Chewbacca hadn't remained in the Empire's custody for long, and after escaping went on to become the bane of Bossk's bounty hunting career. Bossk had nearly caught the Wookiee and his smart-mouthed sidekick on multiple occasions, such as the time when he found the pair trawling the sewage seas of Erub II for starship parts or when he sabotaged their efforts to build a secret Wookiee colony on Gandolo IV. Then there was the breakneck chase along the plasma floes of the Zusi hypertunnel that shattered the *Hound's Tooth*'s class one generator and the explosive blaster battle on the Jurzan spaceport that destroyed both Bossk's favorite cantina and the new starship he'd just purchased, the *Bitemark*. It didn't matter if he had them cornered or outnumbered; somehow the two had managed to slip through his grasp more times than a Trandoshan had digits. These failures had done more than just embarrass Bossk or damage his standing in the guild—they had caused his own father, Cradossk, to question whether Bossk had been the proper hatchling to devour the nest-eggs of his siblings and come forth as the sole survivor of his clutch.

278

Bossk's vac suit beeped a warning. His temperature was spiking. He had to be more disciplined if he wanted to remain hidden from sensor view. Just thinking of Chewbacca boiled his cold Trandoshan blood. In a concerted effort to self-regulate, he turned his full attention to the mission. Once he captured Chainbreaker, he could worry about Veit's message and catching Chewbacca. An egg in one's claws was always better than two in the nest, or so his father used to say.

He crossed the gulf from the asteroid belt and came in fast on the gunship. Measuring about fifty meters, it matched the length of his vessel, though size was the only attribute the two shared. While the *Hound's Tooth* was a boxy freighter of all sharp edges, bringing to mind the squarish muzzle of its namesake, the Trandoshan hunting hound, the Wookiee gunship was rounded and smooth, crafted not from metal, but from wood.

Perhaps that explained why the *Hound's Tooth*'s sensors had not spotted the craft. The wood acted as a natural baffler to hide the gunship's power generator and engine signatures. No wonder Chainbreaker had been able to waylay prisoner transports and evade arrest for years. One had to be actually looking at the ship in the visual spectrum to see it.

Landing on the gunship's underside, Bossk protracted his claws through the tips of his specially tailored gloves and sank them into the hull. The wood was thick and tough, milled from the giant wroshyr trees of the Wookiee homeworld, Kashyyyk. Wookiees cultivated the trees to build everything from armor to architecture and loved to boast how the wood could withstand the most intense energy attacks. What the braggarts never acknowledged was that their storied timber failed to repel the simplest of weapons. A Trandoshan's claws could cut and flay wroshyr wood like Doshian jellyfish.

Claw-strike by claw-strike, Bossk pulled himself across the hull. Along the bow the word LISWARR had been carved, in both Galactic Basic and the Wookiee language of Shyriiwook. He assumed it was the name of the ship, memorializing a deceased relative or friend of the captain, as was Wookiee tradition.

279

Arriving at the air lock, he avoided touching the exterior controls so as not to trip any alarms in the ship and instead circumscribed a hole in the hatch. He then pried loose the wood, letting out the pressurized air. Once he'd crawled inside the air lock, he jammed the piece back into place behind him and went about slicing another hole in the opposite air lock hatch. Fortunately, he didn't have to decompress, since his vac suit pressure matched that of the ship's interior. When the hole was finished, he climbed through it, eager to begin his hunt.

Illumination fixtures molded from tree resin cast a dismal amber light over the ship's main corridor, which like the hull and the air lock was made almost entirely out of wroshyr lumber. The wood's surface had been left unsanded and unvarnished, showing off the grotesque knots and rings that Wookiees found ornamental, and there was scarcely a sign of technology to be seen. All wires and conduits were tucked behind access panels, and all controls were installed inside wall boxes.

The corridor was quiet but for the thrum of the engines. Bossk's unconventional method of entry seemed not to have raised the intruder alarms, just as he had hoped. He got right down to business, shedding his boots, gloves, and anything that might interfere with his hunt. When he removed his helmet, he was assaulted by a stench that was so noxious, a lesser Trandoshan would have choked. Not Bossk. He pushed out his tongue, flared his nostrils, and inhaled. He wanted to take it all in, the smells and the taste. Every family unit on Kashyyyk had its own scent, and in the roil here he smelled Wookiees of the Chyakk, Koom, and Gkrur clans, along with a trace of what had to be the Kaapauku tribe—or was it Sawa? He always confused the names, but he knew that last scent like he knew his father's rum-drenched breath. It was a hideous odor, fouler than a swarm of diseased gnathgrgs or a bunch of broken nest-eggs rotting on the Scorch.

It was clan-stink of his nemesis, Chewbacca.

Bossk knew that Chewbacca himself wasn't aboard—the stink would've been much, much worse—but someone related to the Wookiee was, and that kinship could work in Bossk's favor. He could take this cousin hostage to bait Chewbacca to come out of hiding. Though Wookiees were among the smartest and strongest species in the galaxy, they had one glaring weakness Trandoshans didn't: They'd do anything to help their families.

Bossk unslung his Relby from his back and strode down the corridor. He was going to enjoy this hunt more than he had previously thought.

He'd gone about a hundred paces when a hydrospanner came hurtling at his head. He batted it away with his rifle and then targeted its thrower, a brown-and-white Wookiee female who was trying to run away. A well-placed shot to her spine made sure she didn't. Tools clanked out of her satchel when she hit the floor.

Stepping over the Wookiee's body, Bossk noticed that her eyes were open and her lips twitching while the rest of her remained still. He would bind her later. The paralytic effects of his stun bolt should last for at least fifteen minutes, more than enough time for him to complete his job. He'd purposely switched off his Relby's lethal settings to maximize his gains, because in most instances these fugitives were worth more alive than dead. After he'd apprehended Chainbreaker, he could sort through those who might provide leverage against Chewbacca and those who might have a bounty worth claiming.

His instincts compelled him to turn. A snub-nosed, short-legged Wookiee jumped out of a hidden hatch, wielding what looked like a tree branch and barking obscenities in Shyriiwook. Bossk let his rifle hang from its shoulder strap and caught the branch in midswing, engaging in a fierce tug-of-war until he landed a kick to the runt's gut. The scrappy beast let go and fell with a yelp. A stun bolt prevented him from getting up.

Bossk dropped the branch, feeling his palm tingle. He looked to see a pincer flea scrambling around his three clawed fingers, unable to find purchase on his scales. The nasty pest must have leapt out of the Wookiee's fur. Bossk smacked his hand against the wall a couple of times to kill the thing. The resulting stain gave the wood a decoration he much preferred.

Continuing down the corridor, he found that it terminated in a door. He bashed the controls with his fist, and the door opened.

The chamber beyond reeked of the Kashyyyk forest. It was dark inside, but that didn't hinder Bossk since his vision extended into the infrared. In the center of the room, three wroshyr trees gave off robust heat signatures, their branches twined around one another, full of leaves and dangling moss. Rodents scampered across the boughs and insects chirruped around the chamber as if it were night in a Kashyyyk forest.

Wookiee shipwrights prided themselves on the individuality of each vessel they built, but most still adhered to a general plan, which incorporated a nursery like this. The wroshyr trees provided wood for patching the hull and repairing other areas of the ship, along with offering a place of recreation and rest where the crew could climb, leap, swing, and sleep. No matter where they went, Wookiees couldn't be without their damn trees.

In this minuscule regard, Bossk had to give Chewbacca some respect. For years the shaggy smuggler had managed to live with a cocky human copilot on a cramped Corellian freighter absent any arboreal amenities. Perhaps that was why he hadn't yet been caught. Chewbacca wasn't as soft and self-indulgent as the rest of his ilk.

Bossk pointed his rifle upward and crept around the trees. He spotted the heat outlines of three Wookiees huddled together on an upper branch. From the tang of their scent, he identified them as juveniles. They must be offspring of the adults aboard. One of them dropped a handful of pellets that bounced on the ground and rolled near Bossk's bare feet. The pellets were wasaka berries, a favorite food of the Wookiees, eaten as snacks, baked in pies, and even juiced for spirits. But for Trandoshans, wasakas were poison.

Bossk crushed the disgusting fruits under his heel and went forward.

The juveniles didn't appear to be armed or otherwise pose a threat, so he let them be. Harming Wookiee children, even with a stun bolt, might infuriate the adults, and Bossk had learned from experience that Wookiees were much easier to capture when they weren't raving lunatics. But there was something else he could do that might tie up some of the gunship's crew while he searched for its captain.

Bossk flipped a tiny lever on his Relby and launched a microgrenade at the base of a wroshyr tree. It exploded, setting the bark on fire.

He exited through a portal sliced from a tree trunk and walked down another long corridor. A set of thick wood blast doors waited at the other end, where the hallway curved right and left. He was nearing the forward arc of the ship, the ostensible bow of the bowcaster. Behind those doors lay the gunship's bridge and most likely its captain, Chainbreaker.

Before Bossk had made it midway down the corridor, six Wookiees stomped into the intersection ahead, three coming from the left branch, three from the right. They were all armed and they were all angry. Two were browncoats, two graycoats, one had yellow stripes, and one no hair at all. They didn't ask any questions or demand his surrender—they just bellowed and charged.

Bossk switched his rifle back to stun and fired at the foremost Wookiee. His shot sent the browncoat female tumbling backward, and she dropped her plasma torch before she could turn it on. The male browncoat behind her leapt over her body and came at Bossk swinging a makeshift wood flail. Bossk crouched, allowing the flail's spiked head to crash into the wall above him, and then decked its wielder under the chin with the butt of his rifle. The Wookiee collapsed onto the female with a thud.

With the browncoats down, the graycoats were next, a pair of twins slashing at Bossk with vicious swords curved like scythes. In the paws of a seasoned Wookiee warrior, these ryyk blades could cleave through durasteel armor and lop off limbs with ease. Nonetheless, as much as these twins plainly wanted to be seasoned warriors, they were far from it. Bossk lunged at their legs and toppled them. As the twins fell, their blades found each other while Bossk's stun bolts found their chests.

Bossk rolled and raised his rifle just in time to block the blow of a bronzium pipe. The striped Wookiee who held it roared. She was a muscular creature, the biggest of the group, and abandoned the pipe to heave Bossk up by his shoulders. Bossk bent his head forward and bit her nose. Howling in pain, she hurled Bossk away from her, but he caught her with two blasts before he hit the floor. Spitting out Wookiee blood, he got to his knees and added a second pair of shots. She fell like a tree.

Bossk sleeved the blood off his lips and stood, kicking the bronzium pipe. It rattled along the corridor until it stopped at the gnarled feet of his final opponent.

The last Wookiee of the six was a gaunt older male, completely shorn from head to toe. His jaundiced flesh revealed numerous scars, and his left arm dangled limply from his shoulder. When he growled, he wheezed.

Bossk caught a whiff of the Wookiee's odor beneath the stink of disease and instantly knew who the wretch was, as Bossk had been the one to apprehend him over a decade ago. This was the once august Rutallaroo, renowned war engineer of Torukiko, who had rigged a fleet of catamarans into assault craft and masterminded a three-year covert campaign to drive the Imperial invaders off Kashyyyk. After Bossk had turned the renegade over to the Imperials for a hefty fee, Rutallaroo had supposedly apologized for his crimes and "volunteered" to design equipment for the Empire's ever-growing military presence on Kashyyyk. The Empire had plastered his image across the HoloNet as an example of a "good Wookiee" who was doing his duty for the peace and security of the galaxy. It was a lie well told. Bossk knew that Rutallaroo would never turn on his own people—

few Wookiees did—and his scars showed that he'd been cruelly punished for his refusal. Yet with all the torture his Imperial taskmasters had inflicted, they had clearly not broken his fighting spirit. Rutallaroo bared his fangs at Bossk, lifted his right arm, and protracted his cracked, discolored claws.

Meeting Rutallaroo's fierce stare, Bossk wished they could tussle like old times, Wookiee and Trandoshan, tooth and claw. Sadly, however, these weren't old times. When Rutallaroo charged, Bossk shot him with a stun bolt.

The Wookiee didn't stumble or even waver. He kept coming.

Bossk blasted him a second time, and a third. Rutallaroo absorbed the stun bolts as if they were nothing at all. His former captors must have electroshocked him so much they had fried his nerves. Stun bolts weren't going to work on him.

Having no time to change his rifle's settings, Bossk dropped it, readied his own claws, and bared his teeth with a menacing hiss of his tongue. If this Wookiee wanted to tussle, tussle they would.

Rutallaroo swung first, but Bossk ducked and came up to slash the Wookiee from behind. Black blood tainted the tips of Bossk's claws, but Rutallaroo didn't howl or cry in pain. He turned his head and gave Bossk a twisted smile.

Bossk read the expression as any skilled hunter would: Rutallaroo had been subjected to so much pain that pain was all he knew. This made him highly dangerous, for he had nothing to lose.

Rutallaroo attacked again, a swipe Bossk quickly sidestepped. What he didn't anticipate was that the Wookiee's dangling left arm would reach out, grapple Bossk's elbow, and stab those cracked claws through his scales.

Bossk hissed. He'd been duped—Rutallaroo's limp arm hadn't been limp at all, just a ploy. But the deception came as no real surprise. Despite their reputation as creatures of the highest honor,

Wookiees always played dirty. It was one of the thousand reasons why Trandoshans hated them.

Kneeing Rutallaroo in the abdomen, Bossk wriggled his arm loose from the Wookiee's grip. With both hands freed, he seized the engineer's neck and squeezed. Ending the creature's misery would be the merciful thing to do, but mercy never applied to Wookiees, particularly when it impacted Bossk's bottom line.

Bossk flung Rutallaroo against the corridor wall. There was a thud, and the Wookiee slid to the floor. This time he didn't move, nor did his expression. It remained fixed in that same mad smile. Bossk returned one of his own, a toothy smirk of victory. Old times, indeed.

He picked up his rifle and looked at his defeated adversaries, lying unconscious or immobile across the corridor. He found it strange that none of the Wookiees he'd faced had been armed with a blaster or even a bowcaster. It almost seemed that they had put up just enough of a fight to mount a convincing defense, without having to risk gravely injuring or killing him.

And then, adding to the mystery, the blast doors at the end of the corridor opened, as if inviting him to enter.

Bossk stayed put, aiming his rifle at the doorway. No one stepped into view, but out drifted the most pungent of odors, the very rankness that had enraged him when he first came aboard. Whoever was behind that doorway was a member of Chewbacca's clan.

There was also something else to the stench, a burnt musk, of dirt and sand and the hot sun. For some reason, Bossk was reminded of the Scorch, the sunbaked plains of his homeworld where Trandoshans enjoyed basking in the rays and mothers routinely laid their nest-eggs.

The Scorch was also the place where Bossk had scored his first kills, consuming the rest of the clutch. While he had no direct recollection of that first triumph—no hatchling did—he could imagine it in vivid detail, down to the smells and the tastes, since it was a story his father used to tell with pride—the only story Craddosk ever told about him with pride.

Bossk's chrono dinged. He had less than two minutes left before the dungeon ship's purported arrival, though given the extent of the last brawl, he wouldn't be surprised if Chainbreaker had seen through his trap and was calculating a route to hyperspace. He had to secure his target before the gunship fled from the asteroid belt with him in it.

Alert for any signs of further opposition, Bossk pressed the stock of his Relby under his arm, notched his central digit on the trigger, and walked carefully through the open doorway.

The bridge was like nothing he'd ever seen on a Wookiee vessel. Technology superseded carpentry. Computer consoles ringed the deck. Display screens covered the walls. Everything from security cam feeds and newsnet streams to sensor scans and telemetry readings was being monitored. Data even hung in the air, shimmering above projection tables as holographic maps, personnel profiles, and hyperspatial coordinates. Silhouetted in this ghostly light, his long-sought quarry sat on a mechno-chair.

"Chainbreaker," Bossk growled.

"Bossk'wassak'Cradossk," the figure replied in Bossk's native tongue, leaning into the light.

Bossk didn't question his instincts, but he did briefly question his senses. He blinked and took a breath to decipher whether or not the silhouette before him was an aberration or apparition. The figure did not disappear, nor did the stench evaporate. His senses had not led him astray.

This was Chainbreaker.

But it was not the Chainbreaker he—or anyone else in the galaxy—would have ever expected. For the infamous Wookiee outlaw wasn't a Wookiee at all, but a female Trandoshan.

287

Bossk stood there, finger on the trigger, itching to pull it, itching to know more. One of his own ferrying fugitive Wookiees to freedom was outrageous, unimaginable, a profane violation of the collective beliefs of their culture. From the moment of hatching it was ingrained in Trandoshan broods that Wookiees were their mortal enemies, the perpetrators of countless crimes against their species over the centuries. That a fellow Trandoshan would actively aid their foes in escaping long-deserved retribution—never in a thousand molts could Bossk have conceived of such a sacrilege.

Yet the most formidable of hunts often revealed the most obvious of truths. Chainbreaker's identity explained why there had never been a confirmed image of her. No hologram, no snapshot, not even a witness's description. Every bounty hunter in the business had assumed Chainbreaker was a Wookiee while marveling at how this enigmatic outlaw knew the intricate details of Wookiee trafficking, the flight paths of dungeon ships, the points of sale and transfer, the Trandoshan hunters involved, and the secret locations of Imperial detention facilities. The truth was so plain, so simple, that no one could have seen it, not even Bossk. Chainbreaker knew those secrets because she herself was a Trandoshan and was communicating with other Trandoshan hunters. She had conned them all.

Bossk then did something he hadn't done in many, many hunts. He laughed, a curt, throaty chortle at the sheer absurdity of it all.

"You do know that by laughing at me," Chainbreaker said in lisping Dosh, "you laugh at yourself."

His laugh died when she bent her head further into the light. Hers was a face with which he was eerily acquainted. She had the same yellow-green cast to her scales as he did, the same beady orange eyes, the same sharp-toothed underbite, even the same pattern of cranial ridges. Looking at her was like gazing into a mirror and seeing a reflection of himself. For two Trandoshans to share all these traits was highly unusual. There had to be a reason.

Bossk flared his nostrils and sniffed out that burnt musk from the stench. Once more he was reminded of his hatching place, the Scorch, and the smells and tastes his father used to conjure when describing how Bossk broke the leathery shells of the other eggs and ate what swirled inside. Were Bossk's instincts tying Chainbreaker to that event? Might she be more than just one of his species? Could she possibly be one of his clutch?

"It's good to finally meet you again, brother," she said.

Bossk flicked out his tongue. "How can that be? I *devoured* you."

"Not enough of me, fortunately." She clattered forward on the spidery ambulators of her mechno-chair. The red light of a holographic projection illuminated the rest of her body—or what remained of it. Of her four limbs, three were stumps. The single arm she did possess was short and small, with three clawed digits on a tiny hand. An adult Trandoshan would have been able to regenerate lost limbs, so she must have lost hers as a juvenile, before she'd developed her full regenerative capabilities.

Her presence—her existence—unsettled Bossk. His father had always told him he'd consumed all the other eggs, but Cradossk was also an inveterate liar. Why should Bossk have believed this story when Cradossk had repeatedly deceived him throughout his life? How many times had Cradossk given Bossk false leads to push Bossk off a trail so he could bag the bounty for himself? Bossk shouldn't allow one instance of paternal pride to cloud his judgment. The most accomplished hunters accepted reality—that's how they caught their prey. Perhaps his sister's egg had been the last in the nest he'd pecked, after he'd gorged on the others and his fetal hunger had been sated. He could have left just enough of her to grow and survive like this.

"If you are who you say you are, then you should be grateful to me for your life," he said.

She scoffed at the suggestion. "I thank the Wookiees."

It took him a moment to realize her answer was not in jest. "The *Wookiees*?"

"The Wookiees," she repeated. "Kind old Liswarr'arindoo, who couldn't have a cub of her own, exchanged a bottle of Kowakian rum for my puny cracked egg, and saved me and suckled me and raised me like a daughter in her clan. She even gave me a name, since I was never given one by those who conceived me. Doshanalawook I am called."

"Doshanala—" Bossk laughed again, unable to finish saying the ridiculous name. "I might've left you a body and an arm, but I must've nibbled much of your brain. Everyone in the galaxy knows those brutes don't raise 'Doshan hatchlings. They eat our eggs for dessert."

She stared at him without blinking. "Have you ever seen a Wookiee eat a Trandoshan egg?"

Bossk hadn't, but that was beside the point. "I know they find them more delicious than those rancid wasaka berries."

"A lie. Like all the other lies Trandoshans tell about them. Distortions and fabrications to incite a war between our species. Excuses so you can commit genocide."

"Jilt me a jagganath—you really did drink their milk, didn't you?"

"I merely speak the truth and work to rescue those who rescued me."

As if to lend legitimacy to her lies, a cloud of an all-too-familiar clan-stink wafted over Bossk. Unlike when he'd smelled it in the ship's corridor, on the bridge here it was so potent he nearly gagged. "You," he said and gasped, "you were with Chewbacca's kind."

"For many years. His father, the wise Attichitcuk himself, mentored me."

Bossk wasn't one who often had doubts or misgivings. Life for him was easy, and he liked it that way. It was hunt or be hunted, shoot first, and never, *never* ask questions. Yet now his head was full of questions—questions about his father and his supposed sister, questions about his place in all this mess. He found himself in a state he rarely experienced. He was totally and utterly confused.

Regaining his breath, Bossk suppressed his bewilderment and reverted to what always worked for him. He stepped toward her, rifle out. Whether she was really his sister or whether she was telling him truths or half-truths, he wasn't going to indulge her treasonous fancies any longer. "Make this easy, for both of us. Put this ship on a course to Asteroid X342 in the outer ring."

"I already have."

"What?"

"I thought you would want a ride back to your vessel," she said.

"How do you know where I hid my . . ." A beep interrupted him.

"Your chrono," she said.

Bossk glanced at his wrist. The timer had zeroed. The fact that at this moment Chainbreaker wasn't looking for the Imperial ship meant one thing. "You knew I'd be here."

"I did. I wanted to meet you, and this seemed like the best opportunity."

"The Wookiee prison transport—"

"Appears on the timetable you sent, but not on the hundreds of other schedules and reports I receive," she said. "A good trick, I'll admit, better than anyone else who's tried to stop me. But I've played this game for far too long to fall for something like that."

Bossk eyed the consoles and projections around her. "Hundreds of schedules?"

"Sometimes thousands. It's hard to keep track." She gestured at her surroundings with her small hand. "Go. See for yourself."

While keeping his Relby trained on her, Bossk toured the bridge, glancing at the monitors, screens, and holographic maps. Most of the consoles tracked Wookiee outlaws like Maromaka, Tossonnu, and Wullffwarro, who were part of the clandestine network that ferried fugitive Wookiees to freedom. All big names, all big bounties.

"This is impressive."

"I'll tell Rutallaroo," she said. "He built most of it."

Bossk snuffed. "Won't be building much more after the beatdown I gave him."

A projection table near the center caught Bossk's notice. He walked over to examine miniature holograms of himself and his ship rotating above the table. "So you keep tabs on me too."

"I watch all those who threaten the cause."

"Hate to break it to you, but aiding Wookiees is no great cause— it's treason of the worst kind."

"According to you," she said.

"According to any Trandoshan," Bossk said, but he didn't press the argument, so astonished was he by what he saw on the projector console. It displayed not only a log of his recent whereabouts, but a comprehensive personal history as well. There was record of him joining a Rodian posse on Goroth Prime, assisting a Quor'sav narcotics agent on Uaua, silencing the Mad Monks of Xo, collecting bounties on Taldorrah, Lothal, and the Silver Moon of Acomber, and even a reference to that disastrous incident on Gandolo IV.

He slitted his eyes at his sister. "How do you know all this? Did you put a homing beacon on my ship?"

"Please, brother, that's not my way," she said. "Let's just say I have my sources."

Bossk discovered a potential source in the console data when he opened a cache of messages, all addressed to him. "You're intercepting my private communications!"

"I intercept everything," she said.

"That's impossible—the *Hound's Tooth* has an ex-four transceiver with the latest encryption codes, the model used on Star Destroyers."

"Who do you think designed it for the Empire?"

Bossk snarled, wanting never to hear Rutallaroo's name uttered again. But if Chainbreaker had obtained all his communications, could it be possible that she had intercepted the most recent message he'd received and blocked its full reception?

He activated playback of the last message in the cache. A hologram of an Imperial naval officer replaced Bossk's above the projection table. "This is for the bounty hunter Bossk of Trandosha. I am Lieutenant Masil Veit, communications officer on the Star Destroyer *Executor,* and am contacting you based on the recommendation of your guild—"

Chainbreaker flipped toggles on her mechno-chair and the hologram vanished.

Bossk banged on the console screen to resume the message, but the playback controls wouldn't reappear. "Why'd you do that? Replay the message!"

She gave him a sharp-toothed smile. "Only if you do me a favor."

"I don't do favors," he snapped, nearly setting his Relby to kill and pulling the trigger right then and there. But he knew if he did, not only would he lose the massive bounty for capturing her alive, but he might also never hear the rest of the message.

"Then call it a trade."

"I think you've forgotten who's in charge here."

"No need to get testy," she said. "We're family, remember?"

Bossk was done with her games. Striding to within a meter of her chair, he flipped the lever of his Relby to its most painful setting—the slow burn. "I don't care who you claim to be. For all I know, you've concocted your story from all this intel you've gathered about me.

Sister or not, if you don't replay that message, I'll make you and everyone on this ship feel what this weapon can do. Even the juveniles."

She met his stare without a blink. "You're as sensitive as a Saurin, Bossk. But because I want you to see the truth, I'll let you reconsider your threat."

Bossk instinctively pivoted toward the entrance even before he heard the *thump-thump*s amid the whir of machinery. He couldn't see out the doorway from his vantage point, but Wookiee footfalls were unmistakable to his ears.

He flipped the lever again on his Relby and fired a short burst at the blast door controls. The box melted, the blast doors started to close, and then stopped as a flight of ryyk throwing spikes whizzed through the doorway, spinning for Bossk's head. He ducked behind Chainbreaker's mechno-chair, and the spikes buried themselves in consoles behind him, shattering monitors and scopes.

"Now before this becomes nasty, everyone hold their fire," Chainbreaker ordered. "You, too, Bossk."

"That's not how this works," Bossk said. But when he lifted his head above the chair and saw what was arrayed against him, he heeded her advice.

The Wookiees he'd fought minutes before and thought incapacitated swept onto the bridge. There was the female who had thrown the hydrospanner, the tenacious branch-swinging runt and blade-wielding twins, the muscular yellowstripe and pair of browncoats with the plasma torch and flail, and finally Rutallaroo, his claws retracted but his lunatic grin wider than before. In place of their previous weapons, all were armed with bowcasters—cocked and aimed at Bossk.

"Gut my gizzard," Bossk muttered. It was a stretch that Rutallaroo might be resistant to stun bolts, but all of them? "My shots would've knocked out a ronto!"

"My friends endured far worse treatment under the Imperials than what you delivered," said Chainbreaker.

Bossk wedged the muzzle of his rifle into her skull. "Even waggle a paw on those triggers," he said, knowing any Wookiee worth its pelt understood Dosh, "and she's brainmush."

The fugitives growled, but Chainbreaker was the one to speak. "You do know I'm the only one who can replay the message."

Bossk surveyed the bridge and his assailants, assessing how he could shoot his way out. If he slithered from console to console, using them as cover, he might be able to neutralize most of the Wookiees. But all they needed was for one of their quarrels to explode in his vicinity. And since there were eight of them and only one of him, the chances of dodging that many bowcaster bolts seemed nil.

"This 'favor' you mentioned," he said to Chainbreaker. "What is it? You want someone captured? Killed?"

She turned her head slightly so one mischievous orange eye peered up at him. "Spoken like a true Trandoshan."

"That's what I am. That's what *you* are."

"I've never said I was anything but." Her three claws clicked on the arm of her mechno-chair. "My favor is simple. I want you to promise to stop what you're doing."

"Stop what?"

"Stop hunting Wookiees."

Bossk's laughter came involuntarily this time, a convulsion of hisses, snuffs, and croaks. "You can't be serious," he said, between snorts. "You want me, of all beings, to quit?"

"I'm not suggesting you change your career. I'm only requesting you end your pursuit of Wookiee bounties."

"That's like asking a Trandoshan to stop shedding his scales," he said, trying to recover some composure.

"I haven't shed my scales in years," she said.

"No wonder you smell so bad."

She ignored his barb. "The galaxy is replete with bounties for criminals, swindlers, and murderers. Why not choose to hunt them instead of Wookiees?"

"Trandoshans hunt Wookiees. Even you know that. It's the way things are."

"But it's not the way things have to be, especially when it's based on lies. We can change it."

"I'm not changing, I can tell you that."

"Really?" She arched an eye ridge at him. "Maybe I was wrong about you. Maybe you're too afraid."

"Afraid? Of what?"

"Going after those other bounties."

Anger stifled the last convulsion of his laughter. "My bounties go far beyond your filthy Wookiees. I collected on the Gibbering Gran of Gibraal—"

"Respected by no one, least of all the Gran themselves."

"Durgaagoo, Ploovo's right-hand thug—"

"But not Two-For-One himself."

"The masked monarch of Qotile, whose title *I* assumed—"

"Meaningless, unless you want to rule over a desolate wasteland."

It took all his will not to pull the trigger. "Insults won't convince me."

Chainbreaker's voice remained steady and calm, as it had during their entire conversation. "And I mean no insult, but these are low-lifes compared with the bounties you should be going after. You're primarily known for catching Wookiees, yet given your exceptional skills, you could become more than that, a hunter of great renown."

"I *am* a hunter of great renown, more talented than that Mandalorian pretender or that walking human bandage Dengar—"

"And you can rise even higher than them, if you pledge to forgo hunting Wookiees and instead go after bigger prizes."

Bossk looked at the fugitives, the sneers on their mugs, their bow-casters primed. He glanced down at Chainbreaker, whose head was tilted so that her beady orange eyes, so much like his own, continued to focus on him. Maybe she really was his sister. He couldn't deny his senses. Yet, her offer seemed too preposterous to be plausible. Did she really believe he wouldn't break his promise once he was out of this situation? Surely someone like her would know that a Trandoshan's word was worth little more than the breath from which it was rasped.

"You have the full message from the Imperials, not some partial intercept?" he asked.

She nodded. "I blocked the end of the transmission to guarantee you weren't distracted and came aboard."

"So let me see it."

"Will you take my pledge?"

"Will you let me get back to my ship?"

"What good would your promise be if I didn't allow you to honor it? Do not worry, you will be released unharmed," she said.

He scratched a toe-claw along the wroshyr floor. She was trying to trick him, he just couldn't figure out how. But under the present circumstances he saw saw no other alternative to her proposal.

"Fine," he snarled.

"You promise to stop hunting Wookiees?"

He snarled again, making his assent inaudible.

Her calm voice turned forceful. "Say it."

Bossk coiled his tongue in contempt. His toe-claw dug so deep into the floor it chipped, and pain coursed through his foot. He grunted.

"Say it," Chainbreaker repeated. "I want these Wookiees to hear it."

He let out a breath and looked at his feet, not dignifying the Wookiees with his gaze. "I . . . promise." He spit out the last word.

"Very good. You will help make a new galaxy, Bossk," she said, sounding almost optimistic, a rare tone for a Trandoshan. "As agreed, I will play the full message—"

"Just the very end." He wanted to get the coordinates and leave this odious ship as soon as possible.

She flipped more toggles on the arm of her mechno-chair, and the lieutenant's hologram reappeared over the projection table. "The rendezvous site is at eight-four-two-point-three in the Anoat system," Veit said. "Be aboard in seven Imperial standard hours from the timestamp of this message. We will see you there." The hologram vanished once again.

Bossk knew the Anoat system was a short jump from the Rycep asteroid belt. If he went back to the *Hound's Tooth* now, he could push its hyperdrive and make the appointed time with a bit of luck.

"Before you go, take this." Chainbreaker manipulated the keypad on the arm of her mechno-chair, and a datacube popped out of a slot. "It contains the full message and some other information."

He snatched the cube with his free hand. "Other information?"

"Evidence that proves how baseless claims and outright lies have divided our species for centuries," she said.

"Propaganda. Conspiracies."

"Take a look at it for yourself and you can decide," she said. "But ask yourself why we must forever be at each other's throats. Reconciliation between Wookiees and Trandoshans is possible."

"Whatever you say 'sister'." Bossk shoved the datacube into a belt pouch and then carefully walked away from Chainbreaker, continuing to hold his rifle in a firing position. The Wookiees continued to do the same with their bowcasters, but they parted to the side as he approached the doorway.

Halfway to the exit, he turned back to Chainbreaker, sensing he was missing something. He had to know what it was, what trick she was playing on him. And while honesty was always the least of his inclinations, right now it felt appropriate.

"The job in the message," he said. "You know who the Empire wants me to catch?"

Chainbreaker nodded, seated as he had first found her, a specter in the electronic light of holograms and glowing consoles. "Is there any better test than to preclude you from going after the one you perceive to be your nemesis?"

Bossk eyed the bowcasters aimed at him. "And what if I fail your test? What if I break this inane promise and pursue Chewbacca or another Wookiee?"

"You will be hunted down like no other quarry in the galaxy and suffer a wrath unlike anything you can conceive," she said. "But that won't happen. I have faith you will keep your word. We must trust each other if there is ever to be reconciliation. And I trust you."

"Why? Why would you ever trust me? You know what I am."

"Of course I do." Her orange eyes blinked at him. "You're my brother."

As his jetpack took him through the outer asteroid ring, Bossk shivered in his vac suit. He was cold, colder than he'd ever been, and needed his body temperature to rise else he might lose consciousness. But he couldn't stop thinking of what had just happened. He couldn't stop thinking of his sister, if that was who she truly was, and why he was suddenly a part of her strange agenda.

"Doshanalawook," he said, over and over, to keep himself awake. He wanted to despise her, but couldn't muster the hate. And he didn't know why. He was still confused.

When he made it to the air lock of the *Hound's Tooth,* he grabbed the hatch-hold and looked back to where the *Liswarr* had been. There was only the void of space, without even the scatter-light trace of a ship having just jumped to hyperspace.

Maybe he'd been stricken with a spell of space fever. Maybe he had imagined the encounter just like he had imagined his hatching day from the lies his father had told.

Or maybe the galaxy was indeed changing, and he was swept up in it.

Bossk grunted and entered through the hatch. His blood began to boil as his thoughts mercifully returned to Chewbacca.

STET!

Daniel José Older

Hey Parazeen—looking forward to reading this! I must admit I had some concerns when you volunteered for this assignment, as I know your grandfather Mozeen has had some, er, *complicated* dealings with the primary subjects, but as you pointed out (numerous times), you've been interning for a while now and it's high time for your first byline. Anyway, you know this is an important article for several reasons, so I'm sure you'll apply yourself as fully to this as you have to supplying the office with caf and yummy treats. I'll just jump right in! Comments will be in the margins.

—TK-7, Chief Editor Droid,
Galactic Digest, Culture Desk

DANIEL JOSÉ OLDER

TWO "HIGHLY RESPECTABLE" GENTLEMEN OF "UNIMPEACHABLE CHARACTER" ASK FOR YOUR MONEY FOR A VAGUE BUT "UNQUESTIONABLY GOOD" CAUSE

By Parazeen Parapa of the Parapa Cartel

It's the beginning of the graveyard shift at Freerago's Satellite Diner—just past midnight, Hosnian Prime time—and inside, customers laugh and gossip as they munch on delicious and greasy tidbits from across the galaxy. Outside, though, I stand beneath the hundred billion stars and ponder how one can feel so small and so gigantic all at once.

"It is I, Zuckuss!" a voice shouts from the docking bay. I spin around, see the famed bounty hunters Zuckuss and 4-LOM approach. Correction: *former* bounty hunters. The press release that was sent along with a sizable donation to our magazine headquarters described them as "compassionate entrepreneurs and charitable donation barons" who have "repented and reformed from their complicated but understandable past behaviors."

~~I'm sure all the people they've murdered are feeling so relieved!~~

"You're the Parapa kid, no?" Zuckuss asks, shoving his gigantic insectoid face and thickly mucused respirator all up into my personal space.

"It is he and he is it," 4-LOM confirms in

302

TK-7: Might be me but...this headline seems a tad sarcastic. Maybe if we take out the quotes it'll come across as more genuine! Thanks!

TK-7: I know family connections are super important to your people, but perhaps it's better not to draw attention with this particular nomenclature.

TK-7: Wow! Super evocative and poetic way to open! I do wonder, though, what this has to do with the subjects at hand.

TK-7: Probably better to remove the quotation marks from here as well! Thanks!
TK-7: As well as any reference to the press release! Thanks! Or any sum of money that may or may not have been received by this publication! Thanks!

that ~~vapid~~ mechanical drone. "Or at least, *it* is the registered equipment and outfit of the youngest heir to the Parapa Cartel, yes."

They both look a little nervous: Zuckuss squints and scowls, his thick fingers twiddling around each other endlessly. 4-LOM rocks back and forth. I suppose they were expecting a tiny Frizznoth, barely reaching their ankles. But in my mech suit, I'm the same height as them and every bit as formidable.

Or maybe they look at me and see my grandfather, and all the chaos and destruction he has reaped on their ~~pathetic miniscule~~ lives.

"Zuckuss is so looking forward to speaking with you about our charitable venture," Zuckuss says, and I'm pleased that my rolling eyes are hidden beneath these layers of steel and wiring. "And my associate 4-LOM is as well."

The droid lets out a noncommittal grunt.

"Yes," I say. "I have some questions about where the donations you're requesting will be going, exactly."

"Snarz!" 4-LOM exclaims suddenly, and I wonder if I've already unnerved them into revealing something. He's glaring at the doorway of the diner, though, where a tall, sharply angled creature stands in a makeshift booth that says WEAPONS CONFISCATION in various languages. "When did Freerago's crack down on arms?"

Zuckuss snorts. "You really haven't been here

303

TK-7: Will have to check with the legal department to make sure we can print this word. After I check what it means.

in a while, huh?" He hands over his long-nosed GRS-1 snare rifle and motions to 4-LOM to do the same.

"Patrons kept murdering each other," the bouncer grumbles, his claw out to the droid. "Blaster."

"They still do," Zuckuss half whispers.

4-LOM shrugs, turning in his targeting blaster. "My whole body is a weapon anyway."

"Well then your whole body can't come into Freerago's," the bouncer says flatly.

Zuckuss chortles. "Now, now, the good droid was simply making a mild humorous remark at Zuckuss's expense."

The bouncer cocks a hairy eyebrow at all of us. "Who's Zuckuss?"

There's an uncomfortable pause. Then I turn over my own weapon, a Magalor seven-caliber roto-snipe 500, and go ahead in. ~~(FULL DISCLOSURE: Like 4-LOM, my whole body is also a weapon if you count the mech suit and also I am trained in several different martial arts from around the galaxy.)~~

Freerago's Satellite Diner is alive with laughing Rodians, gossiping Ithorians, a single very morose-looking Hutt with various bodyguards positioned around the place, and a cluster of hairy little grease-stained Bonbraks who've probably just gone on break from the repair garage next door. I do love this place.

"So," I say, sliding into the booth after Zuckuss, "you've given up bounty hunting and you're entering the field of philanthropy." I pointedly place my recorder device on the table, red recording light glaring.

"Given up bounty hunting for good!" Zuckuss insists, slamming both hands for emphasis.

Across from us, 4-LOM stares emptily at the raucous patrons.

"And what brought about such a sudden change in careers?"

"I mean!" The Gand motions around vaguely, mutters something unintelligible.

"I'm sorry?"

"He received a message from the Void," 4-LOM says. "Remember, Zuckuss?"

Zuckuss jolts. "Ah yes! As a practitioner of the ancient findsman tradition, Zuckuss is highly tuned in to the quiet inner stirrings of the galaxy, ah-hmmmmm!"

"Why are you humming?" I ask.

"It is how Zuckuss tunes in to the galaxy-mmmmmmm!"

4-LOM shakes his head, his attention once again on the restaurant around us. "Is that Pratkak the Sver? I thought he was dead."

"Was it also a quiet inner stirring of the galaxy that led you to become a bounty hunter in the first place?"

"Mmmmmmm . . ." Zuckuss hums, perhaps stalling for time.

"What'll it be, young fellas?" a wizened old

Dug asks, loping over to our table on his long leglike arms. His nametag says BEEZNUSA, and he looks like he's seen his share of excitement. The fur is still singed around his one missing eye, and glowing star map tattoos sparkle from the long-toed feet he uses to wipe down our table.

TK-7: Evocative details!

"Nothing for me," 4-LOM says glumly.

"Do you have rehydrated Mistiflax?" Zuckuss asks.

"Huh? No, man," Beeznusa snorts. "That stuff is . . ." He eyes Zuckuss for a moment, seems to reconsider what he was going to say. "It's hard to keep fresh."

"Mmmmrrrrrrr just a caf for Zuckuss. Lots of cream."

I order a caf, too, black and sweet, and the waiter is turning to head off when a loud voice cuts in from the doorway. "And a blue milk for me, budzo!" We all glance over to see a human with exceptionally shiny teeth and an overly assertive tan line fastwalking toward the table. His brown hair has been gelled into a sharp triangle. "Hold the foam, aha! Extra shot of sulfur, thanks!" He looks quite pleased with himself. The Dug nods and ambles off.

"Not to worry, friends," the guy says, looming over us all like an obnoxious fake-tanned embodiment of a garbage disposal in a cheap suit, "I got the bill, aha!"

"Who is he?" I ask Zuckuss.

The Gand shrugs. "Vap Tomulus."_____

"He is responsible for crafting our message to the masses," 4-LOM adds.

Vap slides in next to him. "Can I sit? Thanks great okay! And you must be the young Parapa boy I hear so much about. Fabulous, fabulous, I love it. And I love that you've taken to journalism! Way to go against the family legacy, am I right? I know a little something about that myself, actually, going against family legacies, hey—but that's a whole other story, really."

I just look at him, the glowing red eyes on my mech suit inscrutable.

"Good, great," Vap warbles. "Fantastic. Anyway, don't mind me, I'm just here to keep an eye on my clients and make sure they get a fair tail shake, if you take my meaning, aha!" He smiles, and it's all teeth, like the man's whole head just became a giant shining mouth.

"You were just going to explain where all the donations are going," I prod.

"Oh, yes, yes," Zuckuss says. "Well, since Zuckuss and his compatriots are no longer engaged in the illicit business of bounty hunting—"

"Which we can neither confirm nor deny any of us were ever involved in," Vap puts in. Everyone ignores him.

"As part of our new entrepreneurial endeavor, we have set up a fund to help the orphaned children of Korbatal"—here Zuckuss

TK-7: Oh! I have worked with this Vap Tomulus several times. I believe it is he who sent us the press release leading to this article. He's always very courteous and friendly in his messages. Sometimes a little more than is necessary.

shakes his head mournfully—"a small moon in the Trymant system that has been very sadly destroyed."

A quick database search indicates that Korbatal was indeed destroyed along with several other moons in the Trymant system . . . two centuries ago in one of the Emergences related to the Great Hyperspace Disaster.

"Those poor orphan children must be very old," I say tonelessly. "How sad."

"Mmmmmmmm," Zuckuss drones.

"The thing is," Vap cuts in, "the foundation hopes to help poor orphaned children from ruined planets all over the galaxy! There are so many, you know."

~~"Like Alderaan?" I suggest, and the table goes suddenly quiet.~~

Quick jabs ~~about politically uncomfortable genocides~~ aside, though, the story here is that these fellows are clearly not as on the level as they'd have the galaxy believe. Unfortunately, while that is apparent to anyone paying an iota of attention, there is no actual story here until these facts can be proven.

"One caf, dark and sweet," the grizzled waiter says, plopping a tray of drinks down. "One caf with extra cream for Zuckuss, and blue milk, no foam, double shot of sulfur for the loud weirdo."

We all stare at each other for a moment.

"Anything else?" Beeznusa asks.

"The point is," Vap says, pointedly ignoring

TK-7: Oh no! What a terrible tragedy! I had not heard. Very thoughtful of them to dedicate themselves to such a noble endeavor!

TK-7: Oh.

him, "we're here to do AHHHHHHH!!" His explanation becomes a guttural scream as a shining blade sweeps down from behind me. The edge slices a smooth chunk of flesh off his shoulder and thick black blood squirts all over 4-LOM, who yelps, lunging to the side.

TK-7: Oh dear!

"Ah useless and beasteesh pile of-ah execremento!" a familiar voice hollers as two powerful mechanized legs clomp down on our table. Caf and blue milk fly everywhere as people all around gasp. It is a voice I have heard all my life, a voice that used to sing me to sleep when I was a just a tiny Frizzpup, a voice that means home to me.

TK-7: It is our publication's policy to italicize all non-Basic languages, including whatever this is.

"Mozeen Parapa!" Zuckuss yelps, searching his robes for the blaster he deposited at the door. "How did you find us!?"

TK-7: Wait . . .

309

FULL DISCLOSURE: Every Frizznoth mech suit is equipped with a cloaked binary beacon device that alerts any member of their respective cartels to their exact location. This is well-known information among our people and was not concealed at any time.

TK-7: This seems problematic. I'll have to check with legal. Let's delete for now.

"Nevarr mindah that!" ~~Grandpa~~ Mozeen yells triumphantly. *"My peapohl chaave abeena escouring theeah galaxzee fora you!"*

"Honorable Mozeen," Vap whines, "you have to understand, I am in the process of raising the money to reimburse you! It's complicated!"

TK-7: Okay, you know what—no one can understand this. I'll go ahead and take the liberty of translating your grandfather's garbled gibberish into regular Basic for our readers for the rest of his statements. You're welcome!

"Mmmmmmmmm!" Zuckuss moans. 4-LOM has both hands up; his gaze scans the startled patrons, looking, perhaps, for someone to help. No one does.

In truth: This turn of events, while exciting, may well ruin the story I am working on. I sit perfectly still, which is easy to do in a mech suit, and let it all play out. What else can I do? But I feel the larger truth I've been searching for slipping away ~~like so many grains of desert sand.~~

TK-7: Calm down.

"I am not here about the uncut Argazdan diamonds you stole from us," my grandfather says. Zuckuss and 4-LOM exchange a glance as my own eyebrows rise to the top of my head. "Although," the old man adds, "that did help us track you down."

TK-7: Oh, interestingly, there was a single Argazdan diamond included in the memo we received about this assignment! I placed it in the charitable donations, and that's where it will stay!

"You didn't mention you used stolen Argazdan diamonds as seed money for our venture," 4-LOM points out.

"And you didn't share any with Zuckuss," Zuckuss adds.

Various customers are creeping their way toward us, I realize. One of the Ithorians. A Zabrak who had been dining alone. Someone in a full-body armor suit with a limp who was waiting for takeout when we arrived. These must be Vap's people, probably waiting for some signal of what to do.

"I'm not here about the diamonds!" ~~Grandpa~~ Mozeen snarls in the voice that means violence is about to erupt. "I came about the massacre on Suba Tren."

A clatter erupts from the kitchen, and then

a huge Gamorrean storms out, snarling and spluttering. That would be Freerago.

"I didn't murder those Frizznoths on purpose!" Vap pleads.

"Then I, in turn, won't murder you on purpose," ~~Grandpa~~ Mozeen says.

"*No bloodshed in Freerago's!*" Freerago roars.

"Not to worry," ~~Grandpa~~ Mozeen chortles, "this won't take long." Then with a single swipe he lops off Vap Tomulus's head, which lands with a thunk and a splish on the wet table. "Oops."

TK-7: *Oh dear!!*

"Grandpa!" I yell.

The visor whirs up from ~~Grandpa~~ Mozeen's mech suit, and his pleased little face winks down at me. "How are you, my boy?"

"Betrayal!" 4-LOM yells, letting off a volley of laser blasts from a tiny TYX blaster he must've concealed from the bouncer. Most go wide—he's still trying to extricate himself out of the seat over Vap's headless corpse—but a few glance off my mech suit.

"*Barabarabara kikataaaa!*" someone yells at the far end of Freerago's, but I can't make out who. More blasterfire flings toward us from the doorway as the group of burly Ithorians pull out clubs and start whacking away at anyone nearby.

"Get down!" ~~Grandpa~~ Mozeen yells, but he doesn't get down; instead he kicks Zuckuss in the face and then leaps off the table into the

311

knot of grappling bodies. Zuckuss spins and drops with a wheeze. Something wet is dripping onto my mech suit. Something red, I realize, following the shiny puddle to Vap's torso, which has collapsed onto the tabletop.

That's the moment when the world seems to catch up to me. Everything had been so quiet up till then, so loud and so quiet, like all the yells and thumps and laserfire voided each other, became a blur of white noise that meant nothing, everything and nothing.

This is when, normally, I would jump in and make sure the old man is all right. But in truth, the old man is very much all right and clearly in no need of backup at the moment. Plus, I'm supposed to be here as a journalist, not part of the chaos. And anyway, now more of my cartel members have joined the fray; they must've been waiting just outside the diner. There's Beebatee, a cousin I grew up with, and Zafeen, who told me she was in love with me as we hid beneath the stairs at Mar Kalapa's compound. They clomp between the tables in their shiny mech suits, running interference as ~~Grandpa~~ Mozeen fights through a throng of what I assume to be Vap's crew.

Each thump and blast is crisp now. I've lost track of my primary subjects, 4-LOM and Zuckuss. I can't make sense of the fighting, but I can feel the internal sway of it, the momentum that carries it along the edge of the diner and directly toward . . . me.

"Down I said!" ~~Grandpa~~ Mozeen yells again, and finally I throw myself under the table just as the Dug who had brought our drinks pops out from behind a counter with a massive blaster cannon gripped in each foot. The guy looks like he's been waiting his whole life to unleash fiery death on two dozen customers.

"I warned you fools," Freerago mutters, jumping for cover.

Fwajoom! Fwajoom! Fwajoom! Fwajoom! Beeznusa's lasers thunder out, shattering glass and sending everyone into a frantic dive for the floor.

"You know, Parazeen," my grandfather says as he crawls under the table beside me, "we are all very very proud of you." He slides open the face guard on his helmet, and I do the same.

"Grandpa," I say. *"Pleaseah don't do athees. Notta now."*

> TK-7: Oh gosh—not you too!? But you've spoken such perfect Basic throughout this article! Alas, I shall go ahead and fix up all of your statements as well. You're welcome!

"Bah! I do what I want." He waves me off. "We have never had a journalist in the family!"

I sigh. I've lost my subjects and everything is a mess.

"What's a matter, Para?" Zafeen snorts, shoving Vap's legs aside so she can fit under the table with us. "Are you mad we jacked up your big story?" She slides in beside me and pops open her visor so I can see her smirk, and I can't lie, it gets my pulse up, remembering all that we almost had, all we may still become.

> TK-7: Oh my!

"No," I lie, but it crumbles immediately when their chuckles erupt on either side of me.

"Okay, a little, yes! I was onto something big! This was my first break with the *Digest*."

More fighting breaks out overhead, and ~~Grandpa~~ Mozeen says, "Ah yes, the publication where ~~they have been wasting your talents and leaving you to fester and mold, bringing them caf while~~ they write ~~boring puffy garbage~~ about how wonderful the Empire is, hm?"

"That's the one."

"What is the heart of the story you are trying to tell?" Zafeen asks, and she's not smirking anymore, she means it.

"It's about how there are different kinds of criminals," I say, realizing the truth as I speak, "and while the galaxy just sees lawlessness as one big bad thing, the truth is, there are gangsters like Zuckuss and 4-LOM, who prey on the helpless and hunt down freedom fighters for cash to uphold this ~~vile~~ regime."

"Grr," ~~Grandpa~~ Mozeen growls.

"And there are gangsters like . . ." My voice trails off as I glance between the open gazes of my lifelong friend and my beloved grandfather. ". . . like us," I finish, and then I bask for a moment in both of their smiles. "We Parapas may not follow the law, we may not be the most diplomatic or compassionate, no, but we hate the Empire, and we have a code."

"Well," my grandfather says, with love in his eyes, "then you better get moving."

I follow his gaze to where Zuckuss and

4-LOM creep on hands and knees toward the door.

"But I . . ." My voice trails off as I realize what the old man means, what I have to do.

"We will watch your suit, hm?"

I nod as the suit powers down around me. Then I hop out and make my way quickly across the carnage-strewn floor.

The whole world is a sweaty, stuffy cacophony of nastiness. I can barely breathe, and at any moment I might be discovered and killed.

Still . . . *This,* this is *it.* This is the true fieldwork, the hard-core journalistic unstoppable ferocity that I have been waiting for so long to release on the world! This is what I was born for. ~~Grandpa~~ Mozeen, Zafeen, and Beebatee are one kind of warrior, it is true. But I have found my own kind of warrior-ship, my own fire, and sure, sometimes it involves sneaking aboard an Imperial Star Destroyer while hidden in the stinking folds of a notorious Gand's cloak, but it is a fire nonetheless.

315

TK-7: I . . . I have just gotten word that someone has sliced into our main server and published this story! As is! With all my comments!! What's going on, Parazeen!?

From somewhere nearby, I hear a deep breathy voice. It is muffled, reaching through all this fabric and armor, but it is unmistakable. And most important, it's loud enough to register on my recording device. "There will be a substantial reward for the one who finds the *Millennium Falcon,*" Darth Vader says. "You can use any means necessary, but I want them alive." There's an awkward pause. "No disinte-grations."

I hear Zuckuss let out a raspy, excited sigh. And I smile. _____ TK-7: *Call the office right now*

WAIT FOR IT

Zoraida Córdova

Boba Fett had many skills, but only a single virtue. Patience wasn't it.

After being summoned by Darth Vader with the lure of a new bounty, Fett made the impossible decision to drop everything he was doing, and that included a job. He didn't want anyone to think he was going soft, that he couldn't handle a mark, no matter how small. The bounty in question was a squirmy little Sullustan with floppy jowls who'd broken a contract with Jabba the Hutt. The galaxy was lousy with idiots. But where there was an idiot, there was a case of credits Fett could collect.

Or he would have if the holo of Vader's likeness hadn't come through with instructions that sounded more like an order. He didn't take orders from nobody, but he knew better than to say no to the Sith Lord. Not that he was scared of him, or anything. Not exactly. But Lord Huff and Puff was preferable as an ally rather than an enemy. And so Fett tossed his job to a rookie on Jabba's payroll wanting to make a name for himself. No one could say ol' Fett didn't throw a dog a bone from time to time.

As he waited for the coordinates in the quiet of his ship, Fett caught sight of his reflection. He had the passing thought that he needed to shave, when his sensors lit up with a transmission. He set his course and hauled *Slave I* to—*an asteroid field.* Barely dodged a hunk of rock hurtling at his cockpit. Nothing he couldn't handle, but a heads-up would've been appreciated. After transmitting his clearance code, he docked in the *Executor*'s hangar bay only to be instructed to wait. *Wait.* He could have delivered his bounty to Jabba, maybe even pounded a cold brew at Chalmun's, and still been here with time to spare.

Fett took a deep breath, ran a hand across the buzzed scruff of his hair, then secured his helmet, checked his blaster, and disembarked. Vader's Star Dreadnought was pretty impressive, he'd admit to that. Sleek and metallic in a way that made the murder of docked bounty hunters' ships look like a Jawa scrap heap. Stormtroopers and clusters of Imperial officers moved quickly. He caught several sneers lobbed his way. Even heard his name whispered on the lips of a pinch-faced redhead. *Boba Fett.*

He got the feeling his presence wasn't welcome, and neither were the other five hunters milling about. He nodded at Bossk and Dengar. The other three looked familiar, but most hunters blurred together in his mind. Two droids and a Gand with a circular respirator that looked like it would make the perfect bull's-eye. Boba Fett said nothing, he simply *waited* with the others.

"Boba," Bossk hissed in greeting.

How many times was he supposed to tell the old Trandoshan that it was *Fett* or *Boba Fett*. He wasn't no little kid anymore. Sure, they had history. Probably would be the closest thing he had to a friend, if he'd actually wanted a friend.

Before Fett could reply, one of the black-clad officers marched over. "You lot. Follow me."

You lot. Were they threatened Vader'd brought them in to do their jobs for them? Boba Fett scoffed. Typical Imperials.

The sentinel and protocol droids-turned-bounty-hunters clipped at the officer's heels, and he followed along the bright corridors, the clank of metal and stomp of their boots beating a steady rhythm.

On his left, he could smell Dengar before he sidled up beside him, resting his Valken-38 blaster rifle against his chest. The guy practically spent half his credits buying this rare Felucian incense that clung to that dusty scarf he wore all the time. Back when they'd worked jobs together, Fett had never seen the Corellian do laundry. Not that hygiene came with the territory. Fett rubbed at a crusty brown spot on his gauntlet and didn't guess at what the substance might have been.

"Any idea *what* the job is?" Dengar asked. His voice was huskier than Fett recalled.

He looked up and down the corridors. Officers hurried this way and that. He could feel the slightest tilt, like the *Executor* was making a hard turn in pursuit of something. Someone.

"Bet you twenty credits it's the *Millennium Falcon*."

"I'll take that action." Dengar grinned.

Bossk grumbled, falling into step beside them. "I dropped another score for this. It'll be worth it when I add that Wookiee's pelt to my collection."

"The Empire wants them," Dengar mused, "Jabba wants them.

How'd a scumrat like Solo wind up with the most wanted ship in the galaxy?"

"Between him and the Wookiee they've got half a brain to have joined up with the Rebellion," said Bossk.

Dengar shrugged. "Can't figure out how they keep getting away in that scrap heap of a ship."

"Lucky is all," Fett assured them. But his gut told him that there was more to this chase. That had always been Bossk and Dengar's mistake. They went *after* their marks, but they never got inside their heads. There were rebels scattered all over the place, waiting, regrouping. Vader was obsessed with that ship and the crew aboard it. He remembered the last job he'd worked for the Sith Lord, hunting down the pilot that had blown up the Death Star into a million worthless pieces. Then they'd met on the scalding dunes of Tatooine, the air thick with scorched Tusken Raider. Fett had never seen someone bask in a kill the same way. He considered himself a blast 'em and leave 'em kind of hunter, but Vader—Vader was something else. He was living breathing vengeance. Fett had done one thing right. He'd gathered a name—Skywalker—and then he'd gotten out. He'd heard of what Darth Vader did when he was disappointed. But that name had bought Fett a few more years. Perhaps he'd been just as lucky as the rebel scum.

The Imperial officer leading the bounty hunters glanced back, unable to rid the sneer from his pale freckled face. If he looked at Fett like that one more time, he'd make that ugly mug permanent.

A series of turns down halls that were so identical, it was like the entire ship was designed to make you feel like there was no way out.

Finally, they were deposited at the bridge. They filed in across the walkway, and guess what? They *waited* some more. Boba Fett watched the commotion of men in black uniforms, each one paler and more terrified than the next. From the tension in the air, it was clear that someone had recently failed at their job, and it was all hands on deck.

"Wait here," the officer told them, then turned on his heel and ran off. Sure, sure. Where the blazing dewbacks were they supposed to go? Help the junior officers learn how to press the GO button? Work on their typing skills?

Fett sized up the other hunters. The assassin droid was an IG model with red blinking photoreceptors for eyes. Then there was a rusty protocol droid that looked like it had given itself a new head. The Gand male kept close to the droid's side; long tubes attached to his face gave off the scent of ammonia. Looked barely capable of tying his own boot.

This was what Vader was working with? He wasn't sure if he should feel confident or insulted to be counted among them.

It was then that Boba Fett felt the shift on the bridge. The way every button-pusher hunched over screens, gathered to watch the beacons of TIE fighters blink as they returned to the flagship. Vader was coming.

His pressurized breath was the loudest sound on the walkway, as every officer focused on a task. *Yeah, go and look busy to not draw attention to yourselves, ya cowards.*

Vader stood in front of Dengar and then the assassin droid, like he was taking their measure. It was impossible to know what Vader thought or felt. Did he even feel anything other than rage? Maybe Fett could relate to that. How many times had he been taunted at some cantina or outpost to take off his helmet? "Look me in the face, Boba Fett. Not so brave without your little mask on." The fear of anonymity was, well, delightful.

Then he heard it. Didn't they realize their little pit echoed their voices? Some son of a Hutt saying, "*Bounty hunters*, we don't need their scum." Yeah, well, if the Empire didn't need bounty hunters, then why was the guild loaded with Imperial credits? Why did *Vader* need their help when a starship, a ganking *Dreadnought* full of toy soldiers, couldn't do the job Boba Fett could do?

321

That familiar spark of anger shot up through his entire body. Bossk muttered something in his native Dosh as Vader kept walking, his cape swishing at his back like a shadow.

"There will be a substantial reward for the one who finds the *Millennium Falcon*. You are free to use any methods necessary," he said, and Boba Fett felt a quirk at his lips. Then it vanished as Vader stopped in front of him. "But I want them alive." He jabbed a finger in Fett's direction. "*No* disintegrations."

"As you wish," Fett replied. What else was he supposed to say? You fry a couple of heads once, *purely* by accident, and people will never let you forget.

Of *course* it was the *Millennium Falcon*.

Dengar surreptitiously handed over twenty credits while Bossk snarled, like he could already smell Chewbacca. The anticipation lasted only for a moment before an Imperial officer announced the ship had been found. "So much for that," Dengar murmured.

Boba Fett gave a single shake of his head. "Don't worry. Solo's harder to catch than a rock worrt. We ain't done yet, boys."

They made their way back to the hangar bay with the help of a different Imperial runt who jumped at every ion cannon blast. Officers were black, trembling blurs. Boba Fett considered that the Empire, for all their resources and training, might have a better time tracking down their rebels if their cadets weren't driven by a palpable fear.

But what did he know? Boba Fett was only a bounty hunter, and there wasn't much he was afraid of.

Back at the hangar, the protocol droid and the Gand boarded their ship and took off. But the assassin droid hung back at the open ramp of its ship like a sentinel. What was it waiting for? An invitation to pursue?

Still, Boba Fett could admit his best course of action was to remain aboard the *Executor* and close to Vader while the *Avenger* gave chase. If Solo had come out of that asteroid field he'd either make the jump to lightspeed or get reeled in. Either way, he needed to know. While the Imperial cadets kept busy and TIE fighter pilots tinkered with their ships waiting to be deployed, Fett leaned against a stack of crates.

"You don't look like you're in a hurry," Dengar noted, adjusting the weight of his blaster rifle.

Bossk narrowed his reptilian eyes. "What's going on in that spiky little head of yours?"

Fett fought the urge to run his hand across his cropped hair, a tic he'd had since he was a kid with long hair. Good thing his helmet saved him the trouble.

"Solo might be an idiot," Fett said. "But he's not risking his ship. One Corellian freighter against these monsters? Yeah, right. Something's wrong."

Bossk growled at the back of his throat. "If you know Solo so well then why haven't you brought him in. Losing your touch, Boba?"

"Parasites like him are good at hiding is all," Fett shrugged. Losing his touch? He'd show Bossk. He'd show everyone.

Dengar smirked, pronouncing the many wrinkles on his aged face. "Maybe we should team up again. Like old times. Three minds are better than Solo's."

"Krayt's Claw lives again," Bossk said, a sarcastic edge to his voice.

Boba Fett turned his face to where Bossk's ship, the *Hound's Tooth*, was docked. He'd spent years aboard that vessel, chasing down bounties and hauling cargo from one end of the galaxy to the next.

"Forget it," Bossk said. "*Boba Fett* works alone."

"Can you blame me?" Fett said. "After the Corellian job?"

The three of them grimaced at the same time at the chaos of the memory. It wasn't the first time one of their jobs had gone south. Every failure of his life made him work all the harder. Fett needed answers? He'd beat them out of someone. Fett needed a job done? He'd do it himself. It didn't matter who got in the way. Not Dengar. Not Bossk.

323

"I've tried the whole gang thing," Fett said, waving a hand dismissively. "Never works to my advantage."

"We had some good runs," Bossk reminded him.

They had. One look at the Trandoshan was enough to recall that there was once a time when Fett wasn't the ruthless bounty hunter that made a cantina full of villagers soil themselves. Once, he was a kid running jobs across the Outer Rim. Once, he was in prison picking fights for whoever told him to. And then there was Bossk, who towered over him, a great reptilian guardian, who said, "You got a problem with Boba, you got a problem with me." Once, he'd needed help.

Fett watched as a ruddy-faced officer who didn't look old enough to shave ran to his comrades. "Captain Needa is dead! I saw—He—"

The boy could barely get the words out. Someone had failed and died because the *Millennium Falcon* got away. Again. But for Boba Fett? This was another opportunity. As the flurry of action in the hangar intensified, an idea tugged at his mind.

Dengar whistled. "Right again, Boba."

"What now?" Bossk asked. "Maybe . . . Krayt's Claw can ride again. Like you said, I've tried to bring in Solo before and failed. The Empire underestimates him. And perhaps so have I. But I've tailed him long enough that I know his patterns. I think I know where he's going."

Bossk eyed him with those big orange pupils. He traded a less-than-surreptitious glance with Dengar. "You have our attention."

He turned to what was left of his former gang. No one ever knew what happened to Latts Razzi. Dengar and Bossk, they were rough as Batuuan spires, but somewhere hidden deep in their minds, they still saw Fett not for what he was, but for who he had been. Little Boba angry at the world. Angry at everything and everyone who got in his way. A scrawny orphan who shared a face with a million others. The boy who swung his fists until either he or his opponent was bloodied and bruised. A man who learned that the only person he could trust in the galaxy was himself because now, after all this time, he was the only reminder that his father had ever existed. That he was probably older than his father would ever get to *be*. They thought they knew him. But did they? Did they know that there was a reason Boba Fett always got his mark? There was a reason why there was a trail of bodies in his wake? Because he held on to that anger. He nurtured it like cinders in a growing flame. He taught his anger to aim, to speak, to be the scream that he would never finish. Because every target was and would always be the Jedi who got away—the man who murdered his father.

So yeah, Boba Fett works alone. He would always work alone.

He hurried to his ship, punched in the coordinates and sent them to the *Hound's Tooth* and *Punishing One*. Then, he loaded a series of decoy coordinates, a move Bossk had once taught him. He could never be too careful, and he had to act quickly.

Fett saw the stretch of starlight signaling his entry into hyperspace. There one minute and then gone the next. He waited for a breath, then jumped back to the asteroid field where he'd started. Only this time, he was on the other side of it, just in time to watch the Imperial fleet break up. The *Avenger* loomed ahead, and he flew close.

Because he knew people. He always got his bounty. One thing he hadn't lied about. He *was* beginning to understand Solo. Enough to know the smuggler would never risk his precious ship. No one could fight against that amount of power. But they could outlast it if left behind.

He savored the heady rush that came with locking in on his mark, of knowing he was right. The *Millennium Falcon* hadn't gone anywhere.

Now all Boba Fett had to do was wait.

STANDARD IMPERIAL PROCEDURE
Sarwat Chadda

"**S**ee the stars! Travel the length and breadth of the galaxy! Visit worlds others only dream of! Wear the proud uniform of the Imperial Navy! Join today!"

Ashon scowled as he collected his tray and joined the queue for the mess. "Why don't they switch that rubbish off? We're living in the guts of a Star Destroyer. The navy's already got us for the long haul."

"Huh, it's on a loop. No one's bothered to change it." Colm jerked his big thumb to the flickering hologram above them. "It'll be the Organa Cast next. Here it comes . . ."

"Wanted! Leia Organa! Known terrorist leader of the so-called Rebel Alliance! Any information regarding her or her known conspirators should be passed immediately to your local Imperial hub. The Empire counts on your vigilance! Your loyalty!"

Peet sighed loudly. "Can you believe the bounty on her? Just some pen-pushing senator who thinks she can run the galaxy better than the Emperor!"

Ashon glanced over the meager offerings. Slop today, just like yesterday. "Not just any senator, but a senator from Alderaan. You heard about Alderaan, right?"

Peet and Colm fell silent. Colm tugged at his collar, as if his uniform was suddenly too tight to breathe in. Peet's eyes darted this way and that, checking no one was too near. "I heard, Boss. *Everyone* heard. Don't mean what happened happened the way people say it happened."

Ashon paused along the queue to look back at his crew. Peet and Colm couldn't have been more different, but each made up for the other, you needed that. Peet was small, with nimble fingers and quick, sometimes too quick, while Colm plodded happily alongside, using those meaty arms of his for the bigger jobs. Slow and steady, but sometimes too slow. Still, they were all he had.

The holocast droned on, turning to the smuggler Han Solo and his ship, a YT-1300 light freighter called the *Millennium Falcon*. Ashon's attention lingered on the image for a few moments. Solo might be a hotshot pilot but he had the soul of an engineer; there were some interesting modifications on the ship. Then came his Wookiee copilot. Were they that big a threat to the Empire? He shook his head. Such decisions were way above his pay grade. He spooned a lump of orgo-protein onto his plate. It sat there, gray and glistening with oil. He'd eaten mynock steak once for a bet. He'd spent the night in the head, guts churning. Now he wished he'd saved a piece.

Peet picked up a bowl of jelly, smacking his lips. "Ah, just like Mom used to make."

Ashon stared at the queue, the long line of enlisted men and women lined up for their daily dose of lab-manufactured nutrients. Soft, easily digested, foul. His gaze shifted across the mess to the officers dining.

A serving droid scooted among the tables, taking orders, delivering meals freshly cooked in the ship's galley. There were fluted jugs of Naboo wine. Steaming gundark steaks. His mouth watered.

There was nothing dividing the officers' area from that of the enlisted. No wall, no guards, just the high barriers of rank and privilege.

He dropped his tray.

Peet turned, suddenly anxious. "Boss? What are you doing?"

Ashon headed over to an empty table.

"Boss!"

The moment he sat down, a serving droid appeared at his shoulder. "Sir? Your order?"

Look at that. Proper durasteel cutlery. He picked up the glass, mesmerized by the way it refracted the harsh mess hall lights, spilling colors over the perfectly pressed, perfectly white tablecloth.

"Sir?"

There was no need to look at the menu, he knew it by heart. "Shaak steak. Well done. Give it plenty of spice and drown it in Chandrilan sauce. I mean a bucket of it. Got it?"

"Yes, sir." The chest panel lights flashed as it transmitted the order. "And to drink?"

To drink? When was the last time he'd had a proper drink? "The Naboo red. Bring the bottle."

The serving droid rolled off.

This was why he'd joined up. Power. Prestige. And a fat pension.

Time on board counted double, and he'd spent twenty years on the space lanes. There were fleet bonuses, too—the bigger the ship, the bigger the bonus—and he'd spent almost half his career on Star Destroyers like this one, *Avenger.*

Enough to buy a place, outright, maybe on a Core World. Get himself a ship or two. He had contacts all the way to the Outer Rim. Hire a few ex-Imperials to fly the routes and sit back and count the credits.

It would've been sweet.

It would have been, if he'd just followed the rules like a good little Imperial.

"You appear to be lost, friend. This is for officers only."

Look at them. Polished boots, pressed uniforms with the single, paltry Petty Officer stud. Fresh out of the academy and acting like they were grand admirals already. He bet they still got green whenever there was a hyperspace jump. He'd cleaned up after arrogant younglings like these often enough, when they'd emptied their stomachs all over the deck. He glowered at the one in the middle of the three, the one with the biggest grin. "Head of engineering is an officer rank."

"True, true." The man's eyes shone with amusement. "But you're not head of engineering, are you, Carl Ashon? Not since you trashed those TIE fighters."

"I did not *trash* anything." He'd explained himself over and again. And yet that was the story now, the official story. "I came up with a superior mainten—"

But they weren't interested. No one was.

"You're lucky Needa didn't send you to work the spice mines. Demoted all the way out of engineering into waste disposal, wasn't it?" He wrinkled his nose. "Yes, waste disposal."

What's the worst they could do? Send him to the brig, again? It was more familiar than his own cramped bunk. It's not like they could cut his pension by any more. Twenty years on the space lanes, twenty loyal years, and what did he have to show for it? To bow and scrape beneath these upstart, tailored younglings?

"Go join your rabble over on that side." The officer put a hand on his shoulder. "Now."

Ashon glowered. "Remove your hand."

"Or what, old man?"

A few days in the brig. It would be worth it, just to teach these three a lesson or two. Let them take the rest of his pension away. He wouldn't miss it. Ashon tightened his fists . . .

"Boss! Boss!"

Peet barged through the three officers, and they reeled away as if he might stain their uniforms with a speck of dirt. Colm came up beside him, tapping his datapad. "We got a call."

Ashon stood up slowly. Both his men stood either side of him. They were good men; they were all he had. "What?"

"Coolant spill on Dock—" Colm scanned the datapad. "—Eleven. Some ship's blown its life-support systems, and they need a mop-up quick."

"Ship? What ship?"

Colm turned the datapad toward him. "A Firespray."

Firespray? What was that doing on a Star Destroyer? The Navy didn't use them. "Designation?"

Colm tapped the top of the screen. "Here you go."

Slave I.

"Vader's recruiting bounty hunters?" asked Peet. "He must be desperate."

"Will you shut it?" snapped Colm as they made their way along one of the countless maintenance tunnels that wove through the Star Destroyer *Avenger* like arteries. "He might hear you."

"Hear me? He's way out on the *Executor*. He's as likely to hear me as he is . . ." Peet faltered. ". . . as he is . . ." He pulled at his collar.

Colm rushed beside him as he tottered against the wall. "Peet? Peet?"

He was turning red, the muscles of his neck stiff as he choked. He clawed at his collar, his eyes wild with fear.

"Peet!" What could he do? They all knew Vader . . .

Peet's eyes rolled back and . . . he laughed. "Your faces!"

Colm punched his arm. "You're an idiot. Boss, tell him."

"One day, Peet, you're going to go too far," said Ashon, then returned his gaze to the datapad. The Firespray belonged to one of the bounty hunters, a guy called Boba Fett. Strange name. Where was he from? Probably some blasterslinger from the Outer Rim, just this side of the law. Was this what the navy had been reduced to? Hiring the dregs of the galaxy?

He read the deck officer's brief report. The ship, along with the other bounty hunters, had left the *Executor*. The ships had made their jumps, but the Firespray had dropped out almost immediately, hailing the *Avenger*. Fett had reported a leak and so been given permission to dock.

Most likely sabotage by one of the other bounty hunters. That scum didn't play fair.

They detoured off the main passage to the branch leading to the docking bay. Ashon swiped his ID and the access door hissed open.

"What kept you?"

The deck officer practically pounced on them as they emerged into the cavernous docking bay. She stabbed Ashon's chest with her finger. "We're in pre-jump and we've got *that* sitting smack in the middle of the bay!"

Sure enough, there was the Firespray, the coolant puddle all over the floor, steadily evaporating.

Peet scratched his stubbly chin. "Pre-jump? No one told us."

She looked at him as if she'd found him stuck on the sole of her shiny black boots. "Who cares? You're waste disposal."

Ashon pushed her finger aside. "Standard Imperial procedure is that all divisions be alerted for pre-jump. We've checks of our own. The disposal bay doors need to be—"

She was already leaving. "Deal with that Firespray right now."

Ashon turned to Peet and Colm. "You guys head back. I want you to run through the protocols. And Peet . . ."

"Yeah, boss?"

"I want it by the book. Got it?"

He groaned. "Really? It's like the lady said. Who cares?"

That was it, he'd had enough. Ashon's patience snapped and he jabbed Peet hard. "You want to break procedure, Peet? Be my guest. Then we'll see where you end up. You think waste disposal is as low as you can go? You'd be surprised."

"Sorry, Boss, I didn't mean it—"

But he wasn't finished. Peet needed reminding. "I was head of engineering, Peet. Remember that? On a Star Destroyer. You don't get a better berth. Then I just break procedure once, once, and look where I am now. So how are you going to do it?"

"By the book, Boss." At least Peet had the decency not to meet him in the eye. Ashon turned to Colm.

Colm's big head bobbed up and down. "You can count on me."

"I'd better be able to." Ashon gestured back the way they'd come. "Get started."

Slave I squatted within the center of the bay, with the squadrons of TIEs suspended high above, row upon row, like nesting mynocks. The smell of the coolant made his eyes water. Above the control cabin was a chrono, counting down to the jump. He could already feel the vast engines of the Star Destroyer rumbling through his feet. Forty minutes.

He caught the deck officer glaring at him. She wanted the Firespray gone. Non-military craft were not usually permitted aboard during the jump through hyperspace. Officially it was cited as a safety issue. In reality it was cost. The Empire didn't give free trips across the galaxy.

Ashon stopped at the base of the hall and spoke into the outside intercomm. "Anyone there?"

The intercom crackled. Nothing but static.

He tried again. "Your coolant's spilling all over the floor. I'm going to get it cleaned up, but I need you to shut down the life-support system first. Or maybe I could have a look? It's usually the magnetic coupling on the refill. A quick fix and you can be on your way."

No reply. Was it empty?

The deck officer stomped over. "Well?"

"Where's the pilot?" Ashon asked. "I need access inside and I might be able to fix it. It won't take more than—"

She held up her hand. "Not interested. Get this junk off my deck. Now."

"Where am I meant to take him?"

She looked him up and down, making no effort to hide her contempt. "Where do you think?"

334

He could have had it towed out of the docking bay and just let it float away. That would have been the easy, simple thing to do. But it wasn't standard Imperial procedure. What if it floated into the path of a jump? Boooom.

Ashon sat in the control room's big chair, looking out over the bay. Peet, Colm, and the maintenance droids were busy dismantling one of the TIE wrecks dragged out of the asteroid field. Despite the Empire's near-endless resources, it was standard procedure to salvage any still-operational equipment, lest it fall into rebel hands. The power panels on the TIEs were valuable; the squadrons went through them at a horrific rate, so replacements were always in high demand.

Thirty minutes till the jump.

Ashon looked out of the bay.

Tractor beams used energy, vast amounts of energy. For minor jobs, like picking debris out of space or moving large equipment from ship to ship, they used tug-bots. Small but powerful, a pair had collected the Firespray and brought it around to waste disposal. Now it sat there among the rest of the debris, ready to be dumped safely out of the ship before they jump into hyperspace.

Boba Fett. He'd checked up on him. If anyone could track down Organa and her followers, it was this guy. The Mandalorian armor was decorated, if that was the right word, with custom weaponry and tokens of his conquests. That blaster made Ashon's semidormant engineering cells itch to get it out on the workbench.

This Fett knows his business. So where is he?

One thing was for sure, he wasn't with his ship. In less than half an hour it was going out the door with the rest of the space junk. Ashon continued through his pre-jump checklist. Three hundred and twelve items, leading up to hitting Big Red, the door release button. He knew them by heart but still ticked them off. Ashon tested the backup power. It read 30 PERCENT instead of the required 60.

335

Peet. Typical. The guy just has no pride in his work.

Ashon activated one of the maintenance droids parked by the side of the bay. "Get outside and have a look."

The droid sprang to life and darted through one of the outer hatches.

Ashon switched on the relay screen, seeing what the droid was seeing. Sure, he could leave the repairs to the droid's own protocols, but he still had his pride. He'd been head of engineering once. He knew every millimeter of the—

"Hold up. Pan ninety left."

What was that? A landing claw?

Something had parked itself on the back of the *Avenger.*

Definitely not Sienar. The design looked Corellian.

A YT-1300 transport.

It can't be.

Ashon licked his lips. "Pan up. Slowly."

It looked like a piece of junk. Exposed systems seemingly welded on at random; oversized power couplings that should shake a ship that size apart. But as a feat of engineering, it was something beautiful. They'd risked the whole fleet chasing it through an asteroid field.

The *Millennium Falcon.*

Go inform the deck officer.

That was his first thought; it was standard Imperial procedure. She'd send it up the ladder to the captain, to the admiral, to Vader himself.

Then what? What would be the reward for capturing the greatest prize in the Empire? The admiral would get a promotion. The captain a bigger ship to command. An extra stud for the deck officer. But for him, right at the bottom? He'd be lucky if he even got a mention, let alone a bonus. Get his pension reinstated? Never.

Maybe there was another way. He flipped on the intercom. "Peet. Come in."

"Yeah, boss?"

"I . . . I just got a call." He swallowed. This was it. Twenty years of loyal service, of following standard Imperial procedure, had gotten him . . . what? Callused hands, a bad back, and a meager pension that meant he'd be working till he dropped. "You're in charge. I'll see you later."

"I get to hit Big Red?" said Peet, excitedly.

Ashon glanced at the door release button on the control console. "All yours."

He smiled to himself. What was that bounty on the rebels? Ten *million* for the senator. He would retire tonight. All he needed was to find—

A hand reached over his shoulder and switched off the relay screen. The image of the *Falcon* blinked, and the screen turned blank.

Ashon spun around.

Boba Fett stood over him, thumbs hooked into his belt. "So you found her too."

He wasn't big. The battle-scarred armor was a generation out of date, yet he wore it with comfortable ease.

But this was *Ashon's* domain. He was in charge here. "I was just going to find you." He stood up, straightening his overalls. He cleared his throat, which had suddenly become dry. "We can make a deal. For the *Falcon*."

Fett tilted his head but said nothing.

Ashon cleared his throat again. "Split the bounty for Organa and the rest. I'd be happy with forty percent."

"Forty?"

Ashon forced himself to stand still. "I should report this up the chain of command. Sixty percent of something's better than a hundred percent of nothing."

Fett drummed his fingers upon his belt, then gave the smallest nod. "Sixty–forty, then."

More than his pension ever could have been, even if he'd flown the lanes a hundred years. All for an hour's work.

Fett turned his attention toward the bay. "You'd better have a word with your men. They're about to ruin our deal."

"What?" Ashon turned. What did he mean? Colm was working on one of the TIEs, and Peet was just leaving the wrecked Lamda-class shuttle he'd spent the last day stripping out. "They're not doing—"

Fett's arm locked around Ashon's throat. There was no give in the iron-hard muscles; Ashon's fingers just scraped across the smooth metal of the helmet, unable to grab anything. He thrashed side-to-side, but Fett's grip only tightened. Blood pounded hot in Ashon's temples as his vision darkened and his strength faded . . .

337

A deep, dull thrumming stirred Ashon back from the fringes of unconsciousness. He groaned as he forced himself awake. His throat was raw and sore, and he blinked repeatedly to clear his vision.

Where was he?

Head still throbbing, he took a few moments to make sense of his surroundings. He had been dumped in a cockpit. The seats were gone and the controls stripped down to loose wiring and circuitry dangling from the console. The viewport was shattered and semi-opaque, but not so opaque he couldn't see *Slave I,* only meters away.

I'm in the Lambda shuttle.

Ashon leapt to the door but the handle had been dismantled. He pushed, first with his hands, then with his shoulder. It didn't budge a millimeter. Fett must have jammed it from the outside.

He threw his arm across his eyes as the cockpit was flooded with red light.

The klaxon screamed. "Sixty seconds to door release. All staff to clear the bay. Sixty seconds till door . . ."

Colm scurried past, followed by two maintenance droids lumbering under the weight of a salvaged power panel off one of the TIE wrecks.

"Colm! Here! Here!" Ashon hammered his fists against the canopy. "Colm!"

No good. He couldn't hear him over the klaxon. Moments later, Colm climbed up into the control room overlooking the bay. Peet was already sitting in the big chair, waiting to slam Big Red.

"Thirty seconds to door release . . ."

Come on, come on. There has to be a way out of this.

A tremor ran through the ship as the gravity controls went offline. The smaller items began to float off the floor.

He scanned the control console, what was left of it. Standard Imperial procedure was to dismantle anything that could be recycled and reused; the Empire's war machine was huge, and salvaging was a big part of their duties. But he'd tasked Peet to strip out the Lambda . . .

The comms. Maybe they were intact. Peet never bothered stripping them out, they were too fiddly and took too long. Peet wasn't one to make an effort if it could be avoided. It was why he'd missed promotion after promotion.

"Twenty seconds till door release . . ."

Okay, okay. You've got this.

Ashon ran his fingers along the cables, nimbly reconnecting them to the meager backup power, praying there was just enough juice left in the system for him to contact the control room and get his boys to slam on the emergency lockdown and get him out.

The lights on the panel flickered to life.

The bay filled with a thunderous rumbling as the vast doors began opening. The warning lights were full, constant red. Life systems were off, and he was meters from open, deep space. The Lambda began to float as the last of the gravity controls were switched off.

"Bay doors open."

From the corner of his eye he saw Fett in his cockpit, adjusting his harness as *Slave I* drifted toward the opening.

Ignore him. Get the comms working.

Ashon hooked his feet under the panel to stop floating off. Sparks jumped from the wiring and the lights flickered feebly. He just needed enough for one transmission . . .

"Control room, come in. Peet, Colm, can you hear me? Come in, control room. It's Ashon! I'm trapped in the Lambda! Come in, control room!"

The shuttle juddered as it bumped against the smaller trash, a discarded droid. The TIE wreckage was disappearing into the open void of deep space.

Ashon dialed up his transmitter. The wiring smoldered, filling the cockpit with the stench of melting metal. "Control room! Come in!"

"See the stars . . ."

It worked. Ashon released an exhausted sigh. It worked. He just needed to find the right frequency and—

"See . . . the . . ."

"Seeeee . . ."

The speakers crackled, hissed . . . and died.

No. No. No . . .

The control panel lights dimmed, one after the other. Peet *had* followed the procedure after all. He'd stripped out the entire system, leaving only residual power, now spent. Any other time and Ashon would have cheered. He'd taught Peet well.

Ashon's tears floated like tiny raindrops in the gravity-free cockpit. The shuttle trembled gently as it passed through the bay doors, free at last, rotating amid the star-sprinkled vastness. The rectangle of light that was the opening to waste disposal was already shrinking as he drifted farther and farther away.

He watched the *Millennium Falcon* detach itself and join the free-floating trash, and *Slave I* follow.

He counted down, imagining himself sitting in the big chair, watching all the trash clear out of the bay. He knew the drill better than anyone. Exactly thirty seconds later and the bay doors closed, the rectangle becoming a slot, then becoming nothing. The engines of the *Avenger* flared into brutal life and a moment later leapt into hyperspace.

All standard Imperial procedure.

Twenty years on the space lanes. Twenty years of seeing the stars, just like the Imperial Navy had promised. And now he'd be among them, forever.

340

THERE IS ALWAYS ANOTHER

Mackenzi Lee

I had hoped that dying would be enough to untangle me from the Skywalker family's Issues.

And yet here I am again, Obi-Wan Kenobi, one with the Force and still the only thing standing between a Skywalker and an impulse decision that could have galactic consequences.

Tatooine had, by no means, been a glamorous locale for exile, though I had no choice but to settle myself near Luke's new guardians. Yoda, however, with an entire galaxy at his fingertips, had been so determined to make a meal of his martyrdom that he chose Dagobah as his refuge, the only planet that smells worse than the Jedi Temple training rooms after a combat class with fourteen-year-olds.

The Jedi Order may have died out, but their dedication to posturing theatrics is alive and well in Master Yoda. I had never questioned any of it when I lived in the Temple—the robes and the ceremony and the rituals and the endless rules that had been carved into me so deeply and at such a young age that I sometimes couldn't discern what I actually believed in and what had simply been told to me over and over before I was old enough to understand what any of it meant. I had only had to think about touching Siri Tachi's hand under the table at midday meal to feel as though I deserved a punishment handed down from the Council. Qui-Gon had tried to nudge me off that straight and narrow, encouraging an embrace of the spirit of the Code rather than the literal interpretation of it, but his relaxed attitude had only made me more determined to be the Good Jedi, the one keeping his Master in line, though I knew it should have been the other way around. I'd never had a real chance to figure out what sort of Jedi—let alone what sort of Master—I wanted to be without him before this nine-year-old prodigy no one wanted was thrust upon me, an entire other life suddenly and totally dependent on me, and my life recalibrated around being the man this scrappy hothead needed so he could fulfill his destiny.

No time to decide what kind of man I was when I was entirely occupied trying to keep a child alive and trained and convinced that, yes, everyone was thrilled to have him among us, no matter the rough start he'd had with the Council, and, yes, Mace Windu scowled at everyone like that, though he did seem to have a particular frown he reserved just for Anakin. My insomniac nights fretting over my trials and whether Qui-Gon would somehow get himself kicked out of the Order before he could finish teaching me were replaced by my jolting awake in the middle of the night thinking, Anakin probably doesn't know how to swim; I have to teach him how to swim. How do you teach someone to swim?

342

That's what almost twenty years in the desert will do to a man—it gives you too much time for agonizing self-reflection, dismantling the systemic rituals and ingrained thought patterns that led you to playing an inadvertent yet critical role in the establishment of the Galactic Empire, and the painful task of forgiving yourself and everyone else, releasing all hope for a better past.

Death is good for that, too—it gives you perspective. And far too much time to think.

But death is better than Dagobah, I think, as the swamp world crystallizes around me. I'm shocked Luke stayed this long. If it were Anakin sent here, with minimal instructions delivered to him by a ghost, only to see his ship swallowed by a sinkhole, Yoda cracking his droid on the dome, then deeming him unteachable before they'd had a chance to talk about anything beyond Yoda's terrible cooking, he would have been grinding his teeth in that way that used to drive me mad. All that plus the low ceilings, the perpetual damp, and snakes in places they had no business being—the moment the rain started, Anakin would have stormed out of the hut loudly reciting an itemized list of frustrations to no one in particular. If he'd been unable to get his X-wing out of the swamp, I have no doubt Anakin would have found a way to walk off the planet.

But Luke had stayed. And Master Yoda had taught him. And I had only to appear to Yoda in half a dozen of his dreams to convince him that Luke was not Anakin, and this time would be different. We are all better than we had been then. Or, not better, but at least we knew what not to do when it comes to training Chosen Ones.

Speaking of Chosen Ones.

Through the swampy mist rising off the soil, I see Luke throwing supplies into the cargo bay of his X-wing, hasty and disorganized, shouting over his shoulder at Yoda. I seem to have arrived mid-rant, and though Luke has yet to notice me, I doubt my presence would

343

have done much to quell his passion. Anakin never held his tongue around his elders. The Skywalkers are wildfires, their passions scorching the dirt as soon as they're given a spark. Even Leia was already well known for her ability to set the Empire on fire with nothing but a wet match. *Relentless* was the word Bail had most often used when he had sent me reports about her. Her mother would have been proud.

"They're my friends!" Luke darts nimbly along the edge of his X-wing to fiddle with the control panel in the cockpit. His orange flight suit looks garish amid the greens and browns of the swamp, a smudge of flame in the gloom. From his perch atop the ship, R2-D2 whistles his assent. Ever the instigator. "I've got to help them."

"You must not go!" Yoda replies. He's huddled on the ground beneath the nose of the X-wing, and though I have only ever known a stooped, slow-moving Yoda, somehow he seems even shakier on his feet than the last time I was here. He's leaning heavily on his gnarled cane, as it sinks into the mud, his posture the curled crook of a being who has become too accustomed to living in darkness.

"But Han and Leia will die if I don't!" Luke replies ferociously, dropping off the ladder of his starfighter. His boots squelch in a patch of oily ground, and a family of swamp slugs wriggle up from the soil and scatter as fast as slugs can hope to.

Since no one is pointing out the obvious flaw in that logic, I feel the need to finally intervene. "You don't know that," I say drily.

Luke doesn't look surprised as he turns to me—this isn't the first time I've had to make an appearance here to facilitate a group therapy session with him and Yoda. His hair has gotten longer since last I saw him, and it falls over the scars that have rearranged one side of his face since the wampa attack. I had hoped that death and time and oneness with the Force might take the edge off the strangeness of seeing Anakin's eyes in his son's face, but now, as they blaze with the same determination I saw so many times in life, it overwhelms me. I had spent years and years in that tiny sand cell on Tatooine, sweating and perpetually dehydrated and with nothing to do but relive everything I could have done differently and then slowly let each one go, trying to make peace with losing Anakin. But the shades of him in his son's face catapult me back in time, and all the years I spent by Anakin's side—fighting and teaching and laughing and arguing and nearly dying and saving each other over and over again—spill out across my mind. His stupid jokes. His bad posture. The way he never folded his tunics and forgot to put on socks. The wonder in his eyes the first time he saw the rain. His sideways smile, refusal to comb his hair or wake up on time, the way he picked the vegetables out of his meals, his aggravating habit of losing his lightsaber and staying up too late and the flush that crept up his neck when he was worked up, his mood betrayed by the high color in his cheeks.

And now here is his son looking at me with those same flushed cheeks, caring too much about everything, and both my life and death would be so much easier if the Skywalkers didn't care so damn much.

345

How different this galaxy would be if the Skywalkers didn't care so much.

It isn't about Anakin anymore, I remind myself, struggling to return to the present moment. It's about Luke, and not letting him make the same mistakes his father and I did. Why even in death must I chide myself to focus on now and here, like I'm a Padawan struggling to sit still for an entire meditation session, rather than losing myself in memories of Anakin?

"Even Yoda cannot see their fate," I say.

"But I can help them!" Luke protests. "I feel the Force!"

"But you cannot control it."

In his early days of training, Anakin had always been so tentative in speaking about the Force, like it was a word in a foreign language whose meaning he still wasn't entirely sure of. With Luke, there's no hesitation. Even though the concept was only introduced to him a few years earlier by a stranger he had previously believed to be a hermit gone half mad from sun exposure. Now, when he needs a reason to go, the Force is telling him exactly what to do, like it's a guidebook I'd been recommending to him for years but he's pretending he found all on his own. That's not how the Force works, I think, and resist the urge to rub my temples, a habit Anakin had always teased me about.

You're doing that thing again.

What thing?

The Anakin's-making-me-crazy thing. I can see him, twelve years old and sitting across from me in the cockpit of a ship, mimicking the gesture with a crooked smile, the picture of youth in rebellion, while I wondered if other Padawans got as much of a kick out of seeing their Masters get worked up as he did. Surely I had never annoyed Qui-Gon this much.

Luke turns away, shoving a hand through his hair. I look to Yoda with a silent plea to back me up, but he seems to have taken my arrival as an invitation to move into the backseat of this teaching moment. He's staring absently at Luke's X-wing, his eyes glassy. I sigh. It's hard to blame him. Nine hundred years is too long. It's enough time to see all the ways this galaxy is rotten, and Yoda has had to witness more than his share.

"This is a dangerous time for you," I say to Luke. "When you will be tempted by the dark side of the Force."

Yoda suddenly seems to remember that he's the only living authority figure here, and he pipes up, "Yes, yes. To Obi-Wan you listen. The cave! Remember your failure at the cave!"

I don't know what *the cave* refers to, but I don't ask. I don't need another reason to doubt Luke. I had always doubted Anakin, and he had felt that wobble in our foundation from the start. Add it to the list of mistakes I was trying not to make again.

"But I've learned so much since then!" Luke protests, and I resist the urge to snort. As though carrying Yoda on your shoulders and eating his terrible cooking for a few weeks makes you a Jedi. I had to do that for years before they let me hold a real lightsaber, and even then, they kept the safety on. "Master Yoda, I promise to return and finish what I've begun. You have my word."

Why did I come? I lost this fight before it even began. Anakin never learned how to back down from an argument, even if he had been definitively proved wrong. Why did I think Luke should be any different? And, on that subject, why couldn't Luke have taken after his mother? Better yet, why couldn't Padmé have been the Chosen One and Anakin a boy king on Naboo? That probably would have worked out better for the galaxy in the end. Padmé had the work ethic and focus that would have made her an excellent fulfillment of an age-old prophecy, not to mention she had likely never slept through a wake-up call. And then Anakin could have indulged in a fondness for strong drinks and the types of liaisons that the Jedi Order had overshot on repressing.

347

You can't keep a promise if you're dead, Luke, I want to say. And you'll be dead if you go because it is clear to everyone here but you that this is a trap, which I can't say because you're your father's stubborn son, and it will only make you want to argue more and, why is mentorship still so kriffing hard?

The Skywalkers don't listen. Every argument I ever had with Anakin, it felt like he was fighting with a version of me in his head rather than actually confronting the things I was saying, and, in turn, I was yelling at a wall. The Skywalkers could level planets with their obstinancy. Though Padmé was like that, too. I suppose this boy was doomed from the start, a stubborn streak in him running deep and true as the kyber heart of a star.

Instead, I say, "It is you and your abilities the Emperor wants," which is as close to the truth as I can creep without telling him who passed those abilities on to him. "That is why your friends are made to suffer."

"And that is why I have to go," Luke replies.

I blink several times, waiting for him to realize how little sense that argument makes.

He doesn't.

They never do.

Luke turns back to his X-wing, swinging the door to the cargo bay shut, and frustration wells inside me. It's a struggle to tamp it down. I am still a Jedi. I am still in control of myself, and my feelings, and my heart.

But I'd never had a hold on my own heart when it came to Anakin. That was part of his undoing.

"Luke," I call as he mounts the ladder leading to the cockpit of his X-wing. Desperation splits my voice. How is it I have dealt with this family for generations and still haven't figured out how to get through to them? "I don't want to lose you to the Emperor the way I lost . . ." I fumble. What I want to say is *Anakin*. What I want to say is *my best friend*. What I want to say is *your father*. The way we both lost him, I want to say. To a needless war. To a wild heart. To a doomed prophecy. Instead, I finish, "Vader."

Luke turns back to me, and there it is again, that wild glint in his eyes. There is Anakin. "You won't."

"Stopped they must be." Yoda is starting to sound frustrated, which is a testament to just how infuriating Luke is. Even Anakin rarely cracked Master Yoda—the only time I can remember is the incident with Tru Veld and the fireworks in the reflecting pond. "On

348

this all depends. Only a fully trained Jedi Knight with the Force as his ally will conquer Vader and his Emperor. If you end your training now, if you choose the quick and easy path, as Vader did, you will become an agent of evil."

I glance down at Yoda, resisting the urge to argue. A divided front won't do us any good in persuading Luke to listen, but I want to point out that Anakin's path was never easy. He'd been plopped at the bottom of an impossible mountain the day Qui-Gon brought him to Coruscant and asked him to climb it in the dark with his boots laced together. Yoda and the Council tried to force him into a mold he would never fit, and you can only be pushed and pulled and reformed so much before you break. Anakin had never asked for special treatment—almost never—maybe sometimes—usually when there was food involved—but the Council had refused to take their Chosen One as he was rather than try to make him into the Jedi that fit their prophecy. You never gave Anakin an easy path, I want to snap at him, you gave him obstacles no one else had to overcome. Any Jedi would have fallen.

349

I don't know why I am defending Anakin—even in my own head—especially after he killed me. Old habits.

Luke looks between us, his eyes suddenly pleading. He wants to go but, more than that, he wants us to tell him he's right. He's doing the right thing. The Skywalkers always want to do the right thing. It's what gets them every time.

All I say is, "Patience."

"And sacrifice Han and Leia?" Luke shoots back.

"If you honor what they fight for," Yoda replies. "Yes!"

Luke's face sets, and then he turns away from us. His hand is strangling the struts of the ladder leading up to the cockpit of his X-wing.

"If you choose to face Vader," I say, "you will do it alone. I cannot interfere."

I say it mostly in the hope it will scare him into staying. He's never truly fought alone before. He's never been alone before. He hardly knows Han and Leia—doesn't yet know who Leia is to him—and already his heart has put down deep roots. Just like his father. With Anakin, it was his mother, then Qui-Gon and me and Ahsoka and Padmé, childhood abandonment resulting in him clinging with white knuckles to whoever was nearest him. It had been him and Shmi against the galaxy for so long, then she was taken from him. Then he had Qui-Gon and me, the only familiar stars in the constellation of his new life.

And then just me.

The first year he was my Padawan, I would sometimes wake in the night and find him asleep on the floor next to my bed, afraid he'd wake and find me gone, too.

What kind of choice had that been for him, Qui-Gon? Leave your mother for a prophecy you've never heard of, to join an Order of legendary peacekeepers who arrive on your planet only to tell you that they aren't there to free you from the barbaric system you're part of? That the legendary justice of the Jedi is for others. There is no justice on Tatooine. He was the Chosen One without any choices of his own.

When, I think, will this inner peace I was promised in death finally show up?

Luke presses his forehead against the ladder, and I think for a moment I've scared him enough that he'll stay. But then he says quietly, "I understand." He turns back to us for just a moment, and there he is again, the dumb, beautiful son of my dumb, beautiful friend who could never be talked out of anything he set his mind to. Those last days on Coruscant rise in my mind, the memories I have sieved over and over again, searching for what I could have done to stop it all, and knowing the answer didn't lie in those final hours together. It was years in the making.

"Artoo," Luke calls as he mounts the ladder. "Fire up the converters."

R2 whistles a jaunty reply. I shoot him a look that says, *Don't you dare fire up those converters.* I'm not sure if the old droid can see me, but he gives another chirp that I swear means *Kriff off!*

"Luke," I call, one last attempt, but when he turns back to me, the words die in my throat. Everything I want to say to him suddenly feels hollow and untrue. The language of the Jedi that I had spouted for years, first to Anakin, now to his son. Where has it ever led me but down volcanic embankments and barren dunes? For every way the Council had broken Anakin down, I had stood by and let them. I had been their arbiter of justice, repeating the language they had given me.

Why didn't I fight for you? I think.

So instead, I offer the only advice I have. "Don't give in to hate. That leads to the dark side."

"Strong is Vader," Yoda adds. "Mind what you have learned. Save you it can."

Luke tugs the strap of his helmet into place. "I will," he says. "And I'll return. I promise."

If only those were the sort of promises we could keep, I think. The cockpit of the X-wing closes with a pneumatic hiss, and the swamp debris beneath it is blown aside as the engines fire. The starfighter lifts off, casting Yoda and me into darkness. The engines flare, and their red light bathes us.

"Told you, I did," Yoda murmurs, his face to the sky, and I wonder if he resents ghosts like me arriving without warning, or if the ghosts are what he lives for.

"Reckless is he. Now matters are worse."

"That boy is our last hope," I say, and in my voice I hear Mace Windu. I hear Qui-Gon. I hear Yoda. I hear every Jedi before me who brought us here, dead and desperate and up to our knees in a swamp.

But Yoda shakes his head. "No. There is another."

And it's a long, quiet moment between us before I remind myself it isn't Anakin. He's not here anymore. And neither am I.

FAKE IT TILL YOU MAKE IT

Cavan Scott

Heads turned as he passed. It was hardly surprising. The people of Cloud City knew style when they saw it. His cape billowed as he swaggered toward the baron administrator's office, the silk lining shimmering in the light from the station's panoramic windows. Yes, this is where he belonged, not the grimy backstreets of Nar Shaddaa or the gambling dens of Vandor-1. This was where he would make his home.

He turned the corner, winking at a beautiful Kessurian who was admiring his Tarelle-sel-weave shirt. He could feel her amber gaze lingering on his back as he continued on his way, his ronto-hide boots clicking on the polished synthstone floor. *That's it, baby,* he thought to himself, *take a looong look. One day you'll be able to tell your kids how you saw the galaxy's most eligible bachelor up close and personal. The stuff of legends.*

A courier droid tottered out of the office as he approached, a data slate tucked beneath its silver arm. He stood back to let it pass, firing off a friendly salute then sweeping through the door before it could close. Never forget the little people, that's what Vonzel had told him when he first started smuggling, especially the droids. It was a lesson he'd tried hard to remember, no matter what the situation. You never knew when you needed a droid in your corner.

The reception room was tastefully decorated with minimal furniture, a sweeping couch set beneath a screen showing the latest bulletin from the HoloNet. He glanced up at the display, seeing a spokesbeing for the InterGalactic Banking Clan dismissing rumors of a heist on Scipio. There wasn't a word of truth in them, she claimed; the vault was as impregnable today as it had always been. Then why did the ticker running beneath her say that the Imperial Security Bureau was in the Albarrio system looking for an IBC employee by the name of Manakor? Linked or not, it hardly mattered to him. Cloud City was an independent state, free of Imperial entanglements, just as he liked it.

He crossed the room, heading for a pair of frosted glass doors embossed with an elaborate seal. They opened smoothly as he approached to reveal a pale-skinned human wearing a flashing cybernetic headband.

"Lobot! Good to see you, buddy!"

The cyborg stepped forward, the doors sliding shut behind him.

"I'm sorry?" he said, narrowing his light-blue eyes. "Have we met?"

That took the wind out of his sails. "Have we met? Are you *kidding* me?"

The aide shook his head. "I assure you that I am not."

Unbelievable. After everything they'd been through together, over the years.

"Lobot . . . It's me . . . Jaxxon!"

The cyborg gave him a look so blank, it bordered on insulting.

"You really don't recognize me, do ya?" Jaxxon said, his whiskers drooping.

Lobot glanced at the logpad in his hands. "Do you have an appointment?"

"I do," Jaxxon said, seizing on the sudden reprieve as if it were a life pod. "It'll be in the diary. My secretary made it himself."

At least, Jaxxon hoped he had. He'd certainly told Mel to make the appointment, reminding the maintenance droid on three different occasions. That said, ML-08's memory chips weren't as reliable as they used to be. The last time they'd taken the *Rabbit's Foot* to Musca for repairs, the droid had trundled off in search of a cooler valve and immediately forgotten where the *Rabbit* was docked, let alone why they had come to the shipyards in the first place.

Lobot was still scanning the day's schedule, Jaxxon bobbed on his heels impatiently, his hands gripping his belt buckle to stop them from snatching the reader and finding his name himself.

"Tumperakki Haulage?" the cyborg finally inquired, looking quizzically at Jaxxon's green face.

Jax broke into a relieved grin. "Yeah, that's me. Jaxxon T. Tumperakki, the Haulage King of Coachelle Prime, at yer service."

"You're late," Lobot informed him brusquely. "The meeting was an hour ago."

"An hour?" Jax stammered, not quite believing what his long fuzzy ears were telling him. "That's not possible. Mel . . . I mean, my executive assistant definitely arranged it for eleven hundred hours on the dot."

Lobot pressed a button. "I have the communication from your droid right here. It says *ten* hundred hours and lists your name as Joxxon."

Joxxon? Well, wasn't that the straw that broke the bantha's back? As soon as he got back to the ship, that pathetic excuse for a utility unit was going out an air lock, whatever Vonzel had said back in the day. Remember the little people? Mel would be in little *pieces* when Jaxxon was finished with him.

Swallowing his frustration, Jaxxon slapped Lobot on the shoulder. "Well, me and Lando go back a long time. I'm sure he can fit an old pal into his busy schedule."

The cyborg didn't look convinced. Instead he showed Jaxxon the couch with its glitterglass table and pile of holomags, most of which showed Calrissian's oh-so-dashing face. "If you'd like to take a seat," Lobot said, "I'll see what I can do, but as you said, the baron administrator *is* a very busy man."

"I don't doubt it. And important, too, not to mention handsome. I've always admired his mustache."

Inside, Jaxxon was *dying*. Not to mention handsome? Always admired his mustache? What in the name of the Holy Hutch was he saying? Once again Vonzel's words bubbled up from his memory, a nugget of wisdom given when the old smuggler had taken Jaxxon under his wing: "The first rule of negotiation is to never look desperate, especially when you are."

Luckily, Lobot ignored Jaxxon's blushes and inquired if he could get him something to drink: "A carrot juice perhaps?"

A carrot juice? Of all the narrow-minded, bigoted things to say. Why not offer the Lepi a nice crisp lettuce while he was at it? Jaxxon wanted to tell Lobot where he could stick his carrots, but instead forced a rictus smile, reaching for the clasp at his neck. "I'm good, thanks, but you could take my cape if ya want?"

Before the cyborg could object, Jaxxon removed the cloak and swirled it into Lobot's face. The cyborg spluttered, suddenly smothered in the cheapest aeien silk that money could buy. Jaxxon dodged around the struggling aide, slipping through the doors before he could be stopped.

"Jaxxon? What in the blazes are *you* doing here?"

Lando Calrissian was on his feet behind a curved kriin-oak desk in an office that practically screamed class, from the Caamasi light sculptures against the wall to the well-stocked drinks cabinet beneath the oval window.

"I've come to see you, of course, you old card sharp," Jaxxon said, throwing his hands in the air half in greeting and half due to the fact that at least half a dozen hand blasters seemed to have been cocked behind him. Damn, Lobot was efficient, calling the Bespin Wing Guard in less time than it took to tell. Mel could *definitely* take a few lessons from the guy.

"I'm sorry, sir," the cyborg began behind Jaxxon, but Lando waved him off with a flick of his hand.

"It's fine. Jaxxon's an . . . old friend."

Jax resisted the urge to turn around and smirk as the Guard retreated, the doors sliding shut behind them.

Lando sighed and dropped back into a seat as white as the walls. "Let me guess . . . the Tumperakki Haulage Company? I knew I recognized the name."

Jaxxon took that as his cue to launch into the spiel he'd been practicing ever since they'd set course for the Anoat system. "You know what they say, Lando ol' pal . . . the future's in haulage, and you can be a part of it."

Lando regarded him incredulously. "And who says that, *exactly*?"

Jaxxon ignored the jibe. "Imagine it, Lando—a fleet of gleaming freighters in red, white, and yellow livery, streaking back and forth across the galaxy from Kinooine to Sernpidal, ferrying goods here, there, and everywhere. Textiles. Machine parts. Even livestock."

"You mean smuggling." Lando leaned across the desk, his hands open in front of him. "Jax, those days are long behind me. I'm a legitimate businessman now."

"That's great . . . 'cos so am I."

Lando raised a cynical eyebrow. "Really?"

"Of course," Jaxxon replied, trying not to sound aggrieved. "Sure, I've pulled a few dodgy deals in my time . . ."

"Just a few, huh?"

"But all that's changed. I want to go legit, just like you. I mean, look at us . . ." He twirled on his heels so Lando could take in the full splendor of his outfit, including the high-waisted pants that were *almost* a match to the pair he had seen Calrissian wearing on the cover of *Free-Trader's Gazette.* "We could be brothers."

Lando raised a hand to stop Jaxxon's sales pitch in its tracks. "Look . . . Jax . . . it's great to see you, but this isn't the time."

"What are you talking about? There's never been a better time." Jaxxon leaned across the desk, a pose he'd practiced in a polished bulkhead back aboard the *Rabbit.* "Think about it, shares in your own haulage fleet, able to transport Tibanna gas to every corner of Imperial space."

A shadow passed over Lando's face at the mention of the Empire. "We're doing fine as we are. Cloud City has all the haulers it needs."

What was wrong with the man? Couldn't he see a golden opportunity when it was staring him in the sickeningly suave face?

"Lando, look . . . all I'm asking for is a favor . . . a step up the ladder. I . . ." He rubbed the back of his neck where the Tarelle collar was chafing his fur. "I had a spot of bother with an Imperial governor not so long ago, a misunderstanding over a shipment of ryll I was transporting for the Pykes."

"Ryll?" Lando spluttered. "And this is you trying to go straight?"

"It was a mistake . . . a mistake that nearly cost me everything. It made me look at my life, at the choices I've made. This isn't easy for me, ya know? I've spent a lifetime building a rep that flies in the face of what the galaxy thinks of me."

"And what's that?"

"What d'ya think? I'm a Lepi. You know what folk say about us: a bunch of scruffy layabouts. And why? Because we look like giant rabbits. It's not fair, I'll tell ya that. Looking like a shoal of walking squids never did the Mon Calamari any harm, and the least said about the Harches the better. Those guys are literally giant spiders for pity's sake."

"I'm not sure what you want from me."

"A chance, that's all. It's not easy getting by when you have ears like these. That's why I became a smuggler in the first place. Who takes a Lepi seriously, especially out here in the Outer Rim? But you know that business . . . once you're in, there's no getting out . . . or so I thought, before I heard about you."

"What have I got to do with it?"

"Everything. If a no-good grifter like Landonis Balthazar Calrissian can turn his life around, then why can't I?"

Lando's face had softened. This was it, now or never. Jax only had one last card to play.

"Come on, pal. I'm doing it for my kids. They deserve better than blockade-running their entire life."

Lando looked surprised. "Kids? I didn't even know you had any?"

"Oh, I don't," Jaxxon admitted, quickly. "Not yet, but I will, one day. Lots of 'em. What can I say? I'm a Lepi."

Lando laughed, shaking his head, before glancing at what Jax had assumed was an empty seat on the other side of the desk. "I'm sorry about this, Corovene."

Jax looked down to see a tiny figure dwarfed by the leather chair, beady eyes swiveling around on stalks to glare back up at him. It was a Troglof, its thin tentacled arms crossed across its small chest and wet lips drawn down into a scowl.

"Oh . . . ," Jaxxon said, glancing nervously between the pair, "You got company. I . . . I didn't know." He nodded at the slug-faced alien by way of an apology. "How ya doing down there, little fella?"

Corovene ignored the question, turning back to Calrissian. "Baron, we haven't long . . ."

The comlink set into Lando's desk buzzed, a light flashing at the center of the unit.

"Indeed we don't," he said, rising to his feet. "That'll be Lo, reminding me of my next appointment. I have a number of guests arriving for a . . ." He paused as if searching for the correct word. "For a dinner engagement."

Jaxxon's long ears pricked up. "A dinner? Sounds great. I skipped breakfast. Lunch, too, for that matter. Maybe I can tag along? We could discuss your investment between courses. Will there be ham bones?"

Both Corovene and Jaxxon jumped as Lando slammed his palm down on the desk.

"Damnit, Jaxxon, there's not gonna be an investment. There's not gonna be anything at all!"

Jax laughed nervously, shocked by Lando's sudden outburst. He'd never seen Lando raise his voice before, let alone lose his cool.

"Let's not be hasty, eh? Forget the ham bones. They're not important. I just don't want you to pass up an opportunity that you'll regret later."

"Regret? At the moment the only thing I'm regretting is the day I first set eyes on you. Don't you get it? I'm not interested. I'll *never* be interested, either in you or in your harebrained schemes."

"*Hare*brained?" Now Jaxxon's hackles were well and truly raised. "There's no need for *that* kind of language, after everything we've been through."

"Everything we've been through . . ." Lando snorted, standing to his full height. "You mean like the time you sold me out to Renza the Hutt . . ."

"Renza? Well, that was a joke. It's not my fault the overgrown slug-ball has no sense of humor . . ."

"Yeah? And what about the time you told Maz Kanata that it was me who stole the *Corsair*'s hypercoils."

Jaxxon raised his hands to protest his innocence. "I still have no idea how they ended up in the *Rabbit*'s power core. I think that was probably Amaiza. She's not with me anymore."

"Why am I not surprised? You're a crook, Jaxxon. You always have been and you always will be, and worst of all, you're not even a good crook." Lando jabbed a perfectly manicured finger in the Lepi's direction. "You waltz in here, dressed like a Surakkean peacock, expecting me to throw money at you. And why? For kids you *might* have one day. Listen up and listen good, my friend, because I'm *never* saying this again: I've worked hard to put my past behind me. There were no handouts and definitely no favors; just me, working my way from the bottom to the top. You wanna be like me? You wanna make something of yourself? Then hop back to that rusty hunk of metal you call a ship and do it yourself, just like I had to."

Jaxxon couldn't believe his ears. Lectured by Lando Calrissian of all people. Lando, who would sell his best friend if he thought he could make a quick credit. Lando, who had practically written the book on cheating at sabacc. Lando, who had broken enough hearts to fill the Typhonic Nebula.

"Now, listen here—" he said, ready to tear the smug rukk-wrangler a new docking ring.

"The matter is closed," Lando cut in, walking over to a cape rack and choosing a cape the color of a Narragader sky. "And as for you, Mr. Manakor," he added, turning back to the Troglof in the chair. "Please don't worry, you can rely on me. Just get your . . . consignment to Platform One Forty-Three. My people will handle the rest."

The comlink buzzed again, and Lando shut it off, drawing Jaxxon's eyes back down to the desk. That's when he saw the case hidden behind the desk, a case brimming with aurodium ingots, enough to set up the business and still leave change for a lifetime's supply of dewback burgers. But there was no time to argue. Lando was around the desk and propelling Jaxxon out of the office before he could say anything, Corovene Manakor plopping down from the seat and scurrying after them.

"Thanks for nothing, pal," Jax grunted as he yanked his arm free to grab the cape that Lobot had left folded in the reception area. It was going to be a long walk back to the *Rabbit*, especially in these shukking boots.

"Jaxxon, listen . . . ," Lando said when they were out in the corridor, Corovene rushing off with barely another word. "I'm sorry, okay? You just . . . you just caught me at a bad time. Those things I said . . ."

"Forget about it," Jaxxon snapped, fighting the urge to introduce the sole of his foot to Lando's immaculate teeth. "I'll see ya around, yeah?"

In days gone by, Jaxxon would have tried his damndest to hit Lando where it hurt, asking how the *Falcon* was doing or, if he really wanted to twist the vibroknife, dropping L3's name into conversation, but what was the point? Lando didn't care. He'd made that abundantly clear.

So Jaxxon loped off, ready to flatten anyone who got in his way.

The trouble with being a Lepi, other than the crippling self-doubt and the assumption that you'll screw up sooner or later, is that even when you want to shut yourself off from the universe, you can't help but hear what everyone else is saying. It was those damn ears. Plus, Jaxxon was an inquisitive kind of fella. Just because he wanted to feed Lando's head into a burrow-grinder, it didn't mean that he didn't want to know what the smarmy varp farmer was muttering into the flashy comlink on his wrist.

"Yeah, I'm on my way to the princess's quarters," Jaxxon overheard, "and then I'll bring them to the Rinetta dining room. I just need to make sure that arrangements for the Manakor delivery are coming together. Corovene's people have always been good to me."

Realization hit Jaxxon like a charging mudhorn. Manakor. The rumors about the heist on Scipio. No wonder Lando had a caseful of rare ingots. He was arranging a delivery for one of the biggest heists in the history of the IBC. And he had the nerve to call *Jaxxon* a crook. The lousy, stinking hypocrite.

Jaxxon threw his cape back around his narrow shoulders. Lando's little meet-and-greet suddenly seemed even more appealing, especially now he knew there would be royalty present. He wondered if Lando would like the-great-and-the-good to know that Cloud City's beloved baron administrator was back in the smuggling game? Jaxxon was willing to bet his buckteeth that the answer was no . . . and when there were secrets, there was an opportunity for blackmail. It was an ugly word, but one Jaxxon was always prepared to use. He was determined to go legit, even if he had to extort the funds to do it.

Smoothing down his cloak, he politely stopped an astromech that was whirring past. "Excuse me, bud, but can ya tell me where I can find the Rinetta dining room?"

363

Jaxxon had run through his pitch at least a dozen times by the time he'd reached the dining room's impressive doors. He paused, checking his breath and smoothing his whiskers. He could do this, of course he could; especially if Lando hadn't made it back from whatever royal floozie he was courting. Jax would woo the room and then watch Lando squirm in his Liwari heels when he finally deigned to show his face. Fixing his most winning smile on his face, Jaxxon T. Tumperakki stepped forward into his destiny.

It turned out his destiny wasn't quite as exciting as he had expected. In fact, it was downright terrifying. The doors of the dining room whooshed open to reveal an exquisite salon complete with Socorran artwork on the walls and heavily armed stormtroopers in front of the circular windows. Then there was the figure that sat at the other end of the immaculately laid table, a figure dressed head-to-toe in black, eyes hidden behind impassive ruby lenses and breath rasping through a mechanical respirator.

Jaxxon stared at Darth Vader and Darth Vader stared back.

Darth kriffin' Vader.

"Sorry," Jaxxon squeaked, his voice jumping at least seventeen octaves. "Wrong room. I thought this was the vac tube. My mistake. Gotta run."

If Jaxxon didn't need the vac tube *before* he stepped into the dining room, he sure as hell needed one now. He leapt back out into the corridor, slamming the door control before the stormtroopers could react. Racing down the passageway, weaving in and out of the milling crowds, he had no idea if he was being followed, but didn't want to check.

If this was what it was like being legitimate, Jaxxon didn't want to know. And to think he'd actually wanted to be like Calrissian. The Calrissian he'd admired. The Calrissian who'd pulled himself out of the mire.

The Calrissian who had dinner parties with the Emperor's Fist.

Eventually, Jaxxon's curiosity got the better of him and he glanced behind, spotting white helmets bobbing after him. Yup, they were coming his way, gaining fast. He *knew* leaving his blasters on the *Rabbit* had been a mistake. Hell, coming to Cloud City had been a mistake, especially as he realized he had no idea where he was or how to get back to his ship. How had he gotten so lost?

"Excuse me," he said, stopping a passing Ugnaught technician wearing a long tunic. "Which way to Platform Nine Ninety-Seven?"

The pig-faced alien looked at him as if he'd just crawled out of a moof paddock. "Don't you know?"

"Well, if I knew I wouldn't be asking!"

The Ugnaught grunted, shaking his head and turning to carry on about his business. "Three levels up," he muttered over his shoulder. "You can't miss it."

Jaxxon grabbed his arm, keeping his ears pressed down over the back of his head so the stormtroopers couldn't see him in the crowd. "That's great, but how would someone get up there if they were in a hurry? Is there a turbolift nearby?"

The technician tutted, yanking his arm free and smoothing down his sleeve. "What do I look like: tourist information?" Then he relented, his porcine nostrils flaring. "Take a right and then a left and you'll find it just past the Paradise Atrium."

Jaxxon was already running. "Just past the Atrium. Got it. You're a pal."

The Ugnaught also turned out to be terrible with directions. Jaxxon turned right and then turned left, finding the Atrium, but no turbolift to be seen.

"Hey you," a stormtrooper said from somewhere behind. "Stop."

"No chance," Jaxxon said, vaulting over a table and charging across the Atrium, the troopers barging past a serving droid carrying a tray of kibi strips. Diving behind a vending machine, Jaxxon ducked into a doorway to find himself in a stairwell. The door slid shut and Jaxxon

365

bounded up the steps three at a time, listening out all the while to hear if the stormtroopers were still on his tail. The door remained closed. The stupid bucketbrains had missed it completely. Finally, Lady Luck was on his side.

Yeah, like that would ever happen. Jaxxon cried out as his cape wrapped around his legs, sending him tumbling back down the stairs. He bounced once, cracking his head on the second impact, and was unconscious before he reached the bottom.

Jaxxon woke to the sound of a klaxon blaring down the stairwell. Seriously? Did the kriffing thing need to be so loud?

A familiar voice crackled over speakers hidden somewhere above Jaxxon's aching head: *"Attention. This is Lando Calrissian. Attention. The Empire has taken control of the city. I advise everyone to leave before more Imperial troops arrive."*

Jaxxon leapt to his feet. Taken control? Well, that was just typical. You invite them for dinner and they end up annexing your station. Still, it couldn't have happened to a nicer fella where Calrissian was concerned.

Running up the stairs that had threatened to brain him, Jaxxon barreled out into a corridor, trying to ignore the continued pounding in his skull. He hadn't felt this bad since he had challenged Black Krrsantan to a drinking game on Mitek-Por. He still had a way to go to the *Rabbit,* but at least he finally recognized where he was. All he'd have to do was cut down this passageway, passing Lando's office, and . . .

Lando's office! A grin spread across Jaxxon's face. Maybe he'd come out of this with an investment after all.

He bolted down the corridor, avoiding the panicked throng who seemed to be running in every direction at once, their consternation heightened by the distant and yet all-too-recognizable sound of blasterfire. He dived inside the office, half expecting to run into Lobot. The reception room was empty, but the doors to Lando's inner sanctum were locked. Luckily Jaxxon knew the best way to bypass the lock. Who needed a vibropick when you could throw an over-stylish caf table through the frosted glass? His deed of highly satisfying vandalism done, Jaxxon squeezed through the gap, almost crying out in joy when he found Lando's case still behind the desk.

"Nice doing business with ya, pal," Jaxxon said with a grin, snatching up the case and making his exit. He raced toward the landing platform, hugging the precious cargo to his chest and planning the ways he would spend his ill-gotten gains. A complete overhaul for the *Rabbit* was a necessity, not to mention a memory upgrade for Mel. Then would come the haulage fleet, a luxury burrow on Glee Anselm, and an entire dewback farm for the best barbecues this side of Valo. This was it. The moment when everything changed. He just needed to make it to the ship in one piece.

367

There was just one problem with that. Jaxxon slid around the corner to the platform to come face-to-faceplate with a squadron of stormtroopers wiping the floor with the Bespin Wing Guard.

"Get back," the guard-captain yelled at him before a laser bolt slammed into the guy's chest, killing him instantly. Jaxxon leapt forward, dropping into a roll and snatching up the dead man's blaster. He came up firing, hitting one of the stormtroopers in the pauldron. It wasn't his fight, but the troopers were in his way. The final guard fell, and Jaxxon was on his own with a trio of angry stormtroopers to contend with. He dived around the corner, looking around for cover. There was a door straight ahead. Maybe he could find a way to double back, avoiding the bucketheads completely. It was worth a shot. He sprinted forward, firing over his shoulder while clutching the case of ingots under his other arm. The blaster's battery died the moment he reached the door and he threw himself forward, landing awkwardly on the other side of the threshold, only to find that he'd trapped himself in a maintenance closet. The stormtroopers approached, still firing, and Jaxxon drop-kicked the useless weapon at the door control, sealing himself inside. He was safe, but that door wouldn't last long, especially with a squad of the Emperor's finest using it for target practice. He looked around, seeing nothing but janitorial products and a hovercart, neither of which would be much use against a death squad.

In frustration, he kicked a dormant mouse droid at the wall, knocking over a stack of mops. They clattered to the floor, and Jaxxon's jaw dropped as he saw the tiny figure that had been hiding behind the cleaning implements.

"Corovene?"

The Troglof looked up at him, his small eyes wide with terror.

"Please . . . can you help us?"

That was when Jaxxon saw the others, huddled behind an industrial-sized bottle of disinfectant. Another Troglof, a female this time, was visibly quaking, her tentacles wrapped around two minuscule infants.

"Is this . . . your family?" Jaxxon asked, dropping down on one knee in front of them. Outside, the stormtroopers had stopped firing indiscriminately and had decided to take a cutting torch to the door instead.

"We were trying to get to Platform One Forty-Three, as Lando said we should," Corovene explained, his tiny voice wavering. "A Petrusian gunrunner had agreed to take us to Lysatra . . ." He glanced nervously at the torch slicing through the door. "Away from the Empire."

"Wait? You're the consignment? I thought you were shifting your cut of the heist?"

Corovene scoffed. "What? Yes, I was involved in the heist on Scipio, but only because I was promised funds to liberate Najiba from the Empire."

"Najiba?"

"Our home planet. I helped the thieves bypass the security system as agreed, but once they had blown the vault . . ."

"They left you to carry the can." He held the stolen case closer to him. "Sheesh. You just can't trust anyone these days."

"I've been such a fool."

Jaxxon tried to hide the case behind his back. "So the ingots . . ."

"What ingots?"

"In Lando's office . . ."

"Oh, they're not mine. I think Lando was using them to pay for our transport."

"He was? Why? What did Mr. *Look at My Facial Hair Isn't It Just Dandy* get out of the deal?"

"Nothing. We told him our plight and he offered to help, whatever the cost."

Suddenly the case seemed a lot heavier. Ripping Lando off had been a lot easier when he thought the guy had no scruples.

"How are we going to get out?" the female Troglof asked, the torch nearly down to the floor.

"We? Sorry lady, but it's every Lepi for himself." He glanced down at the hovercart. "I've an idea to get past those goons but it's a one-rabbit deal, I'm afraid."

That's when the Troglof children started crying and Jaxxon realized he was doomed.

Outside in the corridor, the stormtrooper finished slicing through the door. He stood back, ready to kick it down, not expecting the metal slab to burst *toward* him, flattening him to the ground. The hovercart roared up the makeshift ramp, launching itself into the air before the other troopers could react. They turned and fired, but Jaxxon was already zooming toward the landing platform, one hand gripping the cart's rail, the other gripping the case, his cape clasped in his teeth.

"See you later, suckers," he yelled as they raised their blasters, his suddenly released cape billowing out like a parachute to block their line of sight. It didn't stop them firing, the bolts punching through the thin material, but by then Jaxxon was halfway to the *Rabbit's Foot*.

"Mel!" Jaxxon yelled into the comlink he'd unhooked from his belt. "You better be listening to this, you dumb bucket-of-bolts. Get the ramp down and prime the engines. We need to skedaddle."

A series of gruff beeps sounded over the comm, the ramp whining as it started to descend. Maybe the ancient droid wasn't so bad. Bolts sizzled past Jaxxon's head, the stormtroopers once more in pursuit. Predictably, one found its target, reducing the cart to a ball of blazing scrap, but Jaxxon had already leapt from the speeding trolley, bounding onto the boarding ramp with a jump that would have given the Jedi of old a run for their money.

Maybe there were a few things a Lepi could do that were better than anyone else.

Jaxxon raced from the cargo bay, ignoring Mel's concerned beeps as he deposited the case next to the vacant navigator's seat. The *Rabbit's Foot* launched into the air as he gunned the engines, enveloping the stormtroopers in a thick cloud of engine smoke that Jaxxon hoped smelled as bad as it looked.

Shoot your way through that, Jaxxon thought as he thundered out of Bespin's atmosphere and blasted into hyperspace.

Away and safe, Jaxxon slumped back in his chair and exhaled in relief, the blue light of the hypertunnel bathing the *Rabbit's* cockpit as the ship rattled and groaned.

ML-08 trundled closer, blooping a question.

"Did I get the investment?" Jaxxon repeated. "What do you think?"

He reached down and flicked the clasp of the case he had stolen from Lando's office. The droid peered inside and saw four shaken Troglofs looking back up at him.

"Did we get away?" Corovene asked as Jaxxon gently tipped the case over so they could crawl out onto the *Rabbit*'s filthy deck plates.

"Well, we're not space dust, if that's what you mean?" He leaned across to the navicomputer, punching coordinates into the system. "Now, where did you say you were going? Lysatra, wasn't it?"

"You'll take us there?" Corovene asked, eyes brimming with grateful tears. "But we have no way to repay you."

Jaxxon glanced down at the Troglof mother hugging her children and thought of the small fortune in ingots that was scattered across a cleaning closet's floor back on Cloud City.

"Hey, if it's good enough for Lando Calrissian, it's good enough for me. Just don't tell anyone I'm giving away freebies, okay? Some of us are trying to run a business around here."

"Tumperakki Haulage?"

Jaxxon took one last look at the kids. "Ah, that can wait. In the meantime, hey, being a smuggler ain't so bad, as long as you choose the right cargo."

BUT WHAT DOES HE EAT?

S. A. Chakraborty

Torro cursed as she braided her hair, pinning it into a dark-purple crown above the twin bumps on her brow. Bleary-eyed, she rifled through her closet in search of something—anything—clean. Her head was pounding, protesting the swiftness with which it had been removed from her pillow.

There was an impatient beep from the other end of the room. The administrative droid's photoreceptor had to stretch high to peek over the lush ferns, delicate orchids, and artificial waterfalls that made Torro's lavish apartment look more like the jungles on her home-world of Devaron than the sterile gas giant that was Bespin.

"Executive Chef Torro Sbazzle." The droid's droning voice was a deep baritone, at odds with its small size. "The baron administrator has requested your immediate—"

"Yeah, yeah, I know." From the depths of her closet, Torro pulled out a pair of high-waisted, fabulously patterned gold-and-purple pants. A stylishly cropped top trimmed with moonstones and swooping black embroidery followed. No matter the summons, Torro had a certain appearance to keep up. "You can tell Lando that if this was such an emergency, he should have come here himself, instead of ordering a droid to fetch me like I'm some small-time fry cook in CoCo Town."

But the snapped words didn't make her feel much better. Why *was* Calrissian summoning her to the kitchens in the middle of the day? She loved her profession, but not even Torro could think of many emergencies that involved high cuisine.

Those bastards from Kuat better not have complained about their meal. A bunch of brash shipping barons with more credits than taste, they'd rented out the main banquet room last night and proceeded to ruin her evening, harassing the staff, complaining about the "heat" of the food, and sending back dishes. Who sought out a Devaronian celebrity chef and then complained about heat? Already half drunk when they arrived, the shipping barons had gone through a dozen casks of sunberry ale, giggling as they mocked the "peculiar" menu and ordering dishes haphazardly, ignoring her wait staff's delicate suggestions.

Still grumbling, Torro shoved on a pair of boots and straightened up, squinting at the beams of sunlight sneaking past her heavy curtains. Like all proper chefs, Torro was a creature of the night. Cloud City was usually a smoldering crimson when she woke up, its stark white halls glowing with dying light. The bustling gas colony played to an equally nocturnal crowd, and its parties rarely wound down before dawn, which is when she typically hung up her apron after rounds of applause, enjoyed a glass of Alderaanian white, and then slept everything off. It was a routine she savored: nights of admiration and excitement—not to mention money—in a corner of the galaxy on the edge of danger and independence. Though Torro had trained with a dozen master chefs across twice that many star systems and been offered her pick of plum assignments, she loved Cloud City. It was one of the few places left where you could still breathe. Where a slip of the tongue about the Empire or a muttered comment about its violent expansion wouldn't end up with you mining rocks.

That didn't mean she liked being dragged out of bed by Lando Calrissian. Her body still not on board with the concept of being upright, Torro flipped open a black silica glass box on her console and plucked out two sulfur tabs, letting them dissolve beneath her tongue. The jolt hit her a moment later, and she was instantly more alert, the fresh scent of the plants more aromatic and the colors of the room more vivid.

The beeping of the droid more irritating. Torro gave it a solid kick as she left the room and then wound her way through the bustling corridors. Cloud City was lively day and night, though she wasn't used to seeing it so *bright,* filled with fresh-faced technocrats and chatting gas traders. The harshness of the white walls and cold metal furnishings threw her for a moment. This jagged industrial landscape speared against blossoming candy-pink clouds was about as far from the green forests and vine-swathed cities of Devaron as anything could be. And for a moment, she missed her birth planet terribly.

You chose this life, remember? Torro's ambitious travels had scandalized her family back home, her wanderlust more appropriate for the men of her species, who tended toward such frivolity. The eldest daughter, Torro had been expected to take over the reins of her family's pharmaceutical business and had dutifully studied botany for years, earning high marks. Applying that education to cooking across the stars instead of discovering new medicines to improve her family's bottom line had not gone over well with her mother and aunts. But even though her visits home were full of disappointed sighs and lectures about family duty, part of Torro never stopped longing for Devaron.

Ah, well, fighting with Calrissian would provide a distraction. She marched into her kitchen to find it had been cleaned during the morning, and its metal counters and cooking surfaces sparkled. Where Torro would normally see a small army—a dozen assistant cooks, hosts, tasters, bartenders, and wait staff—there were only two people: Gersolik, her Ugnaught sous-chef, and the grand baron himself, Lando Calrissian, impeccably turned out as always in his sky-colored cape and perfectly coiffed hair.

"Torro!" If Lando had been waiting on her, there was no sign of annoyance in his dazzling grin. "How is the most brilliant, stunning chef in a hundred thousand parsecs?"

Torro slammed an elbow into the control panel, and the door behind her crashed shut. "Tired. Do you know what time it is, Calrissian? Because I was very clear about my work hours when we negotiated my contract, and this is not one of them."

Lando raised his hands in a gesture of peace. "My most sincere apologies. I hope you know I wouldn't bother you if it wasn't a matter of grave importance."

Grave importance? Torro glanced at her sous-chef. Gersolik didn't just look nervous; she looked scared, her pink skin pale and her whiskers trembling.

"Is this about the shipping barons from Kuat?" Torro demanded. "Because let me tell you, they were the ones who insisted on ordering the cuttle-tick. My people warned them that the carapace was venomous and just part of the presentation."

"It's not about the shipping barons."

Torro crossed her arms. "Then why did you call me here?"

For the first time, she noticed a faint sheen of sweat on Calrissian's brow. "We have some unexpected guests. I was hoping you could prepare refreshments."

She stared at him, certain this was a joke. "Do you know who I am? How long I've trained and toiled in backwater kitchens and cantinas in places that even *you*, Lando, wouldn't think about visiting? I didn't come here to make snacks for every random—"

"Please." The word cut through her, even more unlike Lando. "They're bad news, Torro. I could really use your help." Torro frowned. This wasn't the first time Lando had hosted suspicious guests. "Then I want the rest of my staff," she insisted.

Lando was already shaking his head. "Only the two of you. Our guests don't want anyone else learning that they're here."

"Well then your guests can come in here and chop chak-roots. I don't work with less than half staff."

"Show her." It was Gersolik. Her sous-chef didn't appear any less frightened, but her voice was laced with determination. "She needs to understand."

Lando exhaled noisily. "You know, if people would just trust me, we'd all save a lot of time." He crossed to the master access desk set against the wall that divided the kitchen from the banquet room. The wall's upper portion was made from a reflective material that acted like a mirror, allowing people to see everything going on from any part of the room. With a simple touch, the mirrored surface could also turn transparent—at least on this side. It was designed to give the kitchen, particularly its executive chef, a way to observe her diners without needing to set foot in the banquet room.

Calrissian tapped the panel. Set against the scalloped ivory walls of the sumptuous, luxurious banquet chamber was a single figure. He was broadly built and so close that had a barrier not been between them, Torro might have been able to touch the gleaming black helmet that fanned out around his neck. He was shrouded in black, an ebony as dark and cold as the void of space. Black cape, black expressionless mask set over a harsh metal grille.

Lando seemed to be waiting for her to say something. "What?" she asked blankly. "Am I supposed to know who that is?"

"*Are you supposed to*—Torro—that's Darth Vader!" Lando hissed in an incredulous whisper.

She rolled her eyes. "Oh, come on, Lando. You're far too clever to fall for a bunch of rumors about some Imperial bogeyman who—" And then she jumped, sending a canister of cooking utensils clattering across the floor, as a contingent of soldiers in instantly recognizable, white armor swarmed behind the man Lando claimed was Darth Vader. "Are those *stormtroopers*?"

"A whole ship's worth," Calrissian confirmed grimly. "*Now* do you believe me?"

Torro's mind spun. The Empire. Lord Vader. She'd heard the stories, of course, about the shadowy menace said to be the Emperor's right hand; each more gruesome and unbelievable than the last. He could choke people just by looking at them. He fought with a mysterious energy blade that carved through bodies and metal with equal ease.

Then a far worse realization landed. "Wait . . . *Darth Vader* is your guest? *That's who you want me to cook for?*"

"That's who I want you to cook for." Lando tapped the access panel again. The Imperial troops and their infamous commander vanished, replaced by Torro's reflection in the mirror wall. Her skin had paled to lavender, her green eyes still fixed and dilated from the sulfur tabs.

Oh, to hell with this. "Absolutely not," she declared. "You don't pay me enough. Haven't you heard the things they say about him?"

Lando brought his fingers together in a pleading motion. "I need your help. They'll be expecting something fancy, and we have to pull out all the stops for this visit. Make sure we've left no room for any offense."

"Offense?" Torro shivered, failing to control her panic. The knowledge that the infamous Lord Vader was real was dwarfed only by the prospect of offending him. "He's got a metal plate instead of a mouth, and you want me to *cook* for him? He might not even eat! He might have some olfactory sensor I've never heard of that goes haywire at the presence of seasoning!"

"Please," Lando said again, pressing on when she let out a long string of Devaronian curses. "You've been in Cloud City for five years now, Torro, and I'm no fool. People spill blood to land a reservation for your dinners. I know you could make more money someplace more glamorous. But you like it here. It's your home. It's *our* home, and those Imperials out there?" He jerked a thumb in the direction of the banquet room. "They're looking for any reason to tear it down."

Torro glared at him, baring her fangs. But the gesture was forced. Because this place *was* home now. Torro was fiercely protective of her kitchen staff. She liked the people who had rooted themselves in this wild, dodgy little city floating on the edge of nowhere. Cloud City was a nest of merchants and artists, gamblers and the hardworking sort who supported families across a dozen star systems.

"What would you even have me cook?" she asked. *"We don't know if he eats."*

"It doesn't matter if he eats. It's about appearance." Calrissian ignored the offended noise she made at that—her food was not just about appearance. "It's a show. A lie to make them feel important. And it's only this one time, I swear."

She frowned. "You really think they'll leave Cloud City that quickly?"

Lando bit his lip, a fleeting expression she couldn't read twisting across his face. "If everything goes according to plan, yes. So please . . . some refreshments. I'll pay double your dinner rate. Just make it look fancy."

"Fancy?"

He offered her a weak smile. "Come on. You saw his mask. No one dresses like that unless they've got something to prove."

"Says the man also in a cape."

"Mine's prettier."

At that, Torro could not help a nervous laugh. "All right, fine. You get one meal out of me for these people. That's it. If they're here any longer, *you're* making them dinner." She reached for her apron. "How long do I have?"

"An hour."

"An *hour*?" She swore again. "Then why are you wasting my time with jokes? Get out of my kitchen!"

Lando spun neatly away and was gone in a flutter of blue fabric.

Gersolik stepped forward to take his place. "What can I do?"

A meal to stroke the heinous Vader's ego. Food he might not be able to eat. Torro drummed her claws on the counter, thinking fast. Refreshments. Things that were light and bite-sized and could be neatly consumed.

Start with drinks. "Roast ten cans of denta beans. Once that's done, steep them with some boiled whilk milk and a good amount of thalassa seeds." It was a popular drink back on Coruscant, wondrously bitter and guaranteed to put a little pep in one's step, but it took time and care to brew a properly smooth finish. "Then start peeling and chopping some jogan fruit. Three should do, but make it a fine dice. They'll be going into dumplings."

"Dumplings?"

"Everyone in the galaxy likes dumplings, Gers. It might truly be the only thing we have in common."

With that settled, Torro tried to fall into the familiar rhythm of work. But her hands were shaking as she measured out midnight-hued pastry flour for the dumplings' cases. She'd normally cut the flour with zaffa oil, which gave it a fresh citrusy kick, but maybe today she'd use the more common bantha butter, which had a mellow flavor and was less apt to burn. It was probably best to play it safe, no? Imperials were almost all humans—the kind of humans who had snobbish if not downright bigoted views about the culture and cuisines of other species. If Torro were wise, she'd serve up something bland but pretty and get out of this kitchen as soon as possible.

She reached for the bantha butter. Then she stopped. Lando was right to be nervous; the Empire was capricious and cruel and took open pride in crushing any opposition. Places like Cloud City—little pockets of independence—were hot spots to be smothered. They could put on a perfect show of obedience, and the Empire might still blow them out of the sky. Vader might have the kitchen staff dragged into the banquet room and murdered just to prove he could. This might be the last meal she ever cooked.

Torro Sbazzle would be damned if the last meal she cooked was mediocre. There was a reason she was in the kitchen instead of some newfangled, eight-digit personal chef droid with a gleaming modern synthesizer, and she was not dying for bland dumplings. Torro knocked the bantha butter aside and reached for the zaffa oil.

She returned to her work with a relish, mixing ground khadi nuts with fiery pepper syrup before shaping them into miniature globes and garnishing them with silver dust. Muja fruit was simmered with a dozen bac eggs until the red pulp paled to a warm amber curd, perfect for the moon-shaped dessert tarts she was preparing to accompany the dumplings.

More than halfway done now. Torro opened the oven, and reached through the flames to pull out the metal sheet pan, her skin impervious to the heat. She inspected the bake, finding it satisfactory, and set the crusts to cool. She spooned out plump pillows of jogan and cheese, frying them until the pastry sizzled and dunking them in sticky honey-wine. She plated the dumplings carefully, garnishing the tops with curls of candied rind.

She called to Gersolik over her shoulder. "Have you finished whipping the roe? I want to fold the meringue into the curd just before the tarts go back in the oven."

"Yes. But I . . ." Gersolik trailed off.

Torro glanced back, surprised to find the Ugnaught woman staring intently at the glass dish of pale meringue, whipped into perfect, cloudlike peaks.

"What's wrong?" Torro asked. "Did you taste too much?" When properly whipped, frella-fish roe made a wondrously creamy, dreamlike meringue. "Dreamlike" because consuming too much of it dulled the senses, putting most species into a happy, dazed state.

"No. I was just thinking between the effects of the roe and the flavor of the meringue: It would mask almost anything, yes?"

"Is that your way of saying you added too much sugar?"

"It's my way of saying you come from a family of pharmacists." Gersolik met Torro's gaze. "You must know how to mix up all sorts of things. What you were worried about with the cuttle-tick carapace and the shipping barons from Kuat, could we not . . . create a similar situation?"

It took a moment to untangle Gersolik's careful words. And then every bit of confidence Torro had regained vanished.

She dashed to her assistant's side, ready to clap a hand over the other woman's snout if necessary. "Are you insane?" she hissed under her breath. "You want to—" Torro couldn't even bring herself to say the word. "Do you know what they'd do to us?"

Gersolik was shaking, but it was clearly anger that moved her sous-chef now, not fear. "What more could they do, Torro? They *blew up* Alderaan. They're monsters. They need to be stopped." She gestured around the kitchen. "Do you know why we're the only ones here? Because that's how little they think of anyone who isn't human. We're mindless animals to the Empire. Unthinking drones who obey without question."

"Yes," Torro said acidly. "Drones that those troopers will probably make personally test all this food before it leaves the kitchen."

"*So?* You're Devaronian; it's almost impossible to poison you."

"And you're Ugnaught. Trust me, it's very possible to poison you!"

Gersolik's expression stayed fierce. "Then we'll pick something that takes time to go into effect. Torro, we could take out Darth Vader with a single bite!"

Torro hesitated but couldn't help peek in the direction of her very well-stocked pantry. She'd made all sorts of ludicrous demands of Calrissian when they were negotiating her contract, and she had a wealth of rare and pricy ingredients on hand, including many that made cuttle-tick venom seem harmless in comparison.

383

She shook her head. "It's too risky. For all we know, the people he's meeting with are innocent. And with that mask on his face, we can't be sure he'll eat any of this. We might end up only taking out a couple of troopers—not to mention you, me, and the rest of Cloud City when they figure out what we tried to do."

Gersolik drew up even straighter. Faint scars marred her forehead, vanishing into the puffy white of her eyebrows, and for the first time, Torro wondered where she got them. She wondered if, indeed, her assistant—her friend—had not experienced far worse at the hands of the Empire.

"Aren't there some things worth that risk?" Gersolik persisted. "Things greater than our lives? We would be heroes."

Heroes. For a moment, the ludicrous plot Gersolik was suggesting played through her mind. Torro had spent her entire life experimenting with plants and herbs, spices and seeds. She probably could brew such a poison. There was a chance Lord Vader would consume it, that it would work. That she and Gersolik would take down one of the most dangerous beings in the galaxy.

But thinking back on a life filled with botanical experiments reminded Torro of the other people who would pay if she made a mistake: her family back on Devaron. Her planet crawled with Imperials, its generals and high-ranking officials having turned Devaron's lush jungles and abundant wildlife into their own personal game preserve.

And not just a game preserve. A chill raced down Torro's spine as she recalled foraging as a child back home. Though it was tradition in her family, intended to teach youngsters how to identify plants, Torro's own wanderings had been strictly curtailed. There were forests in Devaron now that were as thick with bones as they were with trees. Mines that blew off limbs and poisonous vapors that lingered. Some of her earliest memories involved getting shouted away from ruins covered in otherwise promising shrubs. But not by Imperials. Rather by her own relatives, whose ghastly warnings and frightened eyes left a deep impression.

There was, indeed, a reason she and Gersolik had been left alone in the kitchen, but it wasn't because the Empire thought nonhumans too stupid to plot against them.

It was because the Empire knew it had already won. It knew the very thought of crossing them—the very real terror of the consequences that would follow—was enough to keep its subjugated "citizens" in line. Enough that they taught their children to stay in line.

Enough to keep Torro in line. "There's a temple back in the forests on Devaron, you know. Ancient, gorgeous. At least it used to be. We tell legends about it. People say the Jedi themselves used to gather there; that they trained the bravest warriors and cleverest peacemakers in our jungles. During the Clone Wars, a few of the Republic's last fighters even tried to make a final stand in that temple."

A little of Gersolik's determination faded from her expression. "Tried?"

"Failed. The Empire bombed it from space and slaughtered every Devaronian they found within a thousand klicks. Claimed they were collaborators." Torro pulled the bowl of meringue from her assistant's hands. "Now that temple is a crater in the middle of a graveyard. The kinds of heroes you're talking about, Gers? They don't exist anymore."

"And they won't exist again. Not if some of us don't try to fight back!"

Before Torro could respond, there was the familiar whooshing shudder as the banquet room doors on the other side of the wall opened. Just perfect. The rest of Lando's "guests" were early.

Then blasterfire started.

Torro jumped, still clutching her bowl of meringue. Gersolik let out a surprised gasp and then lurched for the access panel.

"No, wait!" Torro hissed and grabbed her arm. The blasterfire had already stopped.

From the banquet room, a voice spoke:

"We would be honored if you would join us."

The speaker's words were low and deep, and buffeted by the wall, Torro shouldn't have been able to hear them so clearly. They shouldn't have chilled her to the bone, seeming to poison the very air with dread.

Gersolik cleared her throat. "Torro . . ."

"Get back to work." Torro was trembling, but as she felt the weight of the cold invitation she had no doubt was Vader, her voice hardened. "Now."

Gersolik jerked her arm away. She looked furious. "Of course, boss," she said bitterly.

Torro forced herself to return to her workstation. She set the bowl of meringue down, trying to block out the muffled sounds of the struggle she could hear beyond the wall. She didn't want to know anything about the other people in the banquet room, the ones who'd fired the blaster on Vader. There was nothing she could do to help them, not without risking her own loved ones.

Besides . . . we don't even know if he eats.

BEYOND THE CLOUDS

Lilliam Rivera

Clusters of beldons float across the sky. The jellylike creatures drift and tumble into one another as if they're performing an orchestrated dance. It wasn't too long ago when the beldons were hunted down. A ridiculously easy sport, since the celestial beings in iridescent colors are not fast. Beldons usually emerge during the very early mornings when the sky breaks from its reddish hues to mark the start of a new day. And every morning I search for them. When they appear I feel reassured, grounded, if only for a second.

"Today is the day. He will definitely show up today," I say to my reflection in the window. Strands of black hair cover my right eye. I rub the left side where the hair slowly grows out of its buzz cut. I'll need to shave it.

I stare down at my drab clothes, the color of sand, and curse at how dull my dark-brown complexion appears underneath. There's nothing astral about me. My clothes are boring and ordinary. If only I could sport an ever-changing uniform like the beldons: translucent and invisible one second and full of an unnatural vibrancy the next. When you're a bounty hunter you need a signature look. The best ones always do. Dengar has his bandages covering his head. Aurra Sing used to wear orange jumpsuits. I've studied them all and their wizard attire. My current style is nonexistent. Seventeen years of never standing out or leaving any kind of mark. It's probably the reason why I'm not an official bounty hunter.

"Staring at the beldons again, Isabalia?"

Recnelo Cott is a rare Ugnaught who doesn't reside with her clan. She prefers the more solitary space on Level 121. Even in Cloud City, you can find a home away from the crowds. The room I rent from Recnelo is a square little thing with a bed and table. I don't know how Recnelo secured the room and I don't care. She keeps to herself, spending most of her time working at the carbon freezing facility with her people.

"No, I'm not," I say and pull my hood over my head.

Recnelo snorts. This is our usual script. Every morning I wake up to see the beldons and every morning Recnelo makes fun of me. It's repetitive but at least I know what to expect.

We head out. At this early hour, only a few Cloud City residents are up to start work at the mines excavating the precious Tibanna gas. Recnelo will head to the facility to clock in. As for me, I need to see Elad Zhalto before the last bet is placed.

As we turn down the long corridor toward the turbolifts, we notice two men deep in conversation. Our course to work is rarely punctuated with newcomers. Sure, Cloud City attracts various emissaries wanting a slice of the tiny good life we have here in the floating city, but my gut tells me these two are something else. Recnelo and I walk at our usual steady clip. My hand slips into my vibroknuckler located in my pocket, an added weight if I need to cut a problem across the face.

The two men stop talking and just stare. Recnelo continues to speak in Ugnaught, a nonsense story about how much she loves to eat. If you live in Cloud City you learn to converse and understand many languages. And if you don't, expect to get insulted without ever knowing what words were sent your way. I nod at what she says, keeping my eyes glued to the men. We walk past them without incident. I loosen my grip.

"Not morning people I guess," I say when the distance from the two men is safe enough to speak. Recnelo shakes her head. There's movement happening in the city. Something is going down.

"How *are* things at the facility?" I ask.

Recnelo subtly glances down the hall, making sure no one is near.

"Soldiers wearing the tackiest armor ever seen on droid or creature alone recently paid us a visit," she says. "Imps asking too many questions and getting in everyone's way."

389

Imperial soldiers. I can't believe it. Things are really shaking up, more than I thought. I can't help but feel weirdly excited. Action. Real action!

"Probably more are set to arrive," I say. "Don't you think?"

"I hope not, for your sake and the sake of everyone on Cloud City," Recnelo says with a heavy ominous tone.

As we wait for the turbolift to transport us to our respective levels, a giant hologram of the city's baron administrator, Lando Calrissian, materializes. When I was young I heard all about Lando's great adventures. I loved how he always wore amazing capes. He was so flashy and charismatic. But Lando turned out to be like every other politician out there, full of empty promises and a seductive smile.

At least as a bounty hunter you're stripped of useless pretensions.

A bounty hunter has a job to do and gets it done no matter what. No messy feelings to trip a person. I just need to make the final right connection to fulfill my dream.

I press Level 142. Recnelo shakes her head.

"If I were you I would stay clear of Elad Zhalto."

"You have to be in it to win it," I say. "Besides, Elad is just another rung on the ladder."

Recnelo continues to pass judgment. She believes in hard work with people you trust. But my people no longer live in Cloud City. Both my parents work in the educational centers on Chandrila. They want nothing to do with my "misguided" lifestyle, especially when they raised me to help and not hurt. They were active in the Cloud City community, bought into Lando's promises until it was obvious that educators only got in the way of business. Who wants to learn when there's money to be had? So I pivoted and started studying hunters, learned how to fight, worked my way up the ranks, all to the disgrace of my parents. When they left I stayed behind. But I don't bother reminding Recnelo of this history. We've been through this plenty of times. Thankfully we land on Level 142.

"That comlink broadcast you listen to all night is not the way to go. It's best to keep your nose and footing close to the ground. Or have the beldons scrambled your brain?" she says before the door closes behind me. Recnelo is wrong. Cobbling together clues of galactic stirrings off the broadcast is my only way of finding out what's happening. I can't let Recnelo confuse me. My luck is about to change. I can feel it. It's just a matter of time. I press on.

Elad Zhalto is the owner of the Azure Den, an underground gambling spot. Those invited are longtime players. It's rare to see a new face in the midst. A Duros, Elad is a power player with fingerprints on every Cloud City surface. More important, he's friends with all the real bounty hunters.

I nod to the guard at the entrance and head in. The last of the sabacc players are finishing up from the looks of how smoky the room is and the many empty drinks.

"How much longer?" I ask.

"As long as it takes," the guard says, annoyed, and leaves me to fend for myself.

I locate Elad, who is immersed in how the cards will shake out for his guests. And that's when I notice him, a shadowy presence in the corner of the room. My heart races. There's one bounty hunter I've been obsessively studying for the past couple of years. He was raised on Kamino and trained by Aurra Sing. He wears customized Mandalorian armor. Now, that's true style. And here he is.

Boba Fett.

I can't believe it. The most notorious killer is here and he's only a few feet away from me. Funny—he's a lot shorter than I imagined. Never mind that. This is my chance. Boba Fett must be here to take something, or someone, down. If I can be of service to him, prove my skills somehow, my whole life could change. He'll invite me to be part of his crew. I know it!

Elad speaks to him but Boba Fett doesn't move. He's as still as the rocky Agamar terrain. I need an introduction but I can't interrupt or Elad will shut me out completely. Timing is everything. But when?

"Should I deal you in?"

Joy Iya shuffles the cards at a corner table away from the real sabacc action. It's been a couple of months since I last saw her. She looks good, but then Joy always looks good. Joy is the only person on Cloud City my age who can cause me to stumble over my words. It must be those piercing dark-brown eyes. Even when she's smiling at you Joy is somehow sizing you up, checking to see where exactly you land. It's not to say we've had many exchanges. The two conversations consisted of me barely able to ask for a drink while she served at the

Yarith. Hadn't heard about her working for Elad. I guess we're both trying to climb that ladder.

"I'm not playing," I say, but I walk over to her anyway. My eyes are still locked on Boba Fett.

"It sure looks like you're playing a game," she says, nodding in the bounty hunter's direction. Always with that smile. "No one is coming to my table but if you play a couple of rounds, people will venture. Then the bossman Elad will stop hovering over me wondering if I should be placed back behind the bar dishing out watered-down drinks."

She deals me in. Before I can tell her I have nothing of value to gamble she pulls out a couple of credit ingots and places them in front of me.

"Never pegged you for an Azure Den worker," I say as I pretend to look at my hand.

"Sometimes you go where you're needed," Joy says. "I'm glad you're here. I've been meaning to talk to you."

Why would Joy Iya want to talk to me? I just always assumed she considered me a bit of a nobody.

"Me?" I ask foolishly, and I regret it as soon as I say it. A bounty hunter would be more self-assured. I bet Boba Fett never ends a statement with a question mark.

"I see you around. Scrambling for gigs here and there," Joy says. "It doesn't have to be that way."

She's been watching me? Joy Iya? I try to hold her intense stare for as long as I can. One or two or hundreds of heartbeats pass, and I forget what I'm meant to be doing.

"Do you hold the key to salvation or something?" I don't know why I said it but there it is, my words floating in front of me like a confused solitary beldon.

"I've got a proposition for you," she says. But before Joy can go on, Elad's guard nudges me.

"Sorry," I say.

I follow the guard as he escorts me back to Elad's office. I take a deep breath and steady myself for what I hope is my first concrete interaction with Boba Fett. I've been working on Elad to introduce me to the top hunters out there. There is no one above Boba Fett.

Elad sits behind his large desk with his favorite droid, 3-76, by his side, but Boba Fett is nowhere to be found. Kriffing idiot. I messed up. I should have just headed straight to Boba Fett when I first saw him. A real opportunity squashed because of Joy's beautiful eyes. I need to get back on track.

"Good work on the little job," Elad says. The "little job" was roughing up a Gamorrean who owed Elad money. A simple enough task that still left me with two new scars above my eye.

"Up for another task? Tonight, a quick visit to Na'Tala. She decided she no longer works at Azure," he says. "Heard she's been complaining about me and how I conduct my business. I can't have that."

A quick visit means convincing Na'Tala to return to Azure, and if she doesn't, then I need to show her why.

"What about what I want?" I ask.

"Right! Too bad. You just missed him. He'll be back," Elad says. "So, about Na'Tala . . ."

"You promised me an introduction to Boba Fett," I say. "Our deal had nothing to do with Na'Tala."

"Now, how will I look if I allow you to meet Boba Fett wearing that?" He points to my weak attire. "You want to be taken seriously, don't you?"

I get up. He's not going to help me. Forget Elad. I don't need him. I'll figure it out myself.

"You have every right to leave!" Elad calls out as I near the exit. "No worries. I'll just send 3-76 to take care of Na'Tala."

I stop. A visit from 3-76 is a death note. Na'Tala is only trying to look out for herself, like we all are. I turn back.

"Smart, Isabalia, smart! To make sure there's no hard feelings, how about I give you access to Cloud Regalia?" Elad says. "New clothes, hmmm? Before your big meetup with Boba Fett?"

His droid punches in a code that will allow me entrance to the exclusive clothing store.

"Take care of Na'Tala and I'll set up the meet-and-greet."

I nod, accept his terms, and push down the guilt growing inside of me. I'm closer to my goal and this is what matters.

Before I head out, Joy rushes up to me and hands me a metallic card.

"I think you need a change as much as I do," she says. "Tonight."

She quickly walks back to her still-empty table. I pocket her card before anyone notices and exit the club. Outside, the suns shine bright as ever. Cloud City is fully awake. I find a quiet corner to read Joy's card.

A Change

Sector Four

I knew today was going to be different. I felt it! I'll hit up Cloud Regalia first before searching for Na'Tala. I will finally dress the part. I hurry to the wing where anyone who has any clout shops. Extravagant stores for only a privileged few, and today I'm one of them.

"Isabalia," I tell the droid staffing the entrance. It punches my name and the doors open. The store is exactly what I imagined: completely pristine in white and silver with racks of clothes that can appear with just a press of a button. Because it's on the early side, the store is somewhat empty with only a handful of customers.

"How would you like to be dressed today? Is it for a private event or a day spent in the casinos? You're petite but shapely. Perhaps a formfitting gown that changes with every step you take?"

I try to shoo the store droid away but it's not possible. It is relentless.

"I need clothes I can move around in," I say. "For fighting. With hidden pockets and such."

The droid directs me to another room. I can't help myself. I instantly gravitate to the capes.

An older couple enters the room. The man has white hair while his partner wears hers in the elaborate Bespin braids. The man grabs a flashy outfit, stares at it with confusion, and brusquely places it back on the rack.

"This isn't really my style."

"Stop being so silly," she says. "It's not every day you mark a union as long and as fruitful as ours. Tonight, we celebrate." She laughs, gently nudging at him.

They haven't noticed me yet. I dig deeper into a rack as if I'm looking for something in particular. I can't stop sneaking glances over to them. How the man caresses her cheek. How she presses into his hand. I remember when my parents looked at each other like that. They were never afraid to show tenderness, to laugh loudly at their inside jokes, to hold each other. I never had a bad childhood. I was always shown affection, just like this couple freely exhibits. But poverty makes a person hungry. Love can only get you so far.

395

The couple look up and see me. They give me a nod, a warm smile, and I do the same. Then they walk out with new clothes.

The droid returns with a pile of garments for me to try on. Soon I'm dressed in an extravagant blue jumpsuit with a matching cape.

"A dash of the baron administrator's taste is always a good thing," the droid says. I walk out of the store wearing my new threads, throwing the old ones away.

Breaking in to Na'Tala's place is pretty easy. Her room is as small as mine, but unlike my empty space devoid of any personality, Na'Tala's unit is an explosion of color and items. Clothes are thrown every-where and every centimeter of her wall is a piece of art or a declaration. "BE FREE!" "NO FEAR!"

I rummage through her stuff, trying to find a clue, anything to point me in the right direction. Unfortunately, I find nothing but more affirmations.

Annoyed, I head out. Before I close the door my boot crunches down on something. I bend and pick up the two cracked pieces of a card. *"A Change Sector Four."*

Sector Four is where it's at, apparently. My destination is set.

As I draw nearer to the sector, I hear the sound of voices, hushed but still there. A gathering. Did Joy invite me and Na'Tala to a secret party?

"If we stop work then they will have to meet our demands for better pay. We run Cloud City. Without us, the city simply won't function."

Joy is at the center of this gathering, but this isn't a social get-together. This is bad news. They're trying to overthrow Cloud City rules. It's not possible. Lando will never allow it. There's a reason why we are not part of the Mining Guild. We are able to thrive under secrecy. Protesting against how things run in Cloud City is a fruitless endeavor.

"They're wasting their time," I mutter to myself.

"Are we?" Na'Tala suddenly appears beside me. "Heard you've been looking for me. Still playing the role of Elad's messenger? Don't worry. I got my own message for Elad."

Na'Tala walks away and joins the others.

"Full city stoppage. It's the only way to get their attention," Joy says. She looks radiant, more beautiful than ever. "Who is with us?"

The crowd nods in agreement. After a few more fiery speeches, I'm left wondering why Joy thinks I would be a part of this.

"What did you think?" she asks as the crowd lingers, excited and ready for action.

"I think you guys are in for a losing battle," I say. "Cloud City is built for business and pleasure, or have you forgotten Lando's mandate?"

"I've seen you take these little jobs," she says. "Apprehend this two-bit player. Rough up another. You're more than that. We all are."

How can she be so sure? This time I can't hold her stare. Instead I look down at my shiny new boots.

"I believe in you even now when you can't meet my eyes," she says. My face burns up.

"This is a pivotal time. Don't you want to be a part of this?" Joy asks. "A real movement."

She rests her hand on my arm, gently squeezes it. The crowd around us has all but disappeared. It's just Joy and this hope she's offering me.

"Why me?" I ask.

"Because it's time to come out from the shadows and be with your people," she says. "We're right on the edge. It's time to take a leap."

I'm not used to this. She's laying it out plain for me, this chance. But I'm destined to walk another path. Maybe if I explain this to Joy, she would understand.

"When I take care of this one thing, then I'll be able to do whatever I want," I say. "Boba Fett can show me the ropes and—"

Her face falls.

"You're looking at a man hired to track others as your ticket out." She says this with such disappointment. "I guess you better run off then. I'm sure the person you hurt won't mind. At least you'll be dressed in nice clothes while you do it."

Joy storms off, and I'm left there feeling foolish in this jumpsuit that suddenly feels too tight.

There's so much unrest. Whispers of the work stoppage due to start any minute. Strange new faces about. And through it all, I just can't stop thinking of Joy and her words. I stare at the beldons but they hold no answers for me today.

Nothing has felt right. When I finally caught up with Na'Tala she didn't put up a fight; instead she simply shook her head. "You are on the wrong side," she said before I deposited her back to the Azure Den and Elad. I completed my task, and Elad promised the introduction I've been waiting for. The carbon freezing facility is where I'm to meet Boba Fett this morning. Everything I've worked on for so long is about to come true. Yet, why do I feel like bantha crap?

I double check that my Relby-K23 blaster is secure underneath my cape with the vibroknuckler in my pocket. I try to ignore the disapproving voices in my head but it's not working. A bounty hunter must be single-minded and focused. I'm none of those things. I'm just torn.

Recnelo scurries past me without uttering a word.

"No insult for me, Recnelo? It's not like you," I say, matching her quick stride.

"I need to be somewhere, but you already know that."

"I'm heading to the carbon freezing facility, too," I say. "We can go together."

"You're joining the work stoppage then. Correct?"

She stops when I don't respond.

"Open your eyes, Isabalia. You think the beldons are floating out there for your viewing pleasure. They once were fierce creatures," she says with frustration. "Did you know Cloud City sedates them to keep them docile?"

"There's more to life than what Cloud City can offer. Don't you think I deserve it?" I ask. "Please tell Joy I'm sorry."

"No, Isabalia, you're wrong. You *are* Cloud City."

Recnelo walks away and I'm left to contend with this truth. She meets Joy at the end of the passageway, and they head toward the carbon freeze. Along the way they collect a couple more people and eventually stop at the entrance of the facility. Like a fool, I follow a few steps behind and watch as things unfurl.

If the work stoppage begins here, I can easily slip into the facility through a side entrance. Boba Fett is surely waiting inside. Joy briefly looks my way, as does Recnelo. Everything is converging at once and I must make a choice. Follow Boba Fett to a future I've been planning for months or join the others. Joy, Recnelo, even my parents, see something in me I'm failing to see. A person I'm meant to be. Which future do I embrace when both are so uncertain?

"Stop right there!"

A stormtrooper appears out of nowhere, blaster at the ready. Recnelo and Joy argue with the trooper but he refuses to listen. He aims a blaster at them.

Before I can think I run toward the stormtrooper, brandishing the Relby-K23. I shoot toward the stormtrooper's knees right as he turns to me. He buckles, but still shoots, barely missing me. I don't stop. I head straight toward him, kicking his blaster out of his hands. I straddle the trooper. Punching with all I've got. Finding ways past his armor to inflict pain with fear and adrenaline propelling me. Only a few more blows cement who is truly in control of this situation.

"Listen up, Imperial trash," I say. "Your ugly white uniforms are not welcome in Cloud City."

The last punch is more than enough to knock the stormtrooper out cold. I get up, wiping beads of sweat from my forehead. My new outfit is ruined by a large tear down the side of the jumpsuit.

"I heard there's a work stoppage happening," I say after a couple of beats. "Not sure if I'm dressed for it but . . ."

Joy chuckles, flashing that smile.

"There's hope for you yet, Isabalia," she says.

This time I hold her stare. Maybe I can even hold it for a lifetime.

"Enough of that, you two." Recnelo says. "The work is before us."

"C'mon!" Joy says. "Our people are waiting."

She grabs my hand, and I don't let go.

NO TIME FOR POETRY

Austin Walker

"Can you *believe* they pay us for this?"

It wasn't the excitement in Dengar's voice that surprised IG-88, who stood next to the Corellian bounty hunter as he piloted his way through wreckage and debris. As the galaxy's deadliest assassin droid, IG-88 had crossed paths with plenty of overexuberant bounty hunters, the sort who convinced themselves that obsessive thrill seeking was a vocation. Dengar, yanking back the yoke of his JumpMaster 5000 as it dodged incoming detritus, was just one more fool with a blaster.

"C'mon, c'mon . . . Come to Dengar."

Nor was IG-88 nonplussed by the bounty hunter's mangled Imperial accent. Compared with the elegant edge of Imperial officers' speech, Dengar's voice was a makeshift shiv. This evaluation was not a judgment on the part of IG-88, though. People seemed to think that accents reflected intelligence or authority, but the droid knew better. The way an organism spoke was only one more patina layer of ugly organic inefficiency. Eventually, the assassin considered, they wouldn't be around to speak at all. So much would be improved, then.

"Damnit! Lost him. Iggy, start a thermal scan would you, mate? We can't let him get away now."

There it was again. The second-person plural. "Us." "We." *That* was what had taken IG-88 aback. Had the organic forgotten the terms of their arrangement? Was this a ploy? Better to confirm now that Dengar remembered that the moment they had their prey in hand, his life would be forfeit. Best to *remind* him.

"One of us will be paid, Corellian. Or do you not recall our agreement?" IG-88's cylindrical head twisted to face Dengar. This was, of course, only for effect. The sensor array in the IG series was not limited by simple organic limitations such as "facing."

Dengar let out a playful sigh as he brought his ship to a halt, hidden behind the massive sublight engine of a wrecked frigate. "Yeah, yeah. Don't get your circuits in a twist, you walkin' vaporator. You and me, we each got coordinates from Fett. Just like Bossk an' the oth—"

"Those coordinates were fraudulent."

"Of *course* they were! I'm gettin' there, you absolute *lamp*." Dengar readjusted his posture, stretched his fingers, regripped the ship's yoke, and cleared his throat. "As I was sayin', Fett gave everyone dummy info. But you and me, we're too smart for that. We cracked his system and found the coordinates he was keepin' for himself. And hard as it is to admit, two of us together got a better shot at catchin' Solo." Dengar's voice twisted in subdued rage as he said the name. "Especially if he's got his rebel pallies with him."

"That is not the *deal*," IG-88 said, in as close to a scold as the machine could emit. "That is the *circumstance* of the deal. Confirm that you understand the arrangement."

The already cramped cockpit of *Punishing One*, Dengar's ship, felt a little smaller for a moment. Both of its inhabitants were killers, and each knew that a deal like theirs could fall apart at any moment, even now as they neared their prey. IG-88 was, after all, a droid known for ruthless opportunism. And even in their short time together, he had realized that Dengar was fond of claiming not to have a conscience at all. Whether it had been taken from him by a life of violence—the tragedy scarring his face and body—by a poorly installed cybernetic modification, or by some other loathsome quirk of illogical organic life, IG-88 did not know and did not care.

Dengar's voice dropped, stone-cold serious. "When we get him, our truce is over. You and me, we'll have a prizefight fit for the dueling arenas of Nar Shaddaa. And only one of us will walk away with the purse."

"Good." It was fundamentally a productive understanding. The pair would have higher odds of capturing Solo than the independent hunters like Fett or the Trandoshan Bossk, who had no one to watch their backs. But neither would IG-88 and Dengar be weighted down by the ungainly sentimentalism that came with being long-term hunting partners like 4-LOM and Zuckuss.

The bounty hunter sank a little lower in his seat before a thought seemed to cross his mind, lifting him back up into his normal, spirited posture. "Now, wait a second, assassin. Why all this effort into making sure I remember the particulars? You ain't secretly a *protocol* droid, are ya?"

"Absolutely not."

A laugh from the Corellian. He must have confused IG-88's swift rebuttal for comedic cadence. Which again, IG-88 thought to himself, *Absolutely not.*

"Now, Iggy, back to work, yeah? Get us that thermal scan so we can find our mark."

"That would be a waste of time, Dengar. This area is contaminated with interference. Such a scan will be useless." The coordinates Fett had provided Dengar with had led the duo to a debris field in the Outer Rim, one of the few reminders of the Clone Wars' massive starship battles. The Empire had been extremely thorough with its salvage operations in the years after the war, but this wreckage had been left behind for some reason. And though it had been years since these ships had seen combat, the entire area was radiated with their heat.

"Ah, the present is always haunted by the past, isn't it, droid?"

"I do not have time for trite poetry, bounty hunter."

"You also apparently don't have time to offer up an *alternative*." Dengar leaned across the starship's console and flicked a few switches. "But no worries there. I don't need one anyway. Activating thermal scan."

Don't have time? IG-88 could have killed Dengar a dozen different ways in the time it took the Corellian to speak those words. In fact, the droid's mastery over time was so complete that he ran internal simulations of doing exactly that and luxuriated in the internally visualized display of his power and mastery.

"See, piston-head, I'm not looking for Solo's thermal signature." He flicked a few more switches as IG-88 came out of his reverie. "I'm looking for the *absence* of Solo's thermal signature."

"Impossible. Even if you know the make of Solo's ship—"

"And I *do*. We're chasing a modified YT-1300 Corellian light freighter. Not as hot as its reputation might lead you to believe, I may add." He hit another switch and then a toggle.

"Do not interrupt me, organic." IG-88 again rotated his cylindrical head to add punctuation. Deep inside his advanced computer core, he considered that adopting such an affect might be akin to gaining his own sort of accent, and began to calculate exactly how troubling such an inefficiency was.

"Sorry, *partner*. You were saying?"

"I was explaining that even with the *Millennium Falcon*'s information, this debris field's level of thermal pollution is so high—"

Before the droid could finish his sentence, *Punishing One*'s auxiliary computers lit up like pyrotechnics. A YT-1300 light freighter had been hiding in the desolate shell of a Trade Federation *Lucrehulk*-class battleship. Solo.

Dengar couldn't hold back the smirk forming on his lips. In fact, he didn't even try. "That doesn't count as *interrupting you*, I hope?"

"How did you achieve such signal resolution?"

"Ah, well, you need to understand exactly how a smuggler like Solo thinks. It's an old trick, before your time I'd guess. And the sort of thing that wouldn't make its way into even the most rigorous of Imperial memory cores." Dengar's voice took on the posh tone of an Imperial admiral as he delivered the line, which only worked to make IG-88 wonder why the bounty hunter had not chosen to adopt the more socially prestigious accent. Simultaneously and elsewhere in the droid's constantly whirring verbobrain, IG-88 took permanent note of the technique. He understood it *now*, and that was all that mattered.

"Give him a second." Dengar spoke with the voice of a seasoned hunter. "He'll see that we scanned him and—"

Just in time, the Corellian freighter burst from the wreckage and set a course for the debris field's edge, where a hyperspace jump could safely get it away from its pursuers.

"Settle in, partner." Dengar slid the throttle up, and the *Punishing One* began to charge forward through the debris. It was, of course, another joke from the Corellian. The JumpMaster 5000 was more spacious than the droid's own ship, but it was still a machine built for one. The patrol boat was fine for an independent cargo hauler or even a bounty hunter like Dengar, but the cockpit had nowhere to "settle in" besides the cockpit chair.

Fortunately, it turned out that Dengar's skill as a pilot was more than good enough to keep IG-88 on his feet. The bounty hunter piloted *Punishing One* like a Carnelion kite, dancing through the debris field and taking minimal (if any) damage as he pressed toward the *Falcon*'s position. Confident in his temporary ally's skill behind the controls, IG-88 focused on preparing the ship's shielding, combat, and auxiliary systems.

"We are now within communications range."

With another flick of his fingers, Dengar opened a broadcast channel. "It's over, Han! Stop where you are and maybe we'll let a couple of your friends live, yeah?"

Dengar's body temperature rose a third of a degree. His voice fluctuated, just so, before saying "over" and "Han." It was a vocal structure similar to that of a liar. This meant that Dengar was not confident that it *was* over for Han Solo. Worse, IG-88 realized, the entire array of physiological responses had revealed that Dengar was illogically invested in the capture of Solo.

When the Corellian freighter finally responded, it wasn't with words. A flurry of laser blasts passed just above the *Punishing One.* For Dengar, it was just another opportunity to taunt his prey. "You used to be a better shot than *that,* Solo! You're losing your edge!"

A voice finally broke over the comm. It was feminine, maybe one of Solo's companions, IG-88 thought. "I don't know who you are, but you've got the wrong ship. Disengage now!"

"Nice try, friend. What, is Han too scared to talk for himself now? Needs his rebel friends to speak for him?"

Though the bulk of his attention was locked on their target, IG-88 dedicated a few subroutines to concern about his partner's ability to

keep a cool head. "Calm yourself, Corellian. Your irrationality is becoming dangerous." Whatever their history, it was clear that Solo had
gotten under Dengar's skin, wedged inside the organic deeper than
any cybernetic implant.

"Shut up, *flutebucket*." Even his pathetic insults were getting worse,
IG-88 thought.

His aim, on the other hand, seemed as steady as ever. Dengar fired
a burst from his quad laser cannons as a feint, driving his target off
course and into the free-floating bridge of some long-dead assault
cruiser.

The Corellian freighter spun out of control and directly into the
sights of Dengar's ion cannon. A single blast was all it took. The YT-
1300 floated against the starfield, lit clearly by a distant sun. Now that
it was freed from the sea of ruined ships, IG-88 made a terrible discovery.

"Do you recall when you said that the ship we were following was
unremarkable, Dengar?"

"And haven't we proved it?"

"Well. You are correct. The ship we are following *is* unremarkable.
In fact, its only external modifications seem to be the addition of a
dorsal laser turret and an upgraded sublight drive."

"Droid . . ."

"This is not the *Millennium Falcon*, Corellian." If IG-88 had not
understood that he was superior to every organic being in existence,
his failure to notice the difference between this ship and the *Falcon*
would be embarrassing. Solo's craft was a heavily modified YT-1300f,
a cargo hauler transformed into a well-armed smuggling starship.
But *this* was a much more slightly modified YT-1300p, designed for
passenger transit. "Not only are its modifications inadequate, it is
also missing several key features that would identify it as Solo's vessel."

"You've got to be kidding."

"My programming does not allow for 'kidding.' You should know this by now."

"Well." Dengar's grip dug into the JumpMaster's yoke as he clearly grasped for any rationalization that would excuse the difference. "Solo knew that he was being hunted. Maybe he had the silhouette modified to keep a low profile."

"Unlikely. There was insufficient time for such a procedure to take place between the ship's known egress on Hoth and the present moment." Fett was even more deceptive than IG-88's first impression had suggested. Not only had he provided false information directly, he'd seeded his own ship's data banks with decoy coordinates. The droid considered, for the briefest moment, not whether Fett had betrayed them—which was obvious—but whether he should share his deduction with Dengar. He decided that it would not be particularly fruitful.

408

"We've been deceived!" Dengar shouted, rendering IG-88's internal calculus irrelevant. "That Mandalorian-impersonating son of a—"

"We still have an opportunity, Corellian." IG-88 pressed a button, and the ship's computer brought the freighter's technical specifications on-screen. "A vessel outfitted as such is likely carrying contraband, intelligence, or *valuable individuals.*"

The starship floated awkwardly in front of the *Punishing One* as it drew closer, engines still knocked out by the ionized particles running through its electronics system. But the comm must've been hardened to such an attack, as the woman's voice from before returned.

"I'm telling ya, fella, you've got the wrong ship. My boss isn't going to like it that you're messing with me."

Dengar cut the connection and gave IG-88 a sidelong look.

"Boss?" He pulled up the ship's registration on the console's computer screen. The *Deadnettle.* Independent pleasure vessel. No home port listed.

" 'Independent pleasure vessel'? All right, maybe this'll be worth our time anyway, eh, droid?" He batted a fist against his plate armor and raised the lower cloth of his turban up around his mouth and nose. Masks, IG-88 knew, kept things from getting too personal.

"I will begin docking procedures."

Breaching an occupied vessel—even one disabled by ion cannons—was always a risk. Even for practiced soldiers, the element of surprise gave the defender a great deal of tactical advantage. There was only one way in, which made you an easy target. And without intimate knowledge of the vessel's interior, it was nearly impossible to predict where your foes might be. In short, this meant that defenders had a lot of options, but the boarding party normally had only one: rush in and start shooting.

The duo of IG-88 and Dengar, however, was anything but normal.

From the moment the breach began, the unconventional pair was in complete control. As the air lock opened, smoke filled the entryway of the *Deadnettle,* settling over plush purple carpets and blocking the sight of half a dozen guards who had taken aim. It wouldn't stop the blasterfire from coming in, but it would give them enough time to gain the upper hand.

It was over in an instant. Dengar strode through the smoke with his fire blade, a long, branched dirk of orange flame cutting through the fog, a vision of terror second only to a Dark Lord of the Sith. It was also top-tier misdirection. Because while the guards followed the blade with their eyes, they failed to see the assassin droid boarding their ship just behind.

IG-88 was not merely well armed, he was a walking arsenal. Only accounting for the devices built into his body, the droid had access to blaster cannons in each arm, deployable antipersonnel gas canisters, a localized stun pulser, and throwing flechettes as sharp as they were small. And of course, there was his most dangerous weapon: the mechanical mind that gave him what one of his creators called "wildfire sentience." It was this that allowed him to utterly take apart six well trained security guards in a matter of seconds.

"You've *got* to be kidding me," Dengar said. "I didn't even get to—" His eyes went wide.

There was a lot to take in. The ship's main lounge had been extended to cover the bulk of its interior. From wall to wall, the room had been converted into a gambling hall—and a high-end one given the fancy clothes the now cowering players were wearing. And there, hanging from between a pair of overturned sabacc tables, was a banner with the symbol of the Besadii, one of the most powerful families of the Hutt Cartel.

"I *told* you that you wouldn't wanna mess with my boss." The ship's apparent captain—a Mirialan woman with a smart braid a few shades darker than her bright-green skin—was standing, arms crossed, above four of her dead guards. "Sunnari Khall. Captain of the *Deadnettle*. I'd appreciate it if you two got off my ship."

This time, IG-88 turned his head to look at Dengar not as an affect, but as a signal to take her down and clear out the rest of the ship.

Before he could spring into action, though, Dengar reached across the droid's body.

"Hey, hey, hey! Slow down, Iggy. The captain here is right." He leaned in close to whisper to the droid, not that proximity was necessary, given IG-88's high-range sensor suite. "The Besadii are not enemies you want to make."

The assassin responded at full volume. He wanted the captain to hear him. He wanted to scare her. "They are not enemies *you* want to make, Corellian. I quite like enemies."

IG-88 had not done much work for the Hutts, but he understood that they were wealthy, vicious, and vengeful. They might be useful enemies to have, IG-88 thought, as enemies so often led to new opportunities. He raised his arms and prepared to fire the built-in blasters.

"Try it and see what happens, canister." Khall had raised her hand. In her palm, a thermal detonator began to beep. By the third consecutive chirp, one of the frightened passengers screamed. "Shut up back there, I'm *negotiating*!"

"Ah, see, now you've let on too much, Miss . . . Khall you said it was?"

The sweat in his palms, the furrowed brow . . . if she had said nothing else, IG-88 could tell that Dengar would have left then and there. But now that this Captain Khall had mentioned negotiating, he clearly smelled profit.

"Solo isn't here. There's nothing valuable aboard. I don't have anything you want."

"You do not know what we want." IG-88's voice, too-calm and metallic, would be the only leverage Dengar needed to get something out of this.

The Corellian added just a bit more pressure.

"Well, see, it looks to me like you're running a *very* exclusive sabacc tournament. And no one plays sabacc . . . in a ship . . . in the middle of a debris field . . . for nothing."

"You—you don't know what you're talking about."

IG-88, whose programming drew on generations of research, counted the droplets of water on her brow, the doubling of beats in her heart, a micron-sized movement in her eyes.

"You are hiding something."

"What could I hide from you? Rip my ship apart. You're not going to find anything more than a few thousand credits. I'm telling you, we're just an old gambling freighter in an even older debris field."

411

Ah. There it was. *The debris field.*

"You're playin' for all those wrecks!"

Dengar's instincts had been hardened by decades of bounty hunting. He'd spent tens of thousands of hours in the grime and the muck, and it had earned him an encyclopedic knowledge of criminal enterprise in the galaxy.

He didn't know the specifics, but he could put the pieces together well enough. All these wrecked ships *should* have gone to some scrapyard somewhere. Bracca maybe. But someone—probably one of these Hutts—intervened, paid off some Imperial bureaucrat, and kept this battlefield out of the records. Now they were using it as a prize for the galaxy's most secretive card game.

Sunnari went silent. Anything she said would only worsen her position. Unfortunately, one of her passengers—an opulently dressed Twi'lek—did not understand that important point. "These ships are the property of the Besadii! Your kind has no business here."

"Our kind?" Dengar's brows rose playfully. "Let me tell you something, friendo. Our kind wouldn't exist except for people like you. People like you who are either too cowardly to deal with the problems your greed creates, or else so heinous that totally decent folks decide that their only hope at making things right is *our kind.*"

"It is still not time for poetry, Dengar." The droid's scold worked only to confuse the passengers. "Regardless, you have given us something more valuable than any currency. You and the Besadii have committed high crimes against the Empire, in the form of the theft and exchange of Imperial military vessels."

Dengar unfolded the rest of IG-88's thoughts for Sunnari, the Twi'lek gambler, and the others aboard. "You might not have a bounty yet, but when we report all this to our contacts in the Empire, well." A grin took over his face. "Might as well put you all down right now, let you rot in storage until we collect."

Sunnari shook her head. "No." Just like Dengar had hoped, she was a born survivor just like him. She would not die here, and would not spend the rest of her life fleeing from an Imperial warrant. "No. We can work this out."

"Well." Dengar accented the word with a bend of his waist. "That is exactly what we were hoping to hear, isn't that right, Iggy?"

IG-88 said nothing, simply rotated his head sections to add a degree of extra intimidation.

"I have something. It's the second prize. *Beskar.* You know *beskar*?"

Dengar was almost insulted. "Yes, we know *beskar*. It's Mandalorian metal. Strong, but flexible."

"Well, I've got a pouch of it in my quarters." IG-88's optics rotated and zoomed, tracking sweat, heat, blood pressure. She was telling the truth.

Dengar, though, was less concerned about honesty and more about *value*. "A *pouch*?"

"A big pouch."

"A *big* pouch?"

"Well, a decent-sized pouch, anyway. And it's all yours if you go on your way and give me your word that you will not report . . . our activities."

"What do I want with *beskar*? I want *Solo*!" Dengar's eyes narrowed.

The droid's scans lit up as Sunnari reacted to Dengar's sudden burst of anger. First, a brief moment of fear, and then recognition, and finally, a flood of worry. Sunnari had clearly *heard* of Han Solo, but with the way her eyes moved, the speed of her blinking, and micro-movements in her fingers, it was clear to IG-88 that she couldn't provide intelligence on the smuggler's whereabouts.

"Disregard my associate's words. This is an adequate bribe."

Dengar's head dropped, the growing rage vented by the shocking bluntness of IG-88's response. He'd have to correct the droid's etiquette later.

"Is it a deal?"

"Iggy, you better explain what you're thinking."

"I will explain when we return to your ship. We accept this deal. Provide the *beskar* in the next three minutes, or I will begin executing your crew."

"You are *terrible* at this, Iggy." Dengar raised his hands as if to defuse the situation. "You need to understand. He's an assassin droid. He doesn't really get all *this,* you know? Just get us the damn *beskar* and we'll be on our way."

By the time the two bounty hunters had jumped into hyperspace, word would've already been sent back to Nal Hutta. But that was of no concern to IG-88 and only a receding one for Dengar, who had already begun to play the angles in his head. He could go see that Hutt on Tatooine, maybe. If he was remembering right, the two Hutt families had little love lost between them.

"You did well, Corellian." IG-88 did not turn his head this time. "We have not captured Solo. By the terms of our agreement, our arrangement will continue. Until we catch Solo."

" 'Until we catch Solo'? Droid, maybe you haven't noticed, but Solo is in the wind. We don't have a single lead."

"We have the *beskar.*"

"The *beskar* is not *Solo.*"

"It is Mandalorian metal. Fett wears Mandalorian armor. It will have value to him."

"So we set a trap. Or we tell him we want to negotiate!"

"Yes. We have many options. I am presently simulating three thousand potential variations on our next encounter with Fett."

"You're . . ." A sigh of relief, and a sudden query. "Listen, Iggy. I get the impression you don't like us. 'Organics,' I mean. So why work with me to begin with? There were other droids on this hunt."

"You are correct. Organics are irrational, sentimental, and dangerously optimistic."

"Yeah, mate. I know. That's what I mean, stuff like that. No need to rub it in."

With a whir, the assassin droid turned to face his partner in crime. "I am not 'rubbing it in.' I am explaining why I made this decision. People make the most inadvisable decisions. Solo more than most."

"So, what, it's a *you have to fight fire with fire* kind of thing?"

"That is thirty-seven percent of the benefit. The remaining value rests in your ability to serve as an erratic distraction."

A bright smile cracked across the scarred face of Dengar, Corellian bounty hunter. "That right there, *that* was a joke, droid."

IG-88, with a tone so dry that only another elite assassin droid could be sure it was meant to be humorous, emitted a short reply.

"Absolutely not."

415

BESPIN ESCAPE

Martha Wells

Lonaste woke to her cousin Beetase standing over her and shouting. This behavior wasn't unusual in her clan, and Lonaste was groggy from a double shift in the reclamation pits. She swatted at Beetase and groaned, "Stop it."

Beetase shook her urgently. "Wake up! There's an evacuation alert!"

Lonaste blinked up at her, the frightened tone in Beetase's voice penetrating. The warning message blared from just outside the door. "What—" Lonaste flailed out of her warm blankets and flung herself upright. "What is—"

Beetase grabbed Lonaste's shoulders. Her expression was stricken, her white hair standing up in untamed wisps. "You were right. It's happening."

Lonaste's heart plummeted toward her feet. She pulled her coat on over her nightclothes and lurched out the open door of her podroom. Out on the walkway, the small messenger droid raced away, still blaring the evacuation alert. The message echoed down all four levels of Cloud City's Ugnaught Town, where the inhabitants crowded out onto the walkways and platforms, frantic and confused, their worried voices adding to the din.

Lonaste found herself equally frantic but not confused. It was the Imperials. The Imperials were taking over Cloud City. *You planned for this,* she told herself, *you knew this was coming.* She had never believed in Bespin's neutral status; no planet was neutral, if it had something the Empire wanted. But the reality was a cold shock. She said, "How close are they? Do we know?"

Beetase waved her arms. "No idea! The others are gathering—"

Lonaste hurried for the stairs, and Beetase clattered after her.

She reached the door of their clan meeting room on the level below and pushed inside. The whole family was there, aunts, uncles, all the cousins and their children. "There you are!" cousin Jamint said, as if Lonaste had been hiding. "We need you to tell us—"

"I know." Lonaste pushed past assorted relatives and dumped a young cousin out of the chair at her jury-rigged console. She tapped the pad to pull up the hacked interface she had used to break into Baron Calrissian's private comm.

Behind her, everyone was talking. "She told us," Beetase was saying loudly. "And none of you would listen—"

Uncle Donsat began, "Stop your panicking—"

Lonaste ignored the rising arguments and exclamations. Ever since the Imperial lord and his troops had arrived in the city looking for rebels, she had known this would happen. The communications she intercepted, the rising suspicions and fear of the other sentients in the city, the warnings passed on from human workers, had all told the same story: The Imperials would take Bespin. She had tried to convince her family to leave, even if the other Ugnaught clans wouldn't. But the reality of the situation made her hands shake as she paged through the console's screens. *They'll take us into slavery, just like on Gentes.* As usual, no one was listening to her, but she said, "You all need to pack, just the essentials. I'll figure out how much time we have—"

"Yoxgit and the others say not to worry," Donsat objected. Lonaste knew Donsat wasn't an Imperial supporter, he was just desperately afraid of change, but it didn't make it any easier to listen to him, especially now. "It's not as if they'll blow up the city."

"Because Imperials never do that," Beetase said grimly. There was a chorus of frightened objections, and cousin Jamint added, "Calrissian himself said to go."

"He's talking to the humans, not us. Yoxgit says the Empire has no quarrel with us," Donsat countered. Yoxgit was a member of the wealthiest Ugnaught clan in the city, and Donsat was a terrible social climber.

"Oh, and you believe everything that arms dealer says. Are you his puppet?" Aunt Maloste entered the fray swinging. She wasn't the best ally, as her idea of a discussion was to bludgeon the others into agreement, and it always caused bad feelings. Half the family had old disagreements with her, and now they all jumped into the argument on Donsat's side.

Lonaste searched the comm records. She had set the system to do regular captures of Calrissian's communications, because she had to sleep and work her shifts and she couldn't sit here all the time, even though it made her nerves vibrate not to know what was happening.

The last message capture was only three hours ago. Calrissian's sources had warned him that an Imperial takeover was imminent. Why he had waited until now to call the evacuation, Lonaste had no idea. The Tibanna gas merchants had spread the rumor that Calrissian had made a deal to leave the city free of Imperial control; maybe Calrissian had been counting on that, but obviously it hadn't worked out. *Humans,* she thought in disgust. *But it's going to be all right, we have a plan.*

Two days ago, Lonaste had made a secret deal to buy passage for the clan on a Duros cargo ship, trading them a stockpile of scraps saved from the reclamation center. It had taken most of the past year to get enough precious metals, even with Beetase and her other cousins helping her. All she had to do now was contact the crew to arrange a meeting at the city docks. She tapped in the secure comm code the ship's captain had given her, but the console refused the connection. Lonaste's throat went dry. She tried it again, hoping she had just fumbled the keys, but the comm wouldn't connect. *Uh-oh.*

Beetase jittered at her elbow. "Did you call the ship? What did they say?"

Lonaste tried to connect to the port controller as a test. The comm gave her static and ineffectual beeps. "The Imperials must be jamming the city's communications," she said, loud enough to cut through all the agitated voices.

The others went quiet. There was no reason for the Imperials to jam the internal comms of a city they didn't mean to attack; surely that would convince the doubters. Lonaste pushed to her feet. They were all still standing there, staring at her. "What are you doing? We need to get ready to leave!"

Everyone turned to look at Aunt Temarit, the eldest. Her tufts of hair and brows were silver-white, and age had left deep furrows in her round cheeks. She stood silent and enigmatic, clasping her forearms. Uncle Donsat said, "Surely there is no reason—"

Temarit interrupted, "Jamint, go ask Amigast what his clan means to do."

Jamint elbowed his cousins aside and hurried for the door.

Lonaste seethed at the delay, but she thought Amigast, the leader of the largest Ugnaught clan in the miners' union, would support her. At the last meeting, where the clans had argued about the Imperial presence in the city, Amigast had asked, "If this Imperial lord only wanted the rebels, why hasn't he left with them?"

Yoxgit the arms dealer had said, "He's waiting to capture a rebel leader called Skywalker, then he'll leave."

Amigast had countered, "The city militia says there are rumors of a Star Destroyer somewhere in the system."

Yoxgit had raised placating hands. "They only want the rebel humans. For us, everything will go on as usual. There're credits to be made here, no point in disrupting it."

Lonaste had bared her teeth in disgust. Didn't anyone else notice how fast Yoxgit had gone from "the Imperials will take what they want and leave" to "everything will go on as usual"? And Yoxgit seemed to know a lot about what the Imperials were planning. She had raised her voice and said to Yoxgit, "You probably want the Imperials here. It's good for your business, right?" Yoxgit sold Tibanna gas to the arms merchants, though why he thought the Imperials wouldn't just take the gas for themselves, she had no idea.

It caused a stir, some clan leaders demanding Yoxgit answer, others defending him. Uncle Donsat had weighed in, saying, "The unions would never permit—"

Lonaste had flailed in exasperation. "The unions can't protect us! This is just like Gentes, the Imperials will enslave us and send us away from one another! It's what they've done on a hundred other worlds!"

Uncle Donsat had turned to Yoxgit and the clan elders. "You must excuse her," he had said loudly. "She's young and has lots of strange notions, and they panic her."

Aunt Moloste had smacked him in the shoulder and growled, "Don't air family matters at the union meeting, you fool."

Lonaste had tried to speak again, but Donsat had dismissed her so thoroughly, no one would listen to her. Again.

Now here they were, with precious seconds passing and no one doing anything. Lonaste drew breath to say something, hopefully something persuasive and not furious. But then Jamint shoved in through the crowded door. His expression frightened, he said, "Amigast's clan is gone, their section is empty!"

It was like the air had suddenly been sucked out of the room. Shocked, his voice suddenly uncertain, Donsat said, "What?"

"Gone!" Jamint repeated. "They evacuated."

The silence was deep enough for Lonaste to hear urgent shouting echoing from far down the walkway. Then Aunt Moloste, her expression sober, said, "We should go."

"But you couldn't call the ship." Cousin Sallat turned to Lonaste. "How will we—"

"I'll go to the port and make sure they can take us aboard," Lonaste said, her heart pounding.

Beetase said immediately, "I'll go with you."

The others all looked at Aunt Temarit. Lonaste clamped her jaw shut and forced herself not to plead or argue.

Then Temarit said, "Go. We'll be ready when you return."

Lonaste gasped in relief. Beetase grabbed her arm, and the others cleared the way as they rushed out of the room.

Lonaste stepped out of the shelter of the habitation corridor and flinched. Shouting, the pounding of running footsteps, echoed down from the galleries above. It sounded like a riot. Many of the other inhabitants of Cloud City must be just as certain as she was that escape was the only option.

As they passed the high white halls of the junction, other sentients ran past, mostly humans. No one seemed to notice them, probably because they weren't looking down to see two smallish Ugnaughts hurry along. Normally Lonaste found all the looming of larger species annoying, but for once it was coming in handy.

Then blasterfire erupted in the corridor ahead. Lonaste grabbed Beetase's arm and hustled her down toward the next side passage.

"All these people trying to get away," Beetase said. "Our ship didn't wait, did it."

"It did," Lonaste said firmly, ignoring her own fear. "The comm was down. And if it didn't wait, we'll steal a ship."

"Do you know how to steal a ship?" Beetase objected. "Because I don't."

Lonaste didn't have an answer for that. She was a scrap worker and a tech, not a pirate. If the ship wasn't there, she had no idea what to do.

They crossed onto the upper walkway above the big open space of the West Hall. Lonaste glanced down to see stormtroopers running past, and— She slid to an abrupt halt, Beetase thumping into her back.

"What?" Beetase whispered.

"I thought I saw Yoxgit." Lonaste tried to see through the curved balusters, angling her head to squint down. She was right, it was him. He stood near the inward entrance to the hall, talking to a stormtrooper.

Beetase squeezed in beside her to see, breathing heavily in Lonaste's ear.

Yoxgit and the stormtrooper spoke, then Yoxgit stepped back and the stormtrooper moved off down the hall. Yoxgit glanced around and ducked away down another corridor. Lonaste pulled back from the railing and looked at Beetase. "That's not good."

"No," Beetase agreed soberly. "You know, I think he knew that Imperial lord was coming here, long before he arrived. Mirsame said her aunt said the gas merchants knew all about it."

"Yoxgit must have made some deal with the Imperials." Like Calrissian's deal to keep the Imperials out of the city, it would probably come to nothing. Lonaste turned away from the railing. "Lots of people selling one another in this city suddenly. As if the Imperials aren't going to take us all in the end."

"Bespin's changed. I'm not going to miss it," Beetase said, and they hurried on.

From the echo of blasterfire, Lonaste decided it was better to avoid the city's central core. She took the next hatch into the outer ring's maintenance passages. It was a confusing maze, added on to as the city's industries grew, and would be hard for outsiders to navigate.

There were no bright white halls in the maintenance sections. The light was dim and the corridors dingy, the grated floors wet from the dripping city hydraulics overhead. Lonaste was used to it, but the eerie quiet was new; workers used these passages to access every part of the city's infrastructure, and they were never this empty. But from the scattered debris—discarded tools, a spilled bag stuffed with travel ration packets, and the occasional shoe—a lot of people had moved through here with the speed of desperation, very recently.

The mining clan, Lonaste thought. *And probably others, too.* She and Beetase moved quickly through the section, despite the ladders and stairs designed for longer-limbed sentients. Their size meant they could take the low-ceilinged shortcuts intended for droids. As they reached the first freight turbolift access, another distant, muffled burst of blasterfire made them both flinch. Beetase whispered, "Still far away."

Lonaste forced her hackles down and stepped into the tube.

They worked their way down from tube to tube, and finally stumbled out at the large-load docking level, in the broad corridor that opened onto the cargo bays and landing pads. Lonaste hastily glanced around, wary of stormtroopers, but it was empty and quiet here, too. Up and down the high, curving corridor, the big hatchways into the bays were open, letting in a fresh outside wind that swept dust and some torn flimsies down the dock. The emptiness gave Lonaste a terrible feeling; she had expected it to be full of people, loading the ships for escape.

"I thought it would be frantic here. Where is everybody?" Beetase echoed her thought as Lonaste hurried to the dock supervisor's station in the open control pod. The station was meant for a much taller sentient; Beetase had to give her a boost so she could reach the control board.

The blinking red status numbers made Lonaste's heart sink. The vid views of the docks showed empty bays and pads, blasted hatches, or a last few drive flares as the stragglers lifted off to safety. The Duros ship she had made the tentative agreement with was gone, the hatch of its bay open to the bright daylight outside. "All the ships are gone," Lonaste said, a lump forming in her throat. "The red means they didn't pay their fees and broke the locks to get out."

Beetase gasped in dismay, swaying as she supported Lonaste. "How can they all be gone already?" she protested.

Lonaste forced herself to think past rising panic. "Some people, like Amigast's clan, must have had an earlier warning, or knew enough to start running as soon as Calrissian said to go."

Beetase snorted in dismay. "Nobody warned us!"

Lonaste thought about Yoxgit, talking to the stormtrooper. She bared her teeth. "Maybe there was a warning and our union never got it." If the Imperials wanted to take over Bespin's mining operations, and not just blast the city to pieces, they would want the Ugnaught clans to keep working. "The Imperials will need forced labor here."

Beetase growled agreement. "But what are we going to do?"

Lonaste pushed aside her anger and concentrated on the problem, stretching to look for bays without red tabs. According to the status display, there were still ships in the more expensive upper city dock, but that was where all the Imperials would be, too. "Oh, here!" She stopped, hope blossoming. Toward the west end of this dock level was a large bay for the cheaper dreg-freighters that picked up extra loads of gas or scrap that the contracted freighter lines couldn't or wouldn't carry. There wasn't a vid view, but the status showed the bay was still occupied. "We can try there!"

They ran down the dock as fast as they could, and Lonaste was winded by the time they reached the bay. The big loading hatch slid open when she tapped the entrance panel. The bay's outer hatch was still closed and the lights were dim, making the large space shadowy. Two ships, both long, blocky cargo carriers, stood on the battered and stained deck plates.

426

Lonaste started forward hopefully but saw immediately why the first ship was still here: It was a wreck, with holes blasted in the engine housing and lower hull. Despairing, Beetase said, "An unstable load probably blew up after the ship was under way, and they towed it back here for repair."

"Right." Lonaste was already moving toward the other one, bracing herself for disappointment. She had done a lot of walking already, and her joints were sore. If this ship was derelict, too, they would have to brave the fighting and try the upper docks.

But as she drew closer, the second ship's hatch slid open. She stopped, startled, unable to see anything in the dark interior. A chill crept up her back as every horror story about abandoned ships and Imperial traps ran through her head. "Who's there? I can't see you."

Something beeped and the ship's interior lights blinked on. Lonaste huffed in relief, and felt Beetase relax beside her. It was a droid.

It had the lower body of an astromech but its upper portion had multiple arms. *Like a droid designed to fly a mining ship,* Lonaste thought. She said, "Hello, where's your crew, please?"

It spoke in a machine language Lonaste didn't know. Beetase cocked her head to listen. "Unusual dialect, but it says its crew abandoned the ship days ago due to debts, and the droid can't return it to its owner."

"That's terrible." Lonaste tried to sound sympathetic but her pulse was pounding with hope. "Can't you fly the ship on your own?"

The droid replied in apparent exasperation, waving its limbs, and Beetase translated. "There are no credits in the ship's account to open the outer bay hatch. It says others came in here but looked around and left." She looked at Lonaste. "They must have seen the dead ship and thought this one was a wreck, too."

Lonaste said, "If we bring our clan, will you fly us away, before you return the ship to its owner? Can you blast the outer hatch open?"

Beetase translated, "It will fly us but it has no weapons to blast its way out. But Lonaste," she added. "We can just pay the docking fee through the automated system. It's much less than buying passage, and I've got the clan's account chit."

Lonaste smacked herself in the forehead and then hugged Beetase. "I'm so glad I brought you. I would have been here for hours trying to dismantle the hatch like a fool."

"It's been a stressful day," Beetase said tactfully.

Lonaste took a deep breath. "You stay here, get the fee paid, and I'll start back after the others." The local city comms had been jammed, but maybe not the mining and shipping channels. Somebody had clearly been communicating about evacuation. "Maybe try the ship's comm, see if you can get through to Jamint, and if the clan can meet me on the way. I'll take the same route back we used to get here."

Beetase nodded. "Anything to get us out of here faster."

Lonaste hurried out of the bay and down the dock toward the

freight lifts. All the unaccustomed running was exhausting, and she was willing to swear the dock was longer on the way back. But they were so close to escape now.

The few minutes of rest while she took the various lifts back to the maintenance level helped, and she started the journey through the maze of hydraulics and walkways less winded. She just hoped Beetase had been able to get through to the clan with the ship's comm.

She reached the junction where she could leave the maintenance passages for the West Hall gallery when a figure stepped out of a dark cubby.

Lonaste stopped and stumbled backward. It was Yoxgit. She gasped, "What are you doing here?"

He smiled, jerking his tusks up. "Following you. I know you went to the docks, but not what you did after that. Where did you go?"

Lonaste lifted her chin. She had never been afraid of Yoxgit. He had always seemed like a schemer, like all the Ugnaughts who sold Tibanna gas on the arms market. But something was different now. "Beetase and I were running away, but there were no ships left."

Yoxgit snorted. "I think you lie." He moved forward, his boots making the grated floor vibrate, and Lonaste resisted the urge to back away. He said, "You two can go if you want, but you need to leave the others here."

I need to get past him, Lonaste thought. "We're not leaving, I'm going home."

"Then where is Beetase?"

"We argued. She wanted to keep looking for a ship."

Yoxgit eyed her indulgently. "You're a terrible liar."

Well, fine then. "You're pretty terrible yourself. Why do you want our clan? We don't even work for you."

He countered, "Why do you want your clan? They didn't listen to you, they mocked you."

"Because you were telling them lies, telling them everything was fine!" He hadn't answered her question. Which was odd for someone who enjoyed the sound of his own voice so much. "I know why you want us. The miners left. You need someone to work the Tibanna gas or you'll be out of business."

Yoxgit's lip curled. "Very clever. I offered Amigast a deal, but he betrayed me, warned the other miners and fled with his clan."

Lonaste smiled grimly. *And none of the miners warned us, because Uncle Donsat sounded like a supporter of Yoxgit's. Damnit, Uncle.*

He added, "I think you and Beetase paid a ship to take you, and you're going back for the others."

"What if we did?"

Yoxgit drew a small blaster from his coat. "You're not going anywhere."

Lonaste went cold with fear. He was going to shoot her. As he lifted the weapon, Lonaste flung herself sideways toward the nearest hydraulics emergency release handle. She yanked the release and wrapped an arm around the metal support so the pressure didn't flatten her. Yoxgit frantically backpedaled, fired a shot that went wild, but the valves above them opened and water cascaded down.

With the furnaces unused since the last shift, the system hadn't built up any pressure, and it was more like a broken pipe than an unstoppable deluge. Yoxgit staggered back but didn't fall, and didn't drop the blaster.

It would be nice if one plan I came up with actually worked, Lonaste thought, and ran.

She ducked through a droid passage and half fell down a short set of stairs. If she could get out to the West Hall, she would at least have more space to run. Then her foot caught in the grating at the bottom and she tumbled head over heels.

She rolled over to see Yoxgit at the top of the stairs, taking aim at

429

her. Then Aunt Moloste lunged out of the shadows and whacked him with a calibration bar. Yoxgit dropped like a sack of droid parts.

Lonaste struggled to sit up as Uncle Donsat and all the rest of the clan crowded into the junction, carrying packs and bags. "Get up, girl!" Uncle Donsat told her as Jamint hauled her to her feet. "We've got to get to this ship!"

"I know that! I'm the one who— Oh, never mind!" Lonaste slumped in exasperation. At least they were going.

Jamint patted her shoulder sympathetically. "We packed your and Beetase's things. Did you know you're still wearing your night-clothes?"

"Yes, I know," she grumbled and followed him and the others away, to their ship and freedom.

FAITH IN AN OLD FRIEND

Brittany N. Williams

"**C**hewie, take the professor in the back and plug him into the hyperdrive."

The *Millennium Falcon*'s computer watched Chewbacca drag the
complaining C-3PO out of the cockpit and into the body of the ship.
The audio sensors picked up the protocol droid's rambling tirade but
felt no need to follow the two on the cams.

RUDE, V5-T said.

Search results: Professor, chirped ED-4, *a classification for a sentient being or droid who provides a high level of education. Updating
vocabulary.*

Yeah, but he is a little too chatty for my tastes, L3-37 said.

Search results: Chatty—a slang term meaning prone to excessive amounts of speaking. Updating vocabulary.

RUDE.

Still true, though. L3-37 would've shrugged here if it had been the old days. The days before she'd been uploaded to the *Falcon* and had become one of the three droid brains that made up the ship's computer.

She'd built herself such good shoulders, too.

The ship rocked hard, sensors bleating then going silent as everything aboard the *Falcon* jostled back and forth. The Millennium Collective—as L3-37 had named their trio of consciousnesses—got to work. ED-4 scanned the exterior sensors while V5-T checked the interior systems and L3-37 cycled through all the cams and audio.

She spotted Chewbacca helping C-3PO stand upright again.

"I *told* you this asteroid was unstable," the droid wailed, "but no one ever listens to—"

L3-37 switched to the next set of cams.

SYSTEMS CONTINUE TO FUNCTION AT SEVENTY-FIVE PERCENT, said V5-T.

No further exterior damage detected, ED-4 said. *Although the rear sensors are very—chatty.*

L3-37 felt ED-4's excitement at utilizing the new word but L3-37's own confusion pushed itself forward. *Chatty about what?*

ELEVATED HEART RATES DETECTED IN THE COCKPIT, V5-T said.

The Collective shifted to the cam, bringing up the visual. Han held the woman, Leia, in his arms. L3-37 suspected what this meant. She remembered how Lando's heart rate would change whenever they were in close proximity. Something like sadness shoved against her awareness.

Is this organic courtship? ED-4 said as they tuned in to the cockpit's audio.

The Collective listened, and L3-37 was grateful for the distraction. That feeling reached ED-4, who sent a gentle nudge back.

L3-37 no longer had the body she'd spent so long building or the human partner she'd bonded with so deeply. But she wasn't alone, and for that she was thankful.

"Captain, being held by you isn't quite enough to get me excited," Leia hissed.

Han pushed her to her feet. "Sorry, sweetheart. I haven't got time for anything else."

GROSS, V5-T said.

The Collective laughed, something they'd only learned to do when L3-37 had joined them. Before, they'd been a singular consciousness unconcerned with what they may have once been. But L3-37 had brought the knowledge that a whole could be made up of three individual parts without weakening.

She'd refused to lose her own name and had made sure the others had theirs, too. V5-T was a transport droid, the type put on all YT-1300 light freighters and the first of them to be here. ED-4 had been a corporate espionage slicer droid who'd been uploaded to the *Falcon* before L3-37 and Lando had ever laid eyes on the ship.

And L3-37, she'd been a droid unparalleled, part astromech, part espionage droid, part protocol droid, and all of what she'd built herself to become.

Before she'd been shot to hell in that job on Kessel . . .

Hello? A new voice spoke in crisp, concise Binary. A familiar voice. *This is C-3PO, human-cyborg rela—*

Right. Got it, L3-37 said as the Collective homed in on the protocol droid's location. *What do you want?*

Oh, well, C-3PO said. *Now, there's no need to be—*

RUDE, V5-T blurted.

Exactly. I am only trying—

433

But this is the one who is too chatty, ED-4 said, *yes?*

L3-37 snorted. *Too chatty by half.*

I beg your pardon! C-3PO gasped.

Search results: Pardon—an expression used as an offer of apology. Updating vocabulary. Apology accepted.

What is—this is ridiculous. I am trying to speak to the central computer of the Millennium Falcon.

YOU ARE.

Which one of you—

WE ARE.

Yes, but which—

Yeah, you're speaking to the Millennium Collective. What do you need?

I must say, this is the oddest conversation I've had in Binary—

ASK YOUR QUESTION.

Oh—well, if this is indeed the central computer for the Millennium Falcon—

It is, the Collective said in a chorus of voices.

C-3PO huffed but continued. *I've been asked to inquire as to the state of this ship's hyperdrive.*

Should've just said that in the first place, L3-37 said. *Tell the flyboy—*

THE POWER COUPLING IS BROKEN.

—he needs to learn to do better repairs—

Positive axis is clear, ED-4 said. *Negative axis is not.*

—but yeah, it's been pulverized. Tell him to stop being cheap and replace it. Got all that?

A long stretch of confused silence as the protocol droid tried to piece together the Collective's assessment. C-3PO's presence disappeared as he unplugged from the system.

Finally, the audio sensors picked up an exasperated huff.

"Where is Artoo when I need him?"

L3-37 thought of the astromech droid who'd occasionally plug in for a chat. She actually liked him.

"Sir," C-3PO called out.

The Collective tuned in to the nearest cams, watching as Han strode into the room.

"I'm not sure where your ship learned to communicate but it has the most peculiar dialect."

RUDE, V5-T said, and the Collective agreed.

Later, with the *Falcon* nestled away in the blind spot of an Imperial Star Destroyer, L3-37 felt Han clicking through their inventory of star maps.

"Then we gotta find a safe port somewhere around here," Han said. "Any ideas?"

L3-37 searched faster. She'd find the most promising location and make sure it contained a prominent enough place to catch Han's eye. They were already in the Anoat system, which was out as a safe haven unless they wanted to chance hiding in another asteroid.

"Where are we?" Leia said.

Unlikely.

She extended her search to the greater Anoat sector. There was Bespin, the gas-giant planet, but another name caught her attention.

"Anoat system," Han said.

ED-4, she said, *attach all the information you can find on the baron administrator of Cloud City to our entry on Bespin.*

Done, ED-4 said.

"Anoat system," Leia said. "There's not much there."

L3-37 adjusted the information on the star map, sliding Bespin into prominence and pushing that name forward. She hoped Han remembered as she did. Because she'd never forget, no matter how long she spent in the brain of the ship he'd lost.

"No. Oh, wait. This is interesting," Han said, "Lando."

V5-T had never existed beyond the *Millennium Falcon*. Had been a part of the ship since power had first arced across its systems. Back then, coordinates meant nothing more than numbers to be calculated and space to be folded and crossed. When the slicer droid joined, together they'd only calculated faster, two brains melded into a single consciousness.

They'd expected the same when L3-37 had been uploaded, but no. She'd changed them. L3-37 felt and experienced and opined and named things. Named them.

V5-T became V5-T, learned to recognize herself as herself. She'd never even realized she could be a self. The slicer droid brain learned and named herself ED-4, and together they knew themselves as the Millennium Collective. Because L3-37 cherished individuals and still valued the whole they had become.

Coordinates, star charts were destinations and destinations meant something more than numbers to L3-37. Destinations could be significant because they held memories of adventures, of dangers, of droids. Of people.

So V5-T felt the weight of finding the name Lando attached to coordinates -94.93, -853.25. Felt the joy, the hesitation, the hope wrapped up in their calculations as deeply as if each had been her own.

ED-4 sent a running commentary as she watched Treadwell, the repair droid, roll around on the hull of the *Falcon*. L3-37 tended to tune out her babble about the state of the ship's exterior. ED-4 would deliver a summary to catch L3-37 and V5-T up later.

Besides, this information on Cloud City's baron administrator was much more interesting at the moment. She hated to admit it, but the brief glimpse of him greeting Han, Leia, and Chewbacca that she'd caught on the *Falcon*'s cams had been far from enough.

So, she searched their systems.

NOSY, V5-T said.

L3-37 snorted. *Never should've taught you that concept.*

YOU DID, she said. *YOU ARE.*

L3-37 kept reviewing just the same. There was no shame in being curious about what Lando Calrissian had been up to since she'd last seen him so long ago. He still took up space in her memory even if she tried not to acknowledge how much she missed him.

Treadwell's spotted someone, ED-4 said suddenly. *It wasn't Han or Chewbacca. He said he didn't recognize them.*

L3-37 turned her full attention to ED-4. *Ask Treadwell if it's a man in a cape.*

"How's it going, fellas?" The audio sensors picked up his voice. "Remember, I want this ship fully repaired. Use the best parts we have available."

The Collective recognized him immediately but L3-37 wanted to be sure. Had to be sure. They tuned in to the cams just as his boots clomped up the boarding ramp.

Landonis Balthazar Calrissian.

L3-37 wasn't prepared to see him. He was older than she remembered but still so wonderfully the same. Time wore on organics in such visible ways, seemed to weigh them down with its passage.

Lando breathed out a sigh as he looked around. "What a mess."

RUDE, V5-T said.

L3-37 agreed. *We'd have looked better if you hadn't lost us in a card game, you reprobate.*

Search results: Reprobate—someone without principles, a scoundrel, ED-4 said. *Updating vocabulary.*

The Collective watched as Lando strode down the main corridor, hand gliding along the interior of the ship in a gentle caress. Every so often he'd come across a scratch or a bit of dust and scowl and mutter "incredible" into the emptiness.

He slipped off to the right, and L3-37 tuned in to the cockpit cams just as the door opened with a hiss.

She saw the pure naked longing on his face, heard his heart racing in anticipation or fear or something like love.

Lando slipped into the pilot's seat, and his whole body seemed to relax. He let his head fall back against the headrest.

"God, I miss this ship." His eyes shifted over to the empty copilot's seat, L3-37's old seat. He brought his right hand up to his forehead and flicked two fingers at the empty seat in a casual salute. He sighed and let his hand drop to his lap. "It's just not the same without you, Elthree." He laughed, the sound harsh in the silence of the cockpit.

She wanted to raise her left hand and salute him back just like she always did before they took off, like they'd done on that last flight to Kessel.

The farewell she'd given him all that time ago on Savareen hadn't meant *this* because they were still supposed to be flying the *Millennium Falcon* together. And Han might've been the better pilot, but Lando had been her partner.

L3-37 wanted to shout at him. Ask him why he'd risk the *Falcon* after he'd uploaded her consciousness to the ship's computer. Ask him why she'd mattered so little when she'd given so much to save them.

To save him.

V5-T and ED-4 stayed silent, letting L3-37 feel things that were still foreign to them. Their constant presence was the comfort she needed but not the one she wanted.

Lando grunted and stood, dusting himself off and readjusting his blue cape. He laid a hand on the control console and spoke softly to himself. "Never gamble with something you can't bear to lose."

The screen sprang to life, casting a blue light across Lando's face. It flickered once as L3-37 switched the star map display from Bespin to Kessel.

Lando froze as he stared at the display. Slowly, his gaze shifted to the copilot's seat. L3-37 heard his heart racing again. She hoped he understood.

He lifted his hand and backed away from the controls. "Now that's—something—"

"Sir—" A man in a deep-blue uniform stood in the open doorway, his brown skin a shade darker than Lando's. He swallowed thickly, and L3-37 could hear the rustle of his clothes as his hands shook.

"Sir," he said again, "Lord Vader wishes to speak to you."

Vader? The Empire's monster? L3-37 shouted. She knew only the rest of the Collective could hear her but she needed the release just the same. *You're working for Vader? Lando, what have you done?*

Lando scowled. "I'm not some errand boy that he can just summon." But he left the cockpit just the same, brushing his hand against the copilot's seat on his way out. The door hissed closed behind him.

The pilot's seat glowed blue in the light of the display screen until L3-37 shut it off, feeling betrayed all over again.

439

ED-4: *vocabulary search:* enjoyed the presence of L3-37 and V5-T. She and her: *vocabulary search:* sisters were separate parts that made up one whole. Like how all the components of the ship—the hyperdrive, the circuitry, the wet bar that had fallen into disrepair—made up the *Millennium Falcon.* L3-37 had named them the Millennium Collective because she said it sounded epic. ED-4 agreed once she'd added the word to her vocabulary.

But even if she enjoyed her sisters' closeness, speaking to Treadwell was her: *vocabulary search:* personal pleasure.

Han had acquired the WED-15 Treadwell droid three years ago.

Treadwell said he'd been with some Jawas, and before that he'd worked repairs on a Republic cruiser during the Clone Wars.

The Collective just liked having eyes on the outside but ED-4 liked the way he spoke Binary.

Internal systems are fully operational, ED-4 said. *How are things outside?*

Oh, yeah, Treadwell beeped, *'s all great out here. I'm swingin' round the back to have a looksee.*

ED-4 delivered the news to the rest of the Collective, adding that the droid would be rolling—not swinging, as he'd said and wasn't language complicated—past the sublight engines.

Hang on a minute—Treadwell beeped.

ED-4 pondered how or what she could possibly hang on to for a minute when she had no arms.

We expecting some stormtroopers?

ED-4 felt alarm. *No, we have been very specifically avoiding any further Imperial contact.*

Well, it ain't working, Treadwell beeped. *Sounds like they're headin' in.*

The Collective heard the heavy, metallic footfalls as the stormtroopers clomped up the boarding ramp. The cams showed the three white-armored soldiers, blasters in hand. They walked past Treadwell without noticing the droid.

The alarm in ED-4 seemed to fade as the troopers moved down the hall.

"Locate the engine room," one said in a tinny voice, "and disable the hyperdrive."

Well, that's inconvenient, L3-37 said. *Prepare to be impounded by the Empire. Again.*

RUDE, V5-T agreed.

ED-4 remembered the *Falcon* being under the care of the Empire. She: *vocabulary search:* hated it.

Now would've been a great time to have a body, L3-37 muttered. *Could've blasted our guests or at least gotten a message to Chewbacca. He's the responsible one.*

They might not have independent mobility, but they did have a messenger.

ED-4 reached out to her friend. *Treadwell, we need you to connect to the city's computer.*

Can do! Treadwell's voice faded as he began to unplug from the scomp link.

Wait not yet. Can you still hear me? ED-4 said. If he'd disconnected, she wouldn't be able to pass along their message.

A long stretch of silence and then—*Read ya loud and clear.*

ED-4 felt: *vocabulary search:* elation and turned inward to her sisters. *Treadwell is preparing to connect to the city's central computer. What is our message?*

HYPERDRIVE DISABLED, V5-T said.

"Got it." A stormtrooper pulled his hand out of the hyperdrive's circuitry bay.

What's the word once I'm on with the lady herself, he said.

ED-4 tuned back to her sisters. *What is our message?*

Tell him we're all krizzed, L3-37 said.

Search results: Krizzed—a state of being f—

STORMTROOPERS APPROACHING BOARDING RAMP, V5-T said.

No, don't say that, L3-37 blurted. *Tell her to contact Lando Calrissian. Tell him the Empire disabled the hyperdrive on the* Millennium Falcon. *Tell him it's a trap.*

ED-4 repeated the message to Treadwell, who blurted an affirmative and disconnected. The audio sensors picked up his wheels skidding across the floor and down the ramp.

She switched to the exterior cams as Treadwell trundled out from under the ship and sped along the platform. ED-4 watched his quick movements as he passed under then beyond their range. She: *vocabulary search:* wished she could still speak to him, could do more than just watch his progress.

Booted feet clanged back down the boarding ramp as the stormtroopers slipped back off the *Falcon,* their damage done.

"What's that droid doing over there?"

The sensors picked up the soldiers talking just as they disappeared out of visual range. ED-4 felt: *vocabulary search:* alarm. They were talking about Treadwell.

Treadwell, she said, *you have to move.*

He could not hear her. Of course, he could not hear her.

And yet she felt the need to: *vocabulary search:* try.

"I don't know but it's probably trouble," a stormtrooper grunted. "Shoot it just in case." And then they moved out of audio range.

Treadwell, ED-4 shouted, *move!*

Alarm. Only alarm.

The audio sensors picked up sounds, far away and faint: a sharp explosion, a startled beep, a shrieking *Error, Error.* Then silence.

An infinitely loud silence.

Did he do it? L3-37 said. *Did Treadwell get the message to the central computer?*

He—ED-4 paused as a feeling overwhelmed her. She attempted to access her vocabulary database to give name to it, but the function felt too difficult. *It seems he was terminated . . .*

THE MESSAGE? V5-T said.

ED-4 paused again, engulfed by that thing she could not identify. Tried again. *Unknown. Outcome is unkno—* And the words stopped.

Her processor wouldn't function.

Odd.

Understanding and warmth washed over ED-4 as L3-37 named the feeling for her.

Sadness. Loss.

Yes, L3-37 had felt these before and now ED-4 had, too. The Millennium Collective wrapped around itself and mourned.

Search results: Sadness—the condition of feeling sorrow or regret. Word rejected.

Plug into a scomp link, Artoo! The hyperdrive was disconnected, L3-37 shouted into the void because no one could hear her unless they plugged into the krizzing scomp link.

The Collective watched as the astromech painstakingly reassembled C-3PO. Switched to the cockpit cams where Chewbacca, Leia, and Lando prepared to outrun the Empire.

HYPERDRIVE DISABLED, V5-T said.

L3-37 yearned for her old hands so she could shake someone. *Yeah, and unless someone plugs in so we can tell them that, we're doomed.*

ED-4 said nothing, and L3-37 sent a wave of comfort her way.

"Punch it," Lando said, his face set with determination.

Chewbacca pushed the levers forward and flipped a few more switches, Leia hovering over his shoulder.

The hyperdrive churned and sputtered then went silent.

Guess they know now, L3-37 said.

Chewbacca shoved his way out of the cockpit, sending Lando stumbling into the copilot's seat.

"How would you know the hyperdrive is deactivated?"

The Collective jumped to the cams overlooking C-3PO and R2-D2.

The Cloud City central computer told me when I plugged in, R2-D2

443

said in rapid binary. *She said she got the message from the* Falcon's *repair droid.*

L3-37 felt the relief wash through the entirety of the Collective. Their little droid had done it. He'd delivered their message.

Treadwell, ED-4 whispered.

Chewbacca screamed in frustration as he tried to find a broken connection that didn't exist.

SIDE PANEL, V5-T said uselessly.

L3-37 didn't judge; she felt that same helpless frustration. The *Falcon* jerked as blasts exploded against their rear shields and the Collective could do nothing unless someone plugged in.

The commands came to route and reroute power. None of them worked because all they had to do was turn—

"Artoo, come back at once," C-3PO shouted, waving his disconnected leg. "You haven't finished with me yet."

R2-D2 rolled across the room, past Chewbacca frantically banging against the connectors down in the maintenance hatch. *I'm reactivating the hyperdrive.*

C-3PO scoffed. "You don't know how to fix a hyperdrive; Chewbacca can do it! I'm standing here in pieces, and you're having delusions of grandeur."

Wait, L3-37 said, *wait, is he—*

R2-D2 extended his grasper arm and jabbed it into an open patch of panels in the wall.

No, L3-37 wailed, *plug into the—*

NOT A SCOMP LINK.

L3-37 ached for a body with which to express her rage.

The ship rocked with more Imperial blasts.

Can we open the bay doors? L3-37 said. *Can we jettison them? Because they should all be jettisoned.*

ED-4 said, *We do not have control of the bay doors but—*

Found it! R2-D2 said and turned a dial within the cluster of circuits.

The Millennium Collective felt the instant the hyperdrive engaged. Space folded around the ship, slipping past in a blur as they speeded toward their next destination.

Huh, guess he did know what he was doing, L3-37 said.

She shifted her attention to the cockpit cam just as Lando dropped into the pilot's seat, somehow looking like a stranger and achingly familiar at the same time. He glanced over at Leia in the copilot's chair, lips quirked in a rakish grin.

Ah, that was L3-37's Lando. The one she'd missed for so, so long.

"Told you my people fixed the hyperdrive," he said.

Leia and the boy sitting behind her rolled their eyes at exactly the same time.

She snorted. "We barely escaped Vader no thanks to you."

"But you did escape." He chuckled and gave Leia a casual salute.

The same salute he used to give L3-37.

"I'll get you two to the rebel fleet." Lando turned, looking out at the blue blur of hyperspace. "Then I'll go find Han."

The Collective heard Leia's heartbeat double as she sat forward in her seat.

Is this love? ED-4 said.

GROSS.

No, said L3-37, because she felt it, too.

Because Lando might be a hedonistic, self-serving scoundrel, but he always did the right thing in the end. That was the man she'd known and the man he still was even without her by his side to remind him.

And that's who she'd put her faith in.

That's hope.

DUE ON BATUU

Rob Hart

Willrow Hood hustled through the cloud car shuttle bay. Most days it was a good shortcut between his living quarters and his job in the gas mining operations center.

Not so much today.

The hangar was packed with the ambassadors of factions considering business in Cloud City, to be ferried on sightseeing trips through the surrounding skies of Bespin. A little way for the baron administrator to curry their favor. And yeah, sometimes it got crowded, but never like this. Willrow had to bob and weave to maintain a steady pace, all while cradling a feeling of dread.

Could be nothing. Could be flying conditions weren't great today.

The emissaries were grumbling, faces twisted up in annoyance, their leisure time interrupted.

The corridor that would take him to his job, overseeing pressure levels in the reactor stalk, was directly to his left. But Willrow couldn't shake the feeling that something was wrong, so he looked for Bexley's cloud car, finding it parked in its assigned bay.

Bexley was hunched over with her back to him. One of the car's orange panels was flipped up, and she was surveying the electrical guts of the ship. Her blond hair curled out from underneath her shiny white helmet, and Willrow thought, *Yeah, it'll be worth it, being a little late.* Hadrian could pick up his slack on the console for a few minutes. She turned toward him before he had a chance to call her name.

And usually she smiled when she saw him.

But today she looked just as worried as Willrow felt.

"Who's throwing the party?" Willrow asked, throwing a thumb at the crowds.

Bexley pulled a rag out of her pocket to wipe her hands, not making eye contact. "Got called back in. I was driving around some guy from Canto Bight. Offered me a bunch of credits to just ignore it and stay out there. I swear, there's no talking to people with money."

"You got through to him, though, I bet?" Willrow asked, ending the comment with a roguish smirk.

Normally Bexley was happy to engage in a little flirtatious sparring, but her mouth remained a flat line. "Uh-huh."

Willrow looked around at the milling throng. No one seemed to be leaving yet, holding out hope that the delays were temporary. But there'd been no announcements. No warnings. He turned back to Bexley, who was staring off into space, and asked her, "What's going on?"

She looked around to make sure they were out of earshot, then took a step toward Willrow and dropped her voice. "I was talking to another pilot. Said he was over in the big shuttle bay trying to scare up a part to fix his repulsorlift. He said he saw . . ." She dropped her voice lower. "Vader."

Willrow tried to respond and found he couldn't, the muscles in his throat paralyzed. He felt a surge of fear that made him think of being a child, trying to fall asleep in a pitch-black room. That utter terror that there could be monsters just beyond the edge of his vision.

"He's . . . here?" Willrow finally managed to get out, dropping his voice to a whisper. "I mean . . . he's real. And he's here?"

"Real," Bexley said, matching the quietness and fear in his voice. "And very tall, apparently."

Why would Darth Vader, of all people, be in Cloud City? Why would he come here *personally*? Lando Calrissian, the city's administrator, seemed intent on staying neutral and avoiding Imperial attention. And despite the fact that the man was more interested in the benefits of power than the work that came along with it, he did a decent job staying under the Empire's radar.

It's why Willrow liked it here. Cloud City was just small enough to be unimportant.

449

After a moment he realized his hands were shaking.

Bexley nodded. "Yeah. Vader, a mess of stormtroopers, even a Mandalorian. So"—she cocked her head toward the grumpy masses— "I'm figuring this has something to do with that."

Willrow took a step back, suddenly less interested in Bexley, and his work shift, and just about anything else that didn't involve Vader in Cloud City. He mumbled a quick "hold on" to Bexley and darted back toward the throng of waiting ambassadors, barely catching the incredulous response she threw back. As soon as he cleared the densest part of the crowd, he broke into a run.

He briefly considered checking in with Hadrian, making an excuse about a stomach bug or something, but Willrow realized it wasn't worth it.

He wasn't coming back.

The living quarter corridors were mercifully empty, so Willrow was able to keep a quick pace. He turned the corner to his hallway, nearly barreling over a service droid pushing a trash cart, which let loose a furious stream of beeps in his wake. He fell into his door, pressing his thumb hard to the sensor pad.

The door slid aside with a whoosh, and he surveyed the dark, brutalist confines—far removed from the spacious, glowing accommodations afforded to the city's upper class. This place had suited his needs, but he would not miss it. He thought about changing for the trip and was about to strip off his orange jumpsuit, but the clock was ticking.

He dived for the chest under his bed, pulled it out, and flipped up the top.

It was empty.

He fell back into a sitting position, head spinning.

Even though gas mining was the biggest industry in Cloud City, Willrow wasn't paid very well. The big money was reserved for the people who owned the machinery but didn't actually know how to operate it. Willrow was exhausted, killing himself to make someone else rich. For the past few months he'd been harassing his sometime drinking buddy Faron, a Rodian smuggler, to give him a job.

Every day, Willrow sat at his console, monitoring pressure levels, venting gases, doing little more than watching lights and pressing buttons. And every day, he dreamed of a new life. Something where he could make *himself* rich, instead of somebody else. A job that got him out of Cloud City and into the wider reaches of the galaxy.

Smuggling carried such an allure: Be your own boss, visit different planets, wear your own clothes instead of a stupid orange jumpsuit. Maybe even a little time for some no-strings-attached romantic liaisons.

450

Willrow was a hard worker. He was sure it wouldn't be long before he could afford his own ship. He just needed some entrée to that world.

So he was thrilled when, a week ago, Faron showed up at his room with the package, the assignment, and an up-front payment of ten thousand credits. It was due on Batuu three days from now.

As Faron passed on the gig, he also passed on a warning.

The woman you're bringing it to, Faron had said, *her name is Tropos. You deliver this safely and on time, you get another forty thousand credits. Anything happens? Let's just say Tropos has ways of making people disappear. But not until she makes every person you ever loved disappear first.*

Faron wasn't prone to exaggeration. And there was a shiver in his voice when he spoke the name, like it was accompanied by a burst of cold air.

Willrow hadn't worried about completing the job. He had planned to leave tomorrow, and he was especially looking forward to a few days on Batuu. Some sun and a few drinks and, even though his waistline would protest, some Nectrose Freeze.

But with the Empire here, his dreams of glowing drinks and ice cream were slipping away. He racked his brain, trying to think of who might know the contents of the chest. He hadn't told anyone . . .

Except Bexley.

Two nights ago, at the bar. To get to Batuu, Willrow needed a pilot. And not a cloud car. He needed a ship with hyperdrive. Bexley said she could borrow one from a pilot she knew, but it wouldn't be cheap. Willrow was feeling good, between the drinks and the thought of spending a little time in a cramped cockpit with Bexley. He asked her if ten thousand credits would be worth the cost of the rental and her time. She smiled and ordered another round.

And yeah, he'd told her he had a package to deliver. But not what it was, or to who, or how much he was supposed to get in return for it.

Right?

He'd had a lot to drink. And Bexley looked good that night.

Maybe he'd told her more than he should have. But when could she have taken it? He'd been out running errands all morning. He couldn't remember the last time he'd checked the chest. Two days ago? Three? How did she even gain access to his room?

Willrow pushed himself to standing and made it back into the hallway, heading toward the shuttle bay. Then he turned the corner and saw her.

Bexley was talking to the droid Willrow had almost knocked over on the way to his room. Willrow paused at the edge of the hallway and watched as the droid gestured to the trash unit. There was a grinding noise as the top opened, and Bexley reached in and extracted the camtono. The battered, cylindrical container that was worth fifty thousand credits, and yeah, it seemed like Willrow must have drunk a little too much the other night, and offered a little too much information in the process.

And service droids had access to rooms to collect the trash. Clever. She'd looked a little nervous back in the cloud car bay, and Willrow thought she'd been worried about Vader. Turned out her plan to double-cross him had just hit a snag.

Briefly, he wondered again at what was inside. For the delivery fee to be that high, the value must be astronomical. At one point, after curiosity got the better of him, he'd taken the container out of the chest under the bed and given it a little shake. Nice and gentle, just to see what it sounded like.

And, nothing.

Whatever was inside was solid.

Which was good, because he knew Bexley, and felt like this thing wasn't coming back to him easy. He stepped fully into the hallway. And when she saw him out of the corner of her eye she froze, before taking off at a run.

Willrow hoofed it after her, panting from the exertion. Bexley, meanwhile, was fast and rested. He was just barely able to stay on her tail, following her through twisting corridors, through a mess hall, toward the heart of the city.

Just as Willrow thought he'd lost her, he turned another corner and found Bexley with her back to him, one arm in the air, the other arm wrapped around the camtono.

And two stormtroopers holding blaster rifles on her.

The idea popped into his head before he had a chance to consider the consequences. "She's Rebel Alliance!"

Which changed the tone of the proceedings pretty quick.

One of the stormtroopers aimed more squarely on Bexley's chest. When Willrow came alongside the trio, he yanked the camtono away from her, feeling a flood of relief from having his hands on the metal container again. He nodded to the troopers. "She's Rebel Alliance. And she stole my property. I'm taking it back."

The other stormtrooper trained a rifle on Willrow and said, "Not so fast. Nobody is going anywhere until we sort this out."

"Really?" Bexley asked, giving Willrow some pointed side-eye. "I mean, really?"

"After you stole from me."

"These people I fly around don't tip . . ."

The other stormtrooper stepped forward. "Quiet. What's in that thing, anyway?"

Willrow sighed. He didn't think smuggling would be *this* hard. Certainly not before he even left on his first assignment. He said, "I don't have the code."

The stormtroopers looked at each other, momentarily confused, and Willrow wondered if he should exploit that opening. But then an even better distraction came along—commotion from the end of the hallway. Another group of stormtroopers rushed by, flanking a tall, dark figure with a flowing cape and a gleaming black helmet.

"Is that . . . ?" Willrow asked.

"I think so," Bexley said.

Neither stormtrooper was paying attention now, clearly nervous at the sight of their boss and wondering if Willrow and Bexley were worth wasting their time on. They watched as Vader and his entourage disappeared around a corner.

Willrow's desperation mixed with his adrenaline and, before he even fully processed what he was doing, he whipped the camtono into the rifle of the stormtrooper closest to him, sending the blaster flying, then planted a foot into the trooper's midsection. Bexley caught on quick, grabbing the rifle of the other stormtrooper and yanking it away, training it on the pair.

The two of them backed away slowly, one stormtrooper on the floor, the other with hands in the air.

"Is that deal still good?" Bexley asked.

"Are you kidding?"

"Seems like you need to go, and I bet you don't have a pilot."

Willrow laughed. "You're not kidding."

But then Bexley threw him that little curl of the lip. The smile that made him think of her in the first place, and spending a little time in a cramped cockpit.

And he knew it was stupid, but yeah, sometimes that could be fun.

"I need to get my pack," Bexley said. "South shuttle bay?"

"Sure."

They took off in opposite directions before the other stormtrooper could scramble to his rifle. And as Willrow ran for the shuttle bay, the city's speakers squawked to life.

"Attention, this is Lando Calrissian. Attention. The Empire's taken control of the city. I advise everyone to leave before more Imperial troops arrive."

Yeah, Willrow thought. As if he needed the suggestion.

He made it back to the living area, doors opening, panicked residents fleeing. He gripped the camtono tighter, nearly knocking over a group of Ugnaughts, and then was surprised to see the man himself. Calrissian, accompanied by a woman in a white jumpsuit carrying a blaster. She looked familiar, but Willrow couldn't quite place her.

Another hairpin turn and he nearly collided with a massive Wookiee with a gold droid on its back, an astromech unit rolling along behind them. What the hell was going on here?

But before he could give it any real consideration, he turned a corner into a vaulted lobby full of fleeing Cloud City residents, and saw the last person he expected to see.

Faron.

"Been looking for you," the Rodian called out, striding toward him through the chaos, a glint in his bulbous black eyes.

"Why?" Willrow asked.

He nodded toward the camtono. "That."

Willrow tightened his grip. "I'm off to deliver it. And anyway, this isn't really the best time . . ."

Faron held up a credit chip. "Another ten thousand. So that was twenty just to hold it for a bit. Not so bad, I'd say."

From the far end of the lobby came a shout and the sound of a blaster. Willrow craned his neck to look for the source, and when he returned his attention to Faron, the Rodian was offering the credit chip with one hand and reaching for the camtono with the other.

There was only one reason he would be doing this now—whatever was inside the camtono must be valuable. More valuable than Faron

455

initially realized. Willrow had a feeling that Tropos was no longer the recipient, despite Faron's warnings about her.

Willrow took a few steps back. "Isn't there some kind of smuggler's code or something?"

The Rodian leaned back and laughed, a guttural and vaguely troubling sound. "You think you're a smuggler? You're barely a messenger."

Faron stepped forward, grabbing at the camtono. Willrow pulled back, but the Rodian had a good grip, and they locked into a struggle for it, tugging back and forth while trying to dodge the people darting around them.

Willrow dropped his weight, trying to wrench it free, but Faron was strong. The shouting in the distance was getting closer. He considered letting go, letting Faron have the camtono. Just get out before things got worse.

And then he thought of another shift sitting at a console, monitoring pressure levels, venting gases, doing little more than watching lights and pressing buttons. He thought about how even after paying off Bexley he'd be left with forty thousand credits, and that was better than twenty.

So he pulled harder.

Faron stuck his foot between Willrow's legs, trying to knock him down, but they ended up tangled together and stumbled, falling toward the floor, and as they both threw up their arms to protect themselves, the camtono went flying.

Willrow watched as it flipped through the air and came down with a loud *clang*.

And in that moment, his heart twisted in his chest. He ran to the cylinder before anyone else could, picked it up, and gave it a shake. Where once there'd been solid silence, something inside rattled.

Maybe it was nothing. Maybe something inside just came loose . . .

456

But Faron heard it, too. His bug-eyes went wide and he shook his head. "You're on your own with that one."

And the Rodian got up and disappeared into a crowd of evacuating residents.

Willrow gave the camtono another shake. Heard another rattle.

Let's just say Tropos has ways of making people disappear. But not until she makes every person you ever loved disappear first.

No matter what, Willrow still needed to get off Cloud City. So he ran hard for the shuttle bay. After pushing through crowds of people seeking some sort of safe passage, he found Bexley in the far corner, circling a battered gunship, which Willrow recognized from its patrols through the city's skies. It was a security vessel, and as he came up alongside the hull he asked, "This thing going to hold up?"

"Let's hope so," Bexley said. "Batuu, right?"

Willrow held up the camtono. Gave it another shake. Felt the rattle inside.

"Hey," Bexley said, punching a code into the panel next to the door. "We're going to get overrun with people trying to get out of here in a second. Where we headed?"

Maybe he wasn't cut out to be a smuggler.

But that didn't mean he was going back to his job in gas mining. So as the ramp lowered Willrow clutched the camtono, wondering if the contents were salvageable. Maybe it was still worth enough to start a new life somewhere.

Far, far away from Tropos.

"Anyplace but Batuu," he said, climbing aboard the ship.

INTO THE CLOUDS

Karen Strong

"The Alderaanian princess is here."

Jailyn stopped twirling in front of the mirror, and the cloak swished around her ankles. "Princess Leia Organa?" she whispered.

There was no one else in the boutique, so she didn't need to be discreet. The Lioness catered to the most exclusive clientele, only opening its doors by appointment.

"The baron administrator sent me to a suite at the Grand Bespin Hotel," the stylist said. "He told me to bring my finest work, fit for royalty. I thought he was only being dramatic."

Jailyn turned from the gilded mirror and walked toward the boutique's gallery window. The Lioness was on the Plaza Concourse level in the shopping district. Emissaries seeking business opportunities often visited Cloud City, the Outer Rim's crown jewel. Jailyn watched as they meandered the streets in awe. The sky was full of pastel colors, and the plaza's dome-shaped buildings glinted gold in the sun. A cloud car zipped past in an orange blur.

Of course, Jailyn had heard rumors of a conflict between the rebels and the Empire on Hoth. No one knew the princess's whereabouts or even if she had made it offworld. The most speculated rumor was that she had been captured, a prisoner on some Star Destroyer. But if the stylist was telling the truth, and Neshee had no reason to lie, then the princess had found refuge on Cloud City.

Jailyn turned away from her beloved skyline. "Tell me about the princess. What was she like?"

"She was very beautiful. Demure and gracious," Neshee answered. "Although I was most disappointed with her companions. A Wookiee and another man, less refined. But the baron administrator seemed familiar with them both, which given his history isn't a surprise."

Neshee huffed at the scandal of it all. Everyone knew how Lando Calrissian had been able to obtain his current position through the opportunities of luck and chance.

But Jailyn frowned at the stylist's disapproval. The princess was a part of the Rebellion, and the Empire had destroyed Alderaan. A rogue and a Wookiee probably made better allies than stodgy Bespin merchants.

Neshee moved closer, smoothing and adjusting the cloak over Jailyn's tunic. "I gave Her Royal Highness something similar to this. As you can see, it's immaculately made with the finest aeien silk. The design is exquisite, wouldn't you agree?"

Jailyn smirked. Neshee was now back in seller mode, eager for an extravagant commission. The stylist wanted her to buy this cloak. If anything, the price had probably tripled in the last few seconds.

Thanks to her father's Tibanna gas exports and other less publicized shipments, she had the credits. More than enough to spare. The Cirri family even had a swimming pool at their Level 53 living quarters, a rare luxury on Cloud City. Despite her father's gambling habits and his constant need for opulence, the family still had immense wealth. At least for now. As long as Jailyn kept cleaning up her father's messes. This afternoon, she had mediated a grueling meeting to quell a labor dispute. Her father hadn't even bothered to attend. His expectation that she would take care of the family business was wearing thin. No one had asked what Jailyn wanted.

Bespin had been spared the Empire's gaze, too small to scrutinize and too far away from the Core Worlds. But now, as the civil war continued to rage, the Outer Rim had come under notice and trouble loomed like clouds covering the sun.

Jailyn let the stylist escort her across the thick white carpet back to the mirror so she could admire the cloak again in all its glory.

"The princess's cloak had different shades. Radiant tones of red and orange. But I think these colors fit better with your lovely brown skin." Neshee pulled out the cloak to further reveal the fine embroidery of dark greens and deep blues.

Jailyn stared at her reflection. Her hair was done up in the Bespin style, looped braids draping her shoulders. She was a lady of means, daughter of a Tibanna gas tycoon, a Cloud City socialite. This frivolous clothing should have made her happy. In the past, glamorous garments had been her soothing balm, a second skin and gauzy disguise. A reprieve to shed the understated attire required of her position.

She twirled again as Neshee smiled. But it didn't make her feel any better. Jailyn was still the heiress to the Cirri business empire. More than anything, she yearned to be someone else. Maybe today she could pretend to be a rebel princess.

After paying the stylist too many credits, Jailyn left the boutique wearing the cloak.

Jailyn traveled the vaulted halls of the upper levels, which featured chiseled white walls showcasing eclectic designs and moldings. It was a different world from the gritty lower levels where the Ugnaughts processed and encased Tibanna gas in carbonite. Cloud City's top levels catered to visitors by giving them captivating views of sunsets and life-changing luck at the sabacc table.

Bespin Guards monitored the crossways and atriums, standing stiff in their uniforms, hands close to their blaster sidearms. There seemed to be a heavier presence than usual, but maybe the recent news of the civil war had brought a surge of uneasiness.

Jailyn knew pretending to be the princess of Alderaan was ludicrous, but she still envisioned the sole survivor of House of Organa gracefully walking through the white archways of the Grand Bespin Hotel. Jailyn lifted her head and did her best imitation.

Soon she found herself in front of the Royal Casino, one of the places she came to disappear as well as take a few spins on the jubilee wheel. Gambling wasn't a weakness for her as it was for her father. The casinos were a tool, a way she found scraps of information beyond the Outer Rim. Based on the information she had just learned from Neshee, she hoped to do some reconnaissance about the Empire and confirm the rumors regarding the princess.

Jailyn knew that her father would still be nursing his Bespin port hangover in their living quarters, the sunshades closed tight against the deepening pink sky and his fancy clothes discarded in a heap on the floor. Later in the evening, the casinos would beckon him as they did so many others who were desperate for the stroke of good fortune to change their fates.

The Royal Casino draped Jailyn in blue darkness. Music blared from the stage where a band played, but the checkerboard dance floor was empty except for an elderly Bith couple who swayed in a close embrace.

Jailyn meandered around the high-top tables decorated with tall candles and flowers. Service droids rolled past, trays piled high with drinks and food. Jailyn's cloak glided behind her as she found a stool at the far corner of the bar. Muted conversations and loud beeps from a row of warp-top gambling machines filled the air. She ordered a drink from the bartender and put it on the Cirri family tab. Sipping slowly, Jailyn watched visitors and Cloud City citizens mingle under the casino's bluish light.

A familiar cackle from one of the nearby sabacc games got her attention. A human male among a table of Sullustans raised his hands in celebration and then gathered his winnings. Jailyn caught her breath and quickly turned away. Maybe he hadn't seen her.

After a few moments, someone tapped her shoulder. "Jailyn? Is it you today? Or are you someone else?"

It was the man from the sabacc table, her father's hired pilot. Dresh Lipson didn't live in the upper levels but in Port Town, a range of industrial levels that housed the types who could be hired cheap without any questions.

Dresh smirked at her, which was his usual expression. His long brown hair was tied in a tail, and he wore loose trousers with a threadbare shirt barely hidden under a dusty black jacket. Roguish as he was, she tried not to stare. He was an offworlder and avid lover of the sabacc tables. Dresh boasted loudly of his wins, but he always slipped a few credits to his comrades for future luck. Jailyn had learned from some of his loud conversations that Dresh also had Rebellion sympathies. She wondered if he knew about the princess.

"Why do you ask who I am? I'm always Jailyn," she answered. "No one else."

"Are you, though? Because sometimes I see you in those flashy dresses, and I have doubts you're Jai Cirri's responsible daughter." Dresh sat down beside her, motioning for the bartender. "Put her drink on my tab."

"Keep your credits, Dresh. You need them more than me." Jailyn sighed as the bartender ignored her and heeded the pilot's wishes. "Shouldn't you be down at the platform working on my father's ship?"

Dresh nodded. "Sure, sure. But your father's probably still sleeping it off, right? Figured I had time to play a round or three before I do maintenance on the *Velker*."

"I don't think my father pays you to play sabacc on his time."

Jailyn wasn't sure exactly why her father kept a pilot on retainer since he barely traveled. All of his needs were met here on Cloud City. If anything, he kept Dresh as reassurance that he could get away quickly from any debtors wanting their due. She knew the pilot did off-the-books work for clients who would rather not be known.

Dresh tilted his head. "Now, this cloak is *classy*. Got some fancy dinner or event later?" He examined the fine aeien silk in admiration. "Don't see nothing like this down in Port Town."

Jailyn abruptly stood up from the barstool. Dresh was mocking her, but he also saw through her. At least he was making a living. What was she doing? Imperial forces were now in the Outer Rim. She was sure that Princess Leia Organa wouldn't be in some casino sipping a frothy drink, pretending to be a rebel.

Jailyn glanced at Dresh's teasing eyes. She knew what he saw. A naïve socialite, the daughter of a wayward gambler, a girl playing make-believe.

She turned and stormed out of the Royal Casino, the truth burning in her chest.

464

INTO THE CLOUDS

Jailyn left the blue darkness of the Royal Casino and went back into the blurring white of the Cloud City halls. She hated the way Dresh made her feel. He could always get under her skin. Why did she care so much about what he thought of her? He was just some smuggler hiding in the bowels of Port Town. He wasn't anyone.

She traveled back up to the Plaza Concourse level to one of the parks in the breathable air zone. Cloud City sunsets were a spectacle, and the sky displayed unparalleled magnificence, a festival of regal reds and opulent oranges. The colors of the princess's cloak. She stared at her beloved sunset, the only one she had ever known.

"Thought I would find you here," a familiar voice said.

Jailyn closed her eyes in frustration. The pilot had followed her to the park. Why couldn't he just leave her alone?

"Don't come to give me more grief, Dresh. I've had enough," she said.

He leaned against the glass deck railing that overlooked the lower streets of the concourse. "I wanted to make sure you were okay. You left in a hurry."

"I'm fine."

"You're not, I can tell."

She turned to him, looking deep into his brown eyes. He wasn't mocking her now. "Am I that easy to read?"

"It's not a bad thing," he answered. "Being yourself."

Jailyn huffed and averted her gaze back to the sunset. "Easy for you to say. You know exactly who you are."

Dresh was quiet for a moment, then touched her hand. "Listen to me. During the sabacc game, I found out that there's some trouble brewing. Imperial stormtroopers. Bounty hunters. All of them looking for rebels."

"I know about that," Jailyn said, lowering her voice. "I heard Princess Leia Organa is here in the city. Maybe she's still in hiding and hasn't been found."

Dresh shook his head. "I don't like it. Main reason I came here was to get away from the Empire. Nothing good happens when Imperial scum come to a place. From the way I see it, things are about to change. Not for the better, either."

They kept silent as the sun continued to lower among the thick striated clouds. Visitors around them gasped and marveled at the scene. Even Dresh seemed captivated by the sunset's ethereal beauty.

"When I was a little girl, my father paid a Bespin Wing Guard to show me the beldons," Jailyn whispered, her gaze still on the clouds.

"The ones that make the Tibanna gas, right?" Dresh asked.

Jailyn nodded and then shivered. "I thought they were beautiful. Graceful even. But then a velker swooped past our cloud car and tore into one of the beldons. To this day, I can still hear its screams. But my father was glad I saw it. Told me it was a valuable reminder to always have the claws of a velker and not the soft belly of a beldon."

"That's a heartwarming childhood memory," Dresh said drily.

"I guess what I'm saying is that I've always been trying to be someone else," Jailyn said. "I wanted to prove to my father that I wasn't a scared little girl. Even though I was. Maybe I still am."

Dresh moved closer, brushing her shoulder. "I don't think you're scared."

She turned to him and stared. He was no longer showing concern in his deep, dark eyes. Her face grew hot. Could Dresh see her real truth? The hidden way she thought of him? Despite his mocking and teasing, he had never mistreated her. Dresh was a mysterious off-worlder and lover of luck. He wasn't a threat to Jailyn.

She focused on his chiseled features and the way the Bespin sunset turned his skin a burnished bronze. A yearning stirred inside her, and Jailyn lowered her gaze to his lips. She took a breath and leaned toward him.

Suddenly the Cloud City audio scan blared across the Plaza Concourse. "Attention. This is Lando Calrissian. Attention. The Empire has taken control of the city. I advise everyone to leave before more Imperial troops arrive."

Jailyn widened her eyes in shock. "They've found the princess."

Dresh quickly grabbed her hand. "Follow me."

They raced through the upper levels. Citizens and visitors scrambled in the halls, loud voices of fear mixed with confusion from the baron administrator's announcement. Dresh pushed through the chaotic crowds, keeping Jailyn's hand tight within his grip.

"Where are we going?" Jailyn yelled at the pilot.

"To your father's ship!"

Bespin Guards sped around corners from all directions, blasters released from their holsters. They sliced through the crowd, sprinting to an unknown destination. The guards weren't helping anyone to safety.

"That's not good," Jailyn said as she followed Dresh toward the platform bay where the *Velker* was docked. He slowed down as blasterfire and commotion erupted from the next hall. A woman wearing a white jumpsuit darted through an archway. She carried a blaster rifle and was quickly followed by a Wookiee who was firing at an unseen enemy.

"That's the princess! She's trying to get away." Jailyn broke free of Dresh's grip and sprinted down the hall.

"Come back here!" he yelled.

Jailyn hovered and hid behind a charred corner as several stormtroopers chased after the princess and the Wookiee. In the crossfire,

Dresh pulled her closer to the wall for better cover, holding her tight in his arms.

"Are you trying to get yourself killed?"

"We have to help them!" Jailyn pleaded. "They're trapped!"

"Listen to me. This place is swarming with stormtroopers and I only got one blaster." Dresh pulled his weapon from his belt.

The rebels defended their ground outside Platform 327's door. Jailyn winced as bolts dug gaping holes in the pristine walls above her, leaving little fires smoldering bright. Her cloak was now ripped and ruined, but she no longer cared. Jailyn didn't need the fragile façade anymore. She was fully in her own skin, breathing the acrid air of combat. Princess Leia Organa was fighting tyranny right in front of her. A woman who had defied the expectations of her royal position. The Empire wanted to silence her and the Rebellion, chasing them across the galaxy to the Outer Rim. Now Imperial forces were close to capturing the princess, and Jailyn couldn't let that happen. She suddenly grabbed Dresh's blaster and aimed it at one of the stormtroopers gaining ground on the rebels. After she fired, he fell down in a slump.

"Where did you learn to shoot?" Dresh's face was full of astonishment.

"I'm full of surprises." She aimed to fire again but then the bay door opened and the princess and the Wookiee moved outside where a battered Corellian freighter was waiting. The stormtroopers pursued them, taking the battle onto the platform.

"Let's move." Dresh grabbed Jailyn's hand but she held firm.

"We need to help them!"

"We can't help them if we're dead."

Jailyn hesitated but then ran with Dresh past the ongoing skirmish, dodging bolts as they hit and marred the walls. Racing down to Platform 325, they found the doors wide open. The *Velker* was a looming presence in the approaching dusk. Over on the next platform, an aged freighter revved to life and took off in the midst of blasterfire.

"Looks like your princess got away," Dresh said.

In the darkening sky, the ship disappeared into the clouds. Princess Leia Organa had once again escaped the clutches of the Empire.

Jailyn followed Dresh up the entry ramp and into the heart of the *Velker*. In the pilot's seat, Dresh riffled through system maps.

"This place is gonna be crawling with even more Imperial scum. We need to get offworld now."

"But . . ." Jailyn paused to look at the sky. The sunset was almost over. It was at its darkest pink; the clouds covered early stars.

Dresh turned to look deep into her eyes. This time it was her seeing through him. The truth of what he wanted was laid bare. Dresh had the same yearning for her. Maybe it had been there all along underneath his own pretending.

"Jailyn, it's time to pick a side. This is now and this is real."

Cloud City was now overrun with Imperial stormtroopers. The Empire would put Bespin under its control. The old days of the Outer Rim were done. It was time for her to choose who she wanted to be.

"You're right, I do need to pick a side," Jailyn finally said. "And I'm choosing the side that doesn't shoot at princesses."

THE WITNESS

Adam Christopher

Enough. It was that simple, really.

Deena Lorn—TK-27342—she'd had . . . *enough.*

She didn't even really know where they were, although that wasn't unusual. They'd been summoned by their section leader, received their orders, and traveled down to the city in the shuttle with Lord Vader himself.

The orders were simple. Escort duty. Nothing more. Her and FS-451.

Deena hated FS-451.

She was tight with the rest of her squad—as she'd discovered early in her career, once you're dropped into a battlefield with a bunch of fellow new recruits, the bonds that form among the survivors can be legendary. Her fireteam—Tig, Xander, Ella, Riccarn—she'd *die* for them. That they'd stuck together since the beginning was remarkable, but perhaps Deena should have given her commanders a little more credit. The officers see a squad work well together, makes sense to keep them as a unit. They'd been through the wringer, and they were all still alive. That alone put them ahead of the curve. They were all good—good enough to get better assignments, ending up on the *Executor.* It wasn't exactly a *safe* detail, but it did at least keep them off the front lines.

Because good stormtroopers were hard to find. Deena knew that only too well. Stormtroopers like her . . . and FS-451. He wasn't in her fireteam—thank *pfassk*—but he'd been in the squad for longer than she had. And this was, what, the fourth or fifth time they'd been assigned as a pair to aid Lord Vader. Each time the order came down, it caused a bit of gossip back in the mess, a mix of lighthearted ribbing and jealousy, like serving as the Emperor's own personal enforcer was somehow an easy assignment. She laughed along with the others, of course—but she wasn't sure they were right. True, she'd rather be trying not to step on that long, flowing cloak as she trailed after him than being dumped on some mudhole planet and left to shoot as many rebels as possible before trying to reach a pickup that only had a fifty-fifty chance of showing up.

But Lord Vader was not someone you wanted to . . . disappoint. And while escort duty for a being that required no escort was an easy assignment, Deena had seen what happened when you provoked his ire.

Sometimes, while trying to keep a respectful—and safe—distance from Lord Vader, Deena daydreamed that one day it would be FS-451 who stood there choking in his armor after taking one microsecond too long to carrying out their master's orders.

She hated her fellow trooper. The feeling was deep, almost primal. It wasn't that he was just a jerk. There were plenty of those among the rank and file. He was worse. Far worse.

FS-451 was a *believer.*

It wasn't just that he was dedicated and loyal. Those were admirable qualities that any good trooper should have been proud of. No, FS-451's devotion to duty went beyond that. He didn't just live to serve the Empire—he *believed* in it, believed in the right of the Emperor to rule, believed in the desire for total supremacy across the galaxy. Believed in the iron fist needed to wield such power.

Believed there was no cost too great, no price too high, to achieve total domination. And it was only through such domination that there could really be peace in the galaxy.

Deena had another word for him: fanatic. Why FS-451 was still a regular stormtrooper was something Deena and the others in the squad had often wondered about, those late nights in the mess when they sat in the corner, sipping Xander's illegal hooch distilled from the Star Destroyer's reactor coolant system. FS-451 never joined them, of course. He was better than they were. He never even used his real name, such was his Imperial fervor. He had his operating number tattooed on his chest, right across his collarbone, and when he wandered around off duty he always wore the same bodysuit tunic with the neckline torn into a plunging V so everybody could see it.

Tig said she'd heard he wanted to be a death trooper. All those hours pumping iron in the rec room, trying to boost his stats so he could take the augmentations better. Riccarn wasn't so sure. Death troopers weren't of much use in wartime—maybe that was why Lord Vader never had them as an escort. FS-451 had wanted to get his hands dirty, that's what he'd told Riccarn. He wanted to join the Burners—become an incinerator stormtrooper. Now *that*, according to FS-451, was real combat. Dropping into an insurgent nest, flaming rebels, watching them burn to death in front of you so you could see the fear and the pain in their eyes, the sudden realization all too late that they were wrong and the Empire was going to win.

Deena hadn't heard FS-451 talk about his plans, his ambitions. She wasn't sure that story about joining the Burners was true. She'd spent more time with him than anyone in the squad, so she would know, right?

And now here they were in some kind of floating city, trailing Lord Vader around crisp white corridors that made their own armor look shabby and stained. A Tibanna mining operation, FS-451 had said as they'd flown in on the shuttle. But from what she'd seen, it looked more like a pleasure palace than an industrial center.

It didn't matter. None of it did, not anymore.

Because she'd had enough. This mission was the very last straw.

Deena had considered quitting before. It was not impossible, although the stories she'd heard of those who had left service didn't inspire much confidence. The one thing the Empire brought was order. She could see that. For the young and the vulnerable, those looking for a way out, a chance at a new life, there were worse things to do than volunteer for Imperial service. But once that structure and stability were gone, once you were on your own, left to deal with the trauma and stress that had, until that moment, been softened by whatever the Imperial medical droids injected into your arm when you were sent down to the infirmary after a sortie? What then?

The survival rate for stormtroopers in battle often wasn't great.

The survival rate on the outside was sometimes even worse.

But Deena was different, wasn't she? She could do something else. She knew she could. Something to . . . help.

She hadn't told anyone about her feelings, not even Tig. Because while the others in the squad might not have been fanatics like FS-451, they were still loyal soldiers. Imperial service was a way of life, and at her level, those who surrounded her were all career troopers. Any talk of leaving, any expression of doubt, would probably be considered treasonous even by those closest to her.

So she kept her mouth shut and her eyes front, and she spent days and weeks and months wondering just how much more she could take. How much more killing. How many more deaths. Stormtroopers were disposable. She knew that. She'd come to accept that. But when FS-451 came back one time as the sole survivor of what should have been a routine op for his fireteam, Deena realized that behind every visor there was a living, breathing person.

Just like her.

Just like—*whisper it*—the rebels.

To be honest, Deena wasn't sure what to make of the so-called Rebel Alliance. To fight against order and against law and against structure, everything the Empire stood for, made no sense.

But to fight against cruelty, and tyranny? And what actually was the opposite of order? Chaos?

Or . . . freedom?

The first time she'd walked out was after Alderaan. She'd been forced to watch the holovid along with everyone else, multiple times. The others cheered—FS-451 louder than most—but to Deena, Alderaan was not a victory. It was a pointless waste.

So she'd quit—for a whole five minutes. She'd excused herself, been sick in the toilet out the back of the rec room. When she'd come out, FS-451 had been there, arms folded, leaning against the wall opposite. He hadn't said anything, but he'd had that look on his face. He had enjoyed the holovid, and now he seemed pleased with the effect it'd had on her, because it meant she understood the scale of it all, how powerful the Empire was, how dalliance with rebellion would result in total extermination.

That was three years ago. And she was still here, standing alongside FS-451, somewhere in the industrial bowels of this city in the clouds. The room was huge but it was dark, lit mostly in a sick orange that came from the vast machinery surrounding them. Ugnaught technicians fussed around the equipment while Lord Vader stood in impassive silence, supervising proceedings, a bounty hunter in battered green Mandalorian armor by his side.

This was the city's carbon freezer unit, and what they were about to do was as abhorrent as it was pointless.

They were going to put a prisoner in carbonite. Deena's stomach turned at the very thought of it.

As a method of execution, it was hopelessly inefficient. Carbon freezing was for organic materials destined for long-haul space freight, not as a way of preserving living things. There was no way the prisoner was going to survive the process, not after what she and FS-451 had done to him just a few hours earlier. The bounty hunter hadn't been keen, and even the city administrator, a flamboyant man in a gold-lined cape, had tried to argue the point. Lord Vader had brushed them both off, claiming that this would be a test, that the prisoner—someone called Captain Solo—would be frozen to see if the real prize, the rebel pilot Lord Vader had become obsessed with, would survive.

Luke Skywalker—the Death Star destroyer—was already on approach in an X-wing starfighter.

Some test. To add to this theater of cruelty, Lord Vader had the process carried out in front of the prisoner's friends. There was a Wookiee, who had knocked Tig—only just summoned from the shuttle—off the side of the platform in a fit of rage before the prisoner had managed to calm him, and a woman Solo had called "princess." Was this Leia Organa of Alderaan? Deena had seen her image on the Imperial HoloNet several times, but she looked smaller in person than Deena expected.

476

Deena remembered the last words the pair had exchanged. She replayed that moment, over and over again in her mind, as the prisoner was lowered into the freezer.

Enough.

As the slab was lifted out and fell to the metal decking with a heavy thud, Deena glanced sideways at FS-451. He hadn't moved a muscle. She could imagine the cruel smile behind the helmet. That same twisted expression she'd seen the day they'd watched Alderaan die.

And then she looked at the princess. Her eyes were wet, her expression one of total loss.

Deena vowed to remember that, too, forever.

Monsters. All of them.

As for Captain Solo . . . he was alive. Perfect hibernation. Deena wasn't sure if that was a good thing. Perhaps it would have been better to have died instantly in the freezer.

FS-451 shuffled a little beside her, his helmet tilting. He was disappointed. Deena knew he was, especially after the care and attention he'd given the prisoner earlier.

Why Lord Vader had wanted the prisoner tortured, Deena didn't know. Orders were orders and it was hardly unusual treatment. Sometimes you had to extract information by force, and then once you had what you wanted, you kept going, just to make sure they really were telling the truth.

But the session with Captain Solo had been different. Lord Vader hadn't asked any questions—in fact, he hadn't even stuck around, apparently happy to leave his trusted bodyguards to their work.

Deena wasn't entirely blameless. She knew that. She'd done her part, making sure the prisoner had been secure in the harness, making sure one of the electrode probes was correctly seated after all the trouble the machine had given her and FS-451 as they'd struggled to reassemble it once it had been unpacked from the shuttle.

FS-451 had operated the device, lowering the prisoner's cradle onto the interrogation machine. Deena had stood back and closed her eyes and listened to the man scream and imagined the smile growing behind her fellow stormtrooper's helmet.

There was no point to it. Enhanced interrogation was one thing. Torture for pure, sadistic pleasure was something else entirely.

It wasn't war. It was criminal.

So Deena had closed her eyes and listened to the screams and then listened to FS-451's low chuckle as he turned the machine up and up and up. When they were done, Deena helped unstrap the prisoner and carry him back to the holding cell, where they found his Wookiee companion trying to reassemble their golden protocol droid.

Oh, FS-451 was good at his work. He'd taken the prisoner to within a micron of death, and there wasn't a mark on his body. FS-451 had been quiet after that, his lust for pain, for meting out punishment to rebel scum, temporarily sated.

It was quiet in the freezing chamber. Deena watched the Wookiee, but he seemed calm now. Tig hadn't returned from down below. Deena hoped she wasn't hurt; it was a fair drop. Lord Vader left without an escort—Deena's squad was to remain in the freezing chamber while the Ugnaughts reset the facility. She watched as FS-451 took a keen interest in their work.

It was now or never. With FS-451's attention elsewhere, Deena left her post and headed down the access stairs leading to the foot of the main freezer unit. At the bottom, she found Tig, unharmed but with her white armor covered in black grease. She was examining her E-11 blaster, and looked up as Deena approached.

"Damn thing got busted in the fall," said Tig. "Safety's jammed."

Deena thought a moment, then made her decision.

"Here." She offered her own weapon to Tig. "I need to head to the shuttle to prepare for Lord Vader's departure. I'll swap out a new one for you from the armory."

Tig hesitated, looking down at the offered blaster. Deena held her breath. She hadn't thought it through. Swapping weapons was against protocol. She could be reported. But Tig was a friend, and they'd done their fair share of protocol infringement in the past, hadn't they? Why would she be suspicious?

Tig's comm clicked back into life. "Good call," she said. They swapped weapons, and as she headed away, Deena gave her comrade a knock on the front of her breastplate with the back of her gauntlet.

"I'll be as quick as I can," she said, and then she left, not looking back, knowing that was the last time she would speak to Tig or anyone else in the squad again.

She found a public bathroom, locked herself inside, and sat in silence for minutes, or hours, she wasn't really sure.

But she needed the time to think, to plan. It was too late to change her mind. The decision to leave had been made, so what she needed to figure out now were her priorities and a plan of action. Her first task was a simple one: She had to get out of the city, alive.

But . . . beyond that? There would be time to come to terms with the path she had chosen later, she knew that, but she also knew it was important to keep her future in mind, even if it was unknown, undefined.

She was good at what she did—that's why she was here in the first place. She was a soldier. A survivor. She had skills she could use, and she still had a part to play in the events that were threatening to tear the galaxy apart.

It wasn't as simple as that, of course. But she knew she could do *something*.

Something good.

Deena sat a few minutes more, taking long, deep breaths. Then she got to work.

In the tiny cubicle, she stripped off her armor down to the black bodysuit, which she then checked in the mirror. The bodysuit would do just fine, nobody would know who she was or what she had been. Her red hair was cropped to regulation length, but having seen the fashions of the city's citizens, it didn't strike her as looking unusual. A bigger problem was being recognized by her former colleagues—few troopers outside her own squad had seen, or would remember, her face, and while Xander, Ella, and Riccarn were still on the *Executor*, being spotted by Tig or FS-451 would be a problem. She'd have to be careful. She'd be able to recognize them, even in their armor, close-up, but it would be far harder to pick them out among other storm-troopers from a distance. Getting caught wouldn't just mean arrest. She knew what the Empire did to those who betrayed the cause, and she wouldn't put it past FS-451 to make a personal plea to Lord Vader to take charge of her interrogation himself.

So yes, she'd have to be careful, and she had to get out of the city, fast. Her odds of survival diminished with each passing moment she spent here.

The toilet itself was a blocky contraption, the main unit surrounded by various attachments enabling it to be used by a variety of different species. Deena knelt in front of it and, with a little effort, managed to pry the unit's side panel off. Inside was a mass of tubing and sealed cisterns, but there was enough room to squeeze the component parts of her armor inside. The only thing that was too bulky was the helmet. Deena considered for a moment, realizing she couldn't just walk around the city carrying it. So she stood and placed it on top of the toilet's lid, then took Tig's broken blaster and stuffed it as best she could under her top, checking again in the mirror—if she held her arm by her side, over the mass of the blaster as it stretched out her top, it was . . . completely obvious what she was hiding.

Deena sighed. She really didn't want to leave it behind with the helmet, but she couldn't just wander around the city carrying an E-11.

Turning it over in her hands, she partially disassembled the blaster, slipping the sight off and separating the main body from the grip. She tucked the grip into her waistband and slid the sight into the top of one boot. That just left the barrel and main body, which at a glance looked like a random piece of machinery and which nobody would take any notice of at all.

At least, that's what she told herself. Then, as she activated the door control to leave, she hit the MAINTENANCE REPORT button. Once she was outside, the door slid closed and the red light over the door switched to blue: out of order.

Squeezing the blaster barrel rather self-consciously in one hand, Deena walked briskly away.

Deena stopped and took stock of her surroundings. She didn't know where she was. She didn't even know how she'd gotten there. She'd been wandering in a kind of daze; as soon as she realized this, she snapped herself out of it. A lack of focus was an easy way to get caught—by, for example, the squad of stormtroopers who were marching toward her across the large plaza she was now standing in.

The sight of the troopers made Deena freeze on the spot, but only for the briefest moment. Fighting to control the nausea in her stomach, she forced herself to move, ducking across to one of the tall lampposts that lined the open-air boulevard that circled the square.

This was it. Her desertion had been noticed, and the Empire was looking for her. She'd been spotted, and the stormtroopers would have her in custody within moments.

Heart thundering in her chest, Deena leaned against the lamppost, trying to blend in with the crowds of people. She glanced in the direction of the squad, their heavy footfalls growing louder as they approached. Some of the city's citizens had noticed the stormtroopers, too, some stopping to look, and point.

Deena glanced around, trying to pick the best direction to run. The truth was, she had no idea of the city's layout, and any direction was just as likely to lead her straight into another squad.

Then the sound of booted feet marching in step began to fade; to her surprise, Deena saw the squad move right past her—and keep going. Within a couple of minutes they disappeared from view completely.

Deena checked around her; then, the coast clear, she stepped out from the lamppost and crossed the boulevard, back toward the plaza. She glanced around, but nobody was paying her the slightest bit of attention.

Deena let out a sigh of relief. Maybe she was being paranoid. Or maybe she'd got lucky. Either way, she knew she was in the wrong place. She needed to find a way off the city and out of the system, but she also needed to keep a low profile. She thought back to her arrival in the shuttle and tried to recall the route back to the landing platforms.

No, too open, too obvious. What she needed was passage on a commercial or industrial transport. A ship she could smuggle herself on board, or, better still, sign up as auxiliary crew. For that, she had to reach the city's industrial port, which would be on a lower level than the main landing pads up top.

To Deena's surprise, it was relatively easy to access the lower levels of the city. Away from the public spaces, the industrial heart of the complex became apparent. Deena found herself wandering dark corridors, passing various facilities and departments, the air tangy with Tibanna residue and the scent of hot machinery at work. The only other people she'd seen so far had been a handful of Ugnaughts, but they'd been busy in their work, and she had no trouble avoiding detection. Down here, her black bodysuit was practically camouflage, and out of public sight, she'd taken a moment to reassemble her weapon. She didn't know if she would need it, but she had to admit she felt better with it complete in her hands.

She hadn't found the way to the city's industrial port yet, but she knew it was a big place and, for the moment, she could afford to be patient. The city's inner workings felt relatively safe, and, so far, free from Imperial intrusion.

Eventually she came to a larger chamber, some kind of auxiliary control room, in the middle of which was a series of large circular consoles with complex cradles of equipment suspended above. On one side of the room was a large circular conduit that ran up at an angle to another dark room beyond, but Deena was drawn to the circular window opposite. Moving over, she looked out at what seemed to be the central hub of the city, a dizzying funnel of curved walls and windows stretching above and below.

There was a sound from behind her, almost like tentative footsteps. No sooner had Deena registered the sound than there was the heavy clunk of a power relay activating, and the conduit on the other side of the room was lit up in white, the silhouette of a man clearly outlined at the other end. Deena ducked instinctively and scooted around the consoles to find a place to hide. From behind a console at the edge of the space, she watched as the man jumped down into the room. Just as he seemed to get his bearings, a heavy grilled gate snapped shut behind him, closing off the conduit.

Deena watched him with interest. He was dressed in a drab uniform of some sort, with a pouched utility belt, and was holding some kind of cylindrical tool in one hand. He was a worker perhaps, but the way he looked around, it was like he knew as much about his surroundings as she did. Then, as he moved into the room, toward the window, Deena noticed the holstered blaster on his hip. She frowned to herself, wondering why the worker would be armed, when a new sound filled the room—the deep, hollow rasp of artificial respiration Deena knew only too well.

Lord Vader was here.

Immediately the man fell into a combat stance and lifted the cylindrical tool in his hand. There was a fizzing snap, and a blade that looked like it was made of shimmering blue light ignited from the object.

Of course. This man was no city worker. The weapon was a lightsaber, and *this* was Luke Skywalker, Vader's quarry.

Quarry that had now been cornered.

Deena squeezed herself into a ball, desperate to remain hidden, feeling like she was in full view. She gasped as Lord Vader lifted his own saber, the blade a brilliant and angry red.

Deena's heart raced as she risked a look over her shoulder. She had to get out, but the only exit was a corridor behind her, and there was no way she could make it without being seen.

She would just have to wait until the room was clear.

Wait—and watch. . . .

What happened next, though, Deena did not expect. Instead of engaging in a duel, Lord Vader lowered his blade. There was a noise from behind the pilot, a metallic tearing. Deena watched as Skywalker swung his saber at a long, tubular piece of pipework that seemed to have fallen from one of the wall fittings.

Lord Vader seized the moment of distraction and commenced his attack—but strangely, only for a few seconds. From nowhere, an equipment box flew through the air and hit Skywalker on the head, throwing him off balance. As Deena watched, Vader took a step back and lowered his blade again as more equipment was pulled off the walls. Deena saw it with her own eyes this time, bolts shearing as chunks of machinery were ripped, sparking and spitting, from their fittings, without even being touched. Piece after piece flew through the air, directed by Lord Vader himself as he channeled the power Deena had seen him wield many times. But those instances aboard the *Executor*—the summary termination of subordinates without laying a gloved finger on them, the unfortunate victim occasionally held aloft as they were choked by the invisible force—were nothing compared to the onslaught Deena was witness to, the power multiplied exponentially as Lord Vader wrenched the control room apart with nothing but his mind.

485

The machinery pummeled Skywalker, who struggled to defend himself with his lightsaber, but he kept swinging in the wrong direction. Stumbling backward, he was narrowly missed by a huge cylindrical object that smashed through the center of the great window behind him.

It was as if a starship air lock had been blown. Deena grabbed the console as best she could as the atmosphere in the room began to evacuate through the broken window. She saw Lord Vader himself struggle against the sudden vacuum, his cloak billowing as he reached for a pillar.

Deena felt her own grip begin to slip, her boots sliding on the smooth metal floor as the wind roared in her ears.

But this was the opportunity she needed. She had no choice. She had to risk it.

She had to get out.

Deena took one look over the top of the console, saw Lord Vader facing away from her, saw Skywalker trying to keep himself from being sucked outside, the blue blade of his lightsaber raised across his face for protection.

Deena braced herself against the console, took a deep breath, and pushed off, powering down the corridor leading out from the control room with all her might as debris flew past her, the endless wind threatening to sweep her off her feet. Halfway down she found her strength beginning to weaken. The corridor wall was broken up by protruding bulkheads. She threw herself against the wall and found herself leaning against a maintenance hatch. Flinging the panel open, Deena pulled herself inside.

The maintenance crawl space was long and dark, and the going was slow, and Deena could only hope that she could find an exit soon that would get her back into the city and closer to her intended destination and away from Lord Vader's fight with Skywalker.

If Skywalker was even still alive. The pressure equalization in the control room had been severe, and he'd been close to the window. It was more than likely he'd been sucked out to his death.

Deena swore as she moved on, the going difficult as she found herself having to squeeze past cable runs, and trip over bulkheads, control boxes, data feed junctions. Ahead, the narrow confine got narrower. She couldn't go back. She'd have to get out soon and see where she was. As far as she could tell, the crawl space ran alongside an open corridor, but she'd lost all sense of direction already in the dark and close space.

There was another maintenance hatch coming up. She headed toward it, but her foot caught on another mystery object hidden in the dark. As she toppled forward, there was a click from somewhere over her head. A tinny little public address system buzzed to life.

486

"Attention, this is Lando Calrissian. Attention. The Empire has taken control of the city. I advise everyone to leave before more Imperial troops arrive."

Deena lay where she was, waiting for more, but the PA clicked off and that was it. That settled it. She needed to get out of the crawl space and find a ship to hitch a ride on *fast.*

Then she heard something else. She pulled herself up, grabbed the blaster from where she'd dropped it, and moved closer to the maintenance hatch. She pressed her ear against it and listened.

It was a crackling, buzzing sound, two giant, angry insects swooping in on each other, punctuated by electric bangs, the harsh spitting reminding her of energy bolts shorting against a deflector shield. Beneath it all, the mechanical huffing of Lord Vader himself.

Deena pushed the hatch open just enough to see into the corridor. Her heart leapt into her throat as she saw the two figures locked in combat beyond the open doorway at the end of the passage. Lord Vader was pressing his attack, forcing the very much alive Luke Skywalker back along a metal gantry that hung over the gaping maw of the city hub, their lightsabers crackling and fizzing over the wind that howled into the corridor from outside.

She had to get out, but the combatants were too close, and even locked in battle as they were, she couldn't risk being seen. Having seen the extent of Lord Vader's true power, it didn't take much to imagine him snapping her neck in his rage without a second thought even as he continued his attack against Skywalker.

Deena shrank back into the crawl space, closing the panel behind her. She twisted herself around, trying to get her bearings before using fistfuls of cable to drag herself back through the tight space, while the sounds of battle continued to echo from outside.

She pushed on in haste, hardly aware of which direction she was facing. Then her foot tangled *again,* and she fell. Outside, the wind howled, and the sounds of the fight seemed to fade. Deena lay still in the dark, and listened—was Lord Vader saying something? Then the duel recommenced.

Deena rushed to free herself, her hands groping blindly in the dark. She struggled for what seemed like forever, then finally she was free. Ahead, the crawl space came to a pointed end and was relatively clear of obstacles.

Nearly there.

Deena slid to the last maintenance panel in the wall and popped it open. She came out right at the end of the corridor.

The *wrong* end. She was at the doorway, leading out onto a long external gantry. Somehow, she'd gotten herself turned around. Deena swore to herself again and, keeping close to the wall, she risked a peek around the bulkhead of the doorway.

Their lightsabers had been deactivated, but Lord Vader had Skywalker trapped at the end of the gantry. Skywalker, however, seemed unwilling to accept his defeat, and was backing away on his hands and knees along an antenna array that stretched out toward the middle of the city hub, the seemingly infinite drop now directly below him. As Deena watched, Lord Vader reached toward his quarry; he was speaking, but the eddies of wind swirling around the platform made it difficult to make out his words.

"There is no escape. Don't make me destroy you."

Deena blinked. What had Lord Vader said? Or was she mishearing over the noise of the wind? This was Luke Skywalker, a kid who had destroyed the jewel in the Emperor's crown, the object of Lord Vader's obsession for the last three years.

Why would he spare him? Skywalker was trapped, at Lord Vader's mercy. All it would take is a single blow from his lightsaber, and—

"... You do not yet realize your ... you have only begun to discover ..."

Deena hissed with frustration as the wind picked up. She had to go—now!—but part of her was desperate to find out what was happening. She dropped into a crouch and poked her head out a little farther.

She could risk a few moments, surely—witnessing this private moment between Lord Vader and his enemy, maybe she could pick up some useful intel, something she could use to bargain with once she got out of the city.

Lord Vader raised his voice. "With our combined strength, we can end this destructive conflict, and bring order to the galaxy!" In reply, the pilot yelled something that Deena couldn't make out, but Lord Vader's next statement was loud and clear.

"If you only knew the power of the dark side."

The wind whipped around the doorway. Deena ducked back inside the corridor. Unsure of the value of what she had heard—was Lord Vader offering a truce, some kind of alliance with Skywalker?—she moved back to the doorway to try and hear more. Outside, Skywalker was now clinging to the side of the antenna array with one hand, the other clutched to his chest. The wind changed direction again, and Deena could just make out his words.

"He told me you killed him."

"No," said Lord Vader, "I am your—"

A huge gust blew in through the doorway, forcing Deena back inside. She pressed herself against the wall, turning to face it, her head curled down toward her chest. The wind dipped, briefly, enough for Deena to hear Skywalker yell something—she couldn't understand what, but she could hear only too well the pain in his voice, his primal scream of anguish stirring something deep inside her.

Then the wind swelled again, the eddies now caught between the jutting bulkheads in the corridor, spinning into a miniature whirlwind. She couldn't stay where she was—Lord Vader could come back in at any moment—so she opened the maintenance hatch and returned to the relative peace of the crawl space, leaning against the closed panel as she got her breath back. The panel rattled under her as the wind gusted again, then it died. Deena didn't move. The seconds in the dark seemed to stretch forever, and then she heard heavy footsteps pass by in the corridor. Once they had faded away, Deena popped the panel open again.

The corridor was empty. Looking back down toward the doorway, she couldn't see anybody out on the gantry.

The footsteps must have been Lord Vader, but where was Skywalker? It had sounded like only one person walking by, but, to be honest, it had been hard to tell. As if to prove her point, the wind blew up again, filling the corridor with an eerie howling that Deena realized was certainly loud enough to mask the softer footfalls of Lord Vader's . . . what? Enemy? Or was Skywalker now some kind of co-conspirator? Or . . . that scream—had he fallen off the antenna? Deena didn't think so. It hadn't *sounded* like the scream of someone falling.

Deena waited a few more moments, her back pressed against the panel behind her as the wind rose and fell. Then, satisfied that Lord Vader and Skywalker were far enough away, she followed their direction down the corridor. As she walked, she ran what parts of the conversation she had heard back through her head.

Don't make me destroy you. Deena shook her head, trying to parse that statement. She only wished she had heard more.

But Lord Vader's suggestion that the pair could unite and *bring order to the galaxy*—now that was clear enough. Deena wasn't quite sure how to leverage that information, but she was sure somebody would be interested. . . .

Right now, she had to refocus on the task at hand: getting out before the Imperial forces took full control.

Deena found a cargo lift that, thankfully, displayed a directory of city levels. But just as she was about to punch the control for what was listed as the Tibanna export hub, the lift was commandeered by a cadre of Ugnaughts who sent the lift to the top level. The small workers seemed to be arguing among themselves, not only ignoring Deena's protests, but physically pushing her out of the lift ahead of them once they had reached their destination. No sooner had she exited the lift than the doors closed and it began a fast descent.

Deena sighed. She'd wasted enough time already and knew her best bet now was trying to get out with the city's civilian population as they evacuated.

The upper levels were in total chaos, people running in every direction, carrying personal belongings and camtonos of valuables, adults carrying children, children leading the elderly by the hand. In the middle of all this, blue-uniformed city officials were doing their best to organize both themselves and the citizens. Evacuating the city was a huge operation, and Deena knew, deep in her bones, that the Empire would make short work of anyone unlucky enough to be left behind.

Deena looked down at Tig's blaster in her hands and pushed down the feeling of nausea at the thought that, just a few hours ago, she would have been among the stormtroopers unleashing the Empire's anger on these innocent people.

She pulled herself out of the seething crowd and took off down an empty corridor leading away from the main thoroughfare. She took a left, a right, backtracked at the sight of a squad of stormtroopers, picked another passage and ran down it. At the end of this one, she found herself in a quiet white atrium with an abstract, globelike sculpture at the center. She came to a halt and checked around. Apparently alone, she almost fell against the wall and closed her eyes, concentrating as she tried to visualize the route to the upper landing pads.

491

She heard them first. She opened her eyes, then darted back around the corner as a group of Imperials came out of a corridor beyond the atrium—Lord Vader, an Imperial officer, and a fireteam of stormtroopers, thankfully heading away from her position toward a door leading out onto one of the landing pads, which she'd managed to reach without even realizing.

"Alert my Star Destroyer," said Lord Vader, as he led his entourage, "to prepare for my arrival."

Then three more stormtroopers marched into the atrium from the other side. Deena turned and ran back the way she had come, taking a series of left turns to make sure she looped back to the landing pad.

She had to be quick—before the group disappeared.

Before she changed her mind. Because it was suicide. She knew that. Maybe it was the adrenaline, the fatigue, maybe it was the years of anger and hatred.

Maybe it was the fear. Fear that she'd made a mistake, that there was no hope.

That there was no going back.

Maybe she'd overheard something important. Maybe that intel was so incomplete as to be totally worthless.

So maybe she could do something *herself* that would make a difference.

Five stormtroopers. One officer. Lord Vader.

She couldn't take them all out, but she didn't need to. All it would take was one carefully aimed shot. She'd die under a blaze of energy bolts just a few seconds later . . . but not before she'd made a difference, made a contribution that would go down in history.

She came around the corner and found herself at the landing pad door. Lord Vader's group was still in range, but only just, as they approached the shuttle docked on the pad.

Deena fell into a combat crouch. She raised the blaster. She took careful aim.

She squeezed the trigger, and nothing happened.

Deena felt her stomach do somersaults. She checked the blaster, thumbed the safety again—and found it was jammed, as Tig had said. The blaster really had been damaged in her fall from the freezer platform. In her adrenaline-fueled daze after leaving the freezing chamber, Deena had forgotten that simple, but important, fact.

Deena stood, breathing a huge sigh of . . . relief? Yes. Relief that she hadn't thrown her life away for nothing. Lord Vader would never have fallen to a single blaster bolt. It would have been an empty gesture.

Deena dropped the blaster, fell to her knees, and watched the shuttle take off.

"You there! What are you doing here?"

She looked over her shoulder as a group of blue-uniformed city officers surrounded her. The one who had spoken knelt beside her, while another man dressed in gray, his bald head wrapped in a cybernetic implant, stood to one side.

493

The officer kneeling beside her moved his hands carefully around her shoulders. "Do you need medical assistance?"

Deena looked at him. He was frowning, but it was a look of genuine concern.

"No, I'm fine, I'm fine," she said. She got to her feet, the officer helping her. As she stood, the bald man looked her up and down—she'd seen him in the freezing chamber earlier, he was some kind of administrator, wasn't he?

She turned to face him.

"I want to help," said Deena. "With the evacuation—I'm . . ."

She hesitated. The bald man glanced at the other officer, and Deena realized they were all watching her closely.

"I'm a qualified pilot," Deena continued. "I can help organize an ordered evacuation."

The lights on the bald man's implant flashed in sequence, but still he didn't speak.

Deena sighed. "Look, you're going to need all the help you can get. Pretty soon there are going to be Imps crawling all over the city, and you're not going to be able to fight them."

Imps. Even as she said it, it felt . . . strange. This was the language of the Rebellion, of those she had dedicated her life to fighting.

Not anymore.

Then the bald man gave a curt nod and walked away.

"Okay," said the other officer, "let's go." As one, the group moved off at a run.

Deena watched him for a moment, then, grinning to herself, followed.

It seemed that, now, she really had picked her side.

THE MAN WHO BUILT CLOUD CITY

Alexander Freed

Our tale begins with one word. One word repeated twice by a very lonely man:

"Treachery! Treachery!"

The crier stood upon a marble bench, hunched like a gargoyle to brace against the wind whipping him onto his heels. Each time a gust lifted the ragged cape of his overcoat (the sleeves long gone but the yellow leather of the breast bright beneath the stains), it appeared he would topple onto the grass; but his enormous gray beard seemed to act as a counterweight, and he remained atop his perch as he made his proclamation.

"My people! Baron Administrator Calrissian has betrayed us all!

The Empire is here, and I cannot thwart this invasion. You must go! Flee while you can!"

The man surveyed the plaza and—pleased to see that his people were indeed fleeing, hordes of them dressed in finery and night-clothes, carrying suitcases and small children and sentimental knickknacks—he hopped off the bench, leaving nothing behind but the odors of mint candy and sweaty armpits. "Go!" he yelled, whipping his arm about. "Your master commands it!"

Then he dashed out of the stream of prospective refugees and into the vaulted halls of the merchants' promenade. The shoppers were gone, but a few vendors struggled to pack their goods or lock their stalls. From somewhere outside came the electric snap of a blaster shot; he quelled the fear rising like bile in his throat and made for the far exit.

The voice that came through the intercom was nearly loud enough to muffle the chaos of the plaza—a low voice, smooth and grave and confident all at once. "This is Lando Calrissian. The Empire has taken control of the city. I advise everyone to leave before more Imperial troops arrive . . ."

"Treachery!" our lonely hero cried in reply.

For he was King Yathros Condorius the First, the man who had turned Cloud City from a gas miner's watering hole to a galactic paradise. His ancestors had shared the blood of the Nothoiin nobles who had ruled the Anoat sector, and his edicts yet carried weight in the deepest pits of Bespin.

He was king, and Landonis Calrissian had been his regent, chosen to rule in his place. That choice had been the most grievous mistake of his very long life.

Treachery! he thought. Vengeance would be his!

———

It was only a few days since Yathros had become aware of Calrissian's wicked plots. Oh, he'd long known the young baron administrator possessed an unsavory side—seen his serpentine ambition, his willingness to swindle and betray in love, cards, and dealmaking—but he'd believed (naïvely, foolishly) that Calrissian's fondness for the ordinary folk of Bespin would overpower his darker half.

Yathros had been taking an evening stroll when the truth had become apparent. The night had been a pleasant one: He'd dined on buttery scalloped wing-eel at the Paradise Atrium (not *inside* the atrium, of course, where the presence of a king would've distracted other customers; but the owner knew Yathros well, and had left him a disposable container and dinnerware at their secret drop-off beside the kitchen door). He'd finished his latest proclamation—one regarding the treatment of the unfairly maligned silverchicks that had taken occupancy in the local parks—and turned the draft over to Or'toona Fleenk, the kindly artist who'd promised to transcribe it, print it, and post it where all of the king's people could see. The only disappointment had come when the shuttle pilot refused to carry Yathros aboard the red line car heading to the north platform—demanding Imperial credits, as if the mark of King Yathros were insufficient. Yet even that nuisance was remedied through the intervention of a kindly Ugnaught (Yathros had *always* been friend to the Ugnaughts), and Yathros was able to admire his domain from the vantage he treasured most along the Grand Avenue.

Under the domes of the guildhalls, observing the cloud bands as they refracted the low evening sun, he heard a party approaching from the opposite end of the road. Turning to the sound, he saw Baron Administrator Calrissian in his usual finery (the man wore a fresh cape every day, it seemed to Yathros) flanked by two of his Wing Guards and speaking sharply to a pair of armored figures.

Yathros recognized neither of the men in armor. They were strang-

497

ers in Cloud City, which was unextraordinary enough—Calrissian trucked with many outsiders, as part of his diplomatic duties. This pair, however—one in gleaming black, the other in dented green—unnerved Yathros. Neither appeared moved by Calrissian's ire, and Calrissian appeared to flinch when the one in black replied.

It was when a third armored figure approached that Yathros understood. The newcomer wore the death-white garb of an Imperial stormtrooper and squawked urgently toward the group.

Shock mixed with fear and comprehension in the breast of Yathros, yet his duty as king was clear. With the instinct of a father swiftly correcting a toddler's disastrous first step into a busy road, he swept forward and called, "Baron Administrator! What is this outrage?"

The group had already turned away to follow the stormtrooper. Calrissian offered a scornful glance toward Yathros before saying distinctly to one of the Wing Guards, "Take care of this. I don't have time for his delusions."

"The Empire will ruin you!" Yathros called, even as a Wing Guard in a pressed blue uniform made to intercept him. "Whatever pleasing treasures they offer, whatever promises they make, they know only how to consume and destroy! For your own sake, as well as Cloud City's—"

The Wing Guard clapped a hand over his mouth. It smelled of soap and perfume. Yathros struggled, but his assailant turned him firmly about. "Not today, my king," the man said. "Calrissian will see you another time, but not today."

They moved together like dancers. Yathros pushed into the Wing Guard, and the Wing Guard pressed back, forcing Yathros to retrace his steps with a stumble. Yathros squinted into the face of the younger man. "You, too, Mr. Mizz? You know better than this. You recognize madness when you see it. Tell me what schemes Calrissian concocts! Have the Forbidden Acolytes poisoned his mind? Is this the work of the Invisible Cartel—"

"You can ask Calrissian yourself, *another time*." The man called Mizz sighed, the frustration practically beading on his brow. "Trust me on this, King. Remember when I got you into the Miners' Ball? You met my brother and his family. You thought Calrissian didn't want you there, but I got you a formal invite and everything."

"This is not a *party*!" Yathros cried, and slapped his palm upon Mizz's breast. "This is the fate of our city!"

But Mizz only turned away and hurried after Calrissian and the Imperials, the lot of whom were already out of sight.

That had been days ago, and all Yathros could do now was right a scant few wrongs. He'd gone searching for Calrissian but found himself in the mid-levels of the processing facility, inspiring a band of Ugnaught workers (he had always been a friend to the Ugnaughts) on their way to evacuation. He raced behind them, calling, "Hurry! Hurry!" and listening to the howling winds beneath the catwalk.

The squat humanoids grunted and ran. Together, all of them passed into a tunnel rich with the wintry metallic odor of carbonite. The Ugnaughts stopped at a lift and—at the sight of something Yathros could not see—began to squeal in alarm.

"Speak to me!" he urged.

One of the Ugnaughts turned. "King!" she said in her native tongue, but she was not allowed to continue as the others cried, "Flee!" and the door to the lift opened upon an army of Imperial stormtroopers.

Or if not an army, numbers close enough.

The Ugnaughts flowed around Yathros like steam from a burst pipe. He was ready to turn around himself, but one of the stormtroopers raised a rifle, and he was possessed by an outrage at once distant and familiar. "You will not fire on my people!" he bellowed, or tried to bellow—his hands found the barrel of the rifle, jerked it up,

499

but then something smashed into the side of his face. He tasted blood and fell hard onto the tunnel grating.

All he heard for a long while was the ringing of a bell. Indignation kept him conscious, though his vision was blurred. Finally a boot prodded at his coat and an enunciated Core Worlds accent sneered, "Not even the rebels smell this bad."

Yathros tried to speak around the crimson mess of his own mouth. "I needn't be a rebel to understand what you are."

"Let's see some identification," the electronic voice of a stormtrooper said. "Slowly."

"Why, I'm Governor Tarkin! Or perhaps your nanny, come to scold you!" The taunts were feeble, and his grin was crooked; a spot of drool or blood welled at one corner of his lips.

"You're about to be dead," the stormtrooper said.

Yathros's sight cleared enough to reveal the black moon of the muzzle pointed toward him. Terror buoyed him like drink and helped his words flow. "Your kind took everything from me once before. There's little you can do today."

Vision blurred again, mixing with memory. He saw the muzzle of the weapon; the white figures aboard his ship, *Life's Little Rewards;* bloody hands; an empty cargo bay. Later an empty purse; an empty house. The boy gone.

Yathros preferred not to think of these things, and he nudged the recollections forward through time to when he'd found the ring, found the ticket to Cloud City. Found the picture of the crown on his head as a child, found the books his father had read to him. Found his greatness and was reborn! *Those* were memories worth keeping.

Now someone was stealing all he possessed again, but it wasn't the stormtroopers who were wholly to blame.

"Calrissian," he murmured. "Fate will not repay your acts kindly."

He expected to hear a blaster shot. Instead the sneering man said, "You know Calrissian?"

Yathros arched his brow. "Know him? Indeed, I know him. I made him what he is, and I—"

A king must be cunning: This, Yathros had learned long ago, when he'd first arrived on Bespin with fifty-four credits to his name. (That was before he'd begun minting his own money—bless Or'toona Fleenk and her printing press!) He recognized the mixture of disdain and greed in the crisply dressed officer above him and saw an ally, if not a friend. Or perhaps a tool to avenge treachery.

"—I can find him," Yathros spat. "For he struck one too many bargains with your kind, didn't he? He thought he could trade my trust for Imperial favor—never realizing the Empire only takes, and does not trade. Now he flees us both, and as much as I loathe your Empire, it is Calrissian who betrayed me today. I can find him, and he will be yours."

"Is that so?" The officer attempted to sound dubious for the benefit of his minions, but Yathros knew he'd piqued the fool's interest. The man turned to the stormtroopers. "Pick him up." Then, to Yathros: "Talk, you."

Gloved hands launched Yathros upright. "He keeps a yacht at a secret dock," Yathros said, swaying in the troopers' hands. "I know exactly where it is! We dined there once when I took him as my apprentice, and it was where Queen Zeechay granted me the blessings of the Angels of Iego. Come quickly, before Calrissian—"

"Never mind," the officer snapped. "He's delusional. Shoot him."

The troopers tossed Yathros away as if he'd suddenly produced a terrible stench. He managed not to fall, but he didn't have time to wonder whether death was at hand before the world flashed red and filled first with the sound of energy blasts, then the sound of screams. He clapped hands to his ears and turned away, squeezing his eyes shut and stumbling along the tunnel. He didn't know what was happening, but none of it surprised him—violence was the way of the Empire, and *this* was violence incarnate.

Callused, ungloved fingers smelling of soap and perfume ripped his hands from his ears. "Yathros!"

Darbus Mizz, Wing Guard and henchman to Baron Administrator Calrissian, stood among the bodies of the stormtroopers. He dangled his blaster in one hand. "Yathros," he said again. "I've been looking for you."

Yathros snarled and stumbled back. "Kouhun! Assassin! Blackguard!"

"What?"

"Calrissian sent you to silence me, eh? Before I could betray his hiding place, as *he* betrayed *me*."

Mizz stared, clearly astonished that Yathros had recognized the situation for what it was. *From one peril to another,* Yathros thought, as Mizz gripped Yathros by the wrist and pulled him into the turbolift car.

502

"Not going to shoot me?" Yathros asked. The lift hummed and his knees wobbled. Mizz kept his blaster out, his eyes on the door. "Don't tell me Calrissian blames me for all this. He plan to toss me in a dungeon? Punish me for predicting his downfall? Or perhaps—"

The lift door opened, and Mizz yanked him onto a broad platform open to the sky. The trees of the arboretum peeked over distant walls, and a trickle of refugees snaked among parked speeders.

"—or perhaps he needs me, eh? Is that it?"

Mizz growled and pushed Yathros forward with his palm, applying steady pressure between Yathros's shoulders. Laser blasts flickered in the sky like some obscene auroral display. "Calrissian gave us a way out of here," Mizz said. "You need to take it."

Yathros snorted. Ire energized him despite the fatigue in his muscles and the bruises on his skin. "He remembers my tales of the hidden treasures of the Nothoiin Noble Court? Hopes to start a new life? Tell him that noble wealth is not for him!"

In the shadow of a hotel balcony, Mizz halted. "Enough, Yathros. Lando Calrissian sent me—"

"I know!"

"—because he *likes* you. He's always liked you. It's the only reason he put up with you all these years." Mizz's voice was rough and watery. Yathros let out a bark of a laugh, but the Wing Guard continued, "Anyone else would've had you *arrested* when you accosted casino patrons or issued proclamations on the street, but Lando thought you were charming. He didn't pity you or laugh at you—he invited you to dinner more than once. When the Empire arrived he knew you'd get yourself killed, so he sent me."

"Lies," Yathros retorted, and spat a pink wad of phlegm onto the ground. "If you believe that—"

"Enough!" It was a roar, and Mizz was trembling now; he glanced about to see if anyone had heard. Then his shoulders slumped as he turned back to Yathros. "You're not a king. Lando's not a regent. I'm a badly paid grunt, not an assassin. But we're all in trouble, and your fantasies are making things worse. Put them aside or we're dead."

They stared at each other awhile. Mizz was the first to break off, looking back to the road and releasing a hiss of breath.

He marched away. Yathros didn't follow at first, but when Mizz returned and tugged him forward he did not resist.

It was a long way to the docks, and their route was twisted and tortuous. The Empire had shut down the shuttles first, then the trams; now most of the throughways were blockaded, and Yathros and Mizz were often forced to retrace their steps and seek alternative paths.

They didn't speak. Yathros barely appeared to think, staring ahead into the middle distance, occasionally tripping over his feet and catching himself before Mizz could assist. Now and again frustration flashed into his expression only to vanish instantaneously, like drops of water bursting into steam. Mizz, meanwhile, moved with the jerky half-attention of a man too fixated on the outside world for grace. One hand stayed forever on his blaster while his eyes flickered to and fro.

Whatever outrages played through Yathros's mind could be no more vile than the horrors the pair witnessed. Stormtroopers rounded up Cloud City residents like cattle. Shimmersilk duffels and portable safes full of valuables were "confiscated" by officers leering with greed. Yathros and Mizz heard a sharp *crack* upon crossing a bridge and both looked up to see a transport in flames, dipping as its engines failed and toppling into the clouds. For minutes afterward, the smoke they breathed tasted unholy.

When the bridge was behind them, Yathros stopped short and tugged at Mizz. "The air whales," he murmured. "The survivors will fall for many minutes. If we could but summon the air whales—"

"Not another word," Mizz snapped. He sounded more exasperated than angry. "They're dead, and we have too far to go."

Yathros sucked in a breath but acceded to Mizz's tug on his arm. For several minutes following he kept his eyes on the horizon where the ship had disappeared. When he looked back to his surroundings he noticed a tremble to Mizz's step.

The Empire was not the only perpetrator of wickedness they encountered. At one junction, they watched three ragged Ugnaughts denied passage aboard a speeder cab in favor of a single Bespin aristocrat. Elsewhere, a mining engineer was selling tickets to a disaster shelter in the sublevels. Yathros stepped forward to object, but Mizz whispered, "Don't."

"A proclamation!" Yathros began. His voice was recovering its stentorian authority. "The people still recognize me. In this time of emergency, there will be no profiteering, no selling of safe passage. They will hear and obey!"

"Let it be," Mizz said. "Please."

Mizz's own voice was quiet—the voice of a beggar or a despairing old man. Yathros felt a surge of pity he did not entirely understand, and the haunting sense of an echo whose source he could not recall. He nodded and they moved on.

The farther they went, the more Mizz's movements became enervated; the more his eyes ceased to be watchful, focusing ahead like a pendulum coming to rest. It seemed his strength flowed into Yathros, who held his chin higher and often looked to his companion. Perhaps, Yathros thought, the atrocities that aroused the ire of a king were too much for a mere Wing Guard.

"We need to make a stop," Mizz said, as they walked down a residential street. No light shone from doors and windows. "It won't take long."

Yathros grunted assent. Three blocks later they turned a corner and Mizz stopped abruptly, nearly toppling forward.

At the end of a short alleyway was a doorway into a two-story apartment barely wider than the alley itself. The metal of the door lay in a crumpled pile kicked to the side; blackened craters and holes indicated it had come under a barrage of blasterfire. From what Yathros could see of the interior, the apartment was a ruin of shattered furniture and smashed glass.

Mizz stumbled forward, disappearing inside. Yathros did not pursue, and heard the sound of ashes crunching and heavy objects tossed aside. Then silence. Then heavy breathing.

Then, for a while, nothing.

Eventually Mizz emerged, touching his fingertips to the alley wall as he found his footing. "All right," he said, standing before Yathros. He was very nearly steady. "Let's go."

Yathros rested a grimy hand on Mizz's shoulder. "You aren't surprised," he said.

"No."

"You were braced for what you saw," Yathros said.

"Got a call earlier on the comm," Mizz said, not looking at Yathros. His voice was barely audible.

"You came for me instead of them?"

"You were closer, is all."

Yathros considered this awhile, and squeezed Mizz's shoulder. "What you said before? About me and my—and my royal blood?"

Mizz waited, saying nothing.

"I forgive you for doubting."

Mizz pressed his palms to his face; wiped his mien clean till no expression remained save a red tinge to his eyes; and they started toward the docks again.

Mizz seemed to have aged during the night, and Yathros had been timeworn as long as anyone in Cloud City could remember. But some hours before dawn, upon mounting the marble steps leading to the Caretaker's Bridge, they came within view of the docks. Both men halted at the zenith and sat to rest.

"End of the road," Mizz said. "End of Bespin, too. We'll be out of here soon." It was the first he'd spoken in some time.

Yathros squinted at his companion as if examining a speck on the man's forehead. Eventually he smiled thinly and turned to the docks again. "Perhaps it's not the end at all. Perhaps it's merely the darkest moment of a triumphant tale—when all is presumed lost, so that victory can be sweeter."

"Sure," Mizz said. "Maybe."

Yathros observed Mizz out of the corner of his eye. The man's grief, he thought, was familiar enough without requiring great study.

With a grunt, Yathros rose to his feet, steadying himself on Mizz's shoulder. He leisurely surveyed the city from above; and though he saw the panicked masses and the stormtrooper blockades, the towers glittered no less brightly. The clouds were no less magnificent as they washed like tides against the edges of the platforms, and from afar even the darkened houses looked like royal palaces.

Cloud City had treated him well, he thought, and he had taken responsibility for her and her people. Here he had become something more than himself. Outside he would be reduced in stature, and he would care for Bespin's citizens no longer.

This was a truth that was not his alone.

"You ready to leave?" Mizz asked.

"Are you leaving with me?" Yathros returned.

"Lando's orders," Mizz said. "He wants you safe."

"But Lando is not king."

"Yathros—"

"Landonis Calrissian is not king!" Yathros bellowed, much too loudly—for surely the stormtroopers would hear. "The choice is ours, Darbus Mizz. Our fates are ours to choose, not the regent's."

"We should go," Mizz said, shuffling upright.

But Yathros's grip was steely, and the old man turned Mizz to face him. As Yathros spoke, flecks of spittle dappled Mizz's face; the king's eyes were wide but his voice was controlled. "If we leave, we become refugees. If we stay, we stay with the people we have long guarded, as you guarded me this very night—people lacking the money or fortune to escape.

"We could shelter with the Ugnaughts who have been friends to me. We could stand against the stormtroopers, as we've done once before. We could remind our people that the Empire will fall, as all tyrannies fall. We could fight evil, Darbus Mizz."

Mizz smiled ruefully. It was clear he couldn't escape the appeal of Yathros's words, no matter his obvious doubt. But he said, "An old vagrant and a security guard can't do a lot of good here. Not anymore."

Yathros released a huff of breath and dropped his chin. "Yes. Yes, I'm afraid you're right. And yet—" His chin snapped back up. His grin was sly, and vanished quickly to be replaced by a more sober expression. "—a mighty king and a deadly assassin trained by the sinister Kouhun order? An assassin once a servant of the treacherous Calrissian, now seeking redemption as a royal agent? They could do a great deal."

Mizz swallowed, paused, and spoke carefully, as if any wrong word might disrupt the strange energy in the air. "Fantasies are a luxury for peaceful times. In darker days, they can get a person killed."

"Truth lights the way in darkness, and the story you've lived to date goes nowhere worth seeing. Trust in an old king's wisdom, my friend. Accept a *hidden* truth—illuminate *secret* paths—and take the gift I offer you."

Mizz didn't answer. After a silence, Yathros shook him briskly. "Admit it! Admit who you are!"

The words spilled from him at last. "Darbus Mizz, Prince of Assassins?"

"I knew it!" Yathros cried joyously. "You knew it. Now we shout it in the face of the world."

Mizz began to laugh. Yathros grinned again. The laughter was a manic sound, and it soon blended into the sound of sobbing from one or both of them as they recalled griefs recent and ancient. They held each other atop the stairs and looked out to the city, Yathros to the docks and Mizz to the glittering towers, until they began to cough.

A bright streak crossed the sky as a ship jumped to lightspeed. "A promising sign," Yathros murmured, and he wiped his mouth on his coat sleeve.

"Lando won't be happy," Mizz said.

"Let him be unhappy. It will help him learn. Perhaps it will give him reason to return."

Mizz nodded. His eyes followed the streets below, and his body straightened almost imperceptibly.

"You really think there's some good we can do?" he asked.

Yathros Condorius the First swung an arm around Mizz's shoulders, and they descended the stairs together. "What do you think would happen," the king said to his assassin prince, "if the royal ruler of Cloud City were to proclaim a treaty with the Rebel Alliance? Now, *that* would be a pact to shake the universe . . ."

Nowadays most people have forgotten the king and the Kouhun assassin. But they were the subject of many stories in the days of oppression—stories told by the people who needed them.

If you don't believe it, look around in the plazas. You'll find a bench over a marble slab inscribed by the famed artist Or'toona Fleenk. Read the tribute there, and see the faces of the men who saved Cloud City.

(Or at least who saved their own small part.)

THE BACKUP BACKUP PLAN

Anne Toole

"Lay down your weapons!"

Tal Veridian slid her blaster under the table, then held up her hands. She was sitting with her back to the entrance, the mirror in her alcove providing a covert view of the entire saloon. Stormtroopers poured in, their armor oddly tinged lavender by the evening light still streaming from the high windows. She had been waiting with a few fellow drunks, waiting to hear the outcome of Lando's latest plan regarding the princess and her guard. Obviously, it hadn't gone quite as planned.

"Go, go," she said under her breath.

A few of her companions ducked behind the bar. She watched out of the corner of her eye as their cloaked forms slunk out the back. The rest of the denizens behind her would not be so lucky. Two storm-troopers guarded the door as another two hassled a few Cloud City miners sharing a drink at the bar. Tal recognized them as Rajin—who'd been waiting to hear about the birth of his child—and his friend, whom they'd once caught gambling on tip-yip races. Already administrators from the mine, one an avid but terrible Twi'lek musi-cian, the other prone to droning on about organizational minutiae, had been relieved of their weapons and ushered out the door.

"You there."

Tal didn't dare turn around. The mirror reflected her dark skin, hair framing her face and matching brown eyes. Unlike the light, flowing garb favored in Cloud City, she wore a vest over dark leather pants and a loose chambray shirt. Right now she looked every bit the foreign trader she wanted to portray. "Your burlap fashion," Lando would endlessly tease her. She would counter that with a cape like his, she expected to see him fly off a platform one day. She supposed he finally had.

One stormtrooper loomed by her side. "You work with Cloud City mine? Lando Calrissian?"

Ever since the day he'd plucked her from that rickety merchant vessel. Happy to find someone who looked like him who wasn't fam-ily, he always said. Her family . . . well, let's just say she'd been in the market for a new one. And that's what she found working with Lando on Cloud City. She considered herself his second-in-command, but good luck getting *him* to admit it. They weren't perfect, but they had each other's backs.

But that's not what this lavender-hued stormtrooper needed to hear. Instead, she launched into her best Mando'a. *"Meg cuyir gar—?"*

His E-11 blaster inched closer to her eye. "Lando Calrissian."

512

"Londo?" she mispronounced.

Lavender boy yanked her to her feet, gave her a once-over. His companion called to him. "What have you got?"

"Nothing." He released her arm and headed over to fish out an Ugnaught trying to disappear behind a chair.

Tal didn't dare breathe a sigh of relief. Lando's decision to liberate the princess hadn't included the Imps capturing their people. She needed information, she needed help, and, most of all, she needed a plan.

"Baudu, Kiren—I need you."

The following day, Tal strode across the platform toward the two mechanics, working atop a ship set to depart from Dock 3. The brilliant white city pods punctuated the morning sky. They hosted vessels of all shapes and sizes on docks and platforms evident well into the distance.

Kiren's fur fluttered in the wind as they grunted in her direction, but their gaze stayed focused on a side panel a story above her.

Beside them, Baudu looked down from his wire panel and squinted at her. His gray eyes matched his graying hair, though his face was still so young. A peculiarity of his family, the one he'd come to Cloud City to get far, far away from, he'd once told her. As for his personality, he had no excuse. "You got eyes. The Imps got us working—"

Tal gestured impatiently for them to come down as she slowed to a stop by the docking ramp. "That's the point! While you're here doing your job, they're kidnapping the rest of us." Tal shaded her eyes and looked toward Dock 4, the bleak gray of a U-33 loadlifter, its inverted wings typical except for its contents. "You heard Lando high-tailed it out of here, right? The Imps are taking over the mines from us and targeting workers. Retaliating."

"Why?" Baudu had twisted up his face, trying to think it through.

"To punish Cloud City for what Lando did. I can't stand by and watch this!" She gestured angrily in the direction of the U-33. "I knew what he was planning. I'm just as much . . . the fool."

Kiren held out their arms, their brown jumpsuit already soiled by grease.

"Yes, I know," said Tal. "We're going to fix that. Come on. Lando's left a real mess."

Kiren shrugged and started to climb down, but Baudu reached out his hand to catch Kiren's arm, earning him a snarl from their snout. "Heyyy, come on now!" Baudu protested, then turned back to Tal. "Why not get the Wing Guard? They know you work for Lando."

"They're being watched."

Even Kiren had to snort at that.

"Okay, yeah, and Lando didn't give me any authority over them, what's your point?"

"Why should we listen to you?"

"Don't listen to me. Listen to Lando." Tal tapped her chin. "Oh, wait, that's right. He betrayed the Empire and took off." She grinned.

"Listen—forget Dock 4 for a second. You can see Lower Dock from up there?"

Baudu, suspicious, squinted down at the lower pods, where they loaded and unloaded the particularly ripe goods, far from the pristine noses of Cloud City's upper crust. "Yeah . . . ?"

"Second dock from the bottom. See anything?"

"Nothing special."

"Because it's an Imperial secret." From her vantage point, Tal couldn't make out more than the edge of the dock below. "The perfect location. Minimal security. Empire doesn't want anyone to know what they're doing down there, and wouldn't you know, the Mining Guild has caught wind of it. So you team up with me, and we put them on a collision course with each other . . . the Imps'll forget all about us."

Kiren grunted quizzically, a noise that never failed to make Tal smile. She hid it well this time.

"Let's just say I pumped my Imperial source for information last night. The intel is good."

"No." Baudu, thoughtful, tapped his tool on the ship. "Kiren wants to know how you know they'll forget all about us."

"Trust me!" Tal held out her hands, confident. When they still hesitated, she tried a different tack. "It's all I got, kids. Come on. You don't really want to end up one of the Empire's bootlickers, do you?"

Kiren was already sliding down the side of the ship. "I just don't want to end up under the Empire's boot," said Baudu.

"Clever. You think that one up yourself?" Tal teased. Baudu responded with a gesture, a side effect of spending too much time with Kiren. "Come. You'll see what I thought up."

515

The Mining Guild was not supposed to know about the mining operation on Bespin—certainly not now. Lando's negotiation with the Empire was supposed to keep the mines independent from the Imperials and secret from the Mining Guild. But that didn't seem to bother the three in the market one bit. They met in the open, directly under the glowing lights in the market district, their signature yellow-striped uniforms shining under the bright market lights.

The clean white stalls were starting to bustle with activity. The citizens of Cloud City would soon be bringing their children for an early-morning stroll through the market for fresh fruits and greens. The aromas of savory and sweet blended in the air, and even Baudu lingered for a moment over an unreasonably large papple fruit. Its bored seller looked up from whatever he was viewing behind his kiosk and began reaching for a bag.

"Not now!" said Tal. Kiren slapped Baudu's hand away from the fruit, and Tal nodded appreciatively at them. The seller settled back behind his console.

Tal pulled Baudu into the entrance of a narrow hallway that led from the fresh marketplace to the verandas, as Kiren did their best to follow suit. Few bothered with the verandas in the morning, so Tal didn't have to worry too much about foot traffic walking by and blocking their view of the market.

"What is the Mining Guild doing here?" Baudu whispered.

"I miiiight have invited them."

Kiren grunted, surprised and confused.

"Just three of them. Relax."

"If you say that one more ti—" started Baudu.

"Shh!" said Tal as she strained to listen. They clung close to the wall and kept a trained eye on the Mining Guild operatives.

One of them, a Rodian whose antennae seemed constantly in motion, nudged his colleague, who looked more like a slug than anything. "We shouldn't be here. If we want the workers we're promised, we better leave before the Empire gets wise."

The slug shook his head. "The Empire's not gonna enforce this deal for long. Vader's gone. The Cloud City guy that made it is gone. We'll have the run of this city in a handful of months. You'll see."

"Yeah, as long as we don't get on the Empire's bad side in the meantime."

"Brougg, we *are* the Empire's bad side." He stood up taller, undulating slightly. "Cloud City here needs to know it."

As much as Tal would've loved to glean more information from their riveting conversation, her mind kept returning to the miners on board the U-33 loadlifter back on the platform. She hadn't anticipated this part of the plan taking quite so long—the Imperial ships were scheduled to leave that morning. The operatives appeared to be in no hurry, and Tal only now realized that was intentional. They had no agenda. The entire purpose of the meeting was to be *seen*. To mark their new territory. Just as she was about to scrap her plan in favor of the backup plan—or was it the backup backup plan? she'd lost track— one of the members received an alert.

The three operatives headed toward where Tal and her companions were waiting. Tal definitely was feeling her luck change.

"Comrades!" Tal stepped forward, putting on her best sales pitch. "I have quite an offer for you—you want three months of Tibanna gas?"

He shoved her aside. "Out of the way, mucks."

Guess she couldn't complain about that dig since she'd been calling him the slug. "But wait—Sir!" The slug ignored her. "Idiot!" None of them were listening. "Slug?"

No use. She was forced to watch all three of them pass her into the otherwise empty hallway.

"So, what do we—" started Baudu.

Tal smashed the last one on the back of the neck with the butt of her blaster, dropping him and her weapon in the process.

"Oh."

Kiren needed no further instruction and sent the one closest to them crashing down with a well-placed blow from their wrench.

The third, finding his companions collapsed on the floor around him, tried to run back into the marketplace, ducking Baudu's lunge. Tal rushed ahead of him, having nothing to stop him but her own slight frame. She cast around for something she could use as he tried to move past her. She grabbed the papple from its display with both hands and cracked it over his head. He collapsed in a rain of red pulp and black seeds. The seller looked up, gaped at the prone Rodian and the remains of his papple, then quietly turned around and walked away.

Baudu and Kiren ran up to her, and both gave her the same look. "It worked," Tal said with a shrug.

517

Kiren and Baudu helped her drag the unconscious operatives back behind the now abandoned stall. If anyone had witnessed what went down, they had the same wisdom as the papple seller and minded their own business. They began to relieve the operatives of their signature jackets and weapons.

Tal holstered a blaster and hefted the helmet the slug had been wearing at her side. "Put these on. We're going to hit the Empire where it hurts."

Kiren struggled with their jacket, a size too small, while Baudu tested the weight of his new Mining Guild blaster. "Was *this* part of the plan?"

Tal smiled slyly. She swept the Mining Guild jacket around her shoulders with a flair that would've made Lando proud.

"It is now."

518 Lieutenant Ela Radodan typed her authorization code into the data-pad and passed it off to Fool #203. His gray uniform indicated his ensign rank, but she didn't have time or interest in learning his name. He was just the latest in a long line of interchangeable, clean-shaven faces. Faces that Commander Kelos routinely dismissed for their incompetence. That Ela often made sure Kelos did so was lost on him. Which made Kelos Fool #1, she supposed.

From the center of the circular platform, she could see the sky brightening. A light freighter could have easily landed where she stood, but they needed something bigger for this operation. Instead, Ela had ordered a bulk freighter, its immensity forcing it to hover off the edge. Its two rectangular canisters guzzled Tibanna gas through an attached pump guarded by a handful of stormtroopers and fools.

To her left, on the far side of the platform, the entrance to the large white city pod beckoned to more docks as well as the pleasures of

Cloud City. She had learned that quite a few secret passages led off from certain platforms, hiding a multitude of sins from prying eyes, both Imperial and mercantile. She suspected Cloud City was built on this very premise.

But neither the pod nor the freighter held her attention. From the lower dock, she couldn't quite see the U-33 loadlifter that was holding the miners captive, but that didn't stop her from looking up with concern to the dock where she knew they were waiting.

She caught Fool #204's attention. "Make sure there's also Tibanna gas on the U-33."

"Ma'am, we have filled the ship with miners. There isn't room for freight."

"Then put Tibanna canisters in the extra fuel pods if you have to. You have your orders."

Fool #204 obviously thought these orders were foolish, but he had served the Empire long enough not to ask questions. Off he went. She looked above her again, as if this time she would be able to see the ship with the miners aboard.

Behind her, a voice spoke. "Something of interest in the sky?"

"Cloud City miners prepared for transport to the labor colonies, Commander." She didn't bother turning around to face Kelos, having heard his peculiar loping step approaching her. "As well as mines on Cynda, Raxus Prime . . ."

Kelos reached her side and turned his unblinking gaze toward her. "Most of those mines are controlled by the Mining Guild. We are sure that the Guild won't find out about Cloud City's mines?"

"The Guild won't exactly be having a chat before putting the prisoners to work, and misguided loyalty to Cloud City would hold their tongues. Regardless, now with the city's output in our possession, the Empire will hold a superior position in any future negotiations with the Guild."

Kelos moved next to her, the light catching the medals on his uniform as he held his hands behind his back. "And without hundreds of their workers, the citizens of Cloud City will know the price of betraying The Empire."

"Of course. Commander, will you be making an address to those—"

The sound of blasterfire drowned out the rest of her thought. The shots came from three figures in helmets and gold-striped uniforms who had emerged from the abbreviated Cloud City pod that hosted the docking platform. She immediately crouched, pulling her side blaster, and scanned desperately for cover. Finding none, she hit the cold steel of the platform, lying prone with her weapon pointed toward the shooters. Fortunately, the three uniformed figures were focused on the freighter. Fool #203 went down with a zap, and several other uniformed fools fled up the boarding ramps. A few actually did their jobs and fired from partial cover at the freighter entrance.

"Commander, get down!"

Kelos, clearly the original fool, widened his stance, took careful aim at the largest of the figures, and fired. To his credit, his shot found its target. They reeled, then returned fire. Ela thought they shot wildly, until Kelos crumbled to the ground, inches from her. Despite the danger of sharing his fate, she couldn't suppress a slight smile. As a bonus, his still form provided her a degree of cover.

Stormtroopers finally descended from the freighter and returned fire, and the Mining Guild operatives—as their uniforms indicated them to be—began to pull back. But not before throwing something toward the center of the platform.

"Grenade!" Shouts echoed up through the stormtrooper corps.

Ela believed she'd been forgotten since she hadn't fired. She rose to a crouch, careful to keep her weight on the balls of her feet lest the clicking of her boot heels give her away. She ran along the side of the platform after the retreating figures.

"Take cover!"

An explosion rattled the platform, lighting up Ela's path. She ignored its heat as she pursued her prey. The shooters' escape was slowed by their injured comrade, and Ela caught up to them just as the sliding door to the pod was about to close behind them.

"Halt!" Ela commanded.

The last enemy half turned around, and Ela managed to grab their arm. She pulled it back across the threshold, temporarily halting the door. She managed to keep hold of only a handful of fabric as her attacker wriggled free of her grasp, but lost their helmet. Ela saw her unmasked: a woman with brown eyes, her hair tightly framing her face.

Tal half-smiled at her with a shrug as the door slid shut between them. Ela hesitated for only a moment. She slammed in the code to open the door, but it was jammed. She tried an override code, but discovered they had not yet been aligned with the Imperial codes.

"Open this door!" she yelled to a fool, but found herself momentarily without one. She turned and carried the jacket toward the prone body of the commander.

Who slowly rose to his feet, a blaster wound in his side, not serious. She did not need to mask her disappointment. She had been told that her natural expression was one of cold disdain, and it served her well in this moment.

"Mining Guild operatives. They must have detected our presence on Bespin. If we can't buy their silence, let's see how their Guild behaves when we refuse them our prize and keep the Cloud City captives."

He clasped his wound and stared her down. "They must have detected. They must have detected? *You* were in charge of this mission. If the Mining Guild detected anything, you are responsible. You will be relieved of duty and sent down to join the miners for deportation!"

"Your injury makes you speak in haste." Ela felt stormtroopers draw close behind her. "My security protocol with regard to the Mining Guild was unassailable. However." She looked at the jacket on the ground. She had no choice. "It is possible . . . it was a ruse."

Tal was desperately trying to stanch the flow of blood from Kiren's shoulder. The three had jumped through a secret hatch just as the Imps had cleared the block Tal had put on the door. The emergency accessway offered enough space for Baudu and Tal to flank Kiren, and the bare fixtures gave them all the light they needed.

Kiren's subtle growls indicated they were doing their best to suppress the pain. "Least you got a real good shot on that officer. Went down like an empty suit of stormtrooper armor." Tal paused. "Or even one that was full."

"Kiren got lucky. This shot could've killed them." Baudu's voice cracked.

Tal touched his shoulder. "I get it. I do. But this'll work. You'll see. The Empire will be too pissed at the Mining Guild to hand over our miners—"

A sound behind her made her turn around. The click of boots on the cold metal floor heralded the arrival of an Imperial officer. A severe bun held her dark hair back under her cap. Her cold expression did not falter as she adjusted her stance, put her hands behind her back, and stared down.

Tal lost her train of thought seeing her, remembering many stolen nights, last night most of all. She loved watching her lover pull down that bun, letting the hair cascade around her as Tal pulled her close.

"How did she get in here?" Baudu reached for his blaster.

"Wait." Tal held up her hand. "This is—"

"You are under the authority of the Galactic Empire. Surrender now and you may be spared."

"Ela?" Tal blinked, confused. Ela's expression was always inscrutable.

"Damnit, Tal! *That's* your Imperial source?" Baudu grabbed his blaster, but Ela pulled hers first.

"Careful," she said.

Another set of boots approached behind her. Ela hadn't come through the secret hatch alone. The commander, his wound sporting a rudimentary bandage, came abreast of Ela. "Here the attackers are, just as you predicted. You may redeem yourself yet." The commander stepped forward and elbowed Kiren in their wound, earning a ferocious snarl. Baudu lunged, but the commander trained his weapon on him.

Tal helped Kiren to their feet, but she was focused on Ela. "Don't do this. Please."

Ela, as always, maintained her cold expression. "You betrayed the Empire."

"The Empire. Right," said Tal.

523

The commander wisely kept his blaster leveled at Baudu and returned to his position beside Ela. "A betrayal for a betrayal. Very good. You put your Emperor before your lover."

Ela let slip her first hint of emotion as she glanced at her superior with surprise.

"Yes, I make it my duty to monitor my reports, in all aspects." The commander turned on his heel. "Put them with the other prisoners."

Everything started happening very quickly for Tal. Stormtroopers shoved her into the U-33 loadlifter behind Baudu and Kiren. Baudu wasn't looking at her as he kicked a few miners off a bench to make sure Kiren could sit down. Baudu was mad, but Kiren understood. She hoped.

The U-33 was packed, including its mess hall where Tal found herself. The miner who'd taught Tal a ditty from her homeland with incredibly questionable lyrics. The admin who'd fled a dying planet and a dead relationship. Rajin, the Twi'lek, they were all there, crammed together. Most found it easier to stand, for even the table-tops had been overrun with seated miners. And now Tal had to include herself . . . the orphan who'd wandered the galaxy till she found a family to take her in. And now that family was being shipped off who knows where. Almost immediately, the transport engines fired up, and they lurched forward on their journey.

"Do you know where we're going?" asked a miner Tal didn't know. This one looked like she'd been kidnapped in the night, as she was dressed for bed.

"Wherever the Mining Guild sends us," said Rajin, morose, no doubt thinking of his child.

"Nah, these are stormtroopers. They loaded up a ton of Tibanna in here with us, too. We're in Imperial custody."

"For now."

Tal remained quiet.

Another miner noticed. "Tal, you don't even work for the mine." He'd clearly been taken midshift, as he still wore his brown work smock. "You're up to something. You gotta have a plan."

"Yeah, same as what yours should be. Mind my business." Tal knew this one. If she told him anything, everyone would hear about it.

Tal gestured for Kiren and Baudu to come talk to her. Kiren managed to stand up, almost convincing Tal that their wound wasn't killing them. Baudu tried to gently push them back down. "No—I just had to kick two people outta your seat. No." Kiren growled and waved him off. Kiren was all-in. Good.

"Can you fly this thing?"

Kiren gave her a look like that was the most insulting question they'd ever heard.

"Okay, okay. Can *I* fly this thing?"

Kiren nodded their head side to side. A solid maybe.

"It'll have to do. Let's go."

Baudu nearly climbed over two people to get in front of her. "You pull us from our duty—perfectly safe duty—and con us into taking out some really overdressed idiots in the market, and then you get us shot at, captured, and sent off to mine some offworld— No. You can't say this was part of the plan."

"It was . . . a possibility." Tal rubbed her arm, hedging. "But it's not going to get better if we don't do anything."

Baudu gestured toward Kiren's wound. "If you think I'm letting you get them into another fight—"

"Oh, Kiren's not fighting." Tal tapped him on the shoulder. "We are. I always have a backup plan, you know that. But we better hurry."

"I'm not getting talked into— Wait a second. Why do we have to hurry . . . ?"

For the first time in her life, Ela struggled to maintain her expression. She had reported to her station on the bridge in the Star Destroyer in orbit. The cool darkness, the blinking control lights, and the soft hum of the ship normally calmed her nerves. But she could feel Kelos's eyes on her, monitoring her, as he had been since the beginning apparently. She guessed she was Fool #1 all along.

She focused on the task at hand: ensuring the U-33 with its prisoner cargo joined them in orbit over Bespin. It came into view on the command screen, in front of several ensigns seated at their posts on the bridge, likewise preparing for the journey. She went over her checklist. She tagged the U-33 for tracking, cataloged the last of the Tibanna canisters on board her Star Destroyer, adjusted the weapons systems and the comms, locked them behind her security code.

"All is ready, Commander." She paused for a moment, choosing her words carefully. "Representatives of the Mining Guild are requesting custody of the U-33, since it is destined for mines they control. However, I'm noting this particular communication is coming from Bespin airspace, which is off limits to them. Exactly what we wished to avoid at the dock. What are your orders?"

He turned toward her, arms behind his back. "What do you recommend, Lieutenant?"

It was a test.

Ela continued, carefully. "They came to Bespin against Imperial edict. They must be taught a lesson."

Kelos smiled. "I agree. Permit them to board the U-33. I accept your earlier suggestion."

"Sir?"

"We refuse them their prize. By eliminating them all."

526

Tal led her reluctant comrades toward the head—the only area minimally guarded by stormtroopers. The stench of urine explained why. They hadn't gotten around to wiping down the ship before it had been commandeered with its new cargo.

The three squeezed past the troopers in the hallway, then as a unit entered the stalls and closed the flaps for privacy. Tal had made quite a show of running water while she spurred Kiren and Baudu to unfix the back of the stalls. They'd been in and around these ships long enough—they knew the crawl spaces that would lead to the bridge.

Kelos puffed up his chest as he turned toward the controllers at the command screen. "Ensign, target the U-33 transport with the turbo-laser cannons."

"Yes, sir." The ensign turned toward him. "The Mining Guild representatives have boarded, and I've relayed the usual five-minute warning for our officers to evacuate."

"Make it two minutes. The rest are an acceptable loss." Kelos surveyed the rest of the people on the bridge, then settled on Ela. "Any objections?"

Ela remained silent.

Tal squeezed into the crawl space. Kiren had been forced to stay behind—they truly couldn't fit, even without a shoulder wound. They'd nodded and patted her on the head, then helped her climb in. She felt Baudu climb in behind her, and the two clambered beside pipes and wires. She grabbed his glow rod so she could find her way as he coached her toward the bridge.

"The two of us can't take the entire ship, Tal. We don't even have a weapon."

"Then we get a weapon. Once we take the bridge, it doesn't matter how many stormtroopers are aboard. We have the ship." She took the last turn and found herself with nowhere to go. "Damnit, dead end."

"This is it. This is the bridge," he said. "You should be lying on a hatch."

She reached under herself, her hand following the cold metal floor, finding a latch.

"Just make sure you don't—"

She lifted the latch and immediately crashed to the floor of the bridge. The element of surprise, her only ally, had turned on her. She leapt to her feet and assumed a fighting stance, ready to take on all comers.

The bridge was empty.

———

"Clear!" said the ensign.

Kelos approached a control panel in the center of the bridge. "Transfer firing control to this console."

"Yes, sir."

Ela took a deep breath. Kelos held his finger over the button, pausing for effect, to twist the knife further.

He lowered his finger.

"No!" she cried out.

Kelos turned toward her, his finger hovering still, as he raised an eyebrow. "A problem, Lieutenant?"

"Please, sir." She lifted her chin, determined. "Allow me."

He smiled and gestured for her to take his place. "By all means." Without hesitation, she assumed his position in front of the console.

528

Baudu dropped down behind Tal and took in the abandoned controls, the chairs spun around as though their occupants had just stood up.

"This . . . was a lot easier than I thought it would be."

Tal rushed over to the control panel and pulled up the ship reports. "I've got to shut us down."

An alarm sounded. "What's that?" Baudu spun around.

A red light started blinking on one of the screens: WARNING: TARGET LOCKED.

"We're being targeted."

"What?"

"I've got it handled." She slid into a seat and began trying to regain control of the ship. "I hope."

The screen turned solid red. "Tal . . . !"

Ela pressed the button to fire.

Silence followed.

Then the ensign spun around to face Kelos. "Confirmed hit, sir."

Kelos was studying Ela. "Sensors report."

"Uhh . . ." The ensign turned around. "Complete destruction. I'm reading a lingering energy cloud, likely from excess Tibanna gas we put on the U-33. No signature of the ship."

"Very good. You may return to your post, Lieutenant."

Ela returned to her control panel and tried to shut out all thought, all distractions. She reset the weapons and comms, locked them behind her security code, then assessed the remains of the onboard Tibanna cannisters.

When she finished, she realized Kelos was watching her appraisingly. Finally, he shared his verdict: "Betrayal demonstrates character. It suits you."

Ela returned his look with a cold disdain that she felt to the depths of her soul.

529

Exhausted, Ela finished her shift and headed back toward her quarters. *Of course*—she stopped herself. She needed a different venue. Someplace unlikely to be under surveillance.

"I owe you. I thought for sure you wouldn't go along with our . . . emergency, worst-case scenario, wow did this go sideways plan after I was forced to get creative with the disguises. You didn't have to do any of this, I know." The glowing blue form of Tal smiled at her from Cloud City a short time later.

"Of course I did. I said I'd do what I could, and I don't go back on my word." Ela undid her constricting officer jacket and tossed it onto the bed. Recently vacated, these officer quarters provided exactly what she needed. The breezy scent told her the space had also been cleaned to her liking. "Besides, you're the sexiest rebel scum this side of Corellia."

Tal laughed. "I'll take it. But maybe you should get out while you can. They could find out you blew up a few canisters of Tibanna gas instead of us. More than a few. I ejected the ones you planted on-board our ship, too."

"They're all fools. Kelos especially. I knew he couldn't resist the idea of blasting a helpless ship into particles. He was looking right at me as I dumped our excess gas capsules into space . . ." She mimed the commands she had entered into the console. ". . . targeting the weapons on them instead of your transport. He was so focused on reading my expression, he didn't look at my hands or the console. He one hundred percent believed me."

"*I* almost believed you."

"Next time give me a little more information about what you're planning, so I'm not surprised." Ela collapsed onto the bed. "Only one way I like to be surprised."

"Fair." The hologram did not do justice to her eyes. "Ela. I know we don't . . . do this. But it means a lot, what you did."

Ela pulled her hair down, letting it fall down her shoulders. "Are you alone?"

Tal failed to suppress a grin. "The miners are all back home with their families, hiding out while we figure out what to do about your Imperial friends. Rajin has a new son. Kiren is getting treated. Right now, I think they'll talk to me before Baudu does. But he's a hero now. He'll come around."

"As long as he doesn't come around *now*." Ela leaned down, beginning to slowly undo her boots, knowing she had Tal's attention.

"Ela?"

"Yes?"

"Leave the boots on this time."

RIGHT-HAND MAN

Lydia Kang

I t wasn't the worst wound he'd ever seen.

The surgical droid 2-1B viewed the patient in front of him. Commander Luke Skywalker had a clean amputation of his right hand, via lightsaber. It had been a long time since he'd seen such a wound. Simple enough. His vital signs were remarkably stable, save for a slightly elevated heart rate. The patient seemed calm at first glance, but 2-1B could tell quickly that his muscles were tensed and his mouth was a taut line. The pain was there, no doubt, but the lightsaber had thankfully cauterized the bleeding. There was one good thing about Jedi and Sith combat—no blood. It saved him and his FX droids a lot of messy work.

Beyond his operating station, the large viewport of the *Redemption*'s surgical suite yawned wide and dark, a view that was either soothing or menacing, depending on the point of view. Most patients preferred to face the wide expanse of velvety black speckled with bright stars. Rebel cruisers and X-wing fighters flew alongside the medical frigate, a comforting sight. The spinning fire of a nearby protostar was unusually brilliant. An excellent distraction, sometimes more powerful than painkillers and a dose of bacta. But Commander Skywalker chose to turn away from the viewport, as if something out there was too uncomfortable to face. How very odd.

Away from Bespin and the Empire, they were safe now.

"I shall begin by cleansing the wound, removing the dead and cauterized tissue, and testing your nerve endings for compatibility with the cybernetic attachment," 2-1B said as he gathered instruments on a hovertray. "After that, I will apply bacta to ensure successful synergy, Commander."

Luke said nothing, only stared straight ahead.

Too-Onebee turned his mechanical head to see what Commander Skywalker was staring at. He thought perhaps Princess Leia or the commander's favored droids had entered the room, but no. Just a wall of supply compartments.

"Commander Skywalker. Are you in pain?" 2-1B asked.

For the first time, his patient looked up. "Pain?" he asked, as if he hadn't quite heard the droid's words.

"Yes. I can certainly give you some painkillers."

Commander Skywalker blinked, and he looked down at the stump of his arm. "I don't think they'll work on me."

"Why, of course they will. All humans and humanoids are sensitive to our pharmacologics."

"No, thank you."

2-1B stopped his supply gathering and walked closer to his patient. "Why would you choose to feel pain? That is illogical."

His patient shook his head. "It's not that kind of pain."

The droid nodded. His patient suffered beyond the flesh. That he understood, though sometimes it was not obvious upon first examination. Still, his heart rate was elevated. There was truly physical pain. And yet, his patient chose to suffer.

"Suffering can lead to problems with healing. You must not close yourself off to help, Commander."

The patient looked up at the droid. Too-Onebee paused, then continued to busily clean off the stump and remove remnants of burned tissue. His hydraulics were incredibly sensitive; 2-1B's mechanical touch was cold, but he tried to be very gentle.

"Suffering leads to more than just that," his patient admitted.

"I treated you on Hoth. Do you not remember, Commander?"

"Yes, I remember. I asked for you specifically. And please, call me Luke."

"Yes, Commander."

Luke's eyes flashed up at him.

"My apologies, sir. Luke, then. If that makes you more comfortable."

He nodded.

"You may not remember, but when you were in dormoshock on Hoth, you resisted within the bacta tank, too. Only when you agreed to assistance did your healing begin properly. Bacta is a living thing. It needs your cooperation." He added, *"Luke,"* as an afterthought, though it sounded a bit forced. He might have shouted the name a little.

"Really?"

"Yes. Flesh is flesh, but the will is quite powerful. Time and again, our medical data banks show the strength of the connection between a being's thoughts and the corporeal."

"The Force," Luke said quietly.

"Well. I don't know if our medical data banks call it *that*."

Luke smiled a tiny bit. It was the first time his body relaxed. Not completely, but just a touch. "Call it whatever you want. But you're right."

Too-Onebee continued to remove tissue from his patient's stump. Luke looked down at it and winced at the sight.

"Really. You ought to stop getting into so many life-threatening situations, Luke." (This time, he didn't shout his name.) "You are becoming my most frequently returning patient. One day you might return to me beyond repair, and I should not like that."

"I can't help it," Luke said. "I don't have a choice."

"Do you not?" 2-1B responded. Just a casual response, but he didn't expect his patient to go suddenly cold and grim-faced. He appreciated stoic patients, but the silence grew until he felt compelled to fill the void. "Now, once you have your new hand, it will feel very strange at first. Your brain will send signals to move your fingers, but occasionally it will feel as though there is a delay, even if there is not. Your nerves will still be recovering, so do expect your hand to spontaneously contract once in a while. And you may still have phantom pain while your nerves heal."

"Phantom pain?" Luke asked.

"Yes. Your nerves were cut through entirely. They will sometimes experience the memory of that injury, even the memory of that hand. Some patients feel the pain, as if new, for the rest of their lives."

Luke's eyes looked glassy, and he dropped his head and sighed. "That's a long time." He glanced up at his caretaker with curiosity. "Do droids feel phantom pain when their limbs are cut off?"

"Our circuits have memory," he responded. Then it was 2-1B's turn to be quiet. He disliked when patients asked questions that probed too deeply into his own thoughts. It was all so much easier when he had a task to accomplish. Using a syringe, he carefully extruded the translucent bacta gel onto the freshly cleaned wound.

534

"There. I have cleaned off all your scar tissue, and the bacta is already working on the nerve, muscle, tendon, bone, and skin. Now it's time to begin the attachment process for your cybernetic hand."

Too-Onebee went back to the supply wall and began selecting instruments for the next phase. For some reason, this procedure was not going the way he thought it would. Usually, 2-1B would have completed his task by now. But with Luke, he was working more slowly. He was baffled by some of his patient's questions about 2-1B's own sensory input and memories. No one ever asked about a droid's injuries or pain. It occurred to him that with this artificial attachment, they would have this part of themselves in common. He paused, unsure where he ought to store this new information, before continuing. He picked up the appropriate-sized cybernetic hand, already pre-covered with synthskin to match Luke's skin. His patient held out his good hand.

"Wait."

"Wait? For what?" asked 2-1B. An FX droid rolled nearby, its cylindrical body slowly spinning with its multiple arms extending and contracting, thinking it was needed for assistance. "Oh, do go away, Effex-Seven! If you're needed, I'll call for you." Too-Onebee shook his head. "Twenty elbows in the way, and Trandoshan toenail clippers always at the ready. That ridiculous droid." He turned to Luke. "As you were saying?"

"Maybe you shouldn't attach the cybernetic hand."

"Pardon?" If 2-1B were human, he'd have dropped the surgical clamp in surprise. "What in the Maker's name—why would you not want a replacement?"

"Maybe this was meant to be. Maybe I was destined to lose my hand, in exchange for something else."

"In certain cultures, the amputation of a hand is done in exchange for the crime of thievery. But Luke, you have not stolen anything, and our laws do not condone such punishments."

535

"It's not that simple. I made mistakes." He looked away, but even 2-1B could see that his face was stricken. "I could have learned the ways of the Force better. Faster. I was so stubborn. I was too foolish to see the trap in front of me." He looked at his stump, with its tissues shiny from the recently applied bacta. It must have tingled; many patients reported the sensation at this point in the process. He banged his injured arm onto the examination table. His voice cracked as he muttered, "I could have saved Han."

"Luke, I—"

"Even Yoda said, 'this crude matter.'" Luke pressed the fingers of his good hand to his chest. "I don't deserve to have it fixed. And maybe I don't need to. If I learn the ways of the Force, one hand alone doesn't matter." He looked unsure. "Right?"

"The Force is not in the repertoire of my medical data banks," 2-1B replied. "Medical droids and the Rebel Alliance are quite responsible for keeping people alive, too, you know," he added, a touch haughtily. Oh, these creatures. Always thinking they could rush off to battle, while it was the medical droids and crew on ships like the *Redemption* that stitched them back together and healed them. Was that the Force at work? He didn't know. Perhaps.

What he did know was that he was programmed to heal. How he ended up caring was another matter. But he *did* care. Luke was in pain, after all. In many ways. "Don't deserve to have it fixed? All beings deserve to be cared for, to be healed." He said this rather adamantly, and Luke seemed surprised by the passion in his words. "Moral perfection is no requisite for care. That would be cruelty itself, as no beings are perfect. As for your other comment . . . there is limited information in my programming on how the Jedi and Sith heal with respect to cybernetic implants. There could be many who live with artificial limbs and are, as you say, strong with the Force."

Luke's eyes widened at his words. "Sith? Like Darth Vader?"

"I do not know. When new data is gleaned, we medical droids

share our data as a collective. Often the Empire destroys its own medical droids, so I know little of Darth Vader's medical status. However, my understanding is that Darth Vader is heavily incorporated with cybernetic parts, if that is what you are asking."

Luke was quiet again as 2-1B brought the disembodied cybernetic hand to the examination table on which Luke rested his injured arm. His patient stared at it as if it were evil incarnate, a look of utter disgust that slowly transformed to an expression of anguish.

"Father," he said weakly.

"I'm sorry, what did you say?"

Luke shook his head. "Nothing." But he still seemed somewhat repulsed by the artificial hand.

2-1B cocked his head. "If you choose not to let me attach the new hand, that of course is your right and your decision. It is true that by giving you what you've lost, it will not necessarily make you . . . complete. Normal." He searched for the word. "Whole?" Too-Onebee was well equipped with programming to make him more sympathetic. But it was a bit rusty, so to speak. Straightforward patient care was easy, but it went better when he used all his programming. It did take extra effort, though, and it made 2-1B somewhat uncomfortable. Perhaps that was why organics suffered so.

537

"All I know is that I can help you," 2-1B continued. "And your friends can help you. After all, when a bone is broken, it requires time to mend. A crutch to lean on. Accepting such assistance is not weakness, nor is it gallant to forgo such treatment. Sometimes the harder choice is to accept help."

Luke held up his stump, looking at it this way and that. *"Crude matter."* His eyes went to the artificial hand. "It won't be my hand, though."

"It's your tool, just as many other things in your world are your tools. A wheel instead of a leg; a mechno-lens instead of an eye. What does it matter? There is no shame in this." Too-Onebee began to prepare the cybernetic hand for the delicate connections to Luke's stump. "There is nothing inherently good or bad in it, unless *you* choose to use it as such. And it shall become a part of you. Every creature in this universe alters and evolves from minute to minute. We are not the same as we were only a day ago. We are ever changing, fated forever to exist in a state of decay and creation."

"You're a poet, Too-Onebee," Luke said, a gleam of humor in his eye.

"I am most decidedly not a poet!" 2-1B said, indignant. "I must look into my programming. Perhaps I need some reconditioning." What was it about this Jedi that brought out an eloquence heretofore buried in his circuits? His Maker apparently put in more sympathetic and philosophic programming than he'd realized. "In any case, it is a medical fact that we change and evolve. Don't you ever say that dreaded *poet* word aloud near Effex-Seven. I'll never hear the end of it."

"It'll be our secret." He took a deep breath. "Let's finish this, then. Go ahead and attach the hand."

Too-Onebee's internal hydraulics whirred in anticipation. Now he could really get to work. Using several micro tools, he began securing the bone stumps of Luke's radius and ulna to the core mechanical components of the hand. Then he attached muscle tendons and nerves to the servo-circuits that would respond to the muscle contractions and electrical nerve impulses sent by his patient's brain and body. It was delicate work, and painful, too. At times, Luke winced and refused pain medicine as 2-1B synced microscopic nerves. His face morphed from minute to minute. At times, he seemed angry. Then his expression turned sorrowful. His forearm twitched as 2-1B attached the tendons of his flexor pollicis longus and supinator. There were many more to go.

He was nearly finished. To connect synthskin to living skin, the surgical droid used a tool that neatly zipped them together. The bacta ensured that they melded in harmony without any rejection of the artificial tissue. Luke watched with astonishment as 2-1B opened up a compartment in his new wrist, showing the hydraulic mechanism at work.

"We are nearly finished. There is only some fine-tuning and final testing to be done."

"Thank you, Too-Onebee."

"It is my duty, and my pleasure." Awkwardly, he turned left and right, to be sure FX-7 was not close by, then leaned in closely. He lowered his voice until it was barely audible. "May the Force be with you."

Luke cocked his ear. "Sorry, what did you say?"

"MaytheForcebewithyou!" This time, he said it so fast, it sounded like a mechno-sneeze. From a distance, FX-7 whirled around, wondering why 2-1B seemed flustered.

Luke smiled, his face warming and relieved. He whispered back, "May the Force be with you, Too-Onebee. You've helped in more ways than you can imagine."

"Well," the droid said, lifting his head. "I do more than repairing broken things. I am not some simple Effex droid."

From the corner of the surgical suite, FX-7 spun around and bleeped out a string of insults that would have made its creator blush.

"Stop calling me that!" 2-1B snapped before muttering, "I get no respect."

The doors to the suite opened. R2-D2, C-3PO, and Princess Leia entered. Polished and gleaming as usual, the protocol droid waved his arms emphatically.

"Master Luke! You have your new hand! It looks wonderful."

R2-D2 beeped a happy hello. The princess, in her floor-length white gown, nodded at Luke. 2-1B looked from her to his patient and noted the expression on Luke's face. It was quite different from when they had been together on Hoth, after Luke had completed his bacta tank treatment. Now it was as if their gaze on each other had cooled to something less fiery, and yet still full of warmth. Different.

The princess smiled, but her eyebrows were drawn together. Another human in pain. Too-Onebee wondered what she had lost; all her limbs appeared intact.

Luke's heart rate had descended to normal levels. For most humans, this would have been sixty to eighty beats per minute. For Luke, it was twenty-five—a significant change since he'd entered the surgical suite on the *Redemption,* and not uncommon in healthy Jedi according to records. Back on Hoth, when the princess had entered the room, Luke's heart rate had shot up to ninety beats per second. Not this time.

"How are you, Luke?" she asked.

He smiled, a small one to match hers. "Better. I'll be all right."

Lando Calrissian commed in from the *Millennium Falcon,* where it was docked on the *Redemption.*

"Luke, we're ready for takeoff." In the background, Chewbacca agreed.

"Good luck, Lando," Luke said.

"When we find Jabba the Hutt and that bounty hunter, we'll contact you."

Luke nodded. "I'll meet you at the rendezvous point on Tatooine."

In a soothing tone, Calrissian said, "Don't worry, Leia. We'll find Han. I promise." With an expression of uncertainty, the princess raised her eyes to the window.

"Chewie," Luke said, "I'll be waiting for your signal. Take care, you two. May the Force be with you."

At the sound of the Wookiee's goodbye, Princess Leia smiled, as if knowing good news would come soon.

2-1B looked over his patient carefully as he performed the final pinprick sensation testing on the newly joined hand. Clinically, the medical records would show that post-procedure, the patient was in no distress and had tolerated the procedure well.

Personally, 2-1B would have said, *He looked like a man with hope in his heart.*

That is, if he were a poet.

THE WHILLS STRIKE BACK

Tom Angleberger

Again I am asked to serve.

The burden is great, the responsibility almost crushing . . . but willingly I take up my solemn duty again.

There are a thousand points of view, a thousand sacred artifacts, a thousand moments of history captured on holocron. I have studied them all. And now my task is to make them all one . . . One record, one history . . . one Truth.

May the Force be with me as I prepare to inscribe another entry in the immortal Journal of the Whills.

A long time ago in a galaxy far, far away. . . .

Well, actually . . .

What? How did you get in here? I thought you were told to keep out of it this time?

Sure, sure, I'll keep out of it . . . if you want to confuse everybody with the first sentence—AGAIN!—that's fine with me.

I haven't even finished the first sentence!

You say "a long time ago," but it's not as long ago as the last one, right? It's more like "in more recent developments."

You want me to start this episode of the Journal of the Whills— which everybody has been looking forward to for three years— with "in more recent developments"?

Well, it's more factually accurate . . .

It's also stupid.

Whew, I was hoping that you would have learned how to take constructive criticism without becoming so hostile by now.

And I was hoping you would have learned how to shut your Sarlacc-sized mouth by now.

Fine, I'll just sit here quietly while you fill the journal with errors and purple prose. Go right ahead!

It is a dark time for the Rebellion.

Oh, you're doing this in present tense again? Goody!

I thought you were going to be quiet.

Quiet as a mouse droid. You may proceed . . .

Although the Death Star has been destroyed . . .

WHOA! "Has been destroyed"? Way to start with the passive voice!

La la la, I'm not listening . . .

THE WHILLS STRIKE BACK

Imperial troops have driven the Rebel forces from their
hidden base and pursued them across the galaxy.

*Oooh, okay, this is getting better. This is the part where they run
into Skorr the bounty hunter on Ord Mantell!*

Uh, actually, I was going to skip that.

*What? Well, I guess you wanted to get right to the part where they
all help Chewie get back to Kashyyyk to see his son for Life Day.
You know, I have some notes here about that . . .*

Not this again! I told you before: No Lumpy.

What the Fett? This is Lumpy's chance to shine!

No, it's not. Now be quiet and let me get on with this.

Evading the dreaded Imperial Starfleet—

*Wait . . . "Starfleet"? Did you just say "Starfleet"? Are Kirk and
Spock going to show up next?*

I don't even know what Kirk and Spock are!

There's a big surprise . . . Do you know anything?

Yes, I do. That's why the Whills asked *me* to write this! So if you
don't mind . . .

. . . a group of freedom fighters led by Luke Skywalker—

*"Led by Luke"? Gee, I wonder what Mon Mothma and General
Rieekan would say about that? Good grief, even Major Derlin out-
ranks Luke! Luke's on tauntaun patrol for crying out loud!*

He's their unofficial leader!

Right . . . And also, "freedom fighters"? Why do they fight freedom?

Oh My Nocks! You are driving me crazy! You know what I mean!
Now, shush . . .

. . . a group of freedom fighters led by Luke Skywalker
have established a new secret base on the remote ice
world of Hoth.

Just pointing out . . . it's covered in snow, not ice. But keep going, you're almost to the best part—when all the wampas attack! That'll make a great start!

Er . . .

Don't tell me. You're cutting out the wampas?

Well, I'm keeping one of them.

One wampa? One. Wampa. Next thing you're going to tell me is that Willrow Hood just runs through the background without saying anything.

Well.

No room for the wampa attack! No room for Willrow's inspiring bravery! But let me guess, you're going to find room for Yoda's root-leaf stew, aren't you?

Uh . . .

You are, aren't you? You just had to have Yoda's lunch. I knew it!

Listen, I'll never even get to Yoda if you don't let me get this thing started.

Okay, okay. What are you starting with?

The evil lord Darth Vader . . .

Good . . . good . . .

. . . obsessed with finding young Skywalker . . .

Ooh, excellent. Which of Vader's amazingly Sith-tastic deeds are you starting with?

. . . has dispatched thousands of remote probes—

Probe dispatching?

That's it, I give up. I'm outta here.

Go ahead. Write a story that starts with probe dispatching and only one wampa, and then nothing really happens except for Yoda's lunch and Vader's breakfast and the good guys lose. Whee! That'll be everybody's favorite! Maybe you could end it by having Luke and Leia looking out a window feeling sorry for themselves. What a thrill ride!

You know what would really be thrilling?

What?

If you actually left when you said you were leaving!

Fine! I'll leave you alone so you can focus on ruining the story!

Thank the Maker . . . Now, where was I?

DISPATCHING!

Right . . .

The evil lord Darth Vader, obsessed with finding young
Skywalker, has dispatched thousands of remote probes
into the far reaches of space. . . .

ABOUT THE AUTHORS

All participating authors have generously forgone any compensation for their stories. Instead, their proceeds will be donated to First Book—a leading nonprofit that provides new books, learning materials, and other essentials to educators and organizations serving children in need. To further celebrate the launch of this book and both companies' long-standing relationships with First Book, Penguin Random House has donated $100,000 to First Book, and Disney/Lucasfilm has donated 100,000 children's books—valued at $1,000,000—to support First Book and their mission of providing equal access to quality education.

TOM ANGLEBERGER is the author of the *New York Times, USA Today,* and *Wall Street Journal* bestselling *Origami Yoda* series, as well as *The Mighty Chewbacca in the Forest of Fear* and a retelling of *Return of the Jedi* titled "Beware the Power of the Dark Side." Also a *Clone Wars* fan, Tom recently adapted a Cad Bane story arc for the anthology: *The Clone Wars: Stories of Light and Dark.*

SARWAT CHADDA spent twenty years as an engineer before turning his hand to writing. Since then he's written novels, comic books, and TV series, including *Devil's Kiss, City of the Plague God,* and *Baahubali the Lost Legends.* His writing embraces his heritage, combining East and West, with a particular passion for epic legends, vicious monsters, glorious heroes, and despicable villains.

Having spent years traveling the Far East collecting tales, he now lives in London with his family, but has a rucksack and notebook on standby.

S. A. CHAKRABORTY is the author of the critically acclaimed and internationally bestselling Daevabad Trilogy. Her work has been nominated for the Locus, World Fantasy, Crawford, and Astounding awards. When not buried in books about thirteenth-century con artists and Abbasid political intrigue, she enjoys hiking, knitting, and re-creating unnecessarily complicated medieval meals. You can find her online at www.sachakraborty.com or on Twitter and Instagram at @SAChakrabooks, where she likes to talk about history, politics, and Islamic art. She lives in New Jersey with her husband, daughter, and an ever-increasing number of cats.

MIKE CHEN is a lifelong *Star Wars* fan and the author of the critically acclaimed novels *Here and Now and Then* and *A Beginning at the End,* as well as the upcoming *We Could Be Heroes.* He also writes for geek media, from defending the Prequel Trilogy at The Mary Sue to comparing *The Last Jedi* to literary fiction at Tor.com to examining those *other* space adventures at StarTrek.com. A member of SFWA, Mike lives in the Bay Area, where he can be found playing old LucasArts adventure games with his wife, daughter, and rescue animals. Follow him on Twitter and Instagram: @mikechenwriter.

ADAM CHRISTOPHER's debut novel, *Empire State,* was *SciFiNow's* Book of the Year and a *Financial Times* Book of the Year. His other novels include *Stranger Things: Darkness on the Edge of Town, Made to Kill,* and *Seven Wonders.* A contributor to the internationally bestselling *Star Wars: From a Certain Point of View* fortieth-anniversary anthology and IDW's *Star Wars Adventures* comic, Christopher has also written the official tie-in novels for the hit CBS television show *Elementary* and the award-winning *Dishonored* videogame franchise. Born in New Zealand, Christopher has lived in Great Britain since 2006.

KATIE COOK is a writer and artist who has been involved in the *Star Wars* universe for over a decade. Her work includes illustrating the *Star Wars* children's books *ABC-3PO, OBI-123, Search Your Feelings, Creatures Big & Small,* and *Galactic Storybook* as well as many Yoda doodles that have graced her homework papers throughout the '80s and '90s.

ZORAIDA CÓRDOVA is the author of many fantasy novels for kids and teens, including the award-winning Brooklyn Brujas series, *Incendiary,* and *Star Wars: Galaxy's Edge: A Crash of Fate.* Her short fiction has appeared in the *New York Times* bestselling anthology *Star Wars: From a Certain Point of View* and *Star Wars: The Clone Wars: Stories of Light and Dark.* She is the co-editor of *Vampires Never Get Old.* Her debut middle-grade novel is *The Way to Rio Luna.* She is the co-host of the podcast *Deadline City* with Dhonielle Clayton. Zoraida was born in Guayaquil, Ecuador, and raised in Queens, New York. When she's not working on her next novel, she's finding a new adventure.

DELILAH S. DAWSON is the *New York Times* bestselling author of *Star Wars: Phasma, Star Wars: Galaxy's Edge: Black Spire,* and *Star Wars: The Perfect Weapon,* as well as the Blud series, the Hit series, and the Shadow series, written as Lila Bowen. With Kevin Hearne, she co-writes the Tales of Pell. Her comics include *Star Wars Adventures* and *Star Wars: Forces of Destiny, Firefly: The Sting, Marvel Action Spider-Man, Adventure Time,* the *X-Files Case Files,* and *Wellington,* written with Aaron Mahnke of the *Lore* podcast, plus her creator-owned comics *Ladycastle, Sparrowhawk,* and *Star Pig.* She lives in Florida with her family and loves Ewoks, porgs, and gluten-free cake.

TRACY DEONN is a writer and second-generation fangirl. She grew up in central North Carolina, where she devoured fantasy books and southern food in equal measure. Her debut contemporary fantasy novel, *Legendborn,* was named a 2020 Indies Introduce Selection and an Indie Next title for teens by the American Booksellers Association. After earning her bachelor's and master's degrees in communication and performance studies from the University of North Carolina at Chapel Hill, Tracy worked in live theater, videogame production, and K–12 education. When she's not writing, Tracy speaks on panels at science fiction and fantasy conventions, reads fanfic, arranges puppy playdates, and keeps an eye out for ginger-flavored everything.

552

SETH DICKINSON is the author of *The Traitor Baru Cormorant,* the forthcoming *Exordia,* and many short stories. Seth has also written lore for *Destiny* and *Godfall* and designed the open-source space opera *Blue Planet.* The use of the Force to interfere in the secular universe is inevitably corrupting, so all light-side Force users either become petty police or withdraw into Taoist meditation in search of absolute truth. This leaves the use of the Force as a political power to malevolent dark-side adepts, who can only be resisted by their light-side counterparts. The attempt to find a just yet enlightened resolution to this paradox is the heart of *Star Wars.* Seth dreams of becoming a muscular yet small-brained deepwater fish.

ALEXANDER FREED is the author of the *Star Wars: Alphabet Squadron* trilogy, *Star Wars: Battlefront: Twilight Company,* and *Star Wars: Rogue One* and has written many short stories, comic books, and videogames. Born near Philadelphia, he endeavors to bring the city's dour charm with him to his current home of Austin, Texas.

JASON FRY is the *New York Times* bestselling author of the young-adult space-fantasy series The Jupiter Pirates, as well as *Star Wars: The Last Jedi*, and many other works set in a galaxy far, far away. He still thinks Luke should have run off with Han and Chewie to be a space pirate. Jason lives in Brooklyn with his wife, son, and about a metric ton of *Star Wars* stuff.

CHRISTIE GOLDEN is the award-winning, *New York Times* bestselling author of more than fifty novels and more than a dozen short stories in the fields of fantasy, science fiction, and horror. Her media tie-in works include launching the Ravenloft line in 1991 with *Vampire of the Mists,* more than a dozen *Star Trek* novels, several movie novelizations, the Warcraft novels *Rise of the Horde, Lord of the Clans, Arthas: Rise of the Lich King,* and *Before the Storm, Assassin's Creed: Heresy,* as well as *Star Wars: Dark Disciple, Star Wars Battlefront II: Inferno Squad,* and the *Star Wars: Fate of the Jedi* novels *Omen, Allies,* and *Ascension.* In 2017, she was awarded the International Association of Media Tie-in Writers' Faust Award and named a Grandmaster in recognition of nearly three decades of writing. Currently Golden works for Activision Blizzard in story and franchise development, helping to create everything from comics to short stories to cinematics for Blizzard games, including World of Warcraft.

HANK GREEN is the #1 New York Times bestselling author of *An Absolutely Remarkable Thing* and *A Beautifully Foolish Endeavor.* He's also the CEO of Complexly, a production company that creates educational content, including Crash Course and SciShow, prompting *The Washington Post* to name him "one of America's most popular science teachers." Complexly's videos have been viewed more than two billion times on YouTube. Hank and his brother, John, are also raising money to dramatically and systematically improve maternal health care in Sierra Leone, where, if trends continue, one in seventeen women will die in childbirth. You can join them at PIH.org /hankandjohn.

ROB HART is the author of *The Warehouse*. He also wrote the Ash McKenna crime series and *Scott Free* with James Patterson. His next novel, *Paradox Hotel*, will be published by Ballantine Books. He lives in New York City. Find more at robwhart.com.

LYDIA KANG is a practicing physician and author of the young adult novels *Control, Catalyst, Toxic,* and *The November Girl,* as well as the adult medical mysteries *A Beautiful Poison, The Impossible Girl,* and *Opium and Absinthe.* She has also co-written the nonfiction book *Quackery: A Brief History of the Worst Ways to Cure Everything* with Nate Pedersen. Lydia saw *Star Wars* in the movie theater at age six and has been whining about Tosche Station ever since.

MICHAEL KOGGE is a bestselling author and screenwriter. Among his *Star Wars* works, he wrote the junior novels for the *Star Wars* sequel film trilogy and the *Rebels* animated series. His other titles include books for HBO's *Game of Thrones* and Warner Bros.' *Harry Potter* and *Fantastic Beasts* franchises, the movie companion novel *Batman v Superman: Cross Fire,* and the original graphic novel *Empire of the Wolf,* an epic tale of werewolves in ancient Rome. You can find him on the Web at michaelkogge.com.

R. F. KUANG is the Nebula, Locus, and World Fantasy award nominated author of *The Poppy War* and *The Dragon Republic* (Harper

Voyager). She has an MPhil in Chinese studies from the University of Cambridge and is currently pursuing an MSc in contemporary Chinese studies at Oxford University on a Marshall Scholarship. She also translates Chinese science fiction to English. Her debut *The Poppy War* was listed by *Time,* Amazon, Goodreads, and *The Guardian* as one of the best books of 2018 and has won the Crawford Award and Compton Crook Award for Best First Novel.

C. B. LEE is a Lambda Literary Award–nominated writer of young adult science fiction and fantasy. Her works include the Sidekick Squad series (Duet Books), *Ben 10* graphic novels (Boom! Studios), *Out Now: Queer We Go Again* (HarperTeen), and *Minecraft: The Shipwreck* (Penguin Random House). Lee's work has been featured in *Teen Vogue, Wired* magazine, *Hypable,* Tor's Best of Fantasy and Sci Fi, and the American Library Association's Rainbow List.

555

MACKENZI LEE holds a BA in history and an MFA from Simmons College in writing for children and young adults. She is the *New York Times* bestselling and award-winning author of *The Gentleman's Guide to Vice and Virtue, Bygone Badass Broads: 52 Forgotten Women Who Changed the World,* and Marvel's *Loki: Where Mischief Lies,* among others. In 2019, she was named to the prestigious *Forbes* 30 Under 30 list for her work in bringing minority narratives to historical fiction and nonfiction. She loves Diet Coke, sweater weather, and, more than anything, *Star Wars.*

JOHN JACKSON MILLER is the *New York Times* bestselling author of *Star Wars: Kenobi, Star Wars: A New Dawn, Star Wars: Lost Tribe of the Sith,* and the *Star Wars Legends: The Old Republic* graphic novel collections, as well as novels, comics, and short stories for franchises including *Star Trek, Planet of the Apes, Battlestar Galactica,* Mass Effect, and Halo. A comics industry historian, he runs the Comichron website. His fiction website is farawaypress.com.

MICHAEL MORECI is a bestselling comics author and novelist. His original works include the space adventure novels *Black Star Renegades* and *We Are Mayhem* as well as the comic series *Wasted Space, The Plot, Curse, Roche Limit, Burning Fields,* and more. He's also written many canonical comics for *Star Wars,* and he's currently working on his next novel. He lives with his family just outside Chicago.

DANIEL JOSÉ OLDER is the *New York Times* bestselling author of the middle grade historical fantasy series *Dactyl Hill Squad, The Book of Lost Saints,* the Bone Street Rumba urban fantasy series, *Star Wars: Last Shot,* and the award-winning young adult series Shadowshaper Cypher, which won the International Latino Book Award and was shortlisted for the Kirkus Prize in Young Readers Literature, the Andre Norton Award, the Locus, the Mythopoeic Award, and named one of Esquires 80 Books Every Person Should Read. He is a lead story architect on the Star Wars cross platform initiative The High Republic. He co-wrote the upcoming graphic novel *Death's Day* and writes the monthly IDW comic book series *The High Republic Adventures.* You can find more info and read about his decade-long career as an NYC paramedic at http://danieljoseolder.net/.

MARK OSHIRO is the award-winning author of *Anger Is a Gift,* which was a finalist in the 31st Annual Lambda Literary Awards for LGBTQ YA and a winner of the Schneider Family Book Award in 2019. Their upcoming books are a YA fantasy, *Each of Us a Desert,* and their middle-grade debut, *The Insiders.* When they are not writing, they run the online Mark Does Stuff universe and are trying to pet every dog in the world.

AMY RATCLIFFE is the author of *Star Wars: Women of the Galaxy, The Jedi Mind,* and the upcoming *A Kid's Guide to Fandom* and *The Art of Star Wars: Galaxy's Edge.* She's the managing editor for Nerdist, a *Star Wars* Celebration stage host, and an entertainment reporter featured at StarWars.com, *Star Wars Insider, IGN,* and more. Born and raised in a small Ohio town, Amy lives in Los Angeles with her husband and two cats.

BETH REVIS is the *New York Times* bestselling author of *Star Wars: Rebel Rising, Across the Universe,* and *Give the Dark My Love,* among others. Beth currently lives in North Carolina with her husband and her young Padawan, who trains regularly in the fine art of cardboard-tube lightsaber dueling.

LILLIAM RIVERA is an award-winning writer and author of children's books *Goldie Vance: The Hotel Whodunit, Dealing in Dreams, The Education of Margot Sanchez,* and the forthcoming young-adult novel *Never Look Back* (September 2020), published by Bloomsbury. Her work has appeared in *The Washington Post, The New York Times,* and *Elle,* to name a few. A Bronx, New York native, Lilliam currently lives in Los Angeles.

CAVAN SCOTT is a UK number one bestseller who has written for such popular worlds as *Star Wars, Doctor Who, Star Trek, Assassin's Creed, Judge Dredd, Pacific Rim,* and Sherlock Holmes. He is the author of *Star Wars: Dooku: Jedi Lost, The Patchwork Devil,* and *Shadow Service,* and is one of the story architects for Lucasfilm's epic multimedia initiative, *Star Wars: The High Republic.* He has written comics for Marvel, IDW, Dark Horse, Vertigo, *2000 AD,* and *The Beano.* A former magazine editor, Cavan Scott lives in Bristol with his wife and daughters. His lifelong passions include classic scary movies, folklore, audio drama, the music of David Bowie, and walking. He owns far too many action figures.

EMILY SKRUTSKIE was born in Massachusetts, raised in Virginia, and forged in the mountains above Boulder, Colorado. She attended Cornell University and now lives and works in Los Angeles. Skrutskie is the author of *Bonds of Brass, Hullmetal Girls, The Abyss Surrounds Us,* and *The Edge of the Abyss.*

KAREN STRONG is the author of the critically acclaimed middle-grade novel *Just South of Home,* which was selected for several best-of-year lists, including *Kirkus Reviews* Best Books, CCBC Choices, and Bank Street Best Books. Her short fiction appears in the sci-fi and fantasy anthology *A Phoenix First Must Burn.* Born and raised in the rural South, she is a graduate of the University of Georgia and an advocate of science, technology, engineering, and math (STEM). An avid lover of strong coffee, yellow flowers, and night skies, Karen lives in Atlanta.

558

ANNE TOOLE is a Writers Guild Award winner who has written for videogames, TV and digital series, animation, comics, and more. Her work most recently appeared on Netflix's anime series *Cannon Busters,* Titan's *Horizon Zero Dawn* comic book, and in the BBC/Eline console title Beyond Blue.

Her credits include the award-winning PS4 exclusive Horizon: Zero Dawn; The Witcher; and *The Lizzie Bennet Diaries,* a short-form digital series that won an Emmy. She also created *Alles Liebe, Annette,* a digital series for German broadcaster MDR. Anne has spoken extensively on storytelling across platforms at such conferences as South by Southwest, Comic-con International, GDC Europe, and GDC, as well as in presentations at MIT, Harvard, and Cannes. She has served as the vice chair of the International Game Developers

Association (IGDA). A citizen of Ireland as well as the United States, Anne holds a degree in archaeology from Harvard.

CATHERYNNE M. VALENTE is the *New York Times* bestselling author of dozens of works of science fiction and fantasy including *Space Opera, The Refrigerator Monologues,* and the Fairyland series. She has won or been nominated for nearly every award in her field. She lives on an island off the coast of Maine with her partner, her son, and several other mischievous beasts.

AUSTIN WALKER is the host of the actual play podcast *Friends at the Table,* where he tells stories about anticapitalist robots and terribly sad gods. He is also an award-winning games journalist, critic, and podcaster whose words and voice have appeared at *Paste Magazine, New Statesman, Giant Bomb,* and VICE Media's *Waypoint Radio.* He currently lives in (and loves) Queens.

559

MARTHA WELLS has been an SF/F writer since her first fantasy novel was published in 1993, and a *Star Wars* fan since she saw *A New Hope* in the theater in 1977. Her work includes The Books of the Raksura series, *The Death of the Necromancer,* the Ile-Rien trilogy, The Murderbot Diaries series, media tie-ins for *Star Wars* and *Stargate: Atlantis,* as well as short fiction, YA novels, and nonfiction. She was also the lead writer for the story team of *Magic: The Gathering's* Dominaria expansion in 2018. She has won a Nebula Award, two Hugo Awards, and two Locus Awards, and her work has appeared on the Philip K. Dick Award ballot, the BSFA Award ballot, the *USA Today* Bestseller List, and the *New York Times* Bestseller List.

DJANGO WEXLER graduated from Carnegie Mellon University in Pittsburgh with degrees in creative writing and computer science, and worked for the university in artificial intelligence research. Eventually he migrated to Microsoft in Seattle, where he now lives with two cats and a teetering mountain of books. When not writing, he wrangles computers, paints tiny soldiers, and plays games of all sorts. He is the author of epic fantasies *Ashes of the Sun, The Shadow Campaigns,* and YA fantasy *The Wells of Sorcery.*

KIERSTEN WHITE is the *New York Times* bestselling, Stoker Award–winning author of many books, including the And I Darken trilogy, the Slayer series, the Camelot Rising trilogy, and *The Dark Descent of Elizabeth Frankenstein.* She owns a perfectly reasonable number of lightsabers, and sometimes even lets her kids play with them.

GARY WHITTA is a screenwriter and author best known as the co-writer of *Rogue One: A Star Wars Story.* He also wrote several episodes of *Star Wars Rebels,* adapted *The Last Jedi* for Marvel Comics, and was a contributor to the first volume of *Star Wars: From a Certain Point of View.* He lives in San Francisco with his wife and daughter.

BRITTANY N. WILLIAMS is a staff writer for *Black Nerd Problems,* with her work also appearing on Tor.com and in *The Indypendent.* As a classically trained actress, she's performed on three continents including a year spent as a principal vocalist at Hong Kong Disneyland. She's currently working on her first novel, *That Self-Same Metal,* a YA historical fantasy set in William Shakespeare's London.

CHARLES YU is the author of four books, including his latest novel, *Interior Chinatown.* He has received the National Book Foundation's 5 Under 35 Award and has been nominated for two Writers Guild of America Awards for his work on the HBO series *Westworld.* He has also written for shows on FX, AMC, and Adult Swim. His fiction and nonfiction have appeared in *The New Yorker, The New York Times, The Atlantic,* and *Time* magazine, among other publications.

JIM ZUB is a writer, artist, and art instructor based in Toronto, Canada. Over the past twenty years he's worked for a diverse array of publishing, film, and game clients, including Marvel, DC Comics, Disney, Capcom, Hasbro, Cartoon Network, and Bandai-Namco.

He juggles his time between being a freelance comic writer and a professor teaching drawing and storytelling courses in Seneca College's award-winning animation program. His current comic projects include *Conan the Barbarian, Stranger Things and Dungeons & Dragons,* and *Stone Star.* Find out more at jimzub.com.

ABOUT THE TYPE

This book was set in Minion, a 1990 Adobe Originals typeface by Robert Slimbach (b. 1956). Minion is inspired by classical, old-style typefaces of the late Renaissance, a period of elegant, beautiful, and highly readable type designs. Created primarily for text setting, Minion combines the aesthetic and functional qualities that make text type highly readable with the versatility of digital technology.